TALES OF MYSTERY & THE SUPERNATURAL

General Editor: David Stuart Davies

THE CASTLE OF OTRANTO
with
VATHEK *and* NIGHTMARE ABBEY

HORACE WALPOLE

The Castle of Otranto

with

WILLIAM BECKFORD: Vathek

THOMAS LOVE PEACOCK:
Nightmare Abbey

with an introduction by
David Stuart Davies

WORDSWORTH EDITIONS

In loving memory of
MICHAEL TRAYLER
the founder of Wordsworth Editions

I

Readers interested in other titles from
Wordsworth Editions are invited to visit our
website at www.wordsworth-editions.com

For our latest list and a full mail-order service contact
Bibliophile Books, Unit 5 Datapoint,
South Crescent, London E16 4TL
Tel: +44 020 74 74 24 74
Fax: +44 020 74 74 85 89
orders@bibliophilebooks.com
www.bibliophilebooks.com

This edition published 2009 by
Wordsworth Editions Limited
8B East Street, Ware,
Hertfordshire SG12 9HJ

ISBN 978 1 84022 184 8

Typeset in Great Britain by Roperford Editorial
Printed by Clays Ltd, St Ives plc

CONTENTS

INTRODUCTION

The Gothic novel, which became the vogue in the late eighteenth and early nineteenth centuries, contains a rich mixture of tragedy and romance, tinged with horror, enacted in or around some form of a medieval or 'Gothick' architecture – a ruined castle, a deserted abbey and the like. The novels feature murky tales of revenge, torture, ancient villainies punished and young sensitive love rewarded usually by supernatural or supposed supernatural means. These tales took the reader into the land of dark dreams and racy scenarios presenting possibilities that the standard novel failed to capture. The Gothic novel was not about real life. Its rich, sensual hallucinatory qualities gave the reader an illicit thrill which still remains as potent and rewarding today.

The creators of these tales wanted to reshape the standard form of literature from the smooth classical structure of the formal novel into a darker, older and more artificial style; as such, Gothic literature is intimately associated with the revival of interest in Gothic architecture during the same era. In a way similar to the Gothic revivalists' rejection of the clarity and rationalism of buildings in the neoclassical style – all smooth clinical lines and regulated forms – the literary Gothic embodies an appreciation of the joys of extreme emotion, the thrills of fear, dark unpredicability, an awe inherent in the recherché and a quest for atmosphere. The ruins of Gothic buildings gave rise to multiple linked emotions by representing the inevitable decay and collapse of human creations. It was a fascination with this architecture and its related art, poetry, that inspired the first wave of Gothic novelists.

The Castle of Otranto (1764), by Horace Walpole (1717–97), is often regarded as the first true Gothic romance. Walpole was obsessed with medieval Gothic architecture, and built his own house in that fashion. Externally the property at Strawberry Hill in Richmond near London seemed to be a blend of two predominant styles: a style based on castles with turrets and battlements, and a style based on

Gothic cathedrals with arched windows and stained glass. It was Walpole's intention to create 'a little Gothic castle'.

Walpole's fascination with the Gothic led to the creation of *The Castle of Otranto*. Indeed, the Gothic castle at the centre of the action in the novel is the true hero of the story, with its antique courts, ruined turrets, deserted chambers and dark corridors.

With this work, Walpole's declared aim was to combine elements of the medieval romance, which he deemed too fanciful, and the modern novel, which he considered to be too confined to strict realism. The basic plot created other elements which became Gothic staples, including a threatening mystery and an ancestral curse, as well as countless trappings such as hidden passages and oft-fainting heroines. Sir Walter Scott called it the 'happy combination of supernatural agency with human interest'.

Horace Walpole, fourth earl of Orford, was the son of Robert Walpole, twice Prime Minister of Britain. An affluent bachelor-aristocrat, his passion for art and literature caused him to be regarded as one of the lynchpins of the literary and political society and a supreme arbiter of taste.

The story goes that the book stemmed from a vivid dream Walpole had which featured a giant hand encased in armour. This image stayed with him for days and became the inspiration for the novel. He recorded his feelings in a letter of 9 March 1765:

> I waked one morning in the beginning of last June from a dream, of which all I could recover was, that I thought myself in an ancient castle (a very natural dream for a head filled like mine with Gothic story) and that on the uppermost bannister of a great staircase I saw a giant hand in armour. In the evening I sat down and began to write, without knowing in the least what I intended to say or relate.

From this mystical beginning, the novel was created. The hand of the dream was transfigured into a gigantic helmet which in the opening of the tale falls and crushes the son of Ferdinand – the novel's protagaonist – on his wedding day, thus prompting a dramatic and fantastic chain of events.

The first edition was disguised as an actual medieval romance from Italy, supposedly discovered and republished by a fictitious translator. When Walpole admitted to his authorship in the second edition, its originally favourable reception by literary reviewers changed into rejection and abuse. While the establishment had been prepared to accept and indeed revel in the rich and gaudy events presented in the novel, believing that it was a genuine historical work, they were outraged when they realised that they had been foxed by this forgery and condemned it as tawdry and shallow.

Nevertheless commercially the novel was a great success and contained all the the essential elements that contributed to form of the Gothic novel. The story is set in medieval Italy, the background influenced by Walpole's protracted Grand Tour of the continent, and features characters placed in a haunted castle with sombre towers and secret passages. Persecuted maidens and spectral appearances set against a background of medieval décor were a dramatic change from the realism of contemporary fiction. Poet Thomas Gray wrote of the book: 'It makes one cry a little, and in all general, afraid to go to bed o' nights.'

With its array of Gothic paraphernalia, the novel provided the template for other writers to use their skills in creating their own Gothic tale, writers such as William Beckford (1759–1844) who created *Vathek*, the second entry in our Gothic feast. The similarities between Walpole and Beckford's background are notable. The son of an influential Whig politican and Lord Mayor of London, Beckford was for a period in the early nineteenth century the richest man in England, with an income from the slave-operated sugar plantations in the West Indies. He used his immense wealth to create what was in essence a small kingdom in Wiltshire where he indulged himself in all the human excesses. Like Walpole he excercised his love of Gothic architecture by creating a monastery-like building on his estate reflecting his passion. One entered the building through doors forty feet high, so carefully counter-weighted that they could be opened by two fantastically garbed dwarfs in Beckford's employ. Through these doors one encountered a true Aladdin's cave: galleries and halls, hundreds of feet long, filled with treasures, paintings, statuary, porcelain, rare books and cabinets of drawings, manuscripts, gems, rare musical instruments, and much else. The entrance to one chamber was gained by a cunning mechanical device – when Beckford approached and stamped his foot, a statue would draw the curtain aside. In this opulent repository, Beckford lived alone, apart from an array of servants. He was living his life as though it were part of one of the tales of the *Arabian Nights*, a work that had fascinated him since his youth. It is therefore not surprising that when he turned his hand to literature he created what is regarded the greatest mock-*Arabian Nights* tale of them all, *Vathek* (1786).

In 1778, after a period of travel and study in Europe, Beckford returned to England, where he later met the eleven-year-old son and heir of Viscount Courtenay, a boy for whom Beckford felt strong attraction. Following a lavish three-day Christmas party held in the boy's honour, Beckford conceived the story of the caliph Vathek, a monarch as impious as he is voluptuous, who builds a tower so high that from it he can survey all the kingdoms of the world. Vathek challenges Mohammed in the seventh heaven and so brings about his own damnation and his banishment to the subterranean kingdom ruled by Eblis, prince of darkness. It was claimed that he completed the novel in outline in three days and two nights. Because it was usual for such oriental tales to be composed in French, Beckford followed the fashion. He later translated it into English but was not satisfied with the result, believing his English prose to be too Gallic, and so he employed the aid of an old scholar, the Reverend Samuel Henley, to help Anglicise it further.

Vathek was written during a time when the European population was entranced by Orientalism. The novel is both an Arabian tale because of the oriental setting and characters and the depiction of oriental cultures, societies, and myths, as well as a Gothic novel because of the emphasis on the supernatural, ghosts and spirits, and the terror it tries to induce in the reader. It is clear that Beckford identified himself with the antihero of his tale. Vathek was a devoutly hedonistic character who put his chosen pleasures above the human needs of those around him, and feeds directly into the Romantic movement's glorification of sensation and experience, so that it is not particularly surprising that Byron referred to it as his 'Bible'.

At the time Beckford wrote this magical work he was married to the beautiful Lady Margaret Gordon and was expecting to be elevated to the peerage in December 1784. However, in the autumn of that year, scandal broke when he was charged with sexual misconduct with the young Courtenay. Reports of the scandal were quickly spread, and, though Beckford's guilt was never proved, in mid-1785 he, with his wife and baby daughter, was forced into exile. In May 1786, in Switzerland, his wife died of puerperal fever after giving birth to a second daughter. About that time, Beckford learned to his anger and despair that Henley, to whom he had entrusted *Vathek* for translation, had arranged for the novel to be published anonymously, with a preface in which Henley claimed that it had been taken directly from the Arabic.

Everett F. Blieler, a pre-eminent authority of supernatural fiction, has stated that *Vathek* ' . . . filled with highly imaginative detail, vaguely allegorical in design . . . uses the mechanisms of an Oriental tale to point a moral – but dwells more lovingly on the horrors involved rather than on the moral. It is remarkable that although the horrors are strong and violent, the tone of the story is light and mocking. The human sacrifices, murders and mutilations are recounted with the most amiable sangfroid. *Vathek* is undoubtedly the finest European imitation of the *Arabian Nights*. No one else has been able to create the bizarre detail, the curious blend of the ludicrous and the horrible, the tongue in cheek wryness of *Vathek*.'

After that description how can you resist devouring the work?

The final course in our Gothic feast is a light pudding: *Nightmare Abbey*, written by Thomas Love Peacock (1775–1866). Unlike the previous authors mentioned, Peacock began life in somewhat lowlier circumstances: he was the son of a London merchant. His formal schooling ended when he was only thirteen, when he became a clerk in an office in the City. However, his passion for learning and in particular literature led him to a close, rigorous study of French, Italian and English literature. He published several volumes of minor poetry and formed a friendship with the poet Percy Bysshe Shelley. It is said that through this close bond of friendship Peacock influenced the direction and tone of Shelley's work.

Nightmare Abbey was written in 1818, and as with many of Peacock's writings it is embedded with a deep vein of satire. In this volume his target is Gothic fiction. The humorous aspect of the work is detected immediately by the use of comical names for the characters. The slender plot of *Nightmare Abbey* follows the fortunes of Christopher Glowry, Esquire, a morose widower who lives with his only son Scythrop in the semi-dilapidated family mansion, Nightmare Abbey in Lincolnshire. Glowry is a melancholy gentleman who likes to surround himself with servants with long faces or dismal names such as Raven, Graves or Deathshead. The few visitors he welcomes to his home are mostly of a similar cast of mind: Mr Flosky, a transcendental philosopher; Mr Toobad, a Manichaean millennarian; the Reverend Mr Larynx, the vicar of nearby Claydyke; Mr Listless, Scythrop's gloomy and misanthropical college friend; and Mr Cypress, a misanthropic poet. The only exception is the sanguine Mr Hilary, who, as Mr Glowry's brother-in-law, is obliged to visit the abbey from family interests. During the course of the book, Peacock gently pokes fun not only at the literary conventions of the time, but also at the opinions and stances of certain writers who he believed created a bleak picture of the the world in their writings. He referred to these as 'morbidities'. After the novel was written and shortly before its publication Walpole wrote to Shelley stating that his object in writing the novel had been, 'merely to bring to a sort of philosophical focus a few of the morbidities of modern literature, and to let a little daylight in on its atrabilarious complexion.' ('atrabilarious' seems to be a self-coined word blending 'atrabilious', which refers to melancholy, and 'hilarious', attaining to something highly comic, thus suggesting that the deep and sombre thoughts of these writers are very amusing, even farcical). In an earlier letter to Shelley, Peacock is more specific, stating that in creating *Nightmare Abbey*, 'I think it is necessary to "make a stand" against the encroachments of black bile. The fourth canto of *Childe Harolde* [the lengthy narrative poem by Lord Byron] is really too bad. I cannot consent to being an *auditor tantum* of this systematic "poisoning" of the mind of the reading public.'

Indeed, the character of Mr Cypress is thinly based on Byron, and in Chapter 11 his gloomy postulations are largely made up of dismal phrases from *Childe Harolde*. However, Byron was not the only specific literary allusion in the novel. Peacock's friend Shelley must have been taken aback by what was so obviously a caricature of his life and opinions in the form of the character Scythrop Glowry, whose romantic entanglements and indecision mirror those of the poet. However Peacock would recall that Shelley found the idea amusing and soon 'took to himself the character of Scythrop'.

As a send-up of Gothic literature and the Romantic movement, this is a joyful, smile-inducing novel, missing out on the trenchant abrasive wit of say Swift or Rabelais.

From *The Castle of Otranto*, with its dark and passionate plot, through *Vathek* with its opulence and improbabilities, to the amusing felicities of *Nightmare Abbey*, this fantastic collection runs the gamut of Gothic fiction, providing the modern reader with a wonderful overview of the genre. As with many trends, Gothic fiction began in earnest, with a tendency perhaps to take itself too seriously. This prompted other writers to experiment with the form, thus inspiring a later set of scribes to gently lampoon it. In this rich trilogy of novels you have examples of each approach, which entertain in their own fascinating fashion.

DAVID STUART DAVIES

THE CASTLE
OF OTRANTO

PREFACE

to the First Edition

The following work was found in the library of an ancient Catholic family in the north of England. It was printed at Naples, in the black letter, in the year 1529. How much sooner it was written does not appear. The principal incidents are such as were believed in the darkest ages of Christianity; but the language and conduct have nothing that savours of barbarism. The style is the purest Italian.

If the story was written near the time when it is supposed to have happened, it must have been between 1095, the era of the First Crusade, and 1243, the date of the last, or not long afterwards. There is no other circumstance in the work that can lead us to guess at the period in which the scene is laid: the names of the actors are evidently fictitious, and probably disguised on purpose: yet the Spanish names of the domestics seem to indicate that this work was not composed until the establishment of the Arragonian Kings in Naples had made Spanish appellations familiar in that country. The beauty of the diction, and the zeal of the author (moderated, however, by singular judgment) concur to make me think that the date of the composition was little antecedent to that of the impression. Letters were then in their most flourishing state in Italy, and contributed to dispel the empire of superstition, at that time so forcibly attacked by the reformers. It is not unlikely that an artful priest might endeavour to turn their own arms on the innovators, and might avail himself of his abilities as an author to confirm the populace in their ancient errors and superstitions. If this was his view, he has certainly acted with signal address. Such a work as the following would enslave a hundred vulgar minds beyond half the books of controversy that have been written from the days of Luther to the present hour.

This solution of the author's motives is, however, offered as a mere conjecture. Whatever his views were, or whatever effects the execution of them might have, his work can only be laid before the public at present as a matter of entertainment. Even as such, some apology for it is necessary. Miracles, visions, necromancy, dreams, and other preternatural events, are exploded now even from romances. That was not the case when our author wrote; much less when the story itself is supposed to have happened. Belief in every kind of prodigy was so established in those dark ages, that an author would not be faithful to the *manners* of the times, who should omit all mention of them. He is not bound to believe them himself, but he must represent his actors as believing them.

If this *air* of the *miraculous* is excused, the reader will find nothing else unworthy of his perusal. Allow the possibility of the facts, and all the actors comport themselves as persons would do in their situation. There is no bombast, no similes, flowers, digressions, or unnecessary descriptions. Everything tends directly to the catastrophe. Never is the reader's attention relaxed. The rules of the drama are almost observed throughout the conduct of the piece. The characters are well drawn, and still better maintained. Terror, the author's principal engine, prevents the story from ever languishing; and it is so often contrasted by pity, that the mind is kept up in a constant vicissitude of interesting passions.

Some persons may perhaps think the characters of the domestics too little serious for the general cast of the story; but besides their opposition to the principal personages, the art of the author is very observable in his conduct of the subalterns. They discover many passages essential to the story, which could not be well brought to light but by their *naïveté* and simplicity. In particular, the womanish terror and foibles of Bianca, in the last chapter, conduce essentially towards advancing the catastrophe.

It is natural for a translator to be prejudiced in favour of his adopted work. More impartial readers may not be so much struck with the beauties of this piece as I was. Yet I am not blind to my author's defects. I could wish he had grounded his plan on a more useful moral than this: that *the sins of fathers are visited on their children to the third and fourth generation.* I doubt whether, in his time any more than at present, ambition curbed its appetite of dominion from the dread of so remote a punishment. And yet this moral is weakened by that less direct insinuation, that even such anathema may be diverted by devotion to St Nicholas. Here the interest of the monk plainly gets the better of the judgment of the author. However, with all its faults, I have no doubt but the English reader will be pleased with a sight of this performance. The piety that reigns throughout, the lessons of virtue that are inculcated, and the rigid purity of the sentiments, exempt this work from the censure to which romances are but too liable. Should it meet with the success I hope for, I may be encouraged to reprint the original Italian, though it will tend to depreciate my own labour. Our language falls far short of the charms of the Italian, both for variety and harmony. The latter is peculiarly excellent for simple narrative. It is difficult in English *to relate* without falling too low or rising too high; a fault obviously occasioned by the little care taken to speak pure language in common conversation. Every Italian or Frenchman of any rank piques himself on speaking his own tongue correctly and with choice. I cannot flatter myself with having done justice to my author in this respect: his style is as elegant as his conduct of the passions is masterly. It is a pity that he did not apply his talents to what they were evidently proper for – the theatre.

I will detain the reader no longer, but to make one short remark. Though the machinery is invention, and the names of the actors imaginary, I cannot but believe that the groundwork of the story is founded on truth. The scene is undoubtedly laid in some real castle. The author seems frequently, without design, to describe particular parts. *The chamber*, says he, *on the right hand; the door on the left hand; the distance from the chapel to Conrad's apartment*: these and other passages are strong presumptions that the author had some certain building in his eye. Curious persons, who have leisure to employ in such researches, may possibly discover in the Italian writers the foundation on which our author has built. If a catastrophe, at all resembling that which he describes, is believed to have given rise to this work, it will contribute to interest the reader, and will make *The Castle of Otranto* a still more moving story.

The favourable manner in which this little piece has been received by the public calls upon the author to explain the grounds on which he composed it. But before he opens those motives, it is fit that he should ask pardon of his readers for having offered his work to them under the borrowed personage of a translator. As diffidence of his own abilities, and the novelty of the attempt, were the sole inducements to assume that disguise, he flatters himself he shall appear excusable. He resigned his performance to the impartial judgment of the public; determined to let it perish in obscurity, if disapproved; nor meaning to avow such a trifle, unless better judges should pronounce that he might own it without a blush.

It was an attempt to blend the two kinds of romance: the ancient and the modern. In the former, all was imagination and improbability; in the latter, nature is always intended to be, and sometimes has been, copied with success. Invention has not been wanting; but the great resources of fancy have been dammed up by a strict adherence to common life. But if in the latter species nature has cramped imagination, she did but take her revenge, having been totally excluded from old romances. The actions, sentiments, conversations, of the heroes and heroines of ancient days, were as unnatural as the machines employed to put them in motion.

The author of the following pages thought it possible to reconcile the two kinds. Desirous of leaving the powers of fancy at liberty to expatiate through the boundless realms of invention, and thence of creating more interesting situations, he wished to conduct the mortal agents in his drama according to the rules of probability; in short, to make them think, speak, and act, as it might be supposed mere men and women would do in extraordinary positions. He had observed, that in all inspired writings, the personages under the dispensation of miracles, and witnesses to the most stupendous phenomena, never lose sight of their human character; whereas, in the productions of romantic story, an improbable event never fails to be attended by an absurd dialogue. The actors seem to lose their senses, the moment the laws of nature have lost their tone. As the public have applauded the attempt, the author must not say he was entirely unequal to the task he had undertaken; yet if the new route he has struck out shall have paved a road for men of brighter talents, he shall own with pleasure and modesty, that he was sensible the plan was capable of receiving greater embellishments than his imagination or conduct of the passions could bestow on it.

With regard to the deportment of the domestics, on which I have touched in the former preface, I will beg leave to add a few words. The simplicity of their behaviour, almost tending to excite smiles, which at first seems not consonant to the serious cast of the work, appeared to me not only not improper, but was marked designedly in that manner. My rule was nature. However grave, important, or even melancholy, the sensations of princes and heroes may be, they do not stamp the same affections on their domestics; at least the latter do not, or should not be made to express their passions in the same dignified tone. In my humble opinion, the contrast between the sublime of the one and the *naïveté* of the other, sets the pathetic of the former in a stronger light. The very impatience which a reader feels while delayed by the coarse pleasantries of vulgar actors from arriving at the knowledge of the important catastrophe he expects, perhaps heightens, certainly proves, that he has been artfully interested in the depending event. But I had higher authority than my own opinion for this conduct. That great master of nature, Shakespeare, was the model I copied. Let me ask if his tragedies of *Hamlet* and *Julius Cæsar* would not lose a considerable share of their spirit and wonderful beauties, if the humour of the grave-diggers, the fooleries of Polonius, and the clumsy jests of the Roman citizens, were omitted, or vested in heroics? Is not the eloquence of Antony, the nobler and affectingly unaffected oration of Brutus, artificially exalted by the rude outbursts of nature from the mouths of their auditors? These touches remind one of the Grecian sculptor, who, to convey the idea of a colossus within the dimensions of a seal, inserted a little boy measuring his thumb.

No, says Voltaire, in his edition of Corneille, this mixture of buffoonery and solemnity is intolerable. – Voltaire is a genius* – but

* The following remark is foreign to the present question. yet excusable in an Englishman, who is willing to think that the severe criticisms of so masterly a

not of Shakespeare's magnitude. Without recurring to disputable authority, I appeal from Voltaire to himself. I shall not avail myself of his former encomiums on our mighty poet, though the French critic has twice translated the same speech in *Hamlet*, some years ago in admiration, latterly in derision; and I am sorry to find that his judgment grows weaker, when it ought to be farther matured. But I shall make use of his own words, delivered on the general topic of the theatre, when he was neither thinking to recommend nor decry Shakespeare's practice; consequently at a moment when Voltaire was impartial. In the preface to his *Enfant prodigue*, that exquisite piece of which I declare my admiration, and which, should I live twenty years longer, I trust I should never attempt to ridicule, he has these words, speaking of comedy (but equally applicable to tragedy, if tragedy is, as surely it ought to be, a picture of human life; nor can I conceive why occasional pleasantry ought more to be banished from the tragic scene, than pathetic seriousness from the comic):

> *On y voit une mélange de sérieux et de plaisanterie, de comique et de touchant; souvent même une seule avanture produit tous ces contrastes. Rien n'est si commun qu'une maison dans laquelle un père gronde, une fille occupée de sa passion pleure; le fils se moque des deux, et quelques parens prennent part différemment à la scène, &c. Nous n'inférons pas de là que toute comédie doive avoir des scènes de bouffonerie et des scènes attendrissantes: il y a beaucoup de très bonnes pièces où il ne régne que de la gayeté; d'autres toutes sérieuses; d'autres mélangées; d'autres où l'attendrissement va jusque aux larmes: il ne faut donner l'exclusion à aucun genre: et si l'on me demandoit, quel genre est le meilleur, je répondrois, celui qui est le mieux traité.*

---

writer as Voltaire on our immortal countryman, may have been the effusions of wit and precipitation, rather than the result of judgment and attention. May not the critic's skill in the force and powers of our language have been as incorrect and incompetent as his knowledge of our history? Of the latter his own pen has dropped glaring evidence. In his preface to Thomas Corneille's *Earl of Essex*, Monsieur de Voltaire allows that the truth of history has been grossly perverted in that piece. In excuse he pleads, that when Corneille wrote, the noblesse of France were much unread in English story; but now, says the commentator, that they study it, such misrepresentation would not be suffered – Yet forgetting that the period of ignorance is lapsed, and that it is not very necessary to instruct the knowing, he undertakes from the overflowing of his own readingto give the nobility of his own country a detail of Queen Elizabeth's favourites – of whom, says he, Robert Dudley was the first, and the Earl of Leicester the second – Could one have believed that it could be necessary to inform Monsieur de Voltaire himself, that Robert Dudley and the Earl of Leicester were the same person?

Surely if a comedy may be *toute sérieuse*, tragedy may now and then, soberly, be indulged in a smile. Who shall proscribe it? Shall the critic, who in self-defence declares that *no kind* ought to be excluded from comedy, give laws to Shakespeare?

I am aware that the preface from whence I have quoted these passages does not stand in Monsieur de Voltaire's name, but in that of his editor; yet who doubts that the editor and the author were the same person? Or where is the editor, who has so happily possessed himself of his author's style and brilliant ease of argument? These passages were indubitably the genuine sentiments of that great writer. In his epistle to Maffei, prefixed to his *Merope*, he delivers almost the same opinion, though I doubt with a little irony. I will repeat his words, and then give my reason for quoting them. After translating a passage in Maffei's *Merope*, Monsieur de Voltaire adds:

> *Tous ces traits sont naifs: tout y est convenable à ceux que vous introduisez sur la scène, et aux moeurs que vous leur donnez. Ces familiarités naturelles eussent été, à ce que je crois, bien reçues dans Athènes; mais Paris et notre parterre veulent une autre espèce de simplicité.*

I doubt, I say, whether there is not a grain of sneer in this and other passages of that epistle; yet the force of truth is not damaged by being tinged with ridicule. Maffei was to represent a Grecian story: surely the Athenians were as competent judges of Grecian manners, and of the propriety of introducing them, as the *parterre* of Paris. On the contrary, says Voltaire (and I cannot but admire his reasoning) there were but ten thousand citizens at Athens, and Paris has near eight hundred thousand inhabitants, among whom one may reckon thirty thousand judges of dramatic works. – Indeed! – But allowing so numerous a tribunal, I believe this is the only instance in which it was ever pretended that thirty thousand persons, living near two thousand years after the era in question, were, upon the mere face of the poll, declared better judges than the Grecians themselves of what ought to be the manner of a tragedy written on a Grecian story.

I will not enter into a discussion of the *espèce de simplicité*, which the *parterre* of Paris demands, nor of the shackles with which *the thirty thousand judges* have cramped their poetry, the chief merit of which, as I gather from repeated passages in *The New Commentary on Corneille*, consists in vaulting in spite of those fetters; a merit which, if true, would reduce poetry from the lofty effort of imagination, to a puerile and most contemptible labour – *difficiles nugae* with a witness! I cannot help however mentioning a couplet, which to my English ears always sounded as the flattest and most trifling instance of circumstantial propriety; but which Voltaire, who has dealt so severely with nine parts in ten of Corneille's works, has singled out to defend in Racine:

> *De son appartement cette porte est prochaine,*
> *Et cette autre conduit dans celui de la* reine.

In English:

> To Caesar's closet through this door you come,
> And t'other leads to the queen's drawing-room.

Unhappy Shakespeare! Hadst thou made Rosencrans inform his compeer Guildenstern of the ichnography of the palace of Copenhagen, instead of presenting us with a moral dialogue between the Prince of Denmark and the grave-digger, the illuminated pit of Paris would have been instructed *a second time* to adore thy talents.

The result of all I have said, is to shelter my own daring under the canon of the brightest genius this country, at least, has produced. I might have pleaded, that having created a new species of romance, I was at liberty to lay down what rules I thought fit for the conduct of it: but I should be more proud of having imitated, however faintly, weakly, and at a distance, so masterly a pattern, than to enjoy the entire merit of invention, unless I could have marked my work with genius as well as with originality. Such as it is, the public have honoured it sufficiently, whatever rank their suffrages allot to it.

SONNET

To the Right Honourable
LADY MARY COKE

The gentle maid, whose hapless tale
These melancholy pages speak;
Say, gracious lady, shall she fail
To draw the tear adown thy cheek?

No; never was thy pitying breast
Insensible to human woes;
Tender, tho' firm, it melts distrest
For weaknesses it never knows.

Oh! guard the marvels I relate
Of fell ambition scourged by fate,
From reason's peevish blame.
Blest with thy smile, my dauntless sail
I dare expand to Fancy's gale,
For sure thy smiles are Fame.

H. W.

Chapter One

Manfred, Prince of Otranto, had one son and one daughter: the latter, a most beautiful virgin, aged eighteen, was called Matilda. Conrad, the son, was three years younger, a homely youth, sickly, and of no promising disposition; yet he was the darling of his father, who never showed any symptoms of affection to Matilda. Manfred had contracted a marriage for his son with the Marquis of Vicenza's daughter, Isabella; and she had already been delivered by her guardians into the hands of Manfred, that he might celebrate the wedding as soon as Conrad's infirm state of health would permit.

Manfred's impatience for this ceremonial was remarked by his family and neighbours. The former, indeed, apprehending the severity of their prince's disposition, did not dare to utter their surmises on this precipitation. Hippolita, his wife, an amiable lady, did sometimes venture to represent the danger of marrying their only son so early, considering his great youth, and greater infirmities; but she never received any other answer than reflections on her own sterility, who had given him but one heir. His tenants and subjects were less cautious in their discourses. They attributed this hasty wedding to the prince's dread of seeing accomplished an ancient prophecy, which was said to have pronounced, *that the castle and lordship of Otranto should pass from the present family, whenever the real owner should be grown too large to inhabit it*. It was difficult to make any sense of this prophecy; and still less easy to conceive what it had to do with the marriage in question. Yet these mysteries, or contradictions, did not make the populace adhere the less to their opinion.

Young Conrad's birthday was fixed for his espousals. The company was assembled in the chapel of the castle, and everything ready for beginning the divine office, when Conrad himself was missing. Manfred, impatient of the least delay, and who had not observed his son retire, despatched one of his attendants to summon the young prince. The servant, who had not stayed long enough to have crossed the court to Conrad's apartment, came running back breathless, in a frantic manner, his eyes staring, and foaming at the month. He said nothing, but pointed to the court.

The company were struck with terror and amazement. The Princess Hippolita, without knowing what was the matter, but anxious for her son, swooned away. Manfred, less apprehensive than enraged at the procrastination of the nuptials, and at the folly of his domestic, asked imperiously what was the matter? The fellow made no answer, but continued pointing towards the courtyard; and at last, after repeated questions put to him, cried out, 'Oh! the helmet! the helmet!'

In the meantime, some of the company had run into the court, from whence was heard a confused noise of shrieks, horror, and surprise. Manfred, who began to be alarmed at not seeing his son, went himself to get information of what occasioned this strange confusion. Matilda remained endeavouring to assist her mother, and Isabella stayed for the same purpose, and to avoid showing any impatience for the bridegroom, for whom, in truth, she had conceived little affection.

The first thing that struck Manfred's eyes was a group of his servants endeavouring to raise something that appeared to him a mountain of sable plumes. He gazed without believing his sight.

'What are ye doing?' cried Manfred, wrathfully; 'where is my son?'

A volley of voices replied, 'Oh! my Lord! The Prince! the Prince! The helmet! the helmet!'

Shocked with these lamentable sounds, and dreading he knew not what, he advanced hastily – but what a sight for a father's eyes! – he beheld his child dashed to pieces, and almost buried under an enormous helmet, an hundred times more large than any casque ever made for human being, and shaded with a proportionable quantity of black feathers.

The horror of the spectacle, the ignorance of all around how this misfortune had happened, and above all, the tremendous phenomenon before him, took away the prince's speech. Yet his silence lasted longer than even grief could occasion. He fixed his eyes on what he wished in vain to believe a vision; and seemed less attentive to his loss, than buried in meditation on the stupendous object that had occasioned it. He touched, he examined the fatal casque; nor could even the bleeding mangled remains of the young prince divert the eyes of Manfred from the portent before him.

All who had known his partial fondness for young Conrad, were as much surprised at their prince's insensibility, as thunderstruck themselves at the miracle of the helmet. They conveyed the disfigured corpse into the hall, without receiving the least direction from Manfred. As little was he attentive to the ladies who remained in the chapel. On the contrary, without mentioning the unhappy princesses, his wife and daughter, the first sounds that dropped from Manfred's lips were, 'Take care of the Lady Isabella.'

The domestics, without observing the singularity of this direction, were guided by their affection to their mistress, to consider it as peculiarly addressed to her situation, and flew to her assistance. They conveyed her to her chamber more dead than alive, and indifferent to all the strange circumstances she heard, except the death of her son.

Matilda, who doted on her mother, smothered her own grief and amazement, and thought of nothing but assisting and comforting her afflicted parent. Isabella, who had been treated by Hippolita like a daughter, and who returned that tenderness with equal duty and affection, was scarce less assiduous about the princess; at the same time endeavouring to partake and lessen the weight of sorrow which she saw Matilda strove to suppress, for whom she had conceived the warmest sympathy of friendship. Yet her own situation could not help finding its place in her thoughts. She felt no concern for the death of young Conrad, except commiseration; and she was not sorry to be delivered from a marriage which had promised her little felicity, either from her destined bridegroom, or from the severe temper of Manfred, who, though he had distinguished her by great indulgence, had imprinted her mind with terror, from his causeless rigour to such amiable princesses as Hippolita and Matilda.

While the ladies were conveying the wretched mother to her bed, Manfred remained in the court, gazing on the ominous casque, and regardless of the crowd which the strangeness of the event had now assembled around him. The few words he articulated, tended solely to inquiries, whether any man knew from whence it could have come? Nobody could give him the least information. However, as it seemed to be the sole object of his curiosity, it soon became so to the rest of the spectators, whose conjectures were as absurd and improbable, as the catastrophe itself was unprecedented. In the midst of their senseless guesses, a young peasant, whom rumour had drawn thither from a neighbouring village, observed that the miraculous helmet was exactly like that on the figure in black marble of Alfonso the Good, one of their former princes, in the church of St Nicholas.

'Villain! what sayest thou?' cried Manfred, starting from his trance in a tempest of rage, and seizing the young man by the collar. 'How darest thou utter such treason? Thy life shall pay for it.'

The spectators, who as little comprehended the cause of the prince's fury as all the rest they had seen, were at a loss to unravel this new circumstance. The young peasant himself was still more astonished, not conceiving how he had offended the prince. Yet recollecting himself, with a mixture of grace and humility he disengaged himself from Manfred's grip, and then with an obeisance, which discovered more jealousy of innocence than dismay, he asked, with respect, of what he was guilty? Manfred, more enraged at the vigour, however decently exerted, with which the young man had shaken off his hold, than appeased by his submission, ordered his attendants to seize him, and, if he had not been withheld by his friends whom he had invited to the nuptials, would have poignarded the peasant in their arms.

During this altercation, some of the vulgar spectators had run to the great church, which stood near the castle, and came back openmouthed, declaring that the helmet was missing from Alfonso's statue. Manfred, at this news, grew perfectly frantic; and, as if he sought a subject on which to vent the tempest within him, he rushed again on the young peasant, crying –

'Villain! Monster! Sorcerer! 'Tis thou hast done this! 'Tis thou hast slain my son!'

The mob, who wanted some object within the scope of their capacities, on whom they might discharge their bewildered reasoning, caught the words from the mouth of their lord, and re-echoed –

'Ay, ay; 'tis he, 'tis he: he has stolen the helmet from good Alfonso's tomb, and dashed out the brains of our young prince with it,' never reflecting how enormous the disproportion was between the marble helmet that had been in the church, and that of steel before their eyes; nor how impossible it was for a youth seemingly not twenty, to wield a piece of armour of so prodigious a weight

The folly of these ejaculations brought Manfred to himself: yet whether provoked at the peasant having observed the resemblance between the two helmets, and thereby led to the farther discovery of the absence of that in the church, or wishing to bury any such rumour under so impertinent a supposition, he gravely pronounced that the young man was certainly a necromancer, and that till the Church could take cognisance of the affair, he would have the magician, whom they had thus detected, kept prisoner under the helmet itself, which he ordered his attendants to raise, and place the young man under it; declaring he should be kept there without food, with which his own infernal art might furnish him.

It was in vain for the youth to represent against this preposterous sentence: in vain did Manfred's friends endeavour to divert him from this savage and ill-grounded resolution. The generality were charmed with their lord's decision, which, to their apprehensions, carried great appearance of justice, as the magician was to be punished by the very instrument with which he had offended: nor were they struck with the least compunction at the probability of the youth being starved, for they firmly believed that, by his diabolic skill, he could easily supply himself with nutriment.

Manfred thus saw his commands even cheerfully obeyed; and appointing a guard with strict orders to prevent any food being conveyed to the prisoner, he dismissed his friends and attendants, and retired to his own chamber, after locking the gates of the castle, in which he suffered none but his domestics to remain.

In the meantime, the care and zeal of the young ladies had brought the Princess Hippolita to herself, who amidst the transports of her own sorrow frequently demanded news of her lord, would have dismissed her attendants to watch over him, and at last enjoined Matilda to leave her, and visit and comfort her father. Matilda, who wanted no affectionate duty to Manfred, though she trembled at his austerity, obeyed the orders of Hippolita, whom she tenderly recommended to Isabella; and inquiring of the domestics for her father, was informed that he was retired to his chamber, and had commanded that nobody should have admittance to him. Concluding that he was immersed in sorrow for the death of her brother, and fearing to renew his tears by the sight of his sole remaining child, she hesitated whether she should break in upon his affliction; yet solicitude for him, backed by the commands of her mother, encouraged her to venture disobeying the orders he had given; a fault she had never been guilty of before.

The gentle timidity of her nature made her pause for some minutes at his door. She heard him traverse his chamber backwards and forwards with disordered steps; a mood which increased her apprehensions. She was, however, just going to beg admittance, when Manfred suddenly opened the door; and as it was now twilight, concurring with the disorder of his mind, he did not distinguish the person, but asked angrily, who it was? Matilda replied, trembling –

'My dearest father, it is I, your daughter.'

Manfred, stepping back hastily, cried, 'Begone! I do not want a daughter;' and flinging back abruptly, clapped the door against the terrified Matilda.

She was too well acquainted with her father's impetuosity to venture a second intrusion. When she had a little recovered the shock of so bitter a reception, she wiped away her tears to prevent the additional stab that the knowledge of it would give to Hippolita, who questioned her in the most anxious terms on the health of Manfred, and how he bore his loss. Matilda assured her he was well, and supported his misfortune with manly fortitude.

'But will he not let me see him?' said Hippolita mournfully; 'will he not permit me to blend my tears with his, and shed a mother's sorrows in the bosom of her Lord? Or do you deceive me, Matilda? I know how Manfred doted on his son: is not the stroke too heavy for him? has he not sunk under it? You do not answer me – alas! I dread the worst! – Raise me, my maidens; I will, I will see my Lord. Bear me to him instantly: he is dearer to me even than my children.'

Matilda made signs to Isabella to prevent Hippolita's rising; and both those lovely young women were using their gentle violence to stop and calm the princess, when a servant, on the part of Manfred, arrived and told Isabella that his Lord demanded to speak with her.

'With me!' cried Isabella.

'Go,' said Hippolita, relieved by a message from her Lord: 'Manfred cannot support the sight of his own family. He thinks you less disordered than we are, and dreads the shock of my grief. Console him, dear Isabella, and tell him I will smother my own anguish rather than add to his.'

As it was now evening the servant who conducted Isabella bore a torch before her. When they came to Manfred, who was walking impatiently about the gallery, he started, and said hastily –

'Take away that light, and begone.'

Then shutting the door impetuously, he flung himself upon a bench against the wall, and bade Isabella sit by him. She obeyed trembling.

'I sent for you, Lady,' said he – and then stopped under great appearance of confusion.

'My Lord!'

'Yes, I sent for you on a matter of great moment,' resumed he. 'Dry your tears, young Lady – you have lost your bridegroom. Yes, cruel fate! and I have lost the hopes of my race! But Conrad was not worthy of your beauty.'

'How, my Lord!' said Isabella; 'sure you do not suspect me of not feeling the concern I ought: my duty and affection would have always – '

'Think no more of him,' interrupted Manfred; 'he was a sickly, puny child, and Heaven has perhaps taken him away, that I might not trust the honours of my house on so frail a foundation. The line of Manfred calls for numerous supports. My foolish fondness for that boy blinded the eyes of my prudence – but it is better as it is. I hope, in a few years, to have reason to rejoice at the death of Conrad.'

Words cannot paint the astonishment of Isabella. At first she apprehended that grief had disordered Manfred's understanding. Her next thought suggested that this strange discourse was designed to ensnare her: she feared that Manfred had perceived her indifference for his son: and in consequence of that idea she replied –

'Good, my Lord, do not doubt my tenderness: my heart would have accompanied my hand. Conrad would have engrossed all my care; and wherever fate shall dispose of me, I shall always cherish his memory, and regard your Highness and the virtuous Hippolita as my parents.'

'Curse on Hippolita!' cried Manfred. 'Forget her from this moment, as I do. In short, Lady, you have missed a husband undeserving of your charms: they shall now be better disposed of. Instead of a sickly boy, you shall have a husband in the prime of his age, who will know how to value your beauties, and who may expect a numerous offspring.'

'Alas, my Lord!' said Isabella, 'my mind is too sadly engrossed by the recent catastrophe in your family to think of another marriage. If ever my father returns, and it shall be his pleasure, I shall obey, as I did when I consented to give my hand to your son: but until his return, permit me to remain under your hospitable roof, and employ the melancholy hours in assuaging yours, Hippolita's, and the fair Matilda's affliction.'

'I desired you once before,' said Manfred angrily, 'not to name that woman: from this hour she must be a stranger to you, as she must be to me. In short, Isabella, since I cannot give you my son, I offer you myself.'

'Heavens!' cried Isabella, waking from her delusion, 'what do I hear? You! my Lord! You! my father-in-law! The father of Conrad! The husband of the virtuous and tender Hippolita!'

'I tell you,' said Manfred imperiously, 'Hippolita is no longer my wife; I divorce her from this hour. Too long has she cursed me by her

unfruitfulness. My fate depends on having sons, and this night I trust
will give a new date to my hopes.'

At those words he seized the cold hand of Isabella, who was half
dead with fright and horror. She shrieked, and started from him,
Manfred rose to pursue her, when the moon, which was now up, and
gleamed in at the opposite casement, presented to his sight the plumes
of the fatal helmet, which rose to the height of the windows, waving
backwards and forwards in a tempestuous manner, and accompanied
with a hollow and rustling sound. Isabella, who gathered courage
from her situation, and who dreaded nothing so much as Manfred's
pursuit of his declaration, cried –

'Look, my Lord! see, Heaven itself declares against your impious
intentions!'

'Heaven nor Hell shall impede my designs,' said Manfred, advancing again to seize the princess.

At that instant the portrait of his grandfather, which hung over the
bench where they had been sitting, uttered a deep sigh, and heaved
its breast.

Isabella, whose back was turned to the picture, saw not the motion,
nor knew whence the sound came, but started, and said –

'Hark, my Lord! What sound was that?' and at the same time made
towards the door.

Manfred, distracted between the flight of Isabella, who had now
reached the stairs, and yet unable to keep his eyes from the picture,
which began to move, had, however, advanced some steps after her,
still looking backwards on the portrait, when he saw it quit its panel,
and descend on the floor with a grave and melancholy air.

'Do I dream?' cried Manfred, returning; 'or are the devils themselves in league against me? Speak, infernal spectre! Or, if thou art my
grandsire, why dost thou too conspire against thy wretched descend-
ant, who too dearly pays for – ' Ere he could finish the sentence, the
vision sighed again, and made a sign to Manfred to follow him.

'Lead on!' cried Manfred; 'I will follow thee to the gulf of perdition.'

The spectre marched sedately, but dejected, to the end of the
gallery, and turned into a chamber on the right hand. Manfred
accompanied him at a little distance, full of anxiety and horror, but
resolved. As he would have entered the chamber, the door was
clapped to with violence by an invisible hand. The prince, collecting
courage from this delay, would have forcibly burst open the door
with his foot, but found that it resisted his utmost efforts.

'Since Hell will not satisfy my curiosity,' said Manfred, 'I will use the human means in my power for preserving my race; Isabella shall not escape me.'

The lady, whose resolution had given way to terror the moment she had quitted Manfred, continued her flight to the bottom of the principal staircase. There she stopped, not knowing whither to direct her steps, nor how to escape from the impetuosity of the prince. The gates of the castle, she knew, were locked, and guards placed in the court. Should she, as her heart prompted her, go and prepare Hippolita for the cruel destiny that awaited her, she did not doubt but Manfred would seek her there, and that his violence would incite him to double the injury he meditated, without leaving room for them to avoid the impetuosity of his passions. Delay might give him time to reflect on the horrid measures he had conceived, or produce some circumstance in her favour, if she could – for that night, at least – avoid his odious purpose. Yet where conceal herself? How avoid the pursuit he would infallibly make throughout the castle?

As these thoughts passed rapidly through her mind, she recollected a subterraneous passage which led from the vaults of the castle to the church of St Nicholas. Could she reach the altar before she was overtaken, she knew even Manfred's violence would not dare to profane the sacredness of the place; and she determined, if no other means of deliverance offered, to shut herself up for ever among the holy virgins whose convent was contiguous to the cathedral. In this resolution, she seized a lamp that burned at the foot of the staircase, and hurried towards the secret passage.

The lower part of the castle was hollowed into several intricate cloisters; and it was not easy for one under so much anxiety to find the door that opened into the cavern. An awful silence reigned throughout those subterraneous regions, except now and then some blasts of wind that shook the doors she had passed, and which, grating on the rusty hinges, were re-echoed through that long labyrinth of darkness. Every murmur struck her with new terror; yet more she dreaded to hear the wrathful voice of Manfred urging his domestics to pursue her.

She trod as softly as impatience would give her leave, yet frequently stopped and listened to hear if she was followed. In one of those moments she thought she heard a sigh. She shuddered, and recoiled a few paces. In a moment she thought she heard the step of some person. Her blood curdled; she concluded it was Manfred. Every suggestion that horror could inspire rushed into her mind.

She condemned her rash flight, which had thus exposed her to his rage in a place where her cries were not likely to draw anybody to her assistance. Yet the sound seemed not to come from behind. If Manfred knew where she was, he must have followed her. She was still in one of the cloisters, and the steps she had heard were too distinct to proceed from the way she had come. Cheered with this reflection, and hoping to find a friend in whoever was not the prince, she was going to advance, when a door that stood ajar, at some distance to the left, was opened gently: but ere her lamp, which she held up, could discover who opened it, the person retreated precipitately on seeing the light.

Isabella, whom every incident was sufficient to dismay, hesitated whether she should proceed. Her dread of Manfred soon outweighed every other terror. The very circumstance of the person avoiding her gave her a sort of courage. It could only be, she thought, some domestic belonging to the castle. Her gentleness had never raised her an enemy, and conscious innocence made her hope that, unless sent by the prince's order to seek her, his servants would rather assist than prevent her flight. Fortifying herself with these reflections, and believing by what she could observe that she was near the mouth of the subterraneous cavern, she approached the door that had been opened; but a sudden gust of wind that met her at the door extinguished her lamp, and left her in total darkness.

Words cannot paint the horror of the princess's situation. Alone in so dismal a place, her mind imprinted with all the terrible events of the day, hopeless of escaping, expecting every moment the arrival of Manfred, and far from tranquil on knowing she was within reach of somebody, she knew not whom, who for some cause seemed concealed thereabouts; all these thoughts crowded on her distracted mind, and she was ready to sink under her apprehensions. She addressed herself to every saint in heaven, and inwardly implored their assistance. For a considerable time she remained in an agony of despair.

At last, as softly as was possible, she felt for the door, and having found it, entered trembling into the vault from whence she had heard the sigh and steps. It gave her a kind of momentary joy to perceive an imperfect ray of clouded moonshine gleam from the roof of the vault, which seemed to be fallen in, and from whence hung a fragment of earth or building, she could not distinguish which, that appeared to have been crushed inwards. She advanced eagerly towards this chasm, when she discerned a human form standing close against the wall.

She shrieked, believing it the ghost of her betrothed Conrad. The figure, advancing, said, in a submissive voice –

'Be not alarmed, Lady; I will not injure you.'

Isabella, a little encouraged by the words and tone of voice of the stranger, and recollecting that this must be the person who had opened the door, recovered her spirits enough to reply –

'Sir, whoever you are, take pity on a wretched princess, standing on the brink of destruction. Assist me to escape from this fatal castle, or in a few moments I may be made miserable for ever.'

'Alas!' said the stranger, 'what can I do to assist you? I will die in your defence; but I am unacquainted with the castle, and want – '

'Oh!' said Isabella, hastily interrupting him; 'help me but to find a trap-door that must be hereabout, and it is the greatest service you can do me, for I have not a minute to lose.'

Saying these words, she felt about on the pavement, and directed the stranger to search likewise, for a smooth piece of brass enclosed in one of the stones.

'That,' said she, 'is the lock, which opens with a spring, of which I know the secret. If we can find that, I may escape – if not, alas! courteous stranger, I fear I shall have involved you in my misfortunes: Manfred will suspect you for the accomplice of my flight, and you will fall a victim to his resentment.'

'I value not my life,' said the stranger, 'and it will be some comfort to lose it in trying to deliver you from his tyranny.'

'Generous youth,' said Isabella, 'how shall I ever requite – '

As she uttered those words, a ray of moonshine, streaming through a cranny of the ruin above, shone directly on the lock they sought.

'Oh! transport!' said Isabella; 'here is the trap-door!' and, taking out the key, she touched the spring, which, starting aside, discovered an iron ring. 'Lift up the door,' said the princess.

The stranger obeyed, and beneath appeared some stone steps descending into a vault totally dark.

'We must go down here,' said Isabella. 'Follow me; dark and dismal as it is, we cannot miss our way; it leads directly to the church of St Nicholas. But, perhaps,' added the princess modestly, 'you have no reason to leave the castle, nor have I farther occasion for your service; in a few minutes I shall be safe from Manfred's rage – only let me know to whom I am so much obliged.'

'I will never quit you,' said the stranger eagerly, 'until I have placed you in safety – nor think me, Princess, more generous than I am; though you are my principal care – '

The stranger was interrupted by a sudden noise of voices that seemed approaching, and they soon distinguished these words –

'Talk not to me of necromancers; I tell you she must be in the castle; I will find her in spite of enchantment.'

'Oh, heavens!' cried Isabella; 'it is the voice of Manfred! Make haste, or we are ruined! and shut the trap-door after you.'

Saying this, she descended the steps precipitately; and as the stranger hastened to follow her, he let the door slip out of his hands: it fell, and the spring closed over it. He tried in vain to open it, not having observed Isabella's method of touching the spring; nor had he many moments to make an essay. The noise of the falling door had been heard by Manfred, who, directed by the sound, hastened thither, attended by his servants with torches.

'It must be Isabella,' cried Manfred, before he entered the vault. 'She is escaping by the subterraneous passage, but she cannot have got far.'

What was the astonishment of the prince when, instead of Isabella, the light of the torches discovered to him the young peasant whom he thought confined under the fatal helmet!

'Traitor!' said Manfred; 'how camest thou here? I thought thee in durance above in the court.'

'I am no traitor,' replied the young man boldly, 'nor am I answerable for your thoughts.'

'Presumptuous villain!' cried Manfred; 'dost thou provoke my wrath? Tell me, how hast thou escaped from above? Thou hast corrupted thy guards, and their lives shall answer it.'

'My poverty,' said the peasant calmly, 'will disculpate them: though the ministers of a tyrant's wrath, to thee they are faithful, and but too willing to execute the orders which you unjustly imposed upon them.'

'Art thou so hardy as to dare my vengeance?' said the prince. 'But tortures shall force the truth from thee. Tell me; I will know thy accomplices.'

'There was my accomplice!' said the youth, smiling, and pointing to the roof.

Manfred ordered the torches to be held up, and perceived that one of the cheeks of the enchanted casque had forced its way through the pavement of the court, as his servants had let it fall over the peasant, and had broken through into the vault, leaving a gap, through which the peasant had pressed himself some minutes before he was found by Isabella.

'Was that the way by which thou didst descend?' said Manfred.

'It was,' said the youth.

'But what noise was that,' said Manfred, 'which I heard as I entered the cloister?'

'A door clapped,' said the peasant. 'I heard it as well as you.'

'What door?' said Manfred hastily.

'I am not acquainted with your castle,' said the peasant; 'this is the first time I ever entered it, and this vault the only part of it within which I ever was.'

'But I tell thee,' said Manfred (wishing to find out if the youth had discovered the trap-door), 'it was this way I heard the noise. My servants heard it too.'

'My Lord,' interrupted one of them officiously, 'to be sure it was the trap-door, and he was going to make his escape.'

'Peace, blockhead!' said the prince angrily; 'if he was going to escape, how should he come on this side? I will know from his own mouth what noise it was I heard. Tell me truly; thy life depends on thy veracity.'

'My veracity is dearer to me than my life,' said the peasant; 'nor would I purchase the one by forfeiting the other.'

'Indeed, young philosopher!' said Manfred contemptuously; 'tell me, then, what was the noise I heard?'

'Ask me what I can answer,' said he, 'and put me to death instantly if I tell you a lie.'

Manfred, growing impatient at the steady valour and indifference of the youth, cried –

'Well, then, thou man of truth, answer! Was it the fall of the trap-door that I heard?'

'It was,' said the youth.

'It was!' said the prince; 'and how didst thou come to know there was a trap-door here?'

'I saw the plate of brass by a gleam of moonshine,' replied he.

'But what told thee it was a lock?' said Manfred. 'How didst thou discover the secret of opening it?'

'Providence, that delivered me from the helmet, was able to direct me to the spring of a lock,' said he.

'Providence should have gone a little farther, and have placed thee out of the reach of my resentment,' said Manfred. 'When Providence had taught thee to open the lock, it abandoned thee for a fool, who did not know how to make use of its favours. Why didst thou not pursue the path pointed out for thy escape? Why didst thou shut the trap-door before thou hadst descended the steps?'

'I might ask you, my Lord,' said the peasant, 'how I, totally unacquainted with your castle, was to know that those steps led to any outlet? But I scorn to evade your questions. Wherever those steps lead to, perhaps I should have explored the way – I could not be in a worse situation than I was. But the truth is, I let the trap-door fall: your immediate arrival followed. I had given the alarm – what imported it to me whether I was seized a minute sooner or a minute later?'

'Thou art a resolute villain for thy years,' said Manfred; 'yet on reflection I suspect thou dost but trifle with me. Thou hast not yet told me how thou didst open the lock.'

'That I will show you, my Lord,' said the peasant; and, taking up a fragment of stone that had fallen from above, he laid himself on the trap-door, and began to beat on the piece of brass that covered it, meaning to gain time for the escape of the princess. This presence of mind, joined to the frankness of the youth, staggered Manfred. He even felt a disposition towards pardoning one who had been guilty of no crime. Manfred was not one of those savage tyrants who wanton in cruelty unprovoked. The circumstances of his fortune had given an asperity to his temper, which was naturally humane; and his virtues were always ready to operate, when his passions did not obscure his reason.

While the prince was in this suspense, a confused noise of voices echoed through the distant vaults. As the sound approached, he distinguished the clamours of some of his domestics, whom he had dispersed through the castle in search of Isabella, calling out –

'Where is my Lord? Where is the Prince?'

'Here I am,' said Manfred, as they came nearer; 'have you found the Princess?'

The first that arrived, replied, 'Oh, my Lord! I am glad we have found you.'

'Found me!' said Manfred; 'have you found the Princess?'

'We thought we had, my Lord,' said the fellow, looking terrified, 'but – '

'But, what?' cried the prince; 'has she escaped?'

'Jaquez and I, my Lord – '

'Yes, I and Diego,' interrupted the second, who came up in still greater consternation.

'Speak one of you at a time,' said Manfred; 'I ask you, where is the Princess?'

'We do not know,' said they both together; 'but we are frightened out of our wits.'

'So I think, blockheads,' said Manfred. 'What is it has scared you thus?'

'Oh! my Lord,' said Jaquez, 'Diego has seen such a sight! your Highness would not believe our eyes.'

'What new absurdity is this?' cried Manfred; 'give me a direct answer, or, by Heaven – '

'Why, my Lord, if it please your Highness to hear me,' said the poor fellow, 'Diego and I – '

'Yes, I and Jaquez – ' cried his comrade.

'Did not I forbid you to speak both at a time?' said the prince: 'you, Jaquez, answer; for the other fool seems more distracted than thou art; what is the matter?'

'My gracious Lord,' said Jaquez, 'if it please your Highness to hear me; Diego and I, according to your Highness's orders, went to search for the young Lady; but being comprehensive that we might meet the ghost of my young Lord, your Highness's son, God rest his soul, as he has not received Christian burial – '

'Sot!' cried Manfred in a rage; 'is it only a ghost, then, that thou hast seen?'

'Oh! worse! worse! my Lord,' cried Diego: 'I had rather have seen ten whole ghosts.'

'Grant me patience!' said Manfred; 'these blockheads distract me. Out of my sight, Diego! and thou, Jaquez, tell me in one word, art thou sober? Art thou raving? Thou wast wont to have some sense: has the other sot frightened himself and thee too? Speak; what is it he fancies he has seen?'

'Why, my Lord,' replied Jaquez, trembling, 'I was going to tell your Highness, that since the calamitous misfortune of my young Lord, God rest his precious soul! not one of us your Highness's faithful servants – indeed we are, my Lord, though poor men – I say, not one of us has dared to set a foot about the castle, but two together: so Diego and I, thinking that my young Lady might be in the great gallery, went up there to look for her, and tell her your Highness wanted something to impart to her.'

'O blundering fools!' cried Manfred; 'and in the meantime, she has made her escape, because you were afraid of goblins! – Why, thou knave! she left me in the gallery; I came from thence myself.'

'For all that, she may be there still for aught I know,' said Jaquez; 'but the devil shall have me before I seek her there again – poor Diego! I do not believe he will ever recover it.'

'Recover what?' said Manfred; 'am I never to learn what it is has terrified these rascals? – but I lose my time; follow me, slave; I will see if she is in the gallery.'

'For Heaven's sake, my dear, good Lord,' cried Jaquez, 'do not go to the gallery. Satan himself I believe is in the chamber next to the gallery.'

Manfred, who hitherto had treated the terror of his servants as an idle panic, was struck at this new circumstance. He recollected the apparition of the portrait, and the sudden closing of the door at the end of the gallery. His voice faltered, and he asked with disorder –

'What is in the great chamber?'

'My Lord,' said Jaquez, 'when Diego and I came into the gallery, he went first, for he said he had more courage than I. So when we came into the gallery we found nobody. We looked under every bench and stool; and still we found nobody.'

'Were all the pictures in their places?' said Manfred.

'Yes, my Lord,' answered Jaquez; 'but we did not think of looking behind them.'

'Well, well!' said Manfred; 'proceed.'

'When we came to the door of the great chamber,' continued Jaquez, 'we found it shut.'

'And could not you open it?' said Manfred.

'Oh! yes, my Lord; would to Heaven we had not!' replied he – 'nay, it was not I neither; it was Diego: he was grown foolhardy, and would go on, though I advised him not – if ever I open a door that is shut again – '

'Trifle not,' said Manfred, shuddering, 'but tell me what you saw in the great chamber on opening the door.'

'I! my Lord!' said Jaquez; 'I was behind Diego; but I heard the noise.'

'Jaquez,' said Manfred, in a solemn tone of voice; 'tell me, I adjure thee by the souls of my ancestors, what was it thou sawest? What was it thou heardest?'

'It was Diego saw it, my Lord, it was not I,' replied Jaquez; 'I only heard the noise. Diego had no sooner opened the door, than he cried out, and ran back. I ran back too, and said, "Is it the ghost?" "The ghost! no, no," said Diego, and his hair stood on end – "it is a giant, I believe; he is all clad in armour, for I saw his foot and part of his leg, and they are as large as the helmet below in the court." As he said these words, my Lord, we heard a violent motion and the rattling of armour, as if the giant was rising, for Diego has told me since that he believes the giant was lying down, for the foot and leg were stretched at length on the floor. Before we could get to the end of the gallery, we heard the door of the great chamber clap behind us, but we did not dare turn back to see if the giant was following us – yet, now I think on it, we must have heard him if he had pursued us – but for Heaven's sake, good my Lord, send for the chaplain, and have the castle exorcised, for, for certain, it is enchanted.'

'Ay, pray do, my Lord,' cried all the servants at once, 'or we must leave your Highness's service.'

'Peace, dotards!' said Manfred, 'and follow me; I will know what all this means.'

'We! my Lord!' cried they with one voice; 'we would not go up to the gallery for your Highness's revenue.' The young peasant, who had stood silent, now spoke.

'Will your Highness,' said he, 'permit me to try this adventure? My life is of consequence to nobody; I fear no bad angel, and have offended no good one.'

'Your behaviour is above your seeming,' said Manfred, viewing him with surprise and admiration – 'hereafter I will reward your bravery – but now,' continued he with a sigh, 'I am so circumstanced, that I dare trust no eyes but my own. However, I give you leave to accompany me.'

Manfred, when he first followed Isabella from the gallery, had gone directly to the apartment of his wife, concluding the princess had retired thither. Hippolita, who knew his step, rose with anxious fondness to meet her Lord, whom she had not seen since the death of their son. She would have flown in a transport mixed of joy and grief to his bosom, but he pushed her rudely off, and said –

'Where is Isabella?'

'Isabella! my Lord!' said the astonished Hippolita.

'Yes, Isabella,' cried Manfred imperiously; 'I want Isabella.'

'My Lord,' replied Matilda, who perceived how much his behaviour had shocked her mother, 'she has not been with us since your Highness summoned her to your apartment.'

'Tell me where she is,' said the prince; 'I do not want to know where she has been.'

'My good Lord,' says Hippolita, 'your daughter tells you the truth: Isabella left us by your command, and has not returned since – but, my good Lord, compose yourself: retire to your rest: this dismal day has disordered you. Isabella shall wait your orders in the morning.'

'What, then, you know where she is!' cried Manfred. 'Tell me
directly, for I will not lose an instant – and you, woman,' speaking to
his wife, 'order your chaplain to attend me forthwith.'

'Isabella,' said Hippolita calmly, 'is retired, I suppose, to her cham-
ber: she is not accustomed to watch at this late hour. Gracious my
Lord,' continued she, 'let me know what has disturbed you. Has
Isabella offended you?'

'Trouble me not with questions,' said Manfred, 'but tell me where
she is.'

'Matilda shall call her,' said the princess. 'Sit down, my Lord, and
resume your wonted fortitude.'

'What, art thou jealous of Isabella?' replied he, 'that you wish to be
present at our interview!'

'Good heavens! my Lord,' said Hippolita, 'what is it your Highness means?'

'Thou wilt know ere many minutes are passed,' said the cruel
prince. 'Send your chaplain to me, and wait my pleasure here.'

At these words he flung out of the room in search of Isabella,
leaving the amazed ladies thunderstruck with his words and frantic
deportment, and lost in vain conjectures on what he was meditating.

Manfred was now returning from the vault, attended by the
peasant and a few of his servants whom he had obliged to accompany
him. He ascended the staircase without stopping till he arrived at
the gallery, at the door of which he met Hippolita and her chaplain.
When Diego had been dismissed by Manfred, he had gone directly
to the princess's apartment with the alarm of what he had seen.
That excellent Lady, who no more than Manfred doubted of the
reality of the vision, yet affected to treat it as a delirium of the
servant. Willing, however, to save her Lord from any additional
shock, and prepared by a series of griefs not to tremble at any
accession to it, she determined to make herself the first sacrifice,
if fate had marked the present hour for their destruction. Dismissing the reluctant Matilda to her rest, who in vain sued for leave
to accompany her mother, and attended only by her chaplain,
Hippolita had visited the gallery and great chamber; and now with
more serenity of soul than she had felt for many hours, she met her
Lord, and assured him that the vision of the gigantic leg and foot
was all a fable; and no doubt an impression made by fear, and the
dark and dismal hour of the night, on the minds of his servants. She
and the chaplain had examined the chamber, and found everything
in the usual order.

Manfred, though persuaded, like his wife, that the vision had been no work of fancy, recovered a little from the tempest of mind into which so many strange events had thrown him. Ashamed, too, of his inhuman treatment of a princess who returned every injury with new marks of tenderness and duty, he felt returning love forcing itself into his eyes; but not less ashamed of feeling remorse towards one against whom he was inwardly meditating a yet more bitter outrage, he curbed the yearnings of his heart, and did not dare to lean even towards pity. The next transition of his soul was to exquisite villainy.

Presuming on the unshaken submission of Hippolita, he flattered himself that she would not only acquiesce with patience to a divorce, but would obey, if it was his pleasure, in endeavouring to persuade Isabella to give him her hand – but ere he could indulge his horrid hope, he reflected that Isabella was not to be found. Coming to himself, he gave orders that every avenue to the castle should be strictly guarded, and charged his domestics on pain of their lives to suffer nobody to pass out. The young peasant, to whom he spoke favourably, he ordered to remain in a small chamber on the stairs, in which there was a pallet-bed, and the key of which he took away himself, telling the youth he would talk with him in the morning. Then dismissing his attendants, and bestowing a sullen kind of half-nod on Hippolita, he retired to his own chamber.

Chapter Two

Matilda, who by Hippolita's order had retired to her apartment, was ill-disposed to take any rest. The shocking fate of her brother had deeply affected her. She was surprised at not seeing Isabella; but the strange words which had fallen from her father, and his obscure menace to the Princess his wife, accompanied by the most furious behaviour, had filled her gentle mind with terror and alarm. She waited anxiously for the return of Bianca, a young damsel that attended her, whom she had sent to learn what was become of Isabella. Bianca soon appeared, and informed her mistress of what she had gathered from the servants, that Isabella was nowhere to be found. She related the adventure of the young peasant who had been discovered in the vault, though with many simple add-itions from the incoherent accounts of the domestics; and she dwelt principally on the gigantic leg and foot which had been seen in the gallery-chamber. This last circumstance had terrified Bianca so much, that she was rejoiced when Matilda told her that she would not go to rest, but would watch till the princess should rise.

The young princess wearied herself in conjectures on the flight of Isabella, and on the threats of Manfred to her mother. 'But what business could he have so urgent with the chaplain?' said Matilda, 'Does he intend to have my brother's body interred privately in the chapel?'

'Oh, Madam!' said Bianca, 'now I guess. As you are become his heiress, he is impatient to have you married: he has always been raving for more sons; I warrant he is now impatient for grandsons. As sure as I live, Madam, I shall see you a bride at last. – Good madam, you won't cast off your faithful Bianca: you won't put Donna Rosara over me now you are a great princess.'

'My poor Bianca,' said Matilda, 'how fast your thoughts amble! I a great princess! What hast thou seen in Manfred's behaviour since my brother's death that bespeaks any increase of tenderness to me? No, Bianca; his heart was ever a stranger to me – but he is my father, and I must not complain. Nay, if Heaven shuts my father's heart against me, it overpays my little merit in the tenderness of my mother – O that dear mother! Yes, Bianca, 'tis there I feel the rugged temper of Manfred. I can support his harshness to me with patience; but it wounds my soul when I am witness to his causeless severity towards her.'

'Oh! Madam,' said Bianca, 'all men use their wives so, when they are weary of them.'

'And yet you congratulated me but now,' said Matilda, 'when you fancied my father intended to dispose of me!'

'I would have you a great Lady,' replied Bianca, 'come what will. I do not wish to see you moped in a convent, as you would be if you had your will, and if my Lady, your mother, who knows that a bad husband is better than no husband at all, did not hinder you. – Bless me! what noise is that! St Nicholas forgive me! I was but in jest.'

'It is the wind,' said Matilda, 'whistling through the battlements in the tower above: you have heard it a thousand times.'

'Nay,' said Bianca, 'there was no harm neither in what I said: it is no sin to talk of matrimony – and so, Madam, as I was saying, if my Lord Manfred should offer you a handsome young prince for a bridegroom, you would drop him a curtsey, and tell him you would rather take the veil?'

'Thank Heaven! I am in no such danger,' said Matilda: 'you know how many proposals for me he has rejected – '

'And you thank him, like a dutiful daughter, do you, Madam? But come, Madam; suppose, tomorrow morning, he was to send for you to the great council chamber, and there you should find at his elbow a lovely young prince, with large black eyes, a smooth white forehead, and manly curling locks like jet; in short, Madam, a young hero resembling the picture of the good Alfonso in the gallery, which you sit and gaze at for hours together – '

'Do not speak lightly of that picture,' interrupted Matilda sighing; 'I know the adoration with which I look at that picture is uncommon – but I am not in love with a coloured panel. The character of that virtuous prince, the veneration with which my mother has inspired me for his memory, the orisons which, I know not why, she has enjoined me to pour forth at his tomb, all have concurred to persuade me that somehow or other my destiny is linked with something relating to him.'

'Lord, Madam! how should that be?' said Bianca; 'I have always heard that your family was in no way related to his: and I am sure I cannot conceive why my Lady, the Princess, sends you in a cold morning or a damp evening to pray at his tomb: he is no saint by the almanack. If you must pray, why does she not bid you address yourself to our great St Nicholas? I am sure he is the saint I pray to for a husband.'

'Perhaps my mind would be less affected,' said Matilda, 'if my mother would explain her reasons to me: but it is the mystery she observes, that inspires me with this – I know not what to call it. As she never acts from caprice, I am sure there is some fatal secret at bottom – nay, I know there is: in her agony of grief for my brother's death she dropped some words that intimated as much.'

'Oh! dear Madam,' cried Bianca, 'what were they?'

'No,' said Matilda, 'if a parent lets fall a word, and wishes it recalled, it is not for a child to utter it.'

'What! was she sorry for what she had said?' asked Bianca; 'I am sure, Madam, you may trust me – '

'With my own little secrets when I have any, I may,' said Matilda; 'but never with my mother's: a child ought to have no ears or eyes but as a parent directs.'

'Well! to be sure, Madam, you were born to be a saint,' said Bianca, 'and there is no resisting one's vocation: you will end in a convent at last. But there is my Lady Isabella would not be so reserved to me: she will let me talk to her of young men: and when a handsome cavalier has come to the castle, she has owned to me that she wished your brother Conrad resembled him.'

'Bianca,' said the princess, 'I do not allow you to mention my friend disrespectfully. Isabella is of a cheerful disposition, but her soul is pure as virtue itself. She knows your idle babbling humour, and perhaps has now and then encouraged it, to divert melancholy, and enliven the solitude in which my father keeps us – '

'Blessed Mary!' said Bianca, starting, 'there it is again! Dear Madam, do you hear nothing? This castle is certainly haunted!'

'Peace!' said Matilda, 'and listen! I did think I heard a voice – but it must be fancy: your terrors, I suppose, have infected me.'

'Indeed! indeed! Madam,' said Bianca, half-weeping with agony, 'I am sure I heard a voice.'

'Does anybody lie in the chamber beneath?' said the princess.

'Nobody has dared to lie there,' answered Bianca, 'since the great astrologer, that was your brother's tutor, drowned himself. For certain, Madam, his ghost and the young prince's are now met in the chamber below – for Heaven's sake let us fly to your mother's apartment!'

'I charge you not to stir,' said Matilda. 'If they are spirits in pain, we may ease their sufferings by questioning them. They can mean no hurt to us, for we have not injured them – and if they should, shall we be more safe in one chamber than in another? Reach me my beads; we will say a prayer, and then speak to them.'

'Oh! dear Lady, I would not speak to a ghost for the world!' cried Bianca. As she said those words they heard the casement of the little chamber below Matilda's open. They listened attentively, and in a few minutes thought they heard a person sing, but could not distinguish the words.

'This can be no evil spirit,' said the princess, in a low voice; 'it is undoubtedly one of the family – open the window, and we shall know the voice.'

'I dare not, indeed, Madam,' said Bianca.

'Thou art a very fool,' said Matilda, opening the window gently herself. The noise the princess made was, however, heard by the person beneath, who stopped; and they concluded had heard the casement open.

'Is anybody below?' said the princess; 'if there is, speak.'

'Yes,' said an unknown voice.

'Who is it?' said Matilda.

'A stranger,' replied the voice.

'What stranger?' said she; 'and how didst thou come there at this unusual hour, when all the gates of the castle are locked?'

'I am not here willingly,' answered the voice. 'But pardon me, Lady, if I have disturbed your rest; I knew not that I was overheard. Sleep had forsaken me; I left a restless couch, and came to waste the irksome hours with gazing on the fair approach of morning, impatient to be dismissed from this castle.'

'Thy words and accents,' said Matilda, 'are of melancholy cast; if thou art unhappy, I pity thee. If poverty afflicts thee, let me know it; I will mention thee to the Princess, whose beneficent soul ever melts for the distressed, and she will relieve thee.'

'I am indeed unhappy,' said the stranger; 'and I know not what wealth is. But I do not complain of the lot which Heaven has cast for me; I am young and healthy, and am not ashamed of owing my support to myself – yet think me not proud, or that I disdain your generous offers. I will remember you in my orisons, and will pray for blessings on your gracious self and your noble mistress – if I sigh, Lady, it is for others, not for myself.'

'Now I have it, Madam,' said Bianca, whispering to the princess; 'this is certainly the young peasant; and, by my conscience, he is in love – Well! this is a charming adventure! – do, Madam, let us sift him. He does not know you, but takes you for one of my Lady Hippolita's women.'

'Art thou not ashamed, Bianca!' said the princess. 'What right have we to pry into the secrets of this young man's heart? He seems virtuous and frank, and tells us he is unhappy. Are those circumstances that authorise us to make a property of him? How are we entitled to his confidence?'

'Lord, Madam! how little you know of love!' replied Bianca. 'Why, lovers have no pleasure equal to talking of their mistress.'

'And would you have *me* become a peasant's confidante?' said the princess.

'Well, then, let me talk to him,' said Bianca; 'though I have the honour of being your Highness's maid of honour, I was not always so great. Besides, if love levels ranks, it raises them too; I have a respect for any young man in love.'

'Peace, simpleton!' said the princess. 'Though he said he was unhappy, it does not follow that he must be in love. Think of all that has happened today, and tell me if there are no misfortunes but what love causes. – Stranger,' resumed the princess, 'if thy misfortunes have not been occasioned by thy own fault, and are within the compass of the Princess Hippolita's power to redress, I will take upon me to answer that she will be thy protectress. When thou art dismissed from this castle, repair to holy Father Jerome, at the convent adjoining to the church of St Nicholas, and make thy story known to him, as far as thou thinkest meet. He will not fail to inform the Princess, who is the mother of all that want her assistance. Farewell; it is not seemly for me to hold farther converse with a man at this unwonted hour.'

'May the saints guard thee, gracious Lady!' replied the peasant; 'but oh! if a poor and worthless stranger might presume to beg a minute's audience farther; am I so happy? The casement is not shut; might I venture to ask – '

'Speak quickly,' said Matilda; 'the morning dawns apace: should the labourers come into the fields and perceive us – what wouldst thou ask?'

'I know not how, I know not if I dare,' said the young stranger, faltering; 'yet the humanity with which you have spoken to me emboldens – Lady! dare I trust you?'

'Heavens!' said Matilda, 'what dost thou mean? With what wouldst thou trust me? Speak boldly, if thy secret is fit to be entrusted to a virtuous breast.'

'I would ask,' said the peasant, recollecting himself, 'whether what I have heard from the domestics is true, that the Princess is missing from the castle?'

'What imports it to thee to know?' replied Matilda. 'Thy first words bespoke a prudent and becoming gravity. Dost thou come hither to pry into the secrets of Manfred? Adieu. I have been mistaken in thee.' Saying these words she shut the casement hastily, without giving the young man time to reply.

'I had acted more wisely,' said the princess to Bianca, with some sharpness, 'if I had let thee converse with this peasant; his inquisitiveness seems of a piece with thy own.'

'It is not fit for me to argue with your Highness,' replied Bianca; 'but perhaps the questions I should have put to him would have been more to the purpose than those you have been pleased to ask him.'

'Oh! no doubt,' said Matilda; 'you are a very discreet personage! May I know what *you* would have asked him?'

'A bystander often sees more of the game than those that play,' answered Bianca. 'Does your Highness think, Madam, that this question about my Lady Isabella was the result of mere curiosity? No, no, Madam, there is more in it than you great folks are aware of. Lopez told me that all the servants believe this young fellow contrived my Lady Isabella's escape; now, pray, Madam, observe: you and I both know that my Lady Isabella never much fancied the Prince your brother. Well! he is killed just in a critical minute – I accuse nobody. A helmet falls from the moon – so my Lord, your father, says; but Lopez and all the servants say that this young spark is a magician, and stole it from Alfonso's tomb – '

'Have done with this rhapsody of impertinence,' said Matilda.

'Nay, Madam, as you please,' cried Bianca; 'yet it is very particular though, that my Lady Isabella should be missing the very same day, and that this young sorcerer should be found at the mouth of the trap-door. I accuse nobody; but if my young Lord came honestly by his death – '

'Dare not on thy duty,' said Matilda, 'to breathe a suspicion on the purity of my dear Isabella's fame.'

'Purity, or not purity,' said Bianca, 'gone she is – a stranger is found that nobody knows; you question him yourself; he tells you he is in love, or unhappy, it is the same thing – nay, he owned he was unhappy about others; and is anybody unhappy about another, unless they are in love with them? And at the very next word, he asks innocently, pour soul! if my Lady Isabella is missing.'

'To be sure,' said Matilda, 'thy observations are not totally without foundation – Isabella's flight amazes me. The curiosity of the stranger is very particular; yet Isabella never concealed a thought from me.'

'So she told you,' said Bianca, 'to fish out your secrets; but who knows, Madam, but this stranger may be some prince in disguise? Do, Madam, let me open the window, and ask him a few questions.'

'No,' replied Matilda, 'I will ask him myself, if he knows aught of Isabella; he is not worthy I should converse farther with him.' She was going to open the casement, when they heard the bell ring at the postern-gate of the castle, which is on the right hand of the tower, where Matilda lay. This prevented the princess from renewing the conversation with the stranger.

After continuing silent for some time, 'I am persuaded,' said she to Bianca, 'that whatever be the cause of Isabella's flight it had no unworthy motive. If this stranger was accessory to it, she must be satisfied with his fidelity and worth. I observed, did not you, Bianca? that his words were tinctured with an uncommon infusion of piety. It was no ruffian's speech; his phrases were becoming a man of gentle birth.'

'I told you, Madam,' said Bianca, 'that I was sure he was some prince in disguise.'

'Yet,' said Matilda, 'if he was privy to her escape, how will you account for his not accompanying her in her flight? Why expose himself unnecessarily and rashly to my father's resentment?'

'As for that, Madam,' replied she, 'if he could get from under the helmet, he will find ways of eluding your father's anger. I do not doubt but he has some talisman or other about him.'

'You resolve everything into magic,' said Matilda; 'but a man who has any intercourse with infernal spirits, does not dare to make use of those tremendous and holy words which he uttered. Didst thou not observe with what fervour he vowed to remember *me* to heaven in his prayers? Yes; Isabella was undoubtedly convinced of his piety.'

'Commend me to the piety of a young fellow and a damsel that consult to elope!' said Bianca. 'No, no, Madam, my Lady Isabella is of another-guess mould than you take her for. She used indeed to sigh and lift up her eyes in your company, because she knows you are a saint; but when your back was turned – '

'You wrong her,' said Matilda; 'Isabella is no hypocrite; she has a due sense of devotion, but never affected a call she has not. On the contrary, she always combated my inclination for the cloister; and though I own the mystery she has made to me of her flight confounds me, though it seems inconsistent with the friendship between us, I cannot forget the disinterested warmth with which she always opposed my taking the veil. She wished to see me married, though my dower would have been a loss to her and my brother's children. For her sake I will believe well of this young peasant.'

'Then you do think there is some liking between them,' said Bianca. While she was speaking, a servant came hastily into the chamber and told the Princess that the Lady Isabella was found.

'Where?' said Matilda.

'She has taken sanctuary in St Nicholas's church,' replied the servant; 'Father Jerome has brought the news himself; he is below with his Highness.'

'Where is my mother?' said Matilda.

'She is in her own chamber, Madam, and has asked for you.'

Manfred had risen at the first dawn of light, and gone to Hippolita's apartment, to inquire if she knew aught of Isabella. While he was questioning her, word was brought that Jerome demanded to speak with him. Manfred, little suspecting the cause of the friar's arrival, and knowing he was employed by Hippolita in her charities, ordered him to be admitted, intending to leave them together, while he pursued his search after Isabella.

'Is your business with me or the Princess?' said Manfred.

'With both,' replied the holy man. 'The Lady Isabella – '

'What of her?' interrupted Manfred, eagerly.

'Is at St Nicholas's altar,' replied Jerome.

'That is no business of Hippolita,' said Manfred with confusion; 'let us retire to my chamber, Father, and inform me how she came thither.'

'No, my Lord,' replied the good man, with an air of firmness and authority that daunted even the resolute Manfred, who could not help revering the saint-like virtues of Jerome; 'my commission is to both, and with your Highness's good-liking, in the presence of both I shall deliver it; but first, my Lord, I must interrogate the Princess, whether she is acquainted with the cause of the Lady Isabella's retirement from your castle.'

'No, on my soul,' said Hippolita; 'does Isabella charge me with being privy to it?'

'Father,' interrupted Manfred, 'I pay due reverence to your holy profession; but I am sovereign here, and will allow no meddling priest to interfere in the affairs of my domestic. If you have aught to say attend me to my chamber; I do not use to let my wife be acquainted with the secret affairs of my state; they are not within a woman's province.'

'My Lord,' said the holy man, 'I am no intruder into the secrets of families. My office is to promote peace, to heal divisions, to preach repentance, and teach mankind to curb their headstrong passions. I forgive your Highness's uncharitable apostrophe; I know my duty, and am the minister of a mightier prince than Manfred. Hearken to him who speaks through my organs.'

Manfred trembled with rage and shame. Hippolita's countenance declared her astonishment and impatience to know where this would end. Her silence more strongly spoke her observance of Manfred.

'The Lady Isabella,' resumed Jerome, 'commends herself to both your Highnesses; she thanks both for the kindness with which she has been treated in your castle: she deplores the loss of your son, and her own misfortune in not becoming the daughter of such wise and noble princes, whom she shall always respect as *parents*; she prays for uninterrupted union and felicity between you,' [Manfred's colour changed] 'but as it is no longer possible for her to be allied to you, she entreats your consent to remain in sanctuary, till she can learn news of her father, or, by the certainty of his death, be at liberty, with the approbation of her guardians, to dispose of herself in suitable marriage.'

'I shall give no such consent,' said the prince, 'but insist on her return to the castle without delay: I am answerable for her person to her guardians, and will not brook her being in any hands but my own.'

'Your Highness will recollect whether that can any longer be proper,' replied the friar.

'I want no monitor,' said Manfred, colouring; 'Isabella's conduct leaves room for strange suspicions – and that young villain, who was at least the accomplice of her flight, if not the cause of it – '

'The cause!' interrupted Jerome; 'was a *young* man the cause?'

'This is not to be borne!' cried Manfred. 'Am I to be bearded in my own palace by an insolent monk? Thou art privy, I guess, to their amours.'

'I would pray to heaven to clear up your uncharitable surmises,' said Jerome, 'if your Highness were not satisfied in your conscience how unjustly you accuse me. I do pray to heaven to pardon that uncharitableness: and I implore your Highness to leave the Princess at peace in that holy place, where she is not liable to be disturbed by such vain and worldly fantasies as discourses of love from any man.'

'Cant not to me,' said Manfred, 'but return and bring the Princess to her duty.'

'It is my duty to prevent her return hither,' said Jerome. 'She is where orphans and virgins are safest from the snares and wiles of this world; and nothing but a parent's authority shall take her thence.'

'I am her parent,' cried Manfred, 'and demand her.'

'She wished to have you for her parent,' said the friar; 'but Heaven that forbad that connection has for ever dissolved all ties betwixt you: and I announce to your Highness – '

'Stop! audacious man,' said Manfred, 'and dread my displeasure.'

'Holy father,' said Hippolita, 'it is your office to be no respecter of persons: you must speak as your duty prescribes: but it is my duty to hear nothing that it pleases not my Lord I should hear. Attend the Prince to his chamber. I will retire to my oratory, and pray to the blessed Virgin to inspire you with her holy counsels, and to restore the heart of my gracious Lord to its wonted peace and gentleness.'

'Excellent woman!' said the friar. 'My Lord, I attend your pleasure.'

Manfred, accompanied by the friar, passed to his own apartment, where shutting the door, 'I perceive, Father,' said he, 'that Isabella has acquainted you with my purpose. Now hear my resolve, and obey. Reasons of state, most urgent reasons, my own and the safety of my people, demand that I should have a son. It is in vain to expect an heir from Hippolita. I have made choice of Isabella. You must bring her back; and you must do more. I know the influence you have with Hippolita: her conscience is in your hands. She is, I allow, a faultless woman: her soul is set on heaven, and scorns the little grandeur of this world: you can withdraw her from it entirely. Persuade her to consent to the dissolution of our marriage, and to retire into a monastery – she shall endow one if she will; and she shall have the means of being as liberal to your order as she or you can wish. Thus you will divert the calamities that are hanging over our heads, and have the merit of saving the principality of Otranto from destruction. You are a prudent man, and though the warmth of my temper betrayed me into some unbecoming expressions, I honour your virtue, and wish to be indebted to you for the repose of my life and the preservation of my family.'

'The will of heaven be done!' said the friar. 'I am but its worthless instrument. It makes use of my tongue to tell thee, Prince, of thy unwarrantable designs. The injuries of the virtuous Hippolita have mounted to the throne of pity. By me thou art reprimanded for thy adulterous intention of repudiating her: by me thou art warned not to pursue the incestuous design on thy contracted daughter. Heaven that delivered her from thy fury, when the judgments so recently fallen on thy house ought to have inspired thee with other thoughts, will continue to watch over her. Even I, a poor and despised friar, am able to protect her from thy violence – I, sinner as I am, and uncharitably reviled by your Highness as an accomplice of I know not what amours, scorn the allurements with which it has pleased thee to tempt mine honesty. I love my order; I honour devout souls; I respect the piety of thy princess – but I will not betray the confidence she reposes in me, nor serve even the cause of religion by foul and sinful compliances – but forsooth! the welfare of the state depends on your Highness having a son! Heaven mocks the shortsighted views of man. But yester-morn, whose house was so great, so flourishing as Manfred's? – Where is young Conrad now? – My Lord, I respect your tears – but I mean not to check them – let them flow, Prince! They will weigh more with heaven toward the welfare of thy subjects, than a marriage which, founded on lust or policy, could never prosper. The sceptre, which passed from the race of Alfonso to thine, cannot be preserved by a match which the church will never allow. If it is the will of the Most High that Manfred's name must perish, resign yourself, my Lord, to its decrees; and thus deserve a crown that can never pass away. Come, my Lord; I like this sorrow – let us return to the Princess: she is not apprised of your cruel intentions; nor did I mean more than to alarm you. You saw with what gentle patience, with what efforts of love, she heard, she rejected hearing, the extent of your guilt. I know she longs to fold you in her arms, and assure you of her unalterable affection.'

'Father,' said the prince, 'you mistake my compunction: true, I honour Hippolita's virtues; I think her a saint; and wish it were for my soul's health to tie faster the knot that has united us – but alas! Father, you know not the bitterest of my pangs! It is some time that I have had scruples on the legality of our union: Hippolita is related to me in the fourth degree – it is true, we had a dispensation: but I have been informed that she had also been contracted to another. This it is that sits heavy at my heart: to this state of unlawful wedlock I impute the visitation that has fallen on me in the death of Conrad! – Ease my conscience of this burden: dissolve our marriage, and accomplish the work of godliness – which your divine exhortations have commenced in my soul.'

How cutting was the anguish which the good man felt, when he perceived this turn in the wily prince! He trembled for Hippolita, whose ruin he saw was determined; and he feared if Manfred had no hope of recovering Isabella, that his impatience for a son would direct him to some other object, who might not be equally proof against the temptation of Manfred's rank. For some time the holy man remained absorbed in thought. At length, conceiving some hopes from delay, he thought the wisest conduct would be to prevent the prince from despairing of recovering Isabella. Her the friar knew he could dispose, from her affection to Hippolita, and from the aversion she had expressed to him for Manfred's addresses, to second his views, till the censures of the church could be fulminated against a divorce. With this intention, as if struck with the prince's scruples, he at length said: 'My Lord, I have been pondering on what your Highness has said; and if in truth it is delicacy of conscience that is the real motive of your repugnance to your virtuous Lady, far be it from me to endeavour to harden your heart. The church is an indulgent mother: unfold your griefs to her: she alone can administer comfort to your soul, either by satisfying your conscience, or upon examination of your scruples, by setting you at liberty, and indulging you in the lawful means of continuing your lineage. In the latter case, if the Lady Isabella can be brought to consent – '

Manfred, who concluded that he had either overreached the good man, or that his first warmth had been but a tribute paid to appearance, was overjoyed at this sudden turn, and repeated the most magnificent promises, if he should succeed by the friar's mediation. The well-meaning priest suffered him to deceive himself, fully determined to traverse his views, instead of seconding them.

'Since we now understand one another,' resumed the prince, 'I expect, Father, that you satisfy me in one point. Who is the youth that I found in the vault? He must have been privy to Isabella's flight: tell me truly, is he her lover? Or is he an agent for another's passion? I have often suspected Isabella's indifference to my son: a thousand circumstances crowd on my mind that confirm that suspicion. She herself was so conscious of it, that while I discoursed her in the gallery, she outran my suspicious, and endeavoured to justify herself from coolness to Conrad.'

The friar, who knew nothing of the youth but what he had learnt occasionally from the princess, ignorant what was become of him, and not sufficiently reflecting on the impetuosity of Manfred's temper, conceived that it might not be amiss to sow the seeds of jealousy in his mind: they might be turned to some use hereafter, either by prejudicing the prince against Isabella, if he persisted in that union, or by diverting his attention to a wrong scent, and employing his thoughts on a visionary intrigue, prevent his engaging in any new pursuit. With this unhappy policy, he answered in a manner to confirm Manfred in the belief of some connection between Isabella and the youth. The prince, whose passions wanted little fuel to throw them into a blaze, fell into a rage at the idea of what the friar suggested.

'I will fathom to the bottom of this intrigue,' cried he; and quitting Jerome abruptly, with a command to remain there till his return, he hastened to the great hall of the castle, and ordered the peasant to be brought before him.

'Thou hardened young impostor!' said the prince, as soon as he saw the youth; 'what becomes of thy boasted veracity now? It was Providence, was it, and the light of the moon, that discovered the lock of the trap-door to thee? Tell me, audacious boy, who thou art, and how long thou hast been acquainted with the Princess – and take care to answer with less equivocation than thou didst last night, or tortures shall wring the truth from thee.'

The young man, perceiving that his share in the flight of the princess was discovered, and concluding that anything he should say could no longer be of any service or detriment to her, replied –

'I am no impostor, my Lord, nor have I deserved opprobrious language. I answered to every question your Highness put to me last night with the same veracity that I shall speak now: and that will not be from fear of your tortures, but because my soul abhors a falsehood. Please to repeat your questions, my Lord; I am ready to give you all the satisfaction in my power.'

'You know my questions,' replied the prince, 'and only want time to prepare an evasion. Speak directly; who art thou? And how long hast thou been known to the Princess?'

'I am a labourer at the next village,' said the peasant; 'my name is Theodore. The Princess found me in the vault last night: before that hour I never was in her presence.'

'I may believe as much or as little as I please of this,' said Manfred; 'but I will hear thy own story before I examine into the truth of it. Tell me, what reason did the Princess give thee for making her escape? Thy life depends on thy answer.'

'She told me,' replied Theodore, 'that she was on the brink of destruction, and that if she could not escape from the castle, she was in danger in a few moments of being made miserable for ever.'

'And on this slight foundation, on a silly girl's report,' said Manfred, 'thou didst hazard my displeasure?'

'I fear no man's displeasure,' said Theodore, 'when a woman in distress puts herself under my protection.'

During this examination, Matilda was going to the apartment of Hippolita. At the upper end of the hall, where Manfred sat, was a boarded gallery with latticed windows, through which Matilda and Bianca were to pass. Hearing her father's voice, and seeing the servants assembled round him, she stopped to learn the occasion. The prisoner soon drew her attention: the steady and composed manner in which he answered, and the gallantry of his last reply, which were the first words she heard distinctly, interested her in his flavour. His person was noble, handsome, and commanding, even in that situation: but his countenance soon engrossed her whole care.

'Heavens! Bianca,' said the princess softly, 'do I dream? Or is not that youth the exact resemblance of Alfonso's picture in the gallery?'

She could say no more, for her father's voice grew louder at every word.

'This bravado,' said he, 'surpasses all thy former insolence. Thou shalt experience the wrath with which thou darest to trifle. Seize him,' continued Manfred, 'and bind him – the first news the Princess hears of her champion shall be, that he has lost his head for her sake.'

'The injustice of which thou art guilty towards me,' said Theodore, 'convinces me that I have done a good deed in delivering the Princess from thy tyranny. May she be happy, whatever becomes of me!'

'This is a lover!' cried Manfred in a rage: 'a peasant within sight of death is not animated by such sentiments. Tell me, tell me, rash boy, who thou art, or the rack shall force thy secret from thee.'

'Thou hast threatened me with death already,' said the youth, 'for the truth I have told thee: if that is all the encouragement I am to expect for sincerity, I am not tempted to indulge thy vain curiosity farther.'

'Then thou wilt not speak?' said Manfred.

'I will not,' replied he.

'Bear him away into the courtyard,' said Manfred; 'I will see his head this instant severed from his body.'

Matilda fainted at hearing those words.

Bianca shrieked, and cried – 'Help! help! the Princess is dead!'

Manfred started at this ejaculation, and demanded what was the matter! The young peasant, who heard it too, was struck with horror, and asked eagerly the same question; but Manfred ordered him to be hurried into the court, and kept there for execution, till he had informed himself of the cause of Bianca's shrieks. When he learned

the meaning, he treated it as a womanish panic, and ordering Matilda
to be carried to her apartment, he rushed into the court, and calling
for one of his guards, bade Theodore kneel down, and prepare to
receive the fatal blow.

The undaunted youth received the bitter sentence with a resignation
that touched every heart but Manfred's. He wished earnestly to know
the meaning of the words he had heard relating to the princess; but
fearing to exasperate the tyrant more against her, he desisted. The
only boon he deigned to ask was, that he might be permitted to have a
confessor, and make his peace with heaven. Manfred, who hoped by
the confessor's means to come at the youth's history, readily granted
his request; and being convinced that Father Jerome was now in his
interest, he ordered him to be called and shrive the prisoner. The holy
man, who had little foreseen the catastrophe that his imprudence
occasioned, fell on his knees to the prince, and adjured him in the
most solemn manner not to shed innocent blood. He accused himself
in the bitterest terms for his indiscretion, endeavoured to disculpate
the youth, and left no method untried to soften the tyrant's rage.
Manfred, more incensed than appeased by Jerome's intercession,
whose retraction now made him suspect he had been imposed upon by
both, commanded the friar to do his duty, telling him he would not
allow the prisoner many minutes for confession.

'Nor do I ask many, my Lord,' said the unhappy young man. 'My
sins, thank heaven, have not been numerous; nor exceed what might be
expected at my years. Dry your tears, good Father, and let us despatch.
This is a bad world; nor have I had cause to leave it with regret.'

'Oh wretched youth!' said Jerome; 'how canst thou bear the sight
of me with patience? I am thy murderer! It is I have brought this
dismal hour upon thee!'

'I forgive thee from my soul,' said the youth, 'as I hope heaven will
pardon me. Hear my confession, Father; and give me thy blessing.'

'How can I prepare thee for thy passage as I ought?' said Jerome.
'Thou canst not be saved without pardoning thy foes – and canst
thou forgive that impious man there?'

'I can,' said Theodore; 'I do.'

'And does not this touch thee, cruel Prince?' said the friar.

'I sent for thee to confess him,' said Manfred, sternly; 'not to plead
for him. Thou didst first incense me against him – his blood be upon
thy head!'

'It will! It will!' said the good main, in an agony of sorrow. 'Thou
and I must never hope to go where this blessed youth is going!'

'Despatch!' said Manfred; 'I am no more to be moved by the whining of priests than by the shrieks of women.'

'What!' said the youth; 'is it possible that my fate could have occasioned what I heard! Is the Princess then again in thy power?'

'Thou dost but remember me of my wrath,' said Manfred. 'Prepare thee, for this moment is thy last.'

The youth, who felt his indignation rise, and who was touched with the sorrow which he saw he had infused into all the spectators, as well as into the friar, suppressed his emotions, and putting off his doublet, and unbuttoning his collar, knelt down to his prayers. As he stooped, his shirt slipped down below his shoulder, and discovered the mark of a bloody arrow.

'Gracious heaven!' cried the holy man, starting. 'What do I see? It is my child! my Theodore!'

The passions that ensued must be conceived; they cannot be painted. The tears of the assistants were suspended by wonder, rather than stopped by joy. They seemed to inquire in the eyes of their Lord what they ought to feel. Surprise, doubt, tenderness, respect, succeeded each other in the countenance of the youth. He received with modest submission the effusion of the old man's tears and embraces. Yet afraid of giving a loose to hope, and suspecting from what had passed the inflexibility of Manfred's temper, he cast a glance towards the prince, as if to say, canst thou be unmoved at such a scene as this?

Manfred's heart was capable of being touched. He forgot his anger in his astonishment; yet his pride forbad his owning himself affected. He even doubted whether this discovery was not a contrivance of the friar to save the youth.

'What may this mean?' said he. 'How can he be thy son? Is it consistent with thy profession or reputed sanctity to avow a peasant's offspring for the fruit of thy irregular amours!'

'Oh, God!' said the holy man, 'dost thou question his being mine? Could I feel the anguish I do if I were not his father? Spare him! good Prince! Spare him! and revile me as thou pleasest.'

'Spare him! spare him!' cried the attendants; 'for this good man's sake!'

'Peace!' said Manfred, sternly. 'I must know more ere I am disposed to pardon. A saint's bastard may be no saint himself.'

'Injurious Lord!' said Theodore, 'add not insult to cruelty. If I am this venerable man's son, though no prince, as thou art, know the blood that flows in my veins – '

'Yes,' said the friar, interrupting him, 'his blood is noble; nor is he that abject thing, my Lord, you speak him. He is my lawful son, and Sicily can boast of few houses more ancient than that of Falconara. But alas! my Lord, what is blood? What is nobility? We are all reptiles, miserable, sinful creatures. It is piety alone that can distinguish us from the dust whence we sprung, and whither we must return.'

'Truce to your sermon,' said Manfred; 'you forget you are no longer Friar Jerome, but the Count of Falconara. Let me know your history; you will have time to moralise hereafter, if you should not happen to obtain the grace of that sturdy criminal there.'

'Mother of God!' said the friar, 'is it possible my Lord can refuse a father the life of his only, his long-lost, child! Trample me, my Lord, scorn, afflict me, accept my life for his, but spare my son!'

'Thou canst feel, then,' said Manfred, 'what it is to lose an only son! A little hour ago thou didst preach up resignation to me: *my* house, if fate so pleased, must perish – but the Count of Falconara – '

'Alas! my Lord,' said Jerome, 'I confess I have offended; but aggravate not an old man's sufferings! I boast not of my family, nor think of such vanities – it is nature that pleads for this boy; it is the memory of the dear woman that bore him. Is she, Theodore, is she dead?'

'Her soul has long been with the blessed,' said Theodore.

'Oh! how?' cried Jerome. 'Tell me – no – she is happy! Thou art all my care now! – Most dread Lord! will you – will you grant me my poor boy's life?'

'Return to thy convent,' answered Manfred; 'conduct the Princess hither; obey me in what else thou knowest; and I promise thee the life of thy son.'

'Oh! my Lord,' said Jerome, 'is my honesty the price I must pay for this dear youth's safety?'

'For me!' cried Theodore. 'Let me die a thousand deaths, rather than stain thy conscience. What is it the tyrant would exact of thee? Is the Princess still safe from his power? Protect her, thou venerable old man; and let all the weight of his wrath fall on me.'

Jerome endeavoured to check the impetuosity of the youth; and ere Manfred could reply, the trampling of horses was heard, and a brazen trumpet, which hung without the gate of the castle, was suddenly sounded. At the same instant the sable plumes on the enchanted helmet, which still remained at the other end of the court, were tempestuously agitated, and nodded thrice, as if bowed by some invisible wearer.

Chapter Three

Manfred's heart misgave him when he beheld the plumage on the miraculous casque shaken in concert with the sounding of the brazen trumpet.

'Father!' said he to Jerome, whom he now ceased to treat as Count of Falconara, 'what mean these portents? If I have offended – ' the plumes were shaken with greater violence than before.

'Unhappy prince that I am,' cried Manfred. 'Holy Father! will you not assist me with your prayers?'

'My Lord,' replied Jerome, 'heaven is no doubt displeased with your mockery of its servants. Submit yourself to the church; and cease to persecute her ministers. Dismiss this innocent youth; and learn to respect the holy character I wear. Heaven will not be trifled with: you see – ' the trumpet sounded again.

'I acknowledge I have been too hasty,' said Manfred. 'Father, do you go to the wicket, and demand who is at the gate.'

'Do you grant me the life of Theodore?' replied the friar.

'I do,' said Manfred; 'but inquire who is without!'

Jerome, falling on the neck of his son, discharged a flood of tears, that spoke the fulness of his soul.

'You promised to go to the gate,' said Manfred.

'I thought,' replied the friar, 'your Highness would excuse my thanking you first in this tribute of my heart.'

'Go, dearest Sir,' said Theodore; 'obey the Prince. I do not deserve that you should delay his satisfaction for me.'

Jerome, inquiring who was without, was answered, 'A herald.'

'From whom?' said he.

'From the Knight of the Gigantic Sabre,' said the herald; 'and I must speak with the usurper of Otranto.'

Jerome returned to the prince, and did not fail to repeat the message in the very words it had been uttered. The first sounds struck Manfred with terror; but when he heard himself styled usurper, his rage rekindled, and all his courage revived.

'Usurper! – insolent villain!' cried he. 'Who dares to question my title? Retire, Father; this is no business for monks: I will meet this presumptuous man myself. Go to your convent and prepare the Princess's return. Your son shall be a hostage for your fidelity: his life depends on your obedience.'

'Good heaven! my Lord,' cried Jerome, 'your Highness did but this instant freely pardon my child – have you so soon forgot the interposition of heaven?'

'Heaven,' replied Manfred, 'does not send heralds to question the title of a lawful prince. I doubt whether it even notifies its will through friars – but that is your affair, not mine. At present you know my pleasure; and it is not a saucy herald that shall save your son, if you do not return with the Princess.'

It was in vain for the holy man to reply. Manfred commanded him to be conducted to the postern-gate, and shut out from the castle. And he ordered some of his attendants to carry Theodore to the top of the black tower, and guard him strictly; scarce permitting the father and son to exchange a hasty embrace at parting. He then withdrew to the hall, and seating himself in princely state, ordered the herald to be admitted to his presence.

'Well! thou insolent!' said the prince, 'what wouldst thou with me?'

'I come,' replied he, 'to thee, Manfred, usurper of the principality of Otranto, from the renowned and invincible knight, the Knight of the Gigantic Sabre: in the name of his Lord, Frederic Marquis of Vicenza, he demands the Lady Isabella, daughter of that prince, whom thou hast basely and traitorously got into thy power, by bribing her false guardians during his absence; and he requires thee to resign the principality of Otranto, which thou hast usurped from the said Lord Frederic, the nearest of blood to the last rightful Lord, Alfonso the Good. If thou dost not instantly comply with these just demands, he defies thee to single combat to the last extremity.' And so saying the herald cast down his warder.

'And where is this braggart who sends thee?' said Manfred.

'At the distance of a league,' said the herald: 'he comes to make good his Lord's claim against thee, as he is a true knight, and thou an usurper and ravisher.'

Injurious as this challenge was, Manfred reflected that it was not his interest to provoke the Marquis. He knew how well founded the claim of Frederic was; nor was this the first time he had heard of it. Frederic's ancestors had assumed the style of Princes of Otranto, from the death of Alfonso the Good without issue; but

Manfred, his father, and grandfather, had been too powerful for the house of Vicenza to dispossess them. Frederic, a martial and amorous young prince, had married a beautiful young lady, of whom he was enamoured, and who had died in childbed of Isabella. Her death affected him so much that he had taken the cross and gone to the Holy Land, where he was wounded in an engagement against the infidels, made prisoner, and reported to be dead. When the news reached Manfred's ears, he bribed the guardians of the Lady Isabella to deliver her up to him as a bride for his son Conrad, by which alliance he had proposed to unite the claims of the two houses. This motive, on Conrad's death, had co-operated to make him so suddenly resolve on espousing her himself; and the same reflection determined him now to endeavour at obtaining the consent of Frederic to this marriage. A like policy inspired him with the thought of inviting Frederic's champion into the castle, lest he should be informed of Isabella's flight, which he strictly enjoined his domestics not to disclose to any of the knight's retinue.

'Herald,' said Manfred, as soon as he had digested these reflections, 'return to thy master, and tell him, ere we liquidate our differences by the sword, Manfred would hold some converse with him. Bid him welcome to my castle, where by my faith, as I am a true knight, he shall have courteous reception, and full security for himself and followers. If we cannot adjust our quarrel by amicable means, I swear he shall depart in safety, and shall have full satisfaction according to the laws of arms: So help me God and His holy Trinity!'

The herald made three obeisances and retired.

During this interview Jerome's mind was agitated by a thousand contrary passions. He trembled for the life of his son, and his first thought was to persuade Isabella to return to the castle. Yet he was scarce less alarmed at the thought of her union with Manfred. He dreaded Hippolita's unbounded submission to the will of her Lord; and though he did not doubt but he could alarm her piety not to consent to a divorce, if he could get access to her; yet should Manfred discover that the obstruction came from him, it might be equally fatal to Theodore. He was impatient to know whence came the herald, who with so little management had questioned the title of Manfred: yet he did not dare absent himself from the convent, lest Isabella should leave it, and her flight be imputed to him. He returned disconsolately to the monastery, uncertain on what conduct to resolve. A monk, who met him in the porch and observed his melancholy air, said – 'Alas! brother, is it then true that we have lost our excellent Princess Hippolita?'

The holy man started, and cried, 'What meanest thou, brother? I come this instant from the castle, and left her in perfect health.'

'Martelli,' replied the other friar, 'passed by the convent but a quarter of an hour ago on his way from the castle, and reported that her Highness was dead. All our brethren are gone to the chapel to pray for her happy transit to a better life, and willed me to wait thy arrival. They know thy holy attachment to that good Lady, and are anxious for the affliction it will cause in thee – indeed we have all reason to weep; she was a mother to our house. But this life is but a pilgrimage; we must not murmur – we shall all follow her! May our end be like hers!'

'Good brother, thou dreamest,' said Jerome. 'I tell thee I come from the castle, and left the Princess well. Where is the Lady Isabella?'

'Poor gentlewoman!' replied the friar; 'I told her the sad news, and offered her spiritual comfort. I reminded her of the transitory condition of mortality, and advised her to take the veil: I quoted the example of the holy Princess Sanchia of Arragon.'

'Thy zeal was laudable,' said Jerome, impatiently; 'but at present it was unnecessary: Hippolita is well – at least I trust in the Lord she is; I heard nothing to the contrary – yet, methinks, the prince's earnestness – Well, brother, but where is the Lady Isabella?'

'I know not,' said the friar; 'she wept much, and said she would retire to her chamber.'

Jerome left his comrade abruptly, and hastened to the princess, but she was not in her chamber. He inquired of the domestics of the convent, but could learn no news of her. He searched in vain throughout the monastery and the church, and despatched messengers round the neighbourhood, to get intelligence if she had been seen; but to no purpose. Nothing could equal the good man's perplexity. He judged that Isabella, suspecting Manfred of having precipitated his wife's death, had taken the alarm, and withdrawn herself to some more secret place of concealment. This new flight would probably carry the prince's fury to the height. The report of Hippolita's death, though it seemed almost incredible, increased his consternation; and though Isabella's escape bespoke her aversion of Manfred for a husband, Jerome could feel no comfort from it, while it endangered the life of his son. He determined to return to the castle, and made several of his brethren accompany him to attest his innocence to Manfred, and, if necessary, join their intercession with his for Theodore.

The prince, in the meantime, had passed into the court, and ordered the gates of the castle to be flung open for the reception of the stranger knight and his train. In a few minutes the cavalcade arrived. First came two harbingers with wands. Next a herald, followed by two pages and two trumpets. Then a hundred foot-guards. These were attended by as many horse. After them fifty footmen, clothed in scarlet and black, the colours of the knight. Then a led horse. Two heralds on each side of a gentleman on horseback bearing a banner with the arms of Vicenza and Otranto quarterly – a circumstance that much offended Manfred – but he stifled his resentment. Two more pages. The knight's confessor telling his beads. Fifty more footmen clad as before. Two knights habited in complete armour, their beavers down, comrades to the principal knight. The squires of the two knights, carrying their shields and devices. The knight's own squire. A hundred gentlemen bearing an enormous sword, and seeming to faint under the weight of it. The knight himself on a chestnut steed, in complete armour, his lance in the rest, his face entirely concealed by his visor, which was surmounted by a large plume of scarlet and black feathers. Fifty foot-guards with drums and trumpets closed the procession, which wheeled off to the right and left to make room for the principal knight.

As soon as he approached the gate he stopped; and the herald advancing, read again the words of the challenge. Manfred's eyes were fixed on the gigantic sword, and he scarce seemed to attend to the cartel: but his attention was soon diverted by a tempest of wind that rose behind him. He turned and beheld the plumes of the enchanted helmet agitated in the same extraordinary manner as before. It required intrepidity like Manfred's not to sink under a concurrence of circumstances that seemed to announce his fate. Yet scorning in the presence of strangers to betray the courage he had always manifested, he said boldly –

'Sir Knight, whoever thou art, I bid thee welcome. If thou art of mortal mould, thy valour shall meet its equal: and if thou art a true knight, thou wilt scorn to employ sorcery to carry thy point. Be these omens from heaven or hell, Manfred trusts to the righteousness of his cause and to the aid of St Nicholas, who has ever protected his house. Alight, Sir Knight, and repose thyself. Tomorrow thou shalt have a fair field, and heaven befriend the juster side!'

The knight made no reply, but dismounting, was conducted by Manfred to the great hall of the castle. As they traversed the court, the knight stopped to gaze on the miraculous casque; and kneeling down, seemed to pray inwardly for some minutes. Rising, he made a sign to the prince to lead on. As soon as they entered the hall, Manfred proposed to the stranger to disarm, but the knight shook his head in token of refusal.

'Sir Knight,' said Manfred, 'this is not courteous, but by my good faith I will not cross thee, nor shalt thou have cause to complain of the Prince of Otranto. No treachery is designed on my part; I hope none is intended on thine; here take my gage' (giving him his ring): 'your friends and you shall enjoy the laws of hospitality. Rest here until refreshments are brought. I will but give orders for the accommodation of your train, and return to you.' The three knights bowed as accepting his courtesy. Manfred directed the stranger's retinue to be conducted to an adjacent hospital, founded by the Princess Hippolita for the reception of pilgrims. As they made the circuit of the court to return towards the gate, the gigantic sword burst from the supporters, and falling to the ground opposite to the helmet, remained immovable. Manfred, almost hardened to preternatural appearances, surmounted the shock of this new prodigy; and returning to the hall, where by this time the feast was ready, he invited his silent guests to take their places. Manfred, however ill his heart was at ease, endeavoured to inspire the company with mirth. He put several questions to them, but was answered only by signs. They raised their visors but sufficiently to feed themselves, and that sparingly.

'Sirs' said the prince, 'ye are the first guests I ever treated within these walls who scorned to hold any intercourse with me: nor has it oft been customary, I ween, for princes to hazard their state and dignity against strangers and mutes. You say you come in the name of Frederic of Vicenza; I have ever heard that he was a gallant and courteous knight; nor would he, I am bold to say, think it beneath him to mix in social converse with a prince that is his equal, and not unknown by deeds in arms. Still ye are silent – well! be it as it may – by the laws of hospitality and chivalry ye are masters under this roof: ye shall do your pleasure. But come, give me a goblet of wine; ye will not refuse to pledge me to the healths of your fair mistresses.'

The principal knight sighed and crossed himself, and was rising from the board.

'Sir Knight,' said Manfred, 'what I said was but in sport. I shall constrain you in nothing: use your good liking. Since mirth is not your mood, let us be sad. Business may hit your fancies better. Let us withdraw, and hear if what I have to unfold may be better relished than the vain efforts I have made for your pastime.'

Manfred then conducting the three knights into an inner chamber, shut the door, and inviting them to be seated, began thus, addressing himself to the chief personage.

'You come, Sir Knight, as I understand, in the name of the Marquis of Vicenza, to re-demand the Lady Isabella, his daughter, who has been contracted in the face of Holy Church to my son, by the consent of her legal guardians; and to require me to resign my dominions to your Lord, who gives himself for the nearest of blood to Prince Alfonso, whose soul God rest! I shall speak to the latter article of your demands first. You must know, your Lord knows, that I enjoy the principality of Otranto from my father, Don Manuel, as he received it from his father, Don Ricardo. Alfonso, their predecessor, dying childless in the Holy Land, bequeathed his estates to my grandfather, Don Ricardo, in consideration of his faithful services.' The stranger shook his head.

'Sir Knight,' said Manfred, warmly, 'Ricardo was a valiant and upright man; he was a pious man; witness his munificent foundation of the adjoining church and two converts. He was peculiarly patronised by St Nicholas – my grandfather was incapable – I say, Sir, Don Ricardo was incapable – excuse me, your interruption has disordered me. I venerate the memory of my grandfather. Well, Sirs, he held this estate; he held it by his good sword and by the favour of St Nicholas – so did my father; and so, Sirs, will I, come what come will. But Frederic, your Lord, is nearest in blood. I have consented to put my title to the issue of the sword. Does that imply a vicious title? I might have asked, where is Frederic your Lord? Report speaks him dead in captivity. You say, your actions say, he lives – I question it not – I might, Sirs, I might – but I do not. Other princes would bid Frederic take his inheritance by force, if he can: they would not stake their dignity on a single combat: they would not submit it to the decision of unknown mutes! – pardon me, gentlemen, I am too warm: but suppose yourselves in my situation: as ye are stout knights, would it not move your choler to have your own and the honour of your ancestors called in question?

'But to the point. Ye require me to deliver up the Lady Isabella. Sirs, I must ask if ye are authorised to receive her?'

The knight nodded.

'Receive her,' continued Manfred; 'well, you are authorised to receive her, but, gentle knight, may I ask if you have full powers?'

The knight nodded.

' 'Tis well,' said Manfred; 'then hear what I have to offer. Ye see, gentlemen, before you, the most unhappy of men!' (he began to weep); 'afford me your compassion; I am entitled to it, indeed I am. Know, I have lost my only hope, my joy, the support of my house – Conrad died yester-morning.'

The knights discovered signs of surprise.

'Yes, Sirs, fate has disposed of my son. Isabella is at liberty.'

'Do you then restore her?' cried the chief knight, breaking silence.

'Afford me your patience,' said Manfred. 'I rejoice to find, by this testimony of your goodwill, that this matter may be adjusted without blood. It is no interest of mine dictates what little I have farther to say. Ye behold in me a man disgusted with the world: the loss of my son has weaned me from earthly cares. Power and greatness have no longer any charms in my eyes. I wished to transmit the sceptre I had received from my ancestors with honour to my son – but that is over! Life itself is so indifferent to me, that I accepted your defiance with joy. A good knight cannot go to the grave with more satisfaction than when falling in his vocation: whatever is the will of heaven, I submit; for alas! Sirs, I am a man of many sorrows. Manfred is no object of envy, but no doubt you are acquainted with my story.'

The knight made signs of ignorance, and seemed curious to have Manfred proceed.

'Is it possible, Sirs,' continued the prince, 'that my story should be a secret to you? Have you heard nothing relating to me and the Princess Hippolita?'

They shook their heads.

'No? Thus, then, Sirs, it is. You think me ambitious: ambition, alas! is composed of more rugged materials. If I were ambitious, I should not for so many years have been a prey to all the hell of conscientious scruples. But I weary your patience: I will be brief. Know, then, that I have long been troubled in mind on my union with the Princess Hippolita. Oh! Sirs, if ye were acquainted with that excellent woman! if ye knew that I adore her like a mistress, and cherish her as a friend – but man was not born for perfect happiness! She shares my scruples, and with her consent I have brought this matter before the church, for we are related within the forbidden degrees. I expect every hour the definitive sentence that must separate us for ever – I am sure you feel for me – I see you do – pardon these tears!'

The knights gazed on each other, wondering where this would end. Manfred continued –

'The death of my son betiding while my soul was under this anxiety, I thought of nothing but resigning my dominions, and retiring for ever from the sight of mankind. My only difficulty was to fix on a successor, who would be tender of my people, and to dispose of the Lady Isabella, who is dear to me as my own blood. I was willing to restore the line of Alfonso, even in his most distant kindred. And though, pardon me, I am satisfied it was his will that Ricardo's lineage should take place of his own relations; yet where was I to search for those relations? I knew of none but Frederic, your Lord; he was a captive to the infidels, or dead; and were he living, and at home, would he quit the flourishing state of Vicenza for the inconsiderable principality of Otranto? If he would not, could I bear the thought of seeing a hard, unfeeling viceroy set over my poor faithful people? For, Sirs, I love my people, and thank heaven am beloved by them. But ye will ask whither tends this long discourse? Briefly, then, thus, Sirs. Heaven in your arrival seems to point out a remedy for these difficulties and my misfortunes. The Lady Isabella is at liberty; I shall soon be so. I would submit to anything for the good of my people. Were it not the best, the only way to extinguish the feuds between our families, if I was to take the Lady Isabella to wife? You start. But though Hippolita's virtues will ever be dear to me, a prince must not consider himself; he is born for his people.' A servant at that instant entering the chamber apprised Manfred that Jerome and several of his brethren demanded immediate access to him.

The prince, provoked at this interruption, and fearing that the friar would discover to the strangers that Isabella had taken sanctuary, was going to forbid Jerome's entrance. But recollecting that he was certainly arrived to notify the princess's return, Manfred began to excuse himself to the knights for leaving them for a few moments, but was prevented by the arrival of the friars. Manfred angrily reprimanded them for their intrusion, and would have forced them back from the chamber; but Jerome was too much agitated to be repulsed. He declared aloud the flight of Isabella, with protestations of his own innocence.

Manfred, distracted at the news, and not less at its coming to the knowledge of the strangers, uttered nothing but incoherent sentences, now upbraiding the friar, now apologising to the knights, earnest to know what was become of Isabella, yet equally afraid of their knowing; impatient to pursue her, yet dreading to have them join in the pursuit. He offered to despatch messengers in quest of her, but the chief knight, no longer keeping silence, reproached Manfred in bitter terms for his dark and ambiguous dealing, and demanded the cause of Isabella's first absence from the castle. Manfred, casting a stern look at Jerome, implying a command of silence, pretended that on Conrad's death he had placed her in sanctuary until he could determine how to dispose of her. Jerome, who trembled for his son's life, did not dare contradict this false-hood, but one of his brethren, not under the same anxiety, declared frankly that she had fled to their church in the preceding night. The prince in vain endeavoured to stop this discovery, which over-whelmed him with shame and confusion. The principal stranger, amazed at the contradictions he heard, and more than half per-suaded that Manfred had secreted the princess, notwithstanding the concern he expressed at her flight, rushing to the door, said –

'Thou traitor prince! Isabella shall be found.'

Manfred endeavoured to hold him, but the other knights assisting their comrade, he broke from the prince, and hastened into the court, demanding his attendants. Manfred, finding it vain to divert him from the pursuit, offered to accompany him, and summoning his attendants, and taking Jerome and some of the friars to guide them, they issued from the castle; Manfred privately giving orders to have the knight's company secured, while to the knight he affected to despatch a messenger to require their assistance.

The company had no sooner quitted the castle than Matilda, who felt herself deeply interested for the young peasant, since she had seen him condemned to death in the hall, and whose thoughts had been taken up with concerting measures to save him, was informed by some of the female attendants that Manfred had despatched all his men various ways in pursuit of Isabella. He had in his hurry given this order in general terms, not meaning to extend it to the guard he had set upon Theodore, but forgetting it. The domestics, officious to obey so peremptory a prince, and urged by their own curiosity and love of novelty to join in any precipitate chase, had to a man left the castle. Matilda disengaged herself from her women, stole up to the black tower, and unbolting the door, presented herself to the astonished Theodore.

'Young man,' said she, 'though filial duty and womanly modesty condemn the step I am taking, yet holy charity, surmounting all other ties, justifies this act. Fly; the doors of thy prison are open: my father and his domestics are absent, but they may soon return. Be gone in safety, and may the angels of heaven direct thy course!'

'Thou art surely one of those angels!' said the enraptured Theodore: 'none but a blessed saint could speak, could act – could look – like thee. May I not know the name of my divine protectress? Methought thou namedst thy father. Is it possible? Can Manfred's blood feel holy pity! Lovely Lady, thou answerest not. But how art thou here thyself? Why dost thou neglect thy own safety, and waste a thought on a wretch like Theodore? Let us fly together: the life thou bestowest shall be dedicated to thy defence.'

'Alas! thou mistakest,' said Matilda, sighing: 'I am Manfred's daughter, but no dangers await me.'

'Amazement!' said Theodore; 'but last night I blessed myself for yielding thee the service thy gracious compassion so charitably returns me now.'

'Still thou art in an error,' said the princess; 'but this is no time for explanation. Fly, virtuous youth, while it is in my power to save thee: should my father return, thou and I both should indeed have cause to tremble.'

'How?' said Theodore; 'thinkest thou, charming maid, that I will accept of life at the hazard of aught calamitous to thee? Better I endured a thousand deaths.'

'I run no risk,' said Matilda, 'but by thy delay. Depart; it cannot be known that I have assisted thy flight.'

'Swear by the saints above,' said Theodore, 'that thou canst not be suspected; else here I vow to await whatever can befall me.'

'Oh! thou art too generous,' said Matilda; 'but rest assured that no suspicion can alight on me.'

'Give me thy beauteous hand in token that thou dost not deceive me,' said Theodore; 'and let me bathe it with the warm tears of gratitude.'

'Forbear!' said the princess; 'this must not be.'

'Alas!' said Theodore, 'I have never known but calamity until this hour – perhaps shall never know other fortune again: suffer the chaste raptures of holy gratitude: 'tis my soul would print its effusions on thy hand.'

'Forbear, and be gone,' said Matilda. 'How would Isabella approve of seeing thee at my feet?'

'Who is Isabella?' said the young man with surprise.

'Ah, me! I fear,' said the princess, 'I am serving a deceitful one. Hast thou forgot thy curiosity this morning?'

'Thy looks, thy actions, all thy beauteous self seem an emanation of divinity,' said Theodore; 'but thy words are dark and mysterious. Speak, Lady; speak to thy servant's comprehension.'

'Thou understandest but too well!' said Matilda; 'but once more I command thee to be gone: thy blood, which I may preserve, will be on my head, if I waste the time in vain discourse.'

'I go, Lady,' said Theodore, 'because it is thy will, and because I would not bring the grey hairs of my father with sorrow to the grave. Say but, adored Lady, that I have thy gentle pity.'

'Stay,' said Matilda; 'I will conduct thee to the subterraneous vault by which Isabella escaped; it will lead thee to the church of St Nicholas, where thou mayst take sanctuary.'

'What?' said Theodore, 'was it another, and not thy lovely self, that I assisted to find the subterraneous passage?'

'It was,' said Matilda; 'but ask no more; I tremble to see thee still abide here; fly to the sanctuary.'

'To sanctuary?' said Theodore. 'No, Princess; sanctuaries are for helpless damsels, or for criminals. Theodore's soul is free from guilt, nor will wear the appearance of it. Give me a sword, Lady, and thy father shall learn that Theodore scorns an ignominious flight.'

'Rash youth!' said Matilda; 'thou wouldst not dare to lift thy presumptuous arm against the Prince of Otranto?'

'Not against thy father; indeed, I dare not,' said Theodore. 'Excuse me, Lady; I had forgotten. But could I gaze on thee, and remember thou art sprung from the tyrant Manfred? But he is thy father, and from this moment my injuries are buried in oblivion.'

A deep and hollow groan, which seemed to come from above, startled the princess and Theodore.

'Good heaven! we are overheard!' said the princess. They listened; but perceiving no further noise, they both concluded it the effect of pent-up vapours. And the princess, preceding Theodore softly, carried him to her father's armoury, where, equipping him with a complete suit, he was conducted by Matilda to the postern-gate.

'Avoid the town,' said the princess, 'and all the western side of the castle. 'Tis there the search must be making by Manfred and the strangers; but hie thee to the opposite quarter. Yonder behind that forest to the east is a chain of rocks, hollowed into a labyrinth of caverns that reach to the sea coast. There thou mayst lie concealed, till thou canst make signs to some vessel to put on shore, and take thee off. Go! heaven be thy guide! – and sometimes in thy prayers remember – Matilda!'

Theodore flung himself at her feet, and seizing her lily hand, which with struggles she suffered him to kiss, he vowed on the earliest opportunity to get himself knighted, and fervently entreated her permission to swear himself eternally her knight. Ere the princess could reply, a clap of thunder was suddenly heard that shook the battlements. Theodore, regardless of the tempest, would have urged his suit: but the princess, dismayed, retreated hastily into the castle, and commanded the youth to be gone with an air that would not be disobeyed. He sighed, and retired, but with eyes fixed on the gate, until Matilda, closing it, put an end to an interview, in which the hearts of both had drunk so deeply of a passion, which both now tasted for the first time.

Theodore went pensively to the convent, to acquaint his father with his deliverance. There he learned the absence of Jerome, and the pursuit that was making after the Lady Isabella, with some particulars of whose story he now first became acquainted. The generous gallantry of his nature prompted him to wish to assist her; but the monks could lend him no lights to guess at the route she had taken. He was not tempted to wander far in search of her, for the idea of Matilda had imprinted itself so strongly on his heart, that he could not bear to absent himself at much distance from her abode. The tenderness Jerome had expressed for him concurred to confirm this reluctance; and he even persuaded himself that filial affection was the chief cause of his hovering between the castle and monastery.

Until Jerome should return at night, Theodore at length determined to repair to the forest that Matilda had pointed out to him. Arriving there, he sought the gloomiest shades, as best suited to the pleasing melancholy that reigned in his mind. In this mood he roved insensibly to the caves which had formerly served as a retreat to hermits, and were now reported round the country to be haunted by evil spirits. He recollected to have heard this tradition; and being of a brave and adventurous disposition, he willingly indulged his curiosity in exploring the secret recesses of this labyrinth. He had not penetrated far before he thought he heard the steps of some person who seemed to retreat before him.

Theodore, though firmly grounded in all our holy faith enjoins to be believed, had no apprehension that good men were abandoned without cause to the malice of the powers of darkness. He thought the place more likely to be infested by robbers than by those infernal agents who are reported to molest and bewilder travellers. He had long burned with impatience to approve his valour. Drawing his sabre, he marched sedately onwards, still directing his steps as the imperfect rustling sound before him led the way. The armour he wore was a like indication to the person who avoided him. Theodore, now convinced that he was not mistaken, redoubled his pace, and evidently gained on the person that fled, whose haste increasing, Theodore came up just as a woman fell breathless before him. He hasted to raise her, but her terror was so great that he apprehended she would faint in his arms. He used every gentle word to dispel her alarms, and assured her that far from injuring, he would defend her at the peril of his life. The lady recovering her spirits from his courteous demeanour, and gazing on her protector, said –

'Sure, I have heard that voice before!'

'Not to my knowledge,' replied Theodore; 'unless, as I conjecture, thou art the Lady Isabella.'

'Merciful heaven!' cried she. 'Thou art not sent in quest of me, art thou?' And saying those words, she threw herself at his feet, and besought him not to deliver her up to Manfred.

'To Manfred!' cried Theodore – 'no, Lady; I have once already delivered thee from his tyranny, and it shall fare hard with me now, but I will place thee out of the reach of his daring.'

'Is it possible,' said she, 'that thou shouldst be the generous unknown whom I met last night in the vault of the castle? Sure thou art not a mortal, but my guardian angel. On my knees, let me thank – '

'Hold! gentle Princess,' said Theodore, 'nor demean thyself before a poor and friendless young man. If heaven has selected me for thy deliverer, it will accomplish its work, and strengthen my arm in thy cause. But come, Lady, we are too near the mouth of the cavern; let us seek its inmost recesses. I can have no tranquillity till I have placed thee beyond the reach of danger.'

'Alas! what mean you, sir?' said she. 'Though all your actions are noble, though your sentiments speak the purity of your soul, is it fitting that I should accompany you alone into these perplexed retreats? Should we be found together, what would a censorious world think of my conduct?'

'I respect your virtuous delicacy,' said Theodore; 'nor do you harbour a suspicion that wounds my honour. I meant to conduct you into the most private cavity of these rocks, and then at the hazard of my life to guard their entrance against every living thing. Besides, Lady,' continued he, drawing a deep sigh, 'beauteous and all perfect as your form is, and though my wishes are not guiltless of aspiring, know, my soul is dedicated to another; and although – '

A sudden noise prevented Theodore from proceeding. They soon distinguished these sounds –

'Isabella! what, ho! Isabella!' The trembling princess relapsed into her former agony of fear. Theodore endeavoured to encourage her, but in vain. He assured her he would die rather than suffer her to return under Manfred's power; and begging her to remain concealed, he went forth to prevent the person in search of her from approaching.

At the mouth of the cavern he found an armed knight, discoursing with a peasant, who assured him he had seen a lady enter the passes of the rock. The knight was preparing to seek her, when Theodore, placing himself in his way, with his sword drawn, sternly forbad him at his peril to advance.

'And who art thou, who darest to cross my way?' said the knight, haughtily.

'One who does not dare more than he will perform,' said Theodore.

'I seek the Lady Isabella,' said the knight, 'and understand she has taken refuge among these rocks. Impede me not, or thou wilt repent having provoked my resentment.'

'Thy purpose is as odious as thy resentment is contemptible,' said Theodore. 'Return whence thou camest, or we shall soon know whose resentment is most terrible.'

The stranger, who was the principal knight that had arrived from the Marquis of Vicenza, had galloped from Manfred as he was busied in getting information of the princess, and giving various orders to prevent her falling into the power of the three knights. Their chief had suspected Manfred of being privy to the princess's absconding, and this insult, from a man who he concluded was stationed by that prince to secrete her, confirming his suspicions, he made no reply, but discharging a blow with his sabre at Theodore, would soon have removed all obstruction, if Theodore, who took him for one of Manfred's captains, and who had no sooner given the provocation than prepared to support it, had not received the stroke on his shield. The valour that had so long been smothered in his breast broke forth at once; he rushed impetuously on the knight, whose pride and wrath were not less powerful incentives to hardy deeds. The combat was furious, but not long. Theodore wounded the knight in three several places, and at last disarmed him as he fainted by the loss of blood.

The peasant, who had fled on the first onset, had given the alarm to some of Manfred's domestics, who, by his orders, were dispersed through the forest in pursuit of Isabella. They came up as the knight fell, whom they soon discovered to be the noble stranger. Theodore, notwithstanding his hatred to Manfred, could not behold the victory he had gained without emotions of pity and generosity. But he was more touched when he learned the quality of his adversary, and was informed that he was no retainer, but an enemy, of Manfred. He assisted the servants of the latter in disarming the knight, and in endeavouring to staunch the blood that flowed from his wounds. The knight recovering his speech, said, in a faint and faltering voice –

'Generous foe, we have both been in an error. I took thee for an instrument of the tyrant; I perceive thou hast made the like mistake. It is too late for excuses. I faint. If Isabella is at hand – call her – I have important secrets to – '

'He is dying!' said one of the attendants. 'Has nobody a crucifix about them? Andrea, do thou pray over him.'

'Fetch some water,' said Theodore, 'and pour it down his throat, while I hasten to the Princess.'

Saying this, he flew to Isabella, and in few words told her modestly that he had been so unfortunate by mistake as to wound a gentleman from her father's court, who wished, ere he died, to impart something of consequence to her.

The princess, who had been transported at hearing the voice of Theodore, as he called to her to come forth, was astonished at what she heard. Suffering herself to be conducted by Theodore, the new proof of whose valour recalled her dispersed spirits, she came where the bleeding knight lay speechless on the ground. But her fears returned when she beheld the domestics of Manfred. She would again have fled if Theodore had not made her observe that they were unarmed, and had not threatened them with instant death if they should dare to seize the Princess.

The stranger, opening his eyes, and beholding a woman, said, 'Art thou – pray tell me truly – art thou Isabella of Vicenza?'

'I am,' said she: 'good heaven restore thee!'

'Then thou – then thou' – said the knight, struggling for utterance – 'seest – thy father. Give me one – '

'Oh! amazement! horror! What do I hear! What do I see!' cried Isabella. 'My father! You my father! How came you here, Sir? For heaven's sake, speak! Oh! run for help, or he will expire!'

' 'Tis most true,' said the wounded knight, exerting all his force; 'I am Frederic thy father. Yes, I came to deliver thee. It will not be. Give me a parting kiss, and take – '

'Sir,' said Theodore, 'do not exhaust yourself; suffer us to convey you to the castle.'

'To the castle!' said Isabella. 'Is there no help nearer than the castle? Would you expose my father to the tyrant? If he goes thither, I dare not accompany him; and yet, can I leave him!'

'My child,' said Frederic, 'it matters not for me whither I am carried. A few minutes will place me beyond danger; but while I have eyes to dote on thee, forsake me not, dear Isabella! This brave knight – I know not who he is – will protect thy innocence. Sir, you will not abandon my child, will you?'

Theodore, shedding tears over his victim, and vowing to guard the princess at the expense of his life, persuaded Frederic to suffer himself to be conducted to the castle. They placed him on a horse belonging to one of the domestics, after binding up his wounds as well as they were able. Theodore marched by his side; and the afflicted Isabella, who could not bear to quit him, followed mournfully behind.

Chapter Four

The sorrowful troop no sooner arrived at the castle, than they were met by Hippolita and Matilda, whom Isabella had sent one of the domestics before to advertise of their approach. The ladies causing Frederic to be conveyed into the nearest chamber, retired, while the surgeons examined his wounds. Matilda blushed at seeing Theodore and Isabella together; but endeavoured to conceal it by embracing the latter, and condoling with her on her father's mischance. The surgeons soon came to acquaint Hippolita that none of the Marquis's wounds were dangerous; and that he was desirous of seeing his daughter and the princesses.

Theodore, under pretence of expressing his joy at being freed from his apprehensions of the combat being fatal to Frederic, could not resist the impulse of following Matilda. Her eyes were so often cast down on meeting his, that Isabella, who regarded Theodore as attentively as he gazed on Matilda, soon divined who the object was that he had told her in the cave engaged his affections. While this mute scene passed, Hippolita demanded of Frederic the cause of his having taken that mysterious course for reclaiming his daughter; and threw in various apologies to excuse her Lord for the match contracted between their children.

Frederic, however incensed against Manfred, was not insensible to the courtesy and benevolence of Hippolita: but he was still more struck with the lovely form of Matilda. Wishing to detain them by his bedside, he informed Hippolita of his story. He told her that, while prisoner to the infidels, he had dreamed that his daughter, of whom he had learned no news since his captivity, was detained in a castle, where she was in danger of the most dreadful misfortunes: and that if he obtained his liberty, and repaired to a wood near Joppa, he would learn more. Alarmed at this dream, and incapable of obeying the direction given by it, his chains became more grievous than ever. But while his thoughts were occupied on the means of obtaining his liberty, he received the agreeable news that the confederate princes who were warring in Palestine had paid his ransom. He instantly set out for the wood that had been marked in his dream.

For three days he and his attendants had wandered in the forest without seeing a human form: but on the evening of the third they came to a cell, in which they found a venerable hermit in the agonies of death. Applying rich cordials, they brought the fainting man to his speech.

'My sons,' said he, 'I am bounden to your charity – but it is in vain – I am going to my eternal rest – yet I die with the satisfaction of performing the will of heaven. When first I repaired to this solitude, after seeing my country become a prey to unbelievers – it is alas! above fifty years since I was witness to that dreadful scene! – St Nicholas appeared to me, and revealed a secret, which he bade me never disclose to mortal man, but on my death-bed. This is that tremendous hour, and ye are no doubt the chosen warriors to whom I was ordered to reveal my trust. As soon as ye have done the last offices to this wretched corse, dig under the seventh tree on the left hand of this poor cave, and your pains will – Oh! good heaven receive my soul!' With those words the devout man breathed his last.

'By break of day,' continued Frederic, 'when we had committed the holy relics to earth, we dug according to direction. But what was our astonishment when about the depth of six feet we discovered an enormous sabre – the very weapon yonder in the court. On the blade, which was then partly out of the scabbard, though since closed by our efforts in removing it, were written the following lines – no; excuse me, Madam,' added the Marquis, turning to Hippolita; 'if I forbear to repeat them: I respect your sex and rank, and would not be guilty of offending your ear with sounds injurious to aught that is dear to you.'

He paused. Hippolita trembled. She did not doubt but Frederic was destined by heaven to accomplish the fate that seemed to threaten her house. Looking with anxious fondness at Matilda, a silent tear stole down her cheek: but recollecting herself, she said – 'Proceed, my Lord; heaven does nothing in vain; mortals must receive its divine behests with lowliness and submission. It is our part to deprecate its wrath, or bow to its decrees. Repeat the sentence, my Lord; we listen resigned.'

Frederic was grieved that he had proceeded so far. The dignity and patient firmness of Hippolita penetrated him with respect, and the tender silent affection with which the princess and her daughter regarded each other, melted him almost to tears. Yet apprehensive that his forbearance to obey would be more alarming, he repeated in a faltering and low voice the following lines:

> Where'er a casque that suits this sword is found,
> With perils is thy daughter compass'd round;
> *Alfonso's* blood alone can save the maid,
> And quiet a long restless prince's shade.

'What is there in these lines,' said Theodore impatiently, 'that affects these princesses? Why were they to be shocked by a mysterious delicacy, that has so little foundation?'

'Your words are rude, young man,' said the Marquis; 'and though fortune has favoured you once – '

'My honoured Lord,' said Isabella, who resented Theodore's warmth, which she perceived was dictated by his sentiments for Matilda, 'discompose not yourself for the glosing of a peasant's son: he forgets the reverence he owes you; but he is not accustomed – '

Hippolita, concerned at the heat that had arisen, checked Theodore for his boldness, but with an air acknowledging his zeal; and changing the conversation, demanded of Frederic where he had left her Lord? As the Marquis was going to reply, they heard a noise without, and rising to inquire the cause, Manfred, Jerome, and part of the troop, who had met an imperfect rumour of what had happened, entered the chamber. Manfred advanced hastily towards Frederic's bed to condole with him on his misfortune, and to learn the circumstances of the combat, when starting in an agony of terror and amazement, he cried –

'Ha! what art thou? Thou dreadful spectre, is my hour come?'

'My dearest, gracious Lord,' cried Hippolita, clasping him in her arms, 'what is it you see! Why do you fix your eyeballs thus?'

'What!' cried Manfred breathless; 'dost thou see nothing, Hippolita? Is this ghastly phantom sent to me alone – to rue, who did not – '

'For mercy's sweetest self, my Lord,' said Hippolita, 'resume your soul, command your reason. There is none here, but us, your friends.'

'What, is not that Alfonso?' cried Manfred. 'Dost thou not see him? Can it be my brain's delirium?'

'This! my Lord,' said Hippolita; 'this is Theodore, the youth who has been so unfortunate.'

'Theodore!' said Manfred mournfully, and striking his forehead; 'Theodore or a phantom, he has unhinged the soul of Manfred. But how comes he here? And how comes he in armour?'

'I believe he went in search of Isabella,' said Hippolita.

'Of Isabella!' said Manfred, relapsing into rage; 'yes, yes, that is not doubtful – But how did he escape from durance, in which I left him? Was it Isabella, or this hypocritical old friar, that procured his enlargement?'

'And would a parent be criminal, my Lord,' said Theodore, 'if he meditated the deliverance of his child?'

Jerome, amazed to hear himself in a manner accused by his son, and without foundation, knew not what to think. He could not comprehend how Theodore had escaped, how he came to be armed, and to encounter Frederic. Still he would not venture to ask any questions that might tend to inflame Manfred's wrath against his son. Jerome's silence convinced Manfred that he had contrived Theodore's release.

'And is it thus, thou ungrateful old man,' said the prince, addressing himself to the friar, 'that thou repayest mine and Hippolita's bounties? And not content with traversing my heart's nearest wishes, thou armest thy bastard, and bringest him into my own castle to insult me!'

'My Lord,' said Theodore, 'you wrong my father: neither he nor I are capable of harbouring a thought against your peace. Is it insolence thus to surrender myself to your Highness's pleasure?' added he, laying his sword respectfully at Manfred's feet. 'Behold my bosom; strike, my Lord, if you suspect that a disloyal thought is lodged there. There is not a sentiment engraven on my heart that does not venerate you and yours.'

The grace and fervour with which Theodore uttered these words interested every person present in his favour. Even Manfred was touched – yet still possessed with his resemblance to Alfonso, his admiration was dashed with secret horror.

'Rise,' said he; 'thy life is not my present purpose. But tell me thy history, and how thou camest connected with this old traitor here.'

'My Lord,' said Jerome eagerly.

'Peace! impostor!' said Manfred; 'I will not have him prompted.'

'My Lord,' said Theodore, 'I want no assistance; my story is very brief. I was carried at five years of age to Algiers with my mother, who had been taken by corsairs from the coast of Sicily. She died of grief in less than a twelvemonth;' the tears gushed from Jerome's eyes, on whose countenance a thousand anxious passions stood expressed. 'Before she died,' continued Theodore, 'she bound a writing about my arm under my garments, which told me I was the son of the Count Falconara.'

'It is most true,' said Jerome; 'I am that wretched father.'

'Again I enjoin thee silence,' said Manfred: 'proceed.'

'I remained in slavery,' said Theodore, 'until within these two years, when attending on my master in his cruises, I was delivered by a Christian vessel, which overpowered the pirate; and discovering myself to the captain, he generously put me on shore in Sicily; but alas! instead of finding a father, I learned that his estate, which was situated on the coast, had, during his absence, been laid waste by the rover who had carried my mother and me into captivity: that his castle had been burnt to the ground, and that my father on his return had sold what remained, and was retired into religion in the kingdom of Naples; but where, no man could inform me. Destitute and friend-less, hopeless almost of attaining the transport of a parent's embrace, I took the first opportunity of setting sail for Naples, from whence, within these six days, I wandered into this province, still supporting myself by the labour of my hands; nor until yester-morn did I believe that heaven had reserved any lot for me but peace of mind and contented poverty. This, my Lord, is Theodore's story. I am blessed beyond my hope in finding a father; I am unfortunate beyond my desert in having incurred your Highness's displeasure.'

He ceased. A murmur of approbation gently arose from the aud-ience.

'This is not all,' said Frederic; 'I am bound in honour to add what he suppresses. Though he is modest, I must be generous; he is one of the bravest youths on Christian ground. He is warm too; and from the short knowledge I have of him, I will pledge myself for his veracity: if what he reports of himself were not true, he would not utter it – and for me, youth, I honour a frankness which becomes thy birth; but now, and thou didst offend me: yet the noble blood which flows in thy veins, may well be allowed to boil out, when it has so recently traced itself to its source. Come, my Lord,' (turning to Manfred), 'if I can pardon him, surely you may; it is not the youth's fault, if you took him for a spectre.'

This bitter taunt galled the soul of Manfred.

'If beings from another world,' replied he haughtily, 'have power to impress my mind with awe, it is more than living man can do; nor could a stripling's arm.'

'My Lord,' interrupted Hippolita, 'your guest has occasion for repose: shall we not leave him to his rest?' Saying this, and taking Manfred by the hand, she took leave of Frederic, and led the com-pany forth.

The prince, not sorry to quit a conversation which recalled to mind the discovery he had made of his most secret sensations, suffered himself to be conducted to his own apartment, after permitting Theodore, though under engagement to return to the castle on the morrow (a condition the young man gladly accepted), to retire with his father to the convent. Matilda and Isabella were too much occupied with their own reflections, and too little content with each other, to wish for farther converse that night. They separated each to her chamber, with more expressions of ceremony and fewer of affection thou had passed between them since their childhood.

If they parted with small cordiality, they did but meet with greater impatience, as soon as the sun was risen. Their minds were in a situation that excluded sleep, and each recollected a thousand questions which she wished she had put to the other overnight. Matilda reflected that Isabella had been twice delivered by Theodore in very critical situations, which she could not believe accidental. His eyes, it was true, had been fixed on her in Frederic's chamber; but that might have been to disguise his passion for Isabella from the fathers of both. It were better to clear this up. She wished to know the truth, lest she should wrong her friend by entertaining a passion for Isabella's lover. Thus jealousy prompted, and at the same time borrowed an excuse from friendship to justify its curiosity.

Isabella, not less restless, had better foundation for her suspicions. Both Theodore's tongue and eyes had told her his heart was engaged; it was true – yet, perhaps, Matilda might not correspond to his passion; she had ever appeared insensible to love: all her thoughts were set on heaven.

'Why did I dissuade her?' said Isabella to herself; 'I am punished for my generosity; but when did they meet? Where? It cannot be; I have deceived myself; perhaps last night was the first time they ever beheld each other; it must be some other object that has prepossessed his affections – if it is, I am not so unhappy as I thought; if it is not my friend Matilda – how? can I stoop to wish for the affection of a man, who rudely and unnecessarily acquainted me with his indifference? And that at the very moment in which common courtesy demanded at least expressions of civility. I will go to my dear Matilda, who will confirm me in this becoming pride. Man is false – I will advise with her on taking the veil: she will rejoice to find me in this disposition; and I will acquaint her that I no longer oppose her inclination for the cloister.'

In this frame of mind, and determined to open her heart entirely to Matilda, she went to that princess's chamber, whom she found already dressed, and leaning pensively on her arm. This attitude, so correspondent to what she felt herself, revived Isabella's suspicions, and destroyed the confidence she had purposed to place in her friend. They blushed at meeting, and were too much novices to disguise their sensations with address. After some unmeaning questions and replies, Matilda demanded of Isabella the cause of her flight? The latter, who had almost forgotten Manfred's passion, so entirely was she occupied by her own, concluding that Matilda referred to her last escape from the convent, which had occasioned the events of the preceding evening, replied –

'Martelli brought word to the convent that your mother was dead.'

'Oh!' said Matilda, interrupting her, 'Bianca has explained that mistake to me: on seeing me faint, she cried out, "The Princess is dead!" and Martelli, who had come for the usual dole to the castle – '

'And what made you faint?' said Isabella, indifferent to the rest. Matilda blushed and stammered –

'My father – he was sitting in judgment on a criminal – '

'What criminal?' said Isabella eagerly.

'A young man,' said Matilda; 'I believe – '

'I think it was that young man that – '

'What, Theodore?' said Isabella.

'Yes,' answered she; 'I never saw him before; I do not know how he had offended my father, but as he has been of service to you, I am glad my Lord has pardoned him.'

'Served me!' replied Isabella; 'do you term it serving me, to wound my father, and almost occasion his death? Though it is but since yesterday that I am blessed with knowing a parent, I hope Matilda does not think I am such a stranger to filial tenderness as not to resent the boldness of that audacious youth, and that it is impossible for me ever to feel any affection for one who dared to lift his arm against the author of my being. No, Matilda, my heart abhors him; and if you still retain the friendship for me that you have vowed from your infancy, you will detest a man who has been on the point of making me miserable for ever.'

Matilda held down her head and replied: 'I hope my dearest Isabella does not doubt her Matilda's friendship: I never beheld that youth until yesterday; he is almost a stranger to me: but as the surgeons have pronounced your father out of danger, you ought not to harbour uncharitable resentment against one, who I am persuaded did not know the Marquis was related to you.'

'You plead his cause very pathetically,' said Isabella, 'considering he is so much a stranger to you! I am mistaken, or he returns your charity.'

'What mean you?' said Matilda.

'Nothing,' said Isabella, repenting that she had given Matilda a hint of Theodore's inclination for her. Then changing the discourse, she asked Matilda what occasioned Manfred to take Theodore for a spectre?

'Bless me,' said Matilda, 'did not you observe his extreme resemblance to the portrait of Alfonso in the gallery? I took notice of it to Bianca even before I saw him in armour; but with the helmet on, he is the very image of that picture.'

'I do not much observe pictures,' said Isabella: 'much less have I examined this young man so attentively as you seem to have done. Ah! Matilda, your heart is in danger, but let me warn you as a friend, he has owned to me that he is in love; it cannot be with you, for yesterday was the first time you ever met – was it not?'

'Certainly,' replied Matilda; 'but why does my dearest Isabella conclude from anything I have said, that' – she paused, then continuing – 'he saw you first, and I am far from having the vanity to think that my little portion of charms could engage a heart devoted to you; may you be happy, Isabella, whatever is the fate of Matilda!'

'My lovely friend,' said Isabella, whose heart was too honest to resist a kind expression, 'it is you that Theodore admires; I saw it; I am persuaded of it; nor shall a thought of my own happiness suffer me to interfere with yours.'

This frankness drew tears from the gentle Matilda; and jealousy that for a moment had raised a coolness between these amiable maidens soon gave way to the natural sincerity and candour of their souls. Each confessed to the other the impression that Theodore had made on her; and this confidence was followed by a struggle of generosity, each insisting on yielding her claim to her friend. At length the dignity of Isabella's virtue reminding her of the preference which Theodore had almost declared for her rival, made her determine to conquer her passion, and cede the beloved object to her friend.

During this contest of amity, Hippolita entered her daughter's chamber.

'Madam,' said she to Isabella, 'you have so much tenderness for Matilda, and interest yourself so kindly in whatever affects our wretched house, that I can have no secrets with my child which are not proper for you to hear.'

The princesses were all attention and anxiety.

'Know then, Madam,' continued Hippolita, 'and you my dearest Matilda, that being convinced by all the events of these two last ominous days, that heaven purposes the sceptre of Otranto should pass from Manfred's hands into those of the Marquis Frederic, I have been perhaps inspired with the thought of averting our total destruction by the union of our rival houses. With this view I have been proposing to Manfred, my lord, to tender this dear, dear child to Frederic, your father.'

'Me to Lord Frederic!' cried Matilda. 'Good heavens! my gracious mother – and have you named it to my father?'

'I have,' said Hippolita; 'he listened benignly to my proposal, and is gone to break it to the Marquis.'

'Ah! wretched Princess!' cried Isabella; 'what hast thou done! What ruin has thy inadvertent goodness been preparing for thyself, for me, and for Matilda!'

'Ruin from me to you and to my child!' said Hippolita. 'What can this mean?'

'Alas!' said Isabella, 'the purity of your own heart prevents your seeing the depravity of others. Manfred, your lord, that impious man – '

'Hold,' said Hippolita; 'you must not in my presence, young lady, mention Manfred with disrespect: he is my lord and husband, and – '

'Will not long be so,' said Isabella, 'if his wicked purposes can be carried into execution.'

'This language amazes me,' said Hippolita. 'Your feeling, Isabella, is warm; but until this hour I never knew it betray you into intemperance. What deed of Manfred authorises you to treat him as a murderer, an assassin?'

'Thou virtuous, and too credulous princess!' replied Isabella; 'it is not thy life he aims at – it is to separate himself from thee! to divorce thee! to – '

'To divorce me!' 'To divorce my mother!' cried Hippolita and Matilda at once.

'Yes,' said Isabella; 'and to complete his crime, he meditates – I cannot speak it!'

'What can surpass what thou hast already uttered?' said Matilda.

Hippolita was silent. Grief choked her speech; and the recollection of Manfred's late ambiguous discourses confirmed what she heard.

'Excellent, dear lady! Madam! Mother!' cried Isabella, flinging herself at Hippolita's feet in a transport of passion; 'trust me, believe me, I will die a thousand deaths sooner than consent to injure you, than yield to so odious – oh! – '

'This is too much!' cried Hippolita: 'What crimes does one crime suggest! Rise, dear Isabella; I do not doubt your virtue. Oh! Matilda, this stroke is too heavy for thee! Weep not, my child; and not a murmur, I charge thee. Remember, he is *thy* father still!'

'But you are my mother too,' said Matilda fervently; 'and *you* are virtuous, *you* are guiltless! – Oh! must not I, must not I complain?'

'You must not,' said Hippolita – 'come, all will yet be well. Manfred, in the agony for the loss of thy brother, knew not what he said; perhaps Isabella misunderstood him; his heart is good – and, my child, thou knowest not all! There is a destiny hangs over us; the hand of Providence is stretched out; oh! could I but save thee from the wreck! Yes,' continued she in a firmer tone, 'perhaps the sacrifice of myself may atone for all; I will go and offer myself to this divorce – it boots not what becomes of me. I will withdraw into the neighbouring monastery, and waste the remainder of life in prayers and tears for my child and – the Prince!'

'Thou art as much too good for this world,' said Isabella, 'as Manfred is execrable; but think not, lady, that thy weakness shall determine for me. I swear, hear me all ye angels – '

'Stop, I adjure thee,' cried Hippolita: 'remember thou dost not depend on thyself; thou hast a father.'

'My father is too pious, too noble,' interrupted Isabella, 'to command an impious deed. But should he command it; can a father enjoin a cursed act? I was contracted to the son, can I wed the father? No, madam, no; force should not drag me to Manfred's hated bed. I loathe him, I abhor him: divine and human laws forbid – and my friend, my dearest Matilda! would I wound her tender soul by injuring her adored mother? my own mother – I never have known another' –

'Oh! she is the mother of both!' cried Matilda. 'Can we, can we, Isabella, adore her too much?'

'My lovely children,' said the touched Hippolita, 'your tenderness overpowers me – but I must not give way to it. It is not ours to make election for ourselves: heaven, our fathers, and our husbands must decide for us. Have patience until you hear what Manfred and Frederic have determined. If the Marquis accepts Matilda's hand, I know she will readily obey. Heaven may interpose and prevent the rest. What means my child?' continued she, seeing Matilda fall at her feet with a flood of speechless tears – 'But no; answer me not, my daughter: I must not hear a word against the pleasure of thy father.'

'Oh! doubt not my obedience, my dreadful obedience to him and to you!' said Matilda. 'But can I, most respected of women, can I experience all this tenderness, this world of goodness, and conceal a thought from the best of mothers?'

'What art thou going to utter?' said Isabella trembling. 'Recollect thyself, Matilda.'

'No, Isabella,' said the princess, 'I should not deserve this incomparable parent, if the inmost recesses of my soul harboured a thought without her permission – nay, I have offended her; I have suffered a passion to enter my heart without her avowal – but here I disclaim it; here I vow to heaven and her – '

'My child! my child,' said Hippolita, 'what words are these! What new calamities has fate in store for us! Thou, a passion? Thou, in this hour of destruction – '

'Oh! I see all my guilt!' said Matilda. 'I abhor myself, if I cost my mother a pang. She is the dearest thing I have on earth – Oh! I will never, never behold him more!'

'Isabella,' said Hippolita, 'thou art conscious to this unhappy secret, whatever it is. Speak!'

'What!' cried Matilda, 'have I so forfeited my mother's love, that she will not permit me even to speak my own guilt? Oh! wretched, wretched Matilda!'

'Thou art too cruel,' said Isabella to Hippolita: 'canst thou behold this anguish of a virtuous mind, and not commiserate it?'

'Not pity my child!' said Hippolita, catching Matilda in her arms – 'Oh! I know she is good, she is all virtue, all tenderness, and duty. I do forgive thee, my excellent, my only hope!'

The princesses then revealed to Hippolita their mutual inclination for Theodore, and the purpose of Isabella to resign him to Matilda. Hippolita blamed their imprudence, and showed them the improbability that either father would consent to bestow his heiress on so poor a man, though nobly born. Some comfort it gave her to find their passion of so recent a date, and that Theodore had had but little cause to suspect it in either. She strictly enjoined them to avoid all correspondence with him. This Matilda fervently promised: but Isabella, who flattered herself that she meant no more than to promote his union with her friend, could not determine to avoid him; and made no reply.

'I will go to the convent,' said Hippolita, 'and order new masses to be said for a deliverance from these calamities.'

'Oh! my mother,' said Matilda, 'you mean to quit us: you mean to take sanctuary, and to give my father an opportunity of pursuing his fatal intention. Alas! on my knees I supplicate you to forbear; will you leave me a prey to Frederic? I will follow you to the convent.'

'Be at peace, my child,' said Hippolita: 'I will return instantly. I will never abandon thee, until I know it is the will of heaven, and for thy benefit.'

'Do not deceive me,' said Matilda. 'I will not marry Frederic until thou commandest it. Alas! what will become of me?'

'Why that exclamation?' said Hippolita. 'I have promised thee to return – '

'Ah! my mother,' replied Matilda, 'stay and save me from myself. A frown from thee can do more than all my father's severity. I have given away my heart, and you alone can make me recall it.'

'No more,' said Hippolita; 'thou must not relapse, Matilda.'

'I can quit Theodore,' said she, 'but must I wed another? Let me attend thee to the altar, and shut myself from the world for ever.'

'Thy fate depends on thy father,' said Hippolita; 'I have ill bestowed my tenderness, if it has taught thee to revere aught beyond him. Adieu! my child: I go to pray for thee.'

Hippolita's real purpose was to demand of Jerome, whether in conscience she might not consent to the divorce. She had oft urged Manfred to resign the principality, which the delicacy of her conscience rendered an hourly burthen to her. These scruples concurred to make the separation from her husband appear less dreadful to her than it would have seemed in any other situation.

Jerome, at quitting the castle overnight, had questioned Theodore severely why he had accused him to Manfred of being privy to his escape. Theodore owned it had been with design to prevent Manfred's suspicion from alighting on Matilda; and added, the holiness of Jerome's life and character secured him from the tyrant's wrath. Jerome was heartily grieved to discover his son's inclination for that princess; and leaving him to his rest, promised in the morning to acquaint him with important reasons for conquering his passion.

Theodore, like Isabella, was too recently acquainted with parental authority to submit to its decisions against the impulse of his heart. He had little curiosity to learn the friar's reasons, and less disposition to obey them. The lovely Matilda had made stronger impressions on him than filial affection. All night he pleased himself with visions of love; and it was not till late after the morning-office, that he recollected the friar's commands to attend him at Alfonso's tomb.

'Young man,' said Jerome, when he saw him, 'this tardiness does not please me. Have a father's commands already so little weight?'

Theodore made awkward excuses, and attributed his delay to having overslept himself.

'And on whom were thy dreams employed?' said the friar sternly. His son blushed. 'Come, come,' resumed the friar, 'inconsiderate youth, this must not be; eradicate this guilty passion from thy breast –'

'Guilty passion!' cried Theodore: 'Can guilt dwell with innocent beauty and virtuous modesty?'

'It is sinful,' replied the friar, 'to cherish those whom heaven has doomed to destruction. A tyrant's race must be swept from the earth to the third and fourth generation.'

'Will heaven visit the innocent for the crimes of the guilty?' said Theodore. 'The fair Matilda has virtues enough –'

'To undo thee:' interrupted Jerome. 'Hast thou so soon forgotten that twice the savage Manfred has pronounced thy sentence?'

'Nor have I forgotten, sir,' said Theodore, 'that the charity of his daughter delivered me from his power. I can forget injuries, but never benefits.'

'The injuries thou hast received from Manfred's race,' said the friar, 'are beyond what thou canst conceive. Reply not, but view this holy image! Beneath this marble monument rest the ashes of the good Alfonso; a prince adorned with every virtue: the father of his people! The delight of mankind! Kneel, headstrong boy, and list, while a father unfolds a tale of horror that will expel every sentiment from thy soul, but sensations of sacred vengeance – Alfonso! much injured prince! let thy unsatisfied shade sit awful on the troubled air, while these trembling lips – Ha! who comes there? – '

'The most wretched of women!' said Hippolita, entering the choir. 'Good Father, art thou at leisure? – But why this kneeling youth? What means the horror imprinted on each countenance? Why at this venerable tomb – alas! hast thou seen aught?'

'We were pouring forth our orisons to heaven,' replied the friar, with some confusion, 'to put an end to the woes of this deplorable province. Join with us, Lady! thy spotless soul may obtain an exemption from the judgments which the portents of these days but too speakingly denounce against thy house.'

'I pray fervently to heaven to divert them,' said the pious princess. 'Thou knowest it has been the occupation of my life to wrest a blessing for my Lord and my harmless children. – One, alas! is taken from me! Would heaven but hear me for my poor Matilda! Father! intercede for her!'

'Every heart will bless her,' cried Theodore with rapture.

'Be dumb, rash youth!' said Jerome. 'And thou, fond Princess, contend not with the Powers above! the Lord giveth, and the Lord taketh away: bless His holy name, and submit to his decrees.'

'I do most devoutly,' said Hippolita; 'but will He not spare my only comfort? Must Matilda perish too? – ah! Father, I came – but dismiss thy son. No ear but thine must hear what I have to utter.'

'May heaven grant thy every wish, most excellent Princess!' said Theodore retiring. Jerome frowned.

Hippolita then acquainted the friar with the proposal she had suggested to Manfred, his approbation of it, and the tender of Matilda that he was gone to make to Frederic. Jerome could not conceal his dislike of the notion, which he covered under pretence of the improbability that Frederic, the nearest of blood to Alfonso, and who was come to claim his succession, would yield to an alliance with the usurper of his right. But nothing could equal the perplexity of the friar, when Hippolita confessed her readiness not to oppose the separation, and demanded his opinion on the legality of her acquiescence. The friar caught eagerly at her request of his advice, and without explaining his aversion to the proposed marriage of Manfred and Isabella, he painted to Hippolita in the most alarming colours the sinfulness of her consent, denounced judgments against her if she complied, and enjoined her in the severest terms to treat any such proposition with every mark of indignation and refusal.

Manfred, in the meantime, had broken his purpose to Frederic, and proposed the double marriage. That weak prince, who had been struck with the charms of Matilda, listened but too eagerly to the offer. He forgot his enmity to Manfred, whom he saw but little hope of dispossessing by force; and flattering himself that no issue might succeed from the union of his daughter with the tyrant, he looked upon his own succession to the principality as facilitated by wedding Matilda. He made faint opposition to the proposal; affecting, for form only, not to acquiesce unless Hippolita should consent to the divorce. Manfred took that upon himself.

Transported with his success, and impatient to see himself in a situation to expect sons, he hastened to his wife's apartment, determined to extort her compliance. He learned with indignation that she was absent at the convent. His guilt suggested to him that she had probably been informed by Isabella of his purpose. He doubted whether her retirement to the convent did not import an intention of remaining there, until she could raise obstacles to their divorce; and the suspicions he had already entertained of Jerome, made him apprehend that the friar would not only traverse his views, but might have inspired Hippolita with the resolution of talking sanctuary. Impatient to unravel this clue, and to defeat its success, Manfred hastened to the convent, and arrived there as the friar was earnestly exhorting the princess never to yield to the divorce.

'Madam,' said Manfred, 'what business drew you hither? why did you not await my return from the Marquis?'

'I came to implore a blessing on your councils,' replied Hippolita.

'My councils do not need a friar's intervention,' said Manfred; 'and of all men living is that hoary traitor the only one whom you delight to confer with?'

'Profane Prince!' said Jerome; 'is it at the altar that thou choosest to insult the servants of the altar? – but, Manfred, thy impious schemes are known. Heaven and this virtuous lady know them – nay, frown not, Prince. The Church despises thy menaces. Her thunders will be heard above thy wrath. Dare to proceed in thy cursed purpose of a divorce, until her sentence be known, and here I lance her anathema at thy head.'

'Audacious rebel!' said Manfred, endeavouring to conceal the awe with which the friar's words inspired him. 'Dost thou presume to threaten thy lawful Prince?'

'Thou art no lawful Prince,' said Jerome; 'thou art no Prince – go, discuss thy claim with Frederic; and when that is done – '

'It is done,' replied Manfred; 'Frederic accepts Matilda's hand, and is content to waive his claim, unless I have no male issue' – as he spoke those words three drops of blood fell from the nose of Alfonso's statue. Manfred turned pale, and the princess sank on her knees.

'Behold!' said the friar; 'mark this miraculous indication that the blood of Alfonso will never mix with that of Manfred!'

'My gracious Lord,' said Hippolita, 'let us submit ourselves to heaven. Think not thy ever-obedient wife rebels against thy authority. I have no will but that of my Lord and the Church. To that revered tribunal let us appeal. It does not depend on us to burst the bonds that unite us. If the Church shall approve the dissolution of our marriage, be it so – I have but few years, and those of sorrow, to pass. Where can they be worn away so well as at the foot of this altar, in prayers for thine and Matilda's safety?'

'But thou shalt not remain here until then,' said Manfred. 'Repair with me to the castle, and there I will advise on the proper measures for a divorce; but this meddling friar comes not thither; my hospitable roof shall never more harbour a traitor – and for thy Reverence's offspring,' continued he, 'I banish him from my dominions. He, I ween, is no sacred personage, nor under the protection of the Church. Whoever weds Isabella, it shall not be Father Falconara's started-up son.'

'They start up,' said the friar, 'who are suddenly beheld in the seat of lawful princes; but they wither away like the grass, and their place knows them no more.'

Manfred, casting a look of scorn at the friar, led Hippolita forth; but at the door of the church whispered one of his attendants to remain concealed about the convent, and bring him instant notice, if anyone from the castle should repair thither.

Chapter Five

Every reflection which Manfred made on the friar's behaviour, conspired to persuade him that Jerome was privy to an amour between
Isabella and Theodore. But Jerome's new presumption, so dissonant
from his former meekness, suggested still deeper apprehensions. The
prince even suspected that the friar depended on some secret support
from Frederic, whose arrival, coinciding with the novel appearance of
Theodore, seemed to bespeak a correspondence. Still more was he
troubled with the resemblance of Theodore to Alfonso's portrait. The
latter he knew had unquestionably died without issue. Frederic had
consented to bestow Isabella on him. These contradictions agitated
his mind with numberless pangs.

He saw but two methods of extricating himself from his difficulties. The one was to resign his dominions to the Marquis – pride,
ambition, and his reliance on ancient prophecies, which had pointed
out a possibility of his preserving them to his posterity, combated
that thought. The other was to press his marriage with Isabella. After
long ruminating on these anxious thoughts, as he marched silently
with Hippolita to the castle, he at last discoursed with that princess
on the subject of his disquiet, and used every insinuating and plausible argument to extract her consent to, even her promise of promot-
ing, the divorce. Hippolita needed little persuasions to bend her to
his pleasure. She endeavoured to win him over to the measure of
resigning his dominions; but finding her exhortations fruitless, she
assured him, that as far as her conscience would allow, she would
raise no opposition to a separation, though without better founded
scruples than what he yet alleged, she would not engage to be active
in demanding it.

This compliance, though inadequate, was sufficient to raise Manfred's hopes. He trusted that his power and wealth would easily
advance his suit at the court of Rome, whither he resolved to engage
Frederic to take a journey on purpose. That prince had discovered so
much passion for Matilda, that Manfred hoped to obtain all he wished
by holding out or withdrawing his daughter's charms, according as

the Marquis should appear more or less disposed to co-operate in his views. Even the absence of Frederic would be a material point gained, until he could take further measures for his security.

Dismissing Hippolita to her apartment, he repaired to that of the Marquis; but crossing the great hall through which he was to pass he met Bianca. The damsel he knew was in the confidence of both the young ladies. It immediately occurred to him to sift her on the subject of Isabella and Theodore. Calling her aside into the recess of the oriel window of the hall, and soothing her with many fair words and promises, he demanded of her whether she knew aught of the state of Isabella's affections.

'I! my Lord! No, my Lord – yes my Lord – poor Lady! she is wonderfully alarmed about her father's wounds; but I tell her he will do well; don't your Highness think so?'

'I do not ask you,' replied Manfred, 'what she thinks about her father; but you are in her secrets. Come, be a good girl and tell me; is there any young man – ha! – you understand me.'

'Lord bless me! understand your Highness? No, not I. I told her a few vulnerary herbs and repose – '

'I am not talking,' replied the prince, impatiently, 'about her father; I know he will do well.'

'Bless me, I rejoice to hear your Highness say so; for though I thought it not right to let my young Lady despond, methought his greatness had a wan look, and a something – I remember when young Ferdinand was wounded by the Venetian – '

'Thou answerest from the point,' interrupted Manfred; 'but here, take this jewel, perhaps that may fix thy attention – nay, no reverences; my favour shall not stop here – come, tell me truly; how stands Isabella's heart?'

'Well! your Highness has such a way!' said Bianca, 'to be sure – but can your Highness keep a secret? If it should ever come out of your lips – '

'It shall not, it shall not,' cried Manfred.

'Nay, but swear, your Highness.'

'By my halidame, if it should ever be known that I said it – '

'Why, truth is truth, I do not think my Lady Isabella ever much affectioned my young Lord your son; yet he was a sweet youth as one should see; I am sure, if I had been a princess – but bless me! I must attend my Lady Matilda; she will marvel what is become of me.'

'Stay,' cried Manfred; 'thou hast not satisfied my question. Hast thou ever carried any message, any letter?'

'I! Good gracious!' cried Bianca; 'I carry a letter? I would not to be a queen. I hope your Highness thinks, though I am poor, I am honest. Did your Highness never hear what Count Marsigli offered me, when he came a-wooing to my Lady Matilda?'

'I have not leisure,' said Manfred, 'to listen to thy tale. I do not question thy honesty. But it is thy duty to conceal nothing from me. How long has Isabella been acquainted with Theodore?'

'Nay, there is nothing can escape your Highness!' said Bianca; 'not that I know any thing of the matter. Theodore, to be sure, is a proper young man, and, as my Lady Matilda says, the very image of good Alfonso. Has not your Highness remarked it?'

'Yes, yes – No – thou torturest me,' said Manfred. 'Where did they meet? When?'

'Who! my Lady Matilda?' said Bianca.

'No, no, not Matilda: Isabella; when did Isabella first become acquainted with this Theodore!'

'Virgin Mary!' said Bianca, 'how should I know?'

'Thou dost know,' said Manfred; 'and I must know; I will – '

'Lord! your Highness is not jealous of young Theodore?' said Bianca.

'Jealous! No, no. Why should I be jealous? Perhaps I mean to unite them – if I were sure Isabella would have no repugnance.'

'Repugnance! No, I'll warrant her,' said Bianca; 'he is as comely a youth as ever trod on Christian ground. We are all in love with him; there is not a soul in the castle but would be rejoiced to have him for our Prince – I mean, when it shall please heaven to call your Highness to itself.'

'Indeed!' said Manfred, 'has it gone so far! Oh! this cursed friar! – but I must not lose time – go, Bianca, attend Isabella; but I charge thee, not a word of what has passed. Find out how she is affected towards Theodore; bring me good news, and that ring has a companion. Wait at the foot of the winding staircase: I am going to visit the Marquis, and will talk further with thee at my return.'

Manfred, after some general conversation, desired Frederic to dismiss the two knights, his companions, having to talk with him on urgent affairs.

As soon as they were alone, he began in artful guise to sound the Marquis on the subject of Matilda; and finding him disposed to his wish, he let drop hints on the difficulties that would attend the celebration of their marriage, unless – at that instant Bianca burst into the room with a wildness in her look and gestures that spoke the utmost terror.

'Oh! my Lord, my Lord!' cried she; 'we are all undone! It is come again! It is come again!'

'What is come again?' cried Manfred amazed.

'Oh! the hand! The giant! The hand! – Support me! I am terrified out of my senses,' cried Bianca. 'I will not sleep in the castle tonight. Where shall I go? My things may come after me tomorrow – would I had been content to wed Francesco! This comes of ambition!'

'What has terrified thee thus, young woman?' said the Marquis. 'Thou art safe here; be not alarmed.'

'Oh! your Greatness is wonderfully good,' said Bianca, 'but I dare not – no, pray let me go – I had rather leave everything behind me, than stay another hour under this roof.'

'Go to, thou hast lost thy senses,' said Manfred. 'Interrupt us not; we were communing on important matters – My Lord, this wench is subject to fits – Come with me, Bianca.'

'Oh! the saints! No,' said Bianca, 'for certain it comes to warn your Highness; why should it appear to me else? I say my prayers morning and evening – oh! if your Highness had believed Diego! 'Tis the same hand that he saw the foot to in the gallery-chamber – Father Jerome has often told us the prophecy would be out one of these days – "Bianca," said he, "mark my words – "'

'Thou ravest,' said Manfred, in a rage; 'be gone, and keep these fooleries to frighten thy companions.'

'What! my Lord,' cried Bianca, 'do you think I have seen nothing? go to the foot of the great stairs yourself – as I live I saw it.'

'Saw what? Tell us, fair maid, what thou hast seen,' said Frederic.

'Can your Highness listen,' said Manfred, 'to the delirium of a silly wench, who has heard stories of apparitions until she believes them?'

'This is more than fancy,' said the Marquis; 'her terror is too natural and too strongly impressed to be the work of imagination. Tell us, fair maiden, what it is has moved thee thus?'

'Yes, my Lord, thank your Greatness,' said Bianca; 'I believe I look very pale; I shall be better when I have recovered myself – I was going to my Lady Isabella's chamber, by his Highness's order – '

'We do not want the circumstances,' interrupted Manfred. 'Since his Highness will have it so, proceed; but be brief.'

'Lord! your Highness thwarts one so!' replied Bianca; 'I fear my hair – I am sure I never in my life – well! as I was telling your

Greatness, I was going by his Highness's order to my Lady Isabella's chamber; she lies in the watchet-coloured chamber, on the right hand, one pair of stairs: so when I came to the great stairs – I was looking on his Highness's present here – '

'Grant me patience!' said Manfred, 'will this wench never come to the point? What imports it to the Marquis, that I gave thee a bauble for thy faithful attendance on my daughter? We want to know what thou sawest.'

'I was going to tell your Highness,' said Bianca, 'if you would permit me. So as I was rubbing the ring – I am sure I had not gone up three steps, but I heard the rattling of armour; for all the world such a clatter as Diego says he heard when the giant turned him about in the gallery-chamber.'

'What giant is this, my Lord?' said the Marquis; 'is your castle haunted by giants and goblins?'

'Lord! what, has not your Greatness heard the story of the giant in the gallery-chamber?' cried Bianca. 'I marvel his Highness has not told you; mayhap you do not know there is a prophecy – '

'This trifling is intolerable,' interrupted Manfred. 'Let us dismiss this silly wench, my Lord! we have more important affairs to discuss.'

'By your favour,' said Frederic, 'these are no trifles. The enormous sabre I was directed to in the wood, yon casque, its fellow – are these visions of this poor maiden's brain?'

'So Jaquez thinks, may it please your Greatness,' said Bianca. 'He says this moon will not be out without our seeing some strange revolution. For my part, I should not be surprised if it was to happen tomorrow; for, as I was saying, when I heard the clattering of armour, I was all in a cold sweat. I looked up, and, if your Greatness will believe me, I saw upon the uppermost banister of the great stairs a hand in armour as big as big. I thought I should have swooned. I never stopped until I came hither – would I were well out of this castle. My Lady Matilda told me but yester-morning that her Highness Hippolita knows something.'

'Thou art an insolent!' cried Manfred. 'Lord Marquis, it much misgives me that this scene is concerted to affront me. Are my own domestics suborned to spread tales injurious to my honour? Pursue your claim by manly daring; or let us bury our feuds, as was proposed, by the intermarriage of our children. But trust me, it ill becomes a prince of your bearing to practise on mercenary wenches.'

'I scorn your imputation,' said Frederic. 'Until this hour I never set eyes on this damsel: I have given her no jewel. My Lord, my

Lord, your conscience, your guilt accuses you, and would throw the suspicion on me; but keep your daughter, and think no more of Isabella. The judgments already fallen on your house forbid me matching into it.'

Manfred, alarmed at the resolute tone in which Frederic delivered these words, endeavoured to pacify him. Dismissing Bianca, he made such submissions to the Marquis, and threw in such artful encomiums on Matilda, that Frederic was once more staggered. However, as his passion was of so recent a date, it could not at once surmount the scruples he had conceived. He had gathered enough from Bianca's discourse to persuade him that heaven declared itself against Manfred. The proposed marriages too removed his claim to a distance; and the principality of Otranto was a stronger temptation than the contingent reversion of it with Matilda. Still he would not absolutely recede from his engagements; but purposing to gain time, he demanded of Manfred if it was true in fact that Hippolita consented to the divorce. The prince, transported to find no other obstacle, and depending on his influence over his wife, assured the Marquis it was so, and that he might satisfy himself of the truth from her own mouth.

As they were thus discoursing, word was brought that the banquet was prepared. Manfred conducted Frederic to the great hall, where they were received by Hippolita and the young princesses. Manfred placed the Marquis next to Matilda, and seated himself between his wife and Isabella. Hippolita comported herself with an easy gravity; but the young ladies were silent and melancholy. Manfred, who was determined to pursue his point with the Marquis in the remainder of the evening, pushed on the feast until it waxed late; affecting unrestrained gaiety, and plying Frederic with repeated goblets of wine. The latter, more upon his guard than Manfred wished, declined his frequent challenges, on pretence of his late loss of blood; while the prince, to raise his own disordered spirits, and to counterfeit unconcern, indulged himself in plentiful draughts, though not to the intoxication of his senses.

The evening being far advanced, the banquet concluded. Manfred would have withdrawn with Frederic; but the latter pleading weakness and want of repose, retired to his chamber, gallantly telling the prince that his daughter should amuse his Highness until himself could attend him. Manfred accepted the party, and to the no small grief of Isabella, accompanied her to her apartment. Matilda waited on her mother to enjoy the freshness of the evening on the ramparts of the castle.

Soon as the company were dispersed their several ways, Frederic, quitting his chamber, inquired if Hippolita was alone, and was told by one of her attendants, who had not noticed her going forth, that at that hour she generally withdrew to her oratory, where he probably would find her. The Marquis, during the repast, had beheld Matilda with increase of passion. He now wished to find Hippolita in the disposition her Lord had promised. The portents that had alarmed him were forgotten in his desires. Stealing softly and unobserved to the apartment of Hippolita, he entered it with a resolution to encourage her acquiescence to the divorce, having perceived that Manfred was resolved to make the possession of Isabella an unalterable condition, before he would grant Matilda to his wishes

The Marquis was not surprised at the silence that reigned in the princess's apartment. Concluding her, as he had been advertised, in her oratory, he passed on. The door was ajar; the evening gloomy and overcast. Pushing open the door gently, he saw a person kneeling before the altar. As he approached nearer, it seemed not a woman, but one in a long woollen weed, whose back was towards him. The person seemed absorbed in prayer. The Marquis was about to return, when the figure, rising, stood some moments fixed in meditation, without regarding him. The Marquis, expecting the holy person to come forth, and meaning to excuse his uncivil interruption, said, 'Reverend Father, I sought the Lady Hippolita.'

'Hippolita!' replied a hollow voice; 'camest thou to this castle to seek Hippolita?' And then the figure, turning slowly round, discovered to Frederic the fleshless jaws and empty sockets of a skeleton, wrapt in a hermit's cowl.

'Angels of grace protect me!' cried Frederic, recoiling.

'Deserve their protection!' said the spectre. Frederic, falling on his knees, adjured the phantom to take pity on him.

'Dost thou not remember me?' said the apparition. 'Remember the wood of Joppa!'

'Art thou that holy hermit?' cried Frederic, trembling. 'Can I do aught for thy eternal peace?'

'Wast thou delivered from bondage,' said the spectre, 'to pursue carnal delights? Hast thou forgotten the buried sabre, and the behest of Heaven engraven on it?'

'I have not, I have not,' said Frederic; 'but say, blest spirit, what is thy errand to me? What remains to be done?'

'To forget Matilda!' said the apparition; and vanished.

Frederic's blood froze in his veins. For some minutes he remained motionless. Then falling prostrate on his face before the altar, he besought the intercession of every saint for pardon. A flood of tears succeeded to this transport; and the image of the beauteous Matilda rushing in spite of him on his thoughts, he lay on the ground in a conflict of penitence and passion. Ere he could recover from this agony of his spirits, the Princess Hippolita with a taper in her hand entered the oratory alone. Seeing a man without motion on the floor, she gave a shriek, concluding him dead. Her fright brought Frederic to himself. Rising suddenly, his face bedewed with tears, he would have rushed from her presence; but Hippolita stopping him, conjured him in the most plaintive accents to explain the cause of his disorder, and by what strange chance she had found him there in that posture.

'Ah, virtuous Princess!' said the Marquis, penetrated with grief, and stopped.

'For the love of Heaven, my Lord,' said Hippolita, 'disclose the cause of this transport! What mean these doleful sounds, this alarming exclamation on my name? What woes has heaven still in store for the wretched Hippolita? Yet silent! By every pitying angel, I adjure thee, noble Prince,' continued she, falling at his feet, 'to disclose the purport of what lies at thy heart. I see thou feelest for me; thou feelest the sharp pangs that thou inflictest – speak, for pity! Does aught thou knowest concern my child?'

'I cannot speak,' cried Frederic, bursting from her. 'Oh, Matilda!'

Quitting the princess thus abruptly, he hastened to his own apartment. At the door of it he was accosted by Manfred, who flushed by wine and love had come to seek him, and to propose to waste some hours of the night in music and revelling. Frederic, offended at an invitation so dissonant from the mood of his soul, pushed him rudely aside, and entering his chamber, flung the door intemperately against Manfred, and bolted it inwards. The haughty prince, enraged at this unaccountable behaviour, withdrew in a frame of mind capable of the most fatal excesses. As he crossed the court, he was met by the domestic whom he had planted at the convent as a spy on Jerome and Theodore. This man, almost breathless with the haste he had made, informed his Lord that Theodore and some lady from the castle were, at that instant, in private conference at the tomb of Alfonso in St Nicholas' church. He had dogged Theodore thither, but the gloominess of the night had prevented his discovering who the woman was.

Manfred, whose spirits were inflamed, and whom Isabella had driven from her on his urging his passion with too little reserve, did not doubt but the inquietude she had expressed had been occasioned by her impatience to meet Theodore. Provoked by this conjecture, and enraged at her father, he hastened secretly to the great church. Gliding softly between the aisles, and guided by an imperfect gleam of moonshine that shone faintly through the illuminated windows, he stole towards the tomb of Alfonso, to which he was directed by indistinct whispers of the persons he sought. The first sounds he could distinguish were –

'Does it, alas! depend on me? Manfred will never permit our union.'

'No, this shall prevent it!' cried the tyrant, drawing his dagger, and plunging it over her shoulder into the bosom of the person that spoke.

'Ah, me, I am slain!' cried Matilda, sinking. 'Good heaven, receive my soul!'

'Savage, inhuman monster, what hast thou done!' cried Theodore, rushing on him, and wrenching his dagger from him.

'Stop, stop thy impious hand!' cried Matilda; 'it is my father!'

Manfred, waking as from a trance, beat his breast, twisted his hands in his locks, and endeavoured to recover his dagger from Theodore to despatch himself. Theodore, scarce less distracted, and only mastering the transports of his grief to assist Matilda, had now by his cries drawn some of the monks to his aid. While part of them endeavoured, in concert with the afflicted Theodore, to stop the blood of the dying princess, the rest prevented Manfred from laying violent hands on himself.

Matilda, resigning herself patiently to her fate, acknowledged with looks of grateful love the zeal of Theodore. Yet oft as her faintness would permit her speech its way, she begged the assistants to comfort her father.

Jerome, by this time, had learnt the fatal news, and reached the church. His looks seemed to reproach Theodore, but turning to Manfred, he said, 'Now, tyrant! behold the completion of woe fulfilled on thy impious and devoted head! The blood of Alfonso cried to heaven for vengeance; and heaven has permitted its altar to be polluted by assassination, that thou mightest shed thy own blood at the foot of that prince's sepulchre!'

'Cruel man!' cried Matilda, 'to aggravate the woes of a parent; may heaven bless my father, and forgive him as I do! My Lord, my gracious Sire, dost thou forgive thy child? Indeed, I came not hither to meet Theodore. I found him praying at this tomb, whither my mother sent me to intercede for thee, for her – dearest father, bless your child, and say you forgive her.'

'Forgive thee! Murderous monster!' cried Manfred, 'can assassins forgive? I took thee for Isabella; but heaven directed my bloody hand to the heart of my child. Oh, Matilda! – I cannot utter it – canst thou forgive the blindness of my rage?'

'I can, I do; and may heaven confirm it!' said Matilda; 'but while I have life to ask it – oh! my mother! what will she feel? Will you comfort her, my Lord? Will you not put her away? Indeed she loves you! Oh, I am faint! Bear me to the castle. Can I live to have her close my eyes?'

Theodore and the monks besought her earnestly to suffer herself to be borne into the convent; but her instances were so pressing to be carried to the castle, that placing her on a litter, they conveyed her thither as she requested. Theodore, supporting her head with his arm, and hanging over her in an agony of despairing love, still endeavoured to inspire her with hopes of life. Jerome, on the other side, comforted her with discourses of heaven, and holding a crucifix before her, which she bathed with innocent tears, prepared her for her passage to immortality. Manfred, plunged in the deepest affliction, followed the litter in despair.

Ere they reached the castle, Hippolita, informed of the dreadful catastrophe, had flown to meet her murdered child; but when she saw the afflicted procession, the mightiness of her grief deprived her of her senses, and she fell lifeless to the earth in a swoon. Isabella and Frederic, who attended her, were overwhelmed in almost equal sorrow. Matilda alone seemed insensible to her own situation: every thought was lost in tenderness for her mother.

Ordering the litter to stop, as soon as Hippolita was brought to herself, she asked for her father. He approached, unable to speak. Matilda, seizing his hand and her mother's, locked them in her own, and then clasped them to her heart. Manfred could not support this act of pathetic piety. He dashed himself on the ground, and cursed the day he was born. Isabella, apprehensive that these struggles of passion were more than Matilda could support, took upon herself to order Manfred to be borne to his apartment, while she caused Matilda to be conveyed to the nearest chamber. Hippolita, scarce more alive than her daughter, was regardless of everything but her; but when the tender Isabella's care would have likewise removed her, while the surgeons examined Matilda's wound, she cried, 'Remove me! Never, never! I lived but in her, and will expire with her.'

Matilda raised her eyes at her mother's voice, but closed them again without speaking. Her sinking pulse and the damp coldness of her hand soon dispelled all hopes of recovery. Theodore followed the surgeons into the outer chamber, and heard them pronounce the fatal sentence with a transport equal to frenzy.

'Since she cannot live mine,' cried he, 'at least she shall be mine in death! Father Jerome! will you not join our hands?' cried he to the friar, who, with the Marquis, had accompanied the surgeons.

'What means thy distracted rashness?' said Jerome. 'Is this an hour for marriage?'

'It is, it is,' cried Theodore. 'Alas! there is no other!'

'Young man, thou art too unadvised,' said Frederic. 'Dost thou think we are to listen to thy fond transports in this hour of fate? What pretensions hast thou to the Princess?'

'Those of a prince,' said Theodore; 'of the sovereign of Otranto. This reverend man, my father, has informed me who I am.'

'Thou ravest,' said the Marquis. 'There is no Prince of Otranto but myself, now Manfred, by murder, by sacrilegious murder, has forfeited all pretensions.'

'My Lord,' said Jerome, assuming an air of command, 'he tells you true. It was not my purpose the secret should have been divulged so soon, but fate presses onward to its work. What his hot-headed passion has revealed, my tongue confirms. Know, Prince, that when Alfonso set sail for the Holy Land – '

'Is this a season for explanations?' cried Theodore. 'Father, come and unite me to the Princess; she shall be mine! In every other thing I will dutifully obey you. My life! my adored Matilda!' continued Theodore, rushing back into the inner chamber, 'will you not be mine? Will you not bless your – '

Isabella made signs to him to be silent, apprehending the princess was near her end.

'What, is she dead?' cried Theodore; 'is it possible!'

The violence of his exclamations brought Matilda to herself. Lifting up her eyes, she looked round for her mother.

'Life of my soul, I am here!' cried Hippolita; 'think not I will quit thee!'

'Oh! you are too good,' said Matilda. 'But weep not for me, my mother! I am going where sorrow never dwells – Isabella, thou hast loved me; wouldst thou not supply my fondness to this dear, dear woman? Indeed I am faint!'

'Oh! my child! my child!' said Hippolita in a flood of tears, 'can I not withhold thee a moment?'

'It will not be,' said Matilda; 'commend me to heaven – Where is my father? Forgive him, dearest mother – forgive him my death; it was an error. Oh! I had forgotten – dearest mother, I vowed never to see Theodore more – perhaps that has drawn down this calamity – but it was not intentional – can you pardon me?'

'Oh! wound not my agonising soul!' said Hippolita; 'thou never couldst offend me – Alas! she faints! help! help!'

'I would say something more,' said Matilda, struggling, 'but it cannot be – Isabella – Theodore – for my sake – Oh! – ' she expired.

Isabella and her women tore Hippolita from the corse; but Theodore threatened destruction to all who attempted to remove him from it. He printed a thousand kisses on her clay-cold hands, and uttered every expression that despairing love could dictate.

Isabella, in the meantime, was accompanying the afflicted Hippolita to her apartment; but, in the middle of the court, they were met by Manfred, who, distracted with his own thoughts, and anxious once more to behold his daughter, was advancing to the chamber where she lay. As the moon was now at its height, he read in the countenances of this unhappy company the event he dreaded.

'What! is she dead?' cried he in wild confusion. A clap of thunder at that instant shook the castle to its foundations; the earth rocked, and the clank of more than mortal armour was heard behind. Frederic and Jerome thought the last day was at hand. The latter, forcing Theodore along with them, rushed into the court. The moment Theodore appeared, the walls of the castle behind Manfred were thrown down with a mighty force, and the form of Alfonso, dilated to an immense magnitude, appeared in the centre of the ruins.

'Behold in Theodore the true heir of Alfonso!' said the vision: and having pronounced those words, accompanied by a clap of thunder, it ascended solemnly towards heaven, where the clouds parting asunder, the form of St Nicholas was seen, and receiving Alfonso's shade, they were soon wrapt from mortal eyes in a blaze of glory.

The beholders fell prostrate on their faces, acknowledging the divine will. The first that broke silence was Hippolita.

'My Lord,' said she to the desponding Manfred, 'behold the vanity of human greatness! Conrad is gone! Matilda is no more! In Theodore we view the true Prince of Otranto. By what miracle he is so

I know not – suffice it to us, our doom is pronounced! Shall we not, can we but dedicate the few deplorable hours we have to live, in deprecating the further wrath of heaven? Heaven ejects us – whither can we fly, but to yon holy cells that yet offer us a retreat.'

'Thou guiltless but unhappy woman! unhappy by my crimes!' replied Manfred, 'my heart at last is open to thy devout admonitions. Oh! could – but it cannot be – ye are lost in wonder – let me at last do justice on myself! To heap shame on my own head is all the satisfaction I have left to offer to offended heaven. My story has drawn down these judgments: Let my confession atone – but, ah! what can atone for usurpation and a murdered child? A child murdered in a consecrated place? List, sirs, and may this bloody record be a warning to future tyrants!

'Alfonso, ye all know, died in the Holy Land – ye would interrupt me; ye would say he came not fairly to his end – it is most true – why else this bitter cup which Manfred must drink to the dregs. Ricardo, my grandfather, was his chamberlain – I would draw a veil over my ancestor's crimes – but it is in vain! Alfonso died by poison. A fictitious will declared Ricardo his heir. His crimes pursued him – yet he lost no Conrad, no Matilda! I pay the price of usurpation for all! A storm overtook him. Haunted by his guilt he vowed to St Nicholas to found a church and two convents, if he lived to reach Otranto. The sacrifice was accepted: the saint appeared to him in a dream, and promised that Ricardo's posterity should reign in Otranto until the rightful owner should be grown too large to inhabit the castle, and as long as issue male from Ricardo's loins should remain to enjoy it – alas! alas! nor male nor female, except myself, remains of all his wretched race! I have done – the woes of these three days speak the rest. How this young man can be Alfonso's heir I know not – yet I do not doubt it. His are these dominions; I resign them – yet I knew not Alfonso had an heir – I question not the will of heaven – poverty and prayer must fill up the woeful space, until Manfred shall be summoned to Ricardo.'

'What remains is my part to declare,' said Jerome. 'When Alfonso set sail for the Holy Land he was driven by a storm to the coast of Sicily. The other vessel, which bore Ricardo and his train, as your *Lordship* must have heard, was separated from him.'

'It is most true,' said Manfred; 'and the title you give me is more than an outcast can claim – well! be it so – proceed.'

Jerome blushed, and continued. 'For three months Lord Alfonso was wind-bound in Sicily. There he became enamoured of a fair virgin named Victoria. He was too pious to tempt her to forbidden pleasures. They were married. Yet deeming this amour incongruous with the holy vow of arms by which he was bound, he determined to conceal their nuptials until his return from the crusade, when he purposed to seek and acknowledge her for his lawful wife. He left her pregnant. During his absence she was delivered of a daughter. But scarce had she felt a mother's pangs ere she heard the fatal rumour of her Lord's death, and the succession of Ricardo. What could a friendless, helpless woman do? Would her testimony avail? – Yet, my lord, I have an authentic writing – '

'It needs not,' said Manfred; 'the horrors of these days, the vision we have but now seen, all corroborate thy evidence beyond a thousand parchments. Matilda's death and my expulsion – '

'Be composed, my Lord,' said Hippolita; 'this holy man did not mean to recall your griefs.' Jerome proceeded.

'I shall not dwell on what is needless. The daughter of which Victoria was delivered, was at her maturity bestowed in marriage on me. Victoria died; and the secret remained locked in my breast. Theodore's narrative has told the rest.'

The friar ceased. The disconsolate company retired to the remaining part of the castle. In the morning Manfred signed his abdication of the principality, with the approbation of Hippolita, and each took on them the habit of religion in the neighbouring convents. Frederic offered his daughter to the new prince, which Hippolita's tenderness for Isabella concurred to promote. But Theodore's grief was too fresh to admit the thought of another love; and it was not until after frequent discourses with Isabella of his dear Matilda, that he was persuaded he could know no happiness but in the society of one with whom he could for ever indulge the melancholy that had taken possession of his soul.

VATHEK

THE HISTORY OF THE CALIPH VATHEK

Vathek, ninth Caliph of the race of the Abassides, was the son of Motassem, and the grandson of Haroun Al Raschid. From an early accession to the throne, and the talents he possessed to adorn it, his subjects were induced to expect that his reign would be long and happy. His figure was pleasing and majestic; but when he was angry one of his eyes became so terrible that no person could bear to behold it, and the wretch upon whom it was fixed instantly fell backward, and sometimes expired. For fear, however, of depopulating his dominions and making his palace desolate, he but rarely gave way to his anger.

Being much addicted to women and the pleasures of the table, he sought by his affability to procure agreeable companions; and he succeeded the better as his generosity was unbounded, and his indulgences unrestrained, for he was by no means scrupulous, nor did he think with the Caliph Omar Ben Abdalaziz that it was necessary to make a hell of this world to enjoy Paradise in the next.

He surpassed in magnificence all his predecessors. The palace of Alkoremmi, which his father Motassem had erected on the hill of Pied Horses, and which commanded the whole city of Samarah, was in his idea far too scanty; he added therefore five wings, or rather other palaces, which he destined for the particular gratification of each of his senses.

In the first of these were tables continually covered with the most exquisite dainties, which were supplied both by night and by day, according to their constant consumption, whilst the most delicious wines and the choicest cordials flowed forth from a hundred fountains that were never exhausted. This palace was called *The Eternal or Unsatiating Banquet.*

The second was styled *The Temple of Melody, or the Nectar of the Soul*. It was inhabited by the most skilful musicians and admired poets of the time, who not only displayed their talents within, but, dispersing in bands without, caused every surrounding scene to reverberate their songs, which were continually varied in the most delightful succession.

The palace named *The Delight of the Eyes, or the Support of Memory*, was one entire enchantment. Rarities collected from every corner of the earth were there found in such profusion as to dazzle and confound, but for the order in which they were arranged. One gallery exhibited the pictures of the celebrated Mani, and statues that seemed to be alive. Here a well-managed perspective attracted the sight; there the magic of optics agreeably deceived it; whilst the naturalist on his part exhibited, in their several classes, the various gifts that Heaven had bestowed on our globe. In a word, Vathek omitted nothing in this palace that might gratify the curiosity of those who resorted to it, although he was not able to satisfy his own, for he was of all men the most curious.

The Palace of Perfumes, which was termed likewise *The Incentive to Pleasure*, consisted of various halls, where the different perfumes which the earth produces were kept perpetually burning in censers of gold. Flambeaux and aromatic lamps were here lighted in open day. But the too-powerful effects of this agreeable delirium might be avoided by descending into an immense garden, where an assemblage of every fragrant flower diffused through the air the purest odours.

The fifth palace, denominated *The Retreat of Joy, or the Dangerous*, was frequented by troops of young females, beautiful as the houris and not less seducing, who never failed to receive with caresses all whom the Caliph allowed to approach them; for he was by no means disposed to be jealous, as his own women were secluded within the palace he inhabited himself.

Notwithstanding the sensuality in which Vathek indulged, he experienced no abatement in the love of his people, who thought that a sovereign immersed in pleasure was not less tolerable to his subjects than one that employed himself in creating them foes. But the unquiet and impetuous disposition of the Caliph would not allow him to rest there; he had studied so much for his amusement in the lifetime of his father as to acquire a great deal of knowledge, though not a sufficiency to satisfy himself; for he wished to know everything, even sciences that did not exist. He was fond of engaging in disputes with the learned, but liked them not to push their opposition with warmth; he stopped the mouths of those with presents whose mouths could be stopped, whilst others, whom his liberality was unable to subdue, he sent to prison to cool their blood: a remedy that often succeeded.

Vathek discovered also a predilection for theological controversy, but it was not with the orthodox that he usually held. By this means he induced the zealots to oppose him, and then persecuted them in return; for he resolved at any rate to have reason on his side.

The great prophet Mahomet, whose vicars the Caliphs are, beheld with indignation from his abode in the seventh heaven the irreligious conduct of such a vicegerent. 'Let us leave him to himself,' said he to the Genii, who are always ready to receive his commands. 'Let us see to what lengths his folly and impiety will carry him; if he run into excess we shall know how to chastise him. Assist him, therefore, to complete the tower which, in imitation of Nimrod, he hath begun, not, like that great warrior, to escape being drowned, but from the insolent curiosity of penetrating the secrets of Heaven; he will not divine the fate that awaits him.'

The Genii obeyed, and when the workmen had raised their structure a cubit in the day-time, two cubits more were added in the night. The expedition with which the fabric arose was not a little flattering to the vanity of Vathek. He fancied that even insensible matter showed a forwardness to subserve his designs, not considering that the successes of the foolish and wicked form the first rod of their chastisement.

His pride arrived at its height when, having ascended for the first time the eleven thousand stairs of his tower, he cast his eyes below, and beheld men not larger than pismires, mountains than shells, and cities than bee-hives. The idea which such an elevation inspired of his own grandeur completely bewildered him; he was almost ready to adore himself, till, lifting his eyes upward, he saw the stars as high above him as they appeared when he stood on the surface of the earth.

He consoled himself, however, for this transient perception of his littleness with the thought of being great in the eyes of others, and flattered himself that the light of his mind would extend beyond the reach of his sight, and transfer to the stars the decrees of his destiny.

With this view the inquisitive prince passed most of his nights on the summit of his tower, till he became an adept in the mysteries of astrology, and imagined that the planets had disclosed to him the most marvellous adventures, which were to be accomplished by an extraordinary personage from a country altogether unknown. Prompted by motives of curiosity, he had always been courteous to strangers, but from this instant he redoubled his attention, and ordered it to be announced by sound of trumpet, through all the streets of Samarah, that no one of his subjects, on peril of displeasure, should either lodge or detain a traveller, but forthwith bring him to the palace.

Not long after this proclamation there arrived in his metropolis a man so hideous that the very guards who arrested him were forced to shut their eyes as they led him along. The Caliph himself appeared startled at so horrible a visage, but joy succeeded to this emotion of terror when the stranger displayed to his view such rarities as he had never before seen, and of which he had no conception.

In reality, nothing was ever so extraordinary as the merchandise this stranger produced; most of his curiosities, which were not less admirable for their workmanship than splendour, had, besides, their several virtues described on a parchment fastened to each. There were slippers which enabled the feet to walk; knives that cut without the motion of a hand; sabres which dealt the blow at the person they were wished to strike; and the whole enriched with gems that were hitherto unknown.

The sabres especially, the blades of which emitted a dazzling radiance, fixed, more than all the rest, the Caliph's attention; who promised himself to decipher at his leisure the uncouth characters engraven on their sides. Without, therefore, demanding their price, he ordered all the coined gold to be brought from his treasury, and commanded the merchant to take what he pleased; the stranger obeyed, took little, and remained silent.

Vathek, imagining that the merchant's taciturnity was occasioned by the awe which his presence inspired, encouraged him to advance, and asked him, with an air of condescension, 'Who he was? Whence he came? And where he obtained such beautiful commodities?' The man, or rather monster, instead of making a reply, thrice rubbed his forehead, which, as well as his body, was blacker than ebony, four times clapped his paunch, the projection of which was enormous, opened wide his huge eyes, which glowed like firebrands, began to laugh with a hideous noise, and discovered his long amber-coloured teeth bestreaked with green.

The Caliph, though a little startled, renewed his inquiries, but without being able to procure a reply; at which, beginning to be ruffled, he exclaimed: 'Knowest thou, varlet, who I am? and at whom thou art aiming thy gibes?' Then, addressing his guards, 'Have ye heard him speak? Is he dumb?'

'He hath spoken,' they replied, 'but to no purpose.'

'Let him speak again, then,' said Vathek, 'and tell me who he is, from whence he came, and where he procured these singular curiosities, or I swear by the ass of Balaam that I will make him rue his pertinacity.'

The menace was accompanied by the Caliph with one of his angry and perilous glances, which the stranger sustained without the slightest emotion, although his eyes were fixed on the terrible eye of the prince.

No words can describe the amazement of the courtiers when they beheld this rude merchant withstand the encounter unshocked. They all fell prostrate with their faces on the ground to avoid the risk of their lives, and continued in the same abject posture till the Caliph exclaimed in a furious tone, 'Up, cowards! seize the miscreant! See that he be committed to prison and guarded by the best of my soldiers! Let him, however, retain the money I gave him; it is not my intent to take from him his property; I only want him to speak.'

No sooner had he uttered these words than the stranger was surrounded, pinioned with strong fetters, and hurried away to the prison of the great tower, which was encompassed by seven empalements of iron bars, and armed with spikes in every direction longer and sharper than spits.

The Caliph, nevertheless, remained in the most violent agitation; he sat down indeed to eat, but of the three hundred covers that were daily placed before him could taste of no more than thirty-two. A diet to which he had been so little accustomed was sufficient of itself to prevent him from sleeping; what then must be its effect when joined to the anxiety that preyed upon his spirits? At the first glimpse of dawn he hastened to the prison, again to importune this intractable stranger; but the rage of Vathek exceeded all bounds on finding the prison empty, the gates burst asunder, and his guards lying lifeless around him. In the paroxysm of his passion he fell furiously on the poor carcases, and kicked them till evening without intermission. His courtiers and viziers exerted their efforts to soothe his extravagance, but finding every expedient ineffectual, they all united in one vociferation: 'The Caliph is gone mad! The Caliph is out of his senses!'

This outcry, which soon resounded through the streets of Samarah, at length reaching the ears of Carathis, his mother, she flew in the utmost consternation to try her ascendency on the mind of her son. Her tears and caresses called off his attention, and he was prevailed upon, by her entreaties, to be brought back to the palace.

Carathis, apprehensive of leaving Vathek to himself, caused him to be put to bed, and seating herself by him, endeavoured by her conversation to heal and compose him. Nor could anyone have attempted it with better success, for the Caliph not only loved her as a mother, but respected her as a person of superior genius; it was she who had induced him, being a Greek herself, to adopt all the sciences and systems of her country, which good Mussulmans hold in such thorough abhorrence. Judicial astrology was one of those systems in which Carathis was a perfect adept; she began, therefore, with reminding her son of the promise which the stars had made him, and intimated an intention of consulting them again.

'Alas!' sighed the Caliph, as soon as he could speak, 'what a fool have I been! Not for having bestowed forty thousand kicks on my guards, who so tamely submitted to death, but for never considering that this extraordinary man was the same the planets had foretold; whom, instead of ill-treating, I should have conciliated by all the arts of persuasion.'

'The past,' said Carathis, 'cannot be recalled, but it behoves us to think of the future; perhaps you may again see the object you so much regret; it is possible the inscriptions on the sabres will afford information. Eat, therefore, and take thy repose, my dear son; we will consider tomorrow in what manner to act.'

Vathek yielded to her counsel as well as he could, and arose in the morning with a mind more at ease. The sabres he commanded to be instantly brought, and poring upon them through a green glass, that their glittering might not dazzle, he set himself in earnest to decipher the inscriptions; but his reiterated attempts were all of them nugatory; in vain did he beat his head and bite his nails, not a letter of the whole was he able to ascertain. So unlucky a disappointment would have undone him again had not Carathis by good fortune entered the apartment.

'Have patience, my son!' said she. 'You certainly are possessed of every important science, but the knowledge of languages is a trifle at best, and the accomplishment of none but a pedant. Issue forth a proclamation that you will confer such rewards as become your greatness upon anyone that shall interpret what you do not understand, and what it is beneath you to learn; you will soon find your curiosity gratified.'

'That may be,' said the Caliph. 'But in the meantime I shall be horribly disgusted by a crowd of smatterers, who will come to the trial as much for the pleasure of retailing their jargon as from the hope of gaining the reward. To avoid this evil it will be proper to add that I will put every candidate to death who shall fail to give satisfaction; for, thank Heaven! I have skill enough to distinguish whether one translates or invents.'

'Of that I have no doubt,' replied Carathis. 'But to put the ignorant to death is somewhat severe, and may be productive of dangerous effects; content yourself with commanding their beards to be burnt – beards in a state are not quite so essential as men.'

The Caliph submitted to the reasons of his mother, and sending for Morakanabad, his prime vizir, said: 'Let the common criers proclaim, not only in Samarah, but throughout every city in my empire, that whosoever will repair hither, and decipher certain characters which appear to be inexplicable, shall experience the liberality for which I am renowned; but that all who fail upon trial shall have their beards burnt off to the last hair. Let them add also that I will bestow fifty beautiful slaves, and as many jars of apricots from the Isle of Kirmith, upon any man that shall bring me intelligence of the stranger.'

The subjects of the Caliph, like their Sovereign, being great admirers of women and apricots from Kirmith, felt their mouths water at these promises, but were totally unable to gratify their hankering, for no one knew which way the stranger had gone.

As to the Caliph's other requisition, the result was different. The learned, the half-learned, and those who were neither, but fancied themselves equal to both, came boldly to hazard their beards, and all shamefully lost them. The exaction of these forfeitures, which found sufficient employment for the eunuchs, gave them such a smell of singed hair as greatly to disgust the ladies of the seraglio, and make it necessary that this new occupation of their guardians should be transferred into other hands.

At length, however, an old man presented himself whose beard was a cubit and a half longer than any that had appeared before him. The officers of the palace whispered to each other, as they ushered him in, 'What a pity, O what a great pity, that such a beard should be burnt!' Even the Caliph, when he saw it, concurred with them in opinion, but his concern was entirely needless. This venerable personage read the characters with facility, and explained them verbatim as follows: 'We were made where everything good is made; we are the least of the wonders of a place where all is wonderful, and deserving the sight of the first potentate on earth.'

'You translate admirably!' cried Vathek. 'I know to what these marvellous characters allude. Let him receive as many robes of honour and thousands of sequins of gold as he hath spoken words. I am in some measure relieved from the perplexity that embarrassed me!' Vathek invited the old main to dine, and even to remain some days in the palace.

Unluckily for him, he accepted the offer; for the Caliph, having ordered him next morning to be called, said: 'Read again to me what you have read already; I cannot hear too often the promise that is made me, the completion of which I languish to obtain.'

The old man forthwith put on his green spectacles, but they instantly dropped from his nose on perceiving that the characters he had read the day preceding had given place to others of different import.

'What ails you?' asked the Caliph. 'And why these symptoms of wonder?'

'Sovereign of the world,' replied the old man, 'these sabres hold another language today from that they yesterday held.'

'How say you?' returned Vathek. 'But it matters not! Tell me, if you can, what they mean.'

'It is this, my lord,' rejoined the old man: 'Woe to the rash mortal who seeks to know that of which he should remain ignorant, and to undertake that which surpasseth his power!'

'And woe to thee!' cried the Caliph, in a burst of indignation. 'Today thou art void of understanding. Begone from my presence; they shall burn but the half of thy beard, because thou wert yesterday fortunate in guessing; my gifts I never resume.'

The old man, wise enough to perceive he had luckily escaped, considering the folly of disclosing so disgusting a truth, immediately withdrew, and appeared not again.

But it was not long before Vathek discovered abundant reason to regret his precipitation; for though he could not decipher the characters himself, yet by constantly poring upon them he plainly perceived that they every day changed, and unfortunately no other candidate offered to explain them. This perplexing occupation inflamed his blood, dazzled his sight, and brought on a giddiness and debility that he could not support. He failed not, however, though in so reduced a condition, to be often carried to his tower, as he flattered himself that he might there read in the stars which he went to consult something more congenial to his wishes: but in this his hopes were deluded, for his eyes, dimmed by the vapours of his head, began to subserve his curiosity so ill, that he beheld nothing but a thick dun cloud, which he took for the most direful of omens.

Agitated with so much anxiety, Vathek entirely lost all firmness; a fever seized him, and his appetite failed. Instead of being one of the greatest eaters, he became as distinguished for drinking. So insatiable was the thirst which tormented him that his mouth, like a funnel, was always open to receive the various liquors that might be poured into it, and especially cold water, which calmed him more than every other.

This unhappy prince, being thus incapacitated for the enjoyment of any pleasure, commanded the palaces of the five senses to be shut up, forbore to appear in public, either to display his magnificence or administer justice, and retired to the inmost apartment of his harem. As he had ever been an excellent husband, his wives, overwhelmed with grief at his deplorable situation, incessantly supplied him with prayers for his health, and water for his thirst.

In the meantime the Princess Carathis, whose affliction no words can describe, instead of confinining herself to sobbing and tears, was closeted daily with the vizir Morakanabad, to find out some cure or mitigation of the Caliph's disease. Under the persuasion that it was caused by enchantment, they turned over together, leaf by leaf, all the books of magic that might point out a remedy, and caused the horrible stranger, whom they accused as the enchanter, to be everywhere sought for with the strictest diligence.

At the distance of a few miles from Samarah stood a high mountain, whose sides were swarded with wild thyme and basil, and its summit overspread with so delightful a plain, that it might be taken for the paradise destined for the faithful. Upon it grew a hundred thickets of eglantine and other fragrant shrubs, a hundred arbours of roses, jessamine, and honeysuckle, as many clumps of orange trees, cedar, and citron, whose branches, interwoven with the palm, the pomegranate, and the vine, presented every luxury that could regale the eye or the taste. The ground was strewed with violets, hare-bells, and pansies, in the midst of which sprang forth tufts of jonquils, hyacinths, and carnations, with every other perfume that impregnates the air. Four fountains, not less clear than deep, and so abundant as to slake the thirst of ten armies, seemed profusely placed here to make the scene more resemble the garden of Eden, which was watered by the four sacred rivers. Here the nightingale sang the birth of the rose, her well-beloved, and at the same time lamented its short-lived beauty; whilst the turtle deplored the loss of more substantial pleasures, and the wakeful lark hailed the rising light that re-animates the whole creation. Here more than anywhere the mingled melodies of birds expressed the various passions they inspired, as if the exquisite fruits which they pecked at pleasure had given them a double energy.

To this mountain Vathek was sometimes brought for the sake of breathing a purer air, and especially to drink at will of the four fountains, which were reputed in the highest degree salubrious and sacred to himself. His attendants were his mother, his wives, and some eunuchs, who assiduously employed themselves in filling capacious bowls of rock crystal, and emulously presenting them to him; but it frequently happened that his avidity exceeded their zeal, insomuch that he would prostrate himself upon the ground to lap up the water, of which he could never have enough.

One day, when this unhappy prince had been long lying in so debasing a posture, a voice, hoarse but strong, thus addressed him: 'Why assumest thou the function of a dog, O Caliph, so proud of thy dignity and power?'

At this apostrophe he raised his head, and beheld the stranger that had caused him so much affliction. Inflamed with anger at the sight, he exclaimed – 'Accursed Giaour! what comest thou hither to do? Is it not enough to have transformed a prince remarkable for his agility into one of those leather barrels which the Bedouin Arabs carry on their camels when they traverse the deserts? Perceivest thou not that I may perish by drinking to excess as well as by thirst?'

'Drink then this draught,' said the stranger, as he presented to him a phial of a red and yellow mixture. 'And, to satiate the thirst of thy soul as well as of thy body, know that I am an Indian, but from a region of India which is wholly unknown.'

The Caliph, delighted to see his desires accomplished in part, and flattering himself with the hope of obtaining their entire fulfilment, without a moment's hesitation swallowed the potion, and instantaneously found his health restored, his thirst appeased, and his limbs as agile as ever. In the transports of his joy Vathek leaped upon the neck of the frightful Indian, and kissed his horrid mouth and hollow cheeks as though they had been the coral lips and the lilies and roses of his most beautiful wives.

Nor would these transports have ceased, had not the eloquence of Carathis repressed them. Having prevailed upon him to return to Samarah, she caused a herald to proclaim as loudly as possible: 'The wonderful stranger hath appeared again; he hath healed the Caliph. He hath spoken! He hath spoken!'

Forthwith all the inhabitants of this vast city quitted their habit-ations, and ran together in crowds to see the procession of Vathek and the Indian, whom they now blessed as much as they had before execrated, incessantly shouting: 'He hath healed our sovereign. He hath spoken! He hath spoken!' Nor were these words forgotten in the public festivals which were celebrated the same evening, to testify the general joy; for the poets applied them as a chorus to all the songs they composed on this interesting subject.

The Caliph in the meanwhile caused the palaces of the senses to be again set open; and, as he found himself prompted to visit that of taste in preference to the rest, immediately ordered a splendid entertainment, to which his great officers and favourite courtiers were all invited. The Indian, who was placed near the prince, seemed to think that as a proper acknowledgment of so distinguished a privilege he could neither eat, drink, nor talk too much. The various dainties were no sooner served up than they vanished, to the great mortification of Vathek, who piqued himself on being the greatest eater alive, and at this time in particular had an excellent appetite.

The rest of the company looked round at each other in amazement; but the Indian, without appearing to observe it, quaffed large bumpers to the health of each of them, sung in a style altogether extravagant, related stories at which he laughed immoderately, and poured forth extemporaneous verses, which would not have been thought bad but for the strange grimaces with which they were uttered. In a word, his loquacity was equal to that of a hundred astrologers; he ate as much as a hundred porters, and caroused in proportion.

The Caliph, notwithstanding the table had been thirty times covered, found himself incommoded by the voraciousness of his guest, who was now considerably declined in the prince's esteem. Vathek, however, being unwilling to betray the chagrin he could hardly disguise, said in a whisper to Bababalouk, the chief of his eunuchs: 'You see how enormous his performances in every way are; what would be the consequence should he get at my wives? Go! redouble your vigilance, and be sure look well to my Circassians, who would be more to his taste than all of the rest.'

The bird of the morning had thrice renewed his song when the hour of the Divan sounded. Vathek, in gratitude to his subjects, having promised to attend, immediately rose from table and repaired thither, leaning upon his vizir, who could scarcely support him, so disordered was the poor prince by the wine he had drunk, and still more by the extravagant vagaries of his boisterous guest.

The vizirs, the officers of the crown and of the law, arranged themselves in a semicircle about their sovereign, and preserved a respectful silence, whilst the Indian, who looked as cool as if come from a fast, sat down without ceremony on the step of the throne, laughing in his sleeve at the indignation with which his temerity had filled the spectators.

The Caliph, however, whose ideas were confused and his head embarrassed, went on administering justice at haphazard, till at length the prime vizir, perceiving his situation, hit upon a sudden expedient to interrupt the audience and rescue the honour of his master, to whom he said in a whisper: 'My Lord, the Princess Carathis, who hath passed the night in consulting the planets, informs you that they portend you evil, and the danger is urgent. Beware lest this stranger, whom you have so lavishly recompensed for his magical gewgaws, should make some attempt on your life; his liquor, which at first had the appearance of effecting your cure, may be no more than a poison of a sudden operation. Slight not this surmise; ask him at least of what it was compounded, whence he procured it, and mention the sabres which you seem to have forgotten.'

Vathek, to whom the insolent airs of the stranger became every moment less supportable, intimated to his vizir by a wink of acquiescence that he would adopt his advice, and at once turning towards the Indian, said: 'Get up and declare in full Divan of what drugs the liquor was compounded you enjoined me to take, for it is suspected to be poison; add also the explanation I have so earnestly desired concerning the sabres you sold me, and thus show your gratitude for the favours heaped on you.'

Having pronounced these words in as moderate a tone as he well could, he waited in silent expectation for an answer. But the Indian, still keeping his seat, began to renew his loud shouts of laughter, and exhibit the same horrid grimaces he had shown them before, without vouchsafing a word in reply. Vathek, no longer able to brook such insolence, immediately kicked him from the steps; instantly descending, repeated his blow, and persisted with such assiduity as incited all who were present to follow his example. Every foot was up and aimed at the Indian, and no sooner had anyone given him a kick than he felt himself constrained to reiterate the stroke.

The stranger afforded them no small entertainment; for, being both short and plump, he collected himself into a ball, and rolled round on all sides at the blows of his assailants, who pressed after him wherever he turned with an eagerness beyond conception, whilst their numbers were every moment increasing. The ball, indeed, in passing from one apartment to another, drew every person after it that came in its way, insomuch that the whole palace was thrown into confusion, and resounded with a tremendous clamour. The women of the harem, amazed at the uproar, flew to their blinds to discover the cause; but no sooner did they catch a glimpse of the ball, than feeling themselves unable to refrain, they broke from the clutches of their eunuchs, who to stop their flight pinched them till they bled, but in vain; whilst themselves, though trembling with terror at the escape of their charge, were as incapable of resisting the attraction.

After having traversed the halls, galleries, chambers, kitchens, gardens, and stables of the palace, the Indian at last took his course through the courts; whilst the Caliph, pursuing him closer than the rest, bestowed as many kicks as he possibly could, yet not without receiving now and then one, which his competitors in their eagerness designed for the ball.

Carathis, Morakanabad, and two or three old vizirs, whose wisdom had hitherto withstood the attraction, wishing to prevent Vathek from exposing himself in the presence of his subjects, fell down in his way to impede the pursuit; but he, regardless of their obstruction, leaped over their heads, and went on as before. They then ordered the muezzins to call the people to prayers, both for the sake of getting them out of the way and of endeavouring by their petitions to avert the calamity; but neither of these expedients was a whit more successful: the sight of this fatal ball was alone sufficient to draw after it every beholder. The muezzins themselves, though they saw it but at a distance, hastened down from their minarets and mixed with the crowd, which continued to increase in so surprising a manner, that scarce an inhabitant was left in Samarah, except the aged, the sick confined to their beds, and infants at the breast, whose nurses could run more nimbly without them. Even Carathis, Morakanabad, and the rest were all become of the party.

The shrill screams of the females, who had broken from their apartments, and were unable to extricate themselves from the pressure of the crowd, together with those of the eunuchs jostling after them, terrified lest their charge should escape from their sight, increased by the execrations of husbands urging forward and menacing both, kicks given and received, stumblings and overthrows at every step; in a word, the confusion that universally prevailed rendered Samarah like a city taken by storm and devoted to absolute plunder. At last the cursed Indian, who still preserved his rotundity of figure, after passing through all the streets and public places, and leaving them empty, rolled onwards to the plain of Catoul, and traversed the valley at the foot of the Mountain of the Four Fountains.

As a continual fall of water had excavated an immense gulf in the valley, whose opposite side was closed in by a steep acclivity, the Caliph and his attendants were apprehensive lest the ball should bound into the chasm, and, to prevent it, redoubled their efforts, but in vain. The Indian persevered in his onward direction, and, as had been apprehended, glancing from the precipice with the rapidity of lightning, was lost in the gulf below.

Vathek would have followed the perfidious Giaour, had not an invisible agency arrested his progress. The multitude that pressed after him were at once checked in the same manner, and a calm instantaneously ensued. They all gazed at each other with an air of astonishment; and, notwithstanding that the loss of veils and turbans, together with torn habits and dust blended with sweat, presented a most laughable spectacle, there was not one smile to be seen; on the contrary, all, with looks of confusion and sadness, returned in silence to Samarah, and retired to their inmost apartments, without ever reflecting that they had been impelled by an invisible power into the extravagance for which they reproached themselves; for it is but just that men, who so often arrogate to their own merit the good of which they are but instruments, should attribute to themselves the absurdities which they could not prevent.

The Caliph was the only person who refused to leave the valley. He commanded his tents to be pitched there, and stationed himself on the very edge of the precipice, in spite of the representations of Carathis and Morakanabad, who pointed out the hazard of its brink giving way, and the vicinity to the magician that had so severely tormented him. Vathek derided all their remonstrances, and, having ordered a thousand flambeaux to be lighted, and directed his attendants to proceed in lighting more, lay down on the slippery margin, and attempted, by help of this artificial splendour, to look through that gloom which all the fires of the empyrean had been insufficient to pervade. One while he fancied to himself voices arising from the depth of the gulf; at another he seemed to distinguish the accents of the Indian, but all was no more than the hollow murmur of waters, and the din of the cataracts that rushed from steep to steep down the sides of the mountain.

Having passed the night in this cruel perturbation, the Caliph at daybreak retired to his tent, where, without taking the least sustenance, he continued to doze till the dusk of evening began again to come on. He then resumed his vigils as before, and persevered in observing them for many nights together. At length, fatigued with so successless an employment, he sought relief from change. To this end he sometimes paced with hasty strides across the plain, and, as he wildly gazed at the stars, reproached them with having deceived him; but, lo! on a sudden the clear blue sky appeared streaked over with streams of blood, which reached from the valley even to the city of Samarah. As this awful phenomenon seemed to touch his tower, Vathek at first thought of repairing thither to view it more distinctly, but feeling himself unable to advance, and being overcome with apprehension, he muffled up his face in the folds of his robe.

Terrifying as these prodigies were, this impression upon him was no more than momentary, and served only to stimulate his love of the marvellous. Instead, therefore, of returning to his palace, he persisted in the resolution of abiding where the Indian vanished from his view. One night, however, while he was walking as usual on the plain, the moon and the stars at once were eclipsed, and a total darkness ensued; the earth trembled beneath him, and a voice came forth, the voice of the Giaour, who, in accents more sonorous than thunder, thus addressed him: 'Wouldest thou devote thyself to me? Adore then the terrestrial influences, and abjure Mahomet. On these conditions I will bring thee to the palace of subterranean fire; there shalt thou behold in immense depositories the treasures which the stars have promised thee, and which will be conferred by those Intelligences whom thou shalt thus render propitious. It was from thence I brought my sabres, and it is there that Soliman Ben Daoud reposes, surrounded by the talismans that control the world.'

The astonished Caliph trembled as he answered, yet in a style that showed him to be no novice in preternatural adventures: 'Where art thou? Be present to my eyes; dissipate the gloom that perplexes me, and of which I deem thee the cause; after the many flambeaux I have burnt to discover thee, thou mayst at least grant a glimpse of thy horrible visage.'

'Abjure then Mahomet,' replied the Indian, 'and promise me full proofs of thy sincerity; otherwise thou shalt never behold me again.'

The unhappy Caliph, instigated by insatiable curiosity, lavished his promises in the utmost profusion. The sky immediately brightened; and by the light of the planets, which seemed almost to blaze,

Vathek beheld the earth open, and at the extremity of a vast black chasm, a portal of ebony, before which stood the Indian, still blacker, holding in his hand a golden key that caused the lock to resound.

'How,' cried Vathek, 'can I descend to thee? Come, take me, and instantly open the portal.'

'Not so fast,' replied the Indian, 'impatient Caliph! Know that I am parched with thirst, and cannot open this door till my thirst be thoroughly appeased. I require the blood of fifty of the most beautiful sons of thy vizirs and great men, or neither can my thirst nor thy curiosity be satisfied. Return to Samarah, procure for me this necessary libation; come back hither, throw it thyself into this chasm, and then shalt thou see!'

Having thus spoken, the Indian turned his back on the Caliph, who, incited by the suggestion of demons, resolved on the direful sacrifice. He now pretended to have regained his tranquillity, and set out for Samarah amidst the acclamations of a people who still loved him, and forbore not to rejoice when they believed him to have recovered his reason. So successfully did he conceal the emotion of his heart, that even Carathis and Morakanabad were equally deceived with the rest. Nothing was heard of but festivals and rejoicings; the ball, which no tongue had hitherto ventured to mention, was again brought on the tapis; a general laugh went round, though many, still smarting under the hands of the surgeon from the hurts received in that memorable adventure, had no great reason for mirth.

The prevalence of this gay humour was not a little grateful to Vathek, as perceiving how much it conduced to his project. He put on the appearance of affability to everyone, but especially to his vizirs and the grandees of his court, whom he failed not to regale with a sumptuous banquet, during which he insensibly inclined the conversation to the children of his guests. Having asked with a good-natured air who of them were blessed with the handsomest boys, every father at once asserted the pretensions of his own, and the contest imperceptibly grew so warm that nothing could have withholden them from coming to blows but their profound reverence for the person of the Caliph. Under the pretence, therefore, of reconciling the disputants, Vathek took upon him to decide; and with this view commanded the boys to be brought.

It was not long before a troop of these poor children made their appearance, all equipped by their fond mothers with such ornaments as might give the greatest relief to their beauty or most advantageously display the graces of their age. But whilst this brilliant assemblage attracted the eyes and hearts of everyone besides, the Caliph scrutinised each in his turn with a malignant avidity that passed for attention, and selected from their number the fifty whom he judged the Giaour would prefer.

With an equal show of kindness as before, he proposed to celebrate a festival on the plain for the entertainment of his young favourites, who he said ought to rejoice still more than all at the restoration of his health, on account of the favours he intended for them.

The Caliph's proposal was received with the greatest delight, and soon published through Samarah; litters, camels, and horses were prepared. Women and children, old men and young, every one placed himself in the station he chose. The cavalcade set forward, attended by all the confectioners in the city and its precincts; the populace following on foot composed an amazing crowd, and occasioned no little noise; all was joy, nor did anyone call to mind what most of them had suffered when they first travelled the road they were now passing so gaily.

The evening was serene, the air refreshing, the sky clear, and the flowers exhaled their fragrance; the beams of the declining sun, whose mild splendour reposed on the summit of the mountain, shed a glow of ruddy light over its green declivity and the white flocks sporting upon it; no sounds were audible save the murmurs of the Four Fountains, and the reeds and voices of shepherds calling to each other from different eminences.

The lovely innocents destined for the sacrifice added not a little to the hilarity of the scene; they approached the plain full of sportiveness, some coursing butterflies, others culling flowers, or picking up the shining little pebbles that attracted their notice. At intervals they nimbly started from each other, for the sake of being caught again, and mutually imparting a thousand caresses.

The dreadful chasm, at whose bottom the portal of ebony was placed, began to appear at a distance; it looked like a black streak that divided the plain. Morakanabad and his companions took it for some work which the Caliph had ordered. Unhappy men! Little did they surmise for what it was destined.

Vathek, not liking they should examine it too nearly, stopped the procession, and ordered a spacious circle to be formed on this side, at some distance from the accursed chasm. The bodyguard of eunuchs was detached to measure out the lists intended for the games, and prepare the rings for the arrows of the young archers. The fifty competitors were soon stripped, and presented to the admiration of the spectators the suppleness and grace of their delicate limbs; their eyes sparkled with a joy which those of their fond parents reflected. Everyone offered wishes for the little candidate nearest his heart, and doubted not of his being victorious; a breathless suspense awaited the contest of these amiable and innocent victims.

The Caliph, availing himself of the first moment to retire from the crowd, advanced towards the chasm, and there heard, yet not without shuddering, the voice of the Indian, who, gnashing his teeth, eagerly demanded: 'Where are they? Where are they? Perceivest thou not how my mouth waters?'

'Relentless Giaour!' answered Vathek, with emotion, 'can nothing content thee but the massacre of these lovely victims! Ah! wert thou to behold their beauty, it must certainly move thy compassion.'

'Perdition on thy compassion, babbler!' cried the Indian. 'Give them me, instantly give them, or my portal shall be closed against thee for ever!'

'Not so loudly,' replied the Caliph, blushing.

'I understand thee,' returned the Giaour, with the grin of an ogre. 'Thou wantest to summon up more presence of mind; I will for a moment forbear.'

During this exquisite dialogue the games went forward with all alacrity, and at length concluded just as the twilight began to over-cast the mountains. Vathek, who was still standing on the edge of the chasm, called out, with all his might: 'Let my fifty little favourites approach me separately, and let them come in the order of their success. To the first I will give my diamond bracelet, to the second my collar of emeralds, to the third my aigret of rubies, to the fourth my girdle of topazes, and to the rest each a part of my dress, even down to my slippers.'

This declaration was received with reiterated acclamations, and all extolled the liberality of a prince who would thus strip himself for the amusement of his subjects and the encouragement of the rising gen-eration. The Caliph in the meantime undressed himself by degrees, and, raising his arm as high as he was able, made each of the prizes glitter in the air; but whilst he delivered it with one hand to the child, who sprang forward to receive it, he with the other pushed the poor innocent into the gulf, where the Giaour, with a sullen muttering, incessantly repeated, 'More! more!'

This dreadful device was executed with so much dexterity that the boy who was approaching him remained unconscious of the fate of his forerunner; and as to the spectators, the shades of evening, together with their distance, precluded them from perceiving any object distinctly. Vathek, having in this manner thrown in the last of the fifty, and expecting that the Giaour on receiving them would have presented the key, already fancied himself as great as Soliman, and consequently above being amenable for what he had done: when, to his utter amazement, the chasm closed, and the ground became as entire as the rest of the plain.

No language could express his rage and despair. He execrated the perfidy of the Indian, loaded him with the most infamous invectives, and stamped with his foot as resolving to be heard; he persisted in this demeanour till his strength failed him, and then fell on the earth like one void of sense. His viziers and grandees, who were nearer than the rest, supposed him at first to be sitting on the grass at play with their amiable children; but at length, prompted by doubt, they advanced towards the spot, and found the Caliph alone, who wildly demanded what they wanted.

'Our children! Our children!' cried they.

'It is assuredly pleasant,' said he, 'to make me accountable for accidents; your children while at play fell from the precipice that was here, and I should have experienced their fate had I not suddenly started back.'

At these words the fathers of the fifty boys cried out aloud, the mothers repeated their exclamations an octave higher, whilst the rest, without knowing the cause, soon drowned the voices of both with still louder lamentations of their own. 'Our Caliph,' said they – and the report soon circulated – 'Our Caliph has played us this trick to gratify his accursed Giaour. Let us punish him for his perfidy! Let us avenge ourselves! Let us avenge the blood of the innocent! Let us throw this cruel prince into the gulf that is near, and let his name be mentioned no more!'

At this rumour and these menaces, Carathis, full of consternation, hastened to Morakanabad, and said: 'Vizir, you have lost two beautiful boys, and must necessarily be the most afflicted of fathers, but you are virtuous; save your master.'

'I will brave every hazard,' replied the vizir, 'to rescue him from his present danger, but afterwards will abandon him to his fate. Bababalouk,' continued he, 'put yourself at the head of your eunuchs; disperse the mob, and, if possible, bring back this unhappy prince to his palace.' Bababalouk and his fraternity, felicitating each other in a low voice on their having been spared the cares as well as the honour of paternity, obeyed the mandate of the vizir; who, seconding their exertions to the utmost of his power, at length accomplished his generous enterprise, and retired as he resolved, to lament at his leisure.

No sooner had the Caliph re-entered his palace than Carathis commanded the doors to be fastened; but, perceiving the tumult to be still violent, and hearing the imprecations which resounded from all quarters, she said to her son: 'Whether the populace be right or wrong, it behoves you to provide for your safety; let us retire to your own apartment, and from thence through the subterranean passage, known only to ourselves, into your tower; there, with the assistance of the mutes who never leave it, we may be able to make some resistance. Bababalouk, supposing us to be still in the palace, will guard its avenues for his own sake; and we shall soon find, without the counsels of that blubberer Morakanabad, what expedient may be the best to adopt.'

Vathek, without making the least reply, acquiesced in his mother's proposal, and repeated as he went: 'Nefarious Giaour! where art thou! Hast thou not yet devoured those poor children? Where are thy sabres? thy golden key? thy talismans?'

Carathis, who guessed from these interrogations a part of the truth, had no difficulty to apprehend in getting at the whole, as soon as he should be a little composed in his tower. This princess was so far from being influenced by scruples that she was as wicked as woman could be, which is not saying a little, for the sex pique themselves on their superiority in every competition. The recital of the Caliph, therefore, occasioned neither terror nor surprise to his mother; she felt no emotion but from the promises of the Giaour, and said to her son: 'This Giaour, it must be confessed, is somewhat sanguinary in his taste, but the terrestrial powers are always terrible; nevertheless, what the one hath promised and the others can confer will prove a sufficient indemnification; no crimes should be thought too dear for such a reward! Forbear then to revile the Indian; you have not fulfilled the conditions to which his services are annexed; for instance, is not a sacrifice to the subterranean Genii required? and should we not be prepared to offer it as soon as the tumult is subsided? This charge I will take on myself, and have no doubt of succeeding by means of your treasures, which, as there are now so many others in store, may without fear be exhausted.'

Accordingly the princess, who possessed the most consummate skill in the art of persuasion, went immediately back through the subterranean passage; and presenting herself to the populace, from a window of the palace, began to harangue them with all the address of which she was mistress, whilst Bababalouk showered money from both hands amongst the crowd, who by these united means were soon appeased; every person retired to his home, and Carathis returned to the tower.

Prayer at break of day was announced, when Carathis and Vathek ascended the steps which led to the summit of the tower, where they remained for some time, though the weather was lowering and wet. This impending gloom corresponded with their malignant dispositions; but when the sun began to break through the clouds they ordered a pavilion to be raised, as a screen from the intrusion of his beams. The Caliph, overcome with fatigue, sought refreshment from repose, at the same time hoping that significant dreams might attend on his slumbers; whilst the indefatigable Carathis, followed by a party of her mutes, descended to prepare whatever she judged proper for the oblation of the approaching night.

By secret stairs, known only to herself and to her son, she first repaired to the mysterious recesses in which were deposited the mummies that had been brought from the catacombs of the ancient Pharaohs; of these she ordered several to be taken. From thence she resorted to a gallery where, under the guard of fifty female negroes, mute and blind of the right eye, were preserved the oil of the most venomous serpents, rhinoceros' horns, and woods of a subtle and penetrating odour procured from the interior of the Indies, together with a thousand other horrible rarities. This collection had been formed for a purpose like the present by Carathis herself, from a presentiment that she might one day enjoy some intercourse with the infernal powers to whom she had ever been passionately attached, and to whose taste she was no stranger.

To familiarise herself the better with the horrors in view, the princess remained in the company of her negresses, who squinted in the most amiable manner from the only eye they had, and leered with exquisite delight at the skulls and skeletons which Carathis had drawn forth from her cabinets, whose key she entrusted to no one; all of them making contortions, and uttering a frightful jargon, but very amusing to the princess; till at last, being stunned by their gibbering, and suffocated by the potency of their exhalations, she was forced to quit the gallery, after stripping it of a part of its abominable treasures.

Whilst she was thus occupied, the Caliph, who, instead of the visions he expected, had acquired in these insubstantial regions a voracious appetite, was greatly provoked at the mutes; for, having totally forgotten their deafness, he had impatiently asked them for food, and seeing them regardless of his demand, he began to cuff, pinch, and bite them, till Carathis arrived to terminate a scene so indecent, to the great content of these miserable creatures, who, having been brought up by her, understood all her signs, and communicated in the same way their thoughts in return.

'Son! what means all this?' said she, panting for breath. 'I thought I heard as I came up the shrieks of a thousand bats tearing from their crannies in the recesses of a cavern; and it was the outcry only of these poor mutes, whom you were so unmercifully abusing. In truth you but ill deserve the admirable provision I have brought you.'

'Give it me instantly,' exclaimed the Caliph. 'I am perishing for hunger!'

'As to that,' answered she, 'you must have an excellent stomach if it can digest what I have been preparing.'

'Be quick,' replied the Caliph. 'But, oh, heavens! what horrors! What do you intend?'

'Come, come,' returned Carathis, 'be not so squeamish, but help me to arrange everything properly, and you shall see that what you reject with such symptoms of disgust will soon complete your felicity. Let us get ready the pile for the sacrifice of tonight, and think not of eating till that is performed; know you not that all solemn rites are preceded by a rigorous abstinence?'

The Caliph, not daring to object, abandoned himself to grief and the wind that ravaged his entrails, whilst his mother went forward with the requisite operations. Phials of serpents' oil, mummies, and bones were soon set in order on the balustrade of the tower; the pile began to rise, and in three hours was as many cubits high. At length darkness approached, and Carathis, having stripped herself to her inmost garment, clapped her hands in an impulse of ecstasy, and struck light with all her force. The mutes followed her example; but Vathek, extenuated with hunger and impatience, was unable to support himself, and fell down in a swoon. The sparks had already kindled the dry wood, the venomous oil burst into a thousand blue flames, the mummies dissolving emitted a thick dun vapour, and the rhinoceros' horns beginning to consume, all together diffused such a stench, that the Caliph, recovering, started from his trance, and gazed wildly on the scene in full blaze around him. The oil gushed forth in a plenitude of streams; and the negresses, who supplied it without intermission, united their cries to those of the princess. At last the fire became so violent, and the flames reflected from the polished marble so dazzling, that the Caliph, unable to withstand the heat and the blaze, effected his escape, and clambered up the imperial standard.

In the meantime the inhabitants of Samarah, scared at the light which shone over the city, arose in haste, ascended their roofs, beheld the tower on fire, and hurried half-naked to the square. Their love to their sovereign immediately awoke; and, apprehending him in danger of perishing in his tower, their whole thoughts were occupied with the means of his safety. Morakanabad flew from his retirement, wiped away his tears, and cried out for water like the rest. Bababalouk, whose olfactory nerves were more familiarised to magical odours, readily conjecturing that Carathis was engaged in her favourite amusements, strenuously exhorted them not to be alarmed. Him, however, they treated as an old poltroon, and forbore not to style him a rascally traitor. The camels and dromedaries were advancing with water, but no one knew by which way to enter the tower. Whilst the populace was obstinate in forcing the doors a violent east wind drove such a volume of flame against them, as at first forced them off, but afterwards re-kindled their zeal; at the same time the stench of the horns and mummies increasing, most of the crowd fell backward in a state of suffocation; those that kept their feet mutually wondered at the cause of the smell, and admonished each other to retire. Morakanabad, more sick than the rest, remained in a piteous condition; holding his nose with one hand, he persisted in his efforts with the other to burst open the doors and obtain admission. A hundred and forty of the strongest and most resolute at length accomplished their purpose; having gained the staircase by their violent exertions, they attained a great height in a quarter of an hour.

Carathis, alarmed at the signs of her mutes, advanced to the staircase, went down a few steps, and heard several voices calling out from below: 'You shall in a moment have water!' Being rather alert, considering her age, she presently regained the top of the tower, and bade her son suspend the sacrifice for some minutes, adding: 'We shall soon be enabled to render it more grateful; certain dolts of your subjects, imagining no doubt that we were on fire, have been rash enough to break through those doors which had hitherto remained inviolate, for the sake of bringing up water; they are very kind, you must allow, so soon to forget the wrongs you have done them, but that is of little moment. Let us offer them to the Giaour; let them come up; our mutes, who neither want strength nor experience, will soon despatch them, exhausted as they are with fatigue.'

'Be it so,' answered the Caliph, 'provided we finish and I dine.'

In fact, these good people, out of breath from ascending eleven thousand stairs in such haste, and chagrined at having spilt by the way the water they had taken, were no sooner arrived at the top than the blaze of the flames and the fumes of the mummies at once overpowered their senses. It was a pity; for they beheld not the agreeable smile with which the mutes and the negresses adjusted the cord to their necks; these amiable personages rejoiced, however, no less at the scene; never before had the ceremony of strangling been performed with so much facility; they all fell without the least resistance or struggle, so that Vathek in the space of a few moments found himself surrounded by the dead bodies of his faithfullest subjects, all which were thrown on the top of the pile.

Carathis, whose presence of mind never forsook her, perceiving that she had carcases sufficient to complete her oblation, commanded the chains to be stretched across the staircase, and the iron doors barricaded, that no more might come up.

No sooner were these orders obeyed than the tower shook, the dead bodies vanished in the flames, which at once changed from a swarthy crimson to a bright rose colour; an ambient vapour emitted the most exquisite fragrance, the marble columns rang with harmonious sounds, and the liquefied horns diffused a delicious perfume. Carathis, in transports, anticipated the success of her enterprise, whilst her mutes and negresses, to whom these sweets had given the colic, retired grumbling to their cells.

Scarcely were they gone when, instead of the pile, horns, mummies, and ashes, the Caliph both saw and felt, with a degree of pleasure which he could not express, a table covered with the most magnificent repast; flagons of wine and vases of exquisite sherbet floating on snow. He availed himself without scruple of such an entertainment and had already laid hands on a lamb stuffed with pistachios, whilst Carathis was privately drawing from a filigree urn a parchment that seemed to be endless, and which had escaped the notice of her son; totally occupied in gratifying an importunate appetite he left her to peruse it without interruption, which, having finished, she said to him in an authoritative tone, 'Put an end to your gluttony, and hear the splendid promises with which you are favoured!' She then read as follows: 'Vathek, my well-beloved, thou hast surpassed my hopes; my nostrils have been regaled by the savour of thy mummies, thy horns, and still more by the lives devoted on the pile. At the full of the moon cause the bands of thy musicians and thy tymbals to be heard; depart from thy palace surrounded by all the pageants of majesty: thy most faithful slaves, thy best beloved wives, thy most magnificent litters, thy richest laden camels, and set forward on thy way to Istakar; there await I thy coming; that is the region of wonders; there shalt thou receive the diadem of Gian Ben Gian, the talismans of Soliman, and the treasures of the pre-Adamite sultans; there shalt thou be solaced with all kinds of delight. But beware how thou enterest any dwelling on thy route, or thou shalt feel the effects of my anger.'

The Caliph, notwithstanding his habitual luxury, had never before dined with so much satisfaction. He gave full scope to the joy of these golden tidings, and betook himself to drinking anew. Carathis, whose antipathy to wine was by no means insuperable, failed not to supply a reason for every bumper, which they ironically quaffed to the health of Mahomet. This infernal liquor completed their impious temerity, and prompted them to utter a profusion of blasphemies; they gave a loose to their wit at the expense of the ass of Balaam, the dog of the seven sleepers, and the other animals admitted into the paradise of Mahomet. In this sprightly humour they descended the eleven thousand stairs, diverting themselves as they went at the anxious faces they saw on the square through the barbacans and loopholes of the tower; and at length arrived at the royal apartments by the subterranean passage. Bababalouk was parading to and fro, and issuing his mandates with great pomp to the eunuchs, who were snuffing the lights and painting the eyes of the Circassians. No sooner did he catch sight of the Caliph and his mother than he exclaimed, 'Hah! you have then, I perceive, escaped from the flames; I was not, however, altogether out of doubt.'

'Of what moment is it to us what you thought, or think?' cried Carathis. 'Go, speed, tell Morakanabad that we immediately want him; and take care how you stop by the way to make your insipid reflections.'

Morakanabad delayed not to obey the summons, and was received by Vathek and his mother with great solemnity; they told him, with an air of composure and commiseration, that the fire at the top of the tower was extinguished; but that it had cost the lives of the brave people who sought to assist them.

'Still more misfortunes,' cried Morakanabad, with a sigh. 'Ah, Commander of the Faithful, our holy Prophet is certainly irritated against us! It behoves you to appease him.'

'We will appease him hereafter!' replied the Caliph, with a smile that augured nothing of good. 'You will have leisure sufficient for your supplications during my absence; for this country is the bane of my health; I am disgusted with the Mountain of the Four Fountains, and am resolved to go and drink of the stream of Rocnabad; I long to refresh myself in the delightful valleys which it waters. Do you, with the advice of my mother, govern my dominions, and take care to supply whatever her experiments may demand; for you well know that our tower abounds in materials for the advancement of science.'

The tower but ill suited Morakanabad's taste. Immense treasures had been lavished upon it; and nothing had he ever seen carried thither but female negroes, mutes, and abominable drugs. Nor did he know well what to think of Carathis, who, like a chameleon, could assume all possible colours; her cursed eloquence had often driven the poor Mussulman to his last shifts. He considered, however, that if she possessed but few good qualities, her son had still fewer; and that the alternative on the whole would be in her favour. Consoled, therefore, with this reflection, he went in good spirits to soothe the populace, and make the proper arrangements for his master's journey.

Vathek, to conciliate the spirits of the subterranean palace, resolved that his expedition should be uncommonly splendid. With this view he confiscated on all sides the property of his subjects, whilst his worthy mother stripped the seraglios she visited of the gems they contained. She collected all the sempstresses and embroiderers of Samarah and other cities to the distance of sixty leagues, to prepare pavilions, palanquins, sofas, canopies, and litters for the train of the monarch. There was not left in Masulipatam a single piece of chintz, and so much muslin had been bought up to dress out Bababalouk and the other black eunuchs, that there remained not an ell in the whole Irak of Babylon.

During these preparations Carathis, who never lost sight of her great object, which was to obtain favour with the Powers of Darkness, made select parties of the fairest and most delicate ladies of the city; but in the midst of their gaiety she contrived to introduce serpents amongst them, and to break pots of scorpions under the table; they all bit to a wonder; and Carathis would have left them to die, were it not that, to fill up the time, she now and then amused herself in curing their wounds with an excellent anodyne of her own invention, for this good princess abhorred being indolent.

Vathek, who was not altogether so active as his mother, devoted his time to the sole gratification of his senses, in the palaces which

were severally dedicated to them; he disgusted himself no more with
the Divan or the mosque. One half of Samarah followed his example,
whilst the other lamented the progress of corruption.

In the midst of these transactions the embassy returned which had
been sent in pious times to Mecca. It consisted of the most reverend
mullahs, who had fulfilled their commission and brought back one of
those precious besoms which are used to sweep the sacred Cahaba: a
present truly worthy of the greatest potentate on earth!

The Caliph happened at this instant to be engaged in an apartment
by no means adapted to the reception of embassies. He heard the
voice of Bababalouk, calling out from between the door and the
tapestry that hung before it: 'Here are the excellent Mahomet Ebn
Edris al Shafei, and the seraphic Al Mouhateddin, who have brought
the besom from Mecca, and with tears of joy entreat they may
present it to your majesty in person.'

'Let them bring the besom hither; it may be of use,' said Vathek.

'How?' said Bababalouk, half aloud and amazed.

'Obey,' replied the Caliph, 'for it is my sovereign will; go instantly,
vanish! For here will I receive the good folk who have thus filled
thee with joy.'

The eunuch departed muttering, and bade the venerable train
attend him. A sacred rapture was diffused amongst these reverend
old men. Though fatigued with the length of their expedition, they
followed Bababalouk with an alertness almost miraculous, and felt
themselves highly flattered, as they swept along the stately porticoes,
that the Caliph would not receive them like ambassadors in ordinary
in his hall of audience. Soon reaching the interior of the harem
(where, through blinds of Persian, they perceived large soft eyes,
dark and blue, that went and came like lightning), penetrated with
respect and wonder, and full of their celestial mission, they advanced
in procession towards the small corridors that appeared to terminate
in nothing, but nevertheless led to the cell where the Caliph expected their coming.

'What! is the Commander of the Faithful sick?' said Ebn Edris al
Shafei in a low voice to his companion.

'I rather think he is in his oratory,' answered Al Mouhateddin.

Vathek, who heard the dialogue, cried out: 'What imports it you
how I am employed? Approach without delay.'

They advanced, and Bababalouk almost sunk with confusion, whilst
the Caliph, without showing himself, put forth his hand from behind
the tapestry that hung before the door, and demanded of them the

besom. Having prostrated themselves as well as the corridor would
permit, and even in a tolerable semicircle, the venerable Al Shafei,
drawing forth the besom from the embroidered and perfumed scarves
in which it had been enveloped, and secured from the profane gaze of
vulgar eyes, arose from his associates, and advanced, with an air of the
most awful solemnity, towards the supposed oratory; but with what
astonishment! with what horror was he seized! Vathek, bursting out
into a villainous laugh, snatched the besom from his trembling hand,
and, fixing upon some cobwebs that hung suspended from the ceiling,
gravely brushed away till not a single one remained. The old men,
overpowered with amazement, were unable to lift their heards from
the ground; for, as Vathek had carelessly left the tapestry between
them half drawn, they were witnesses to the whole transaction; their
tears gushed forth on the marble; Al Mouhateddin swooned through
mortification and fatigue; whilst the Caliph, throwing himself backward on his seat, shouted and clapped his hands without mercy. At
last, addressing himself to Bababalouk: 'My dear black,' said he, 'go,
regale these pious poor souls with my good wine from Shiraz; and, as
they can boast of having seen more of my palace than anyone besides,
let them also visit my office courts, and lead them out by the back
steps that go to my stables.' Having said this, he threw the besom in
their face, and went to enjoy the laugh with Carathis. Bababalouk did
all in his power to console the ambassadors, but the two most infirm
expired on the spot; the rest were carried to their beds, from whence,
being heartbroken with sorrow and shame, they never arose.

The succeeding night Vathek, attended by his mother, ascended
the tower to see if everything were ready for his journey; for he had
great faith in the influence of the stars. The planets appeared in their
most favourable aspects. The Caliph, to enjoy so flattering a sight,
supped gaily on the roof, and fancied that he heard during his repast
loud shouts of laughter resound through the sky, in a manner that
inspired the fullest assurance.

All was in motion at the palace; lights were kept burning through
the whole of the night; the sound of implements and of artisans
finishing their work, the voices of women and their guardians who
sung at their embroidery, all conspired to interrupt the stillness of
nature and infinitely delight the heart of Vathek, who imagined
himself going in triumph to sit upon the throne of Soliman. The
people were not less satisfied than himself; all assisted to accelerate
the moment which should rescue them from the wayward caprices of
so extravagant a master.

The day preceding the departure of this infatuated prince was employed by Carathis in repeating to him the decrees of the mysterious parchment, which she had thoroughly gotten by heart, and in recommending him not to enter the habitation of anyone by the way. 'For well thou knowest,' added she, 'how liquorish thy taste is after good dishes and young damsels; let me, therefore, enjoin thee to be content with thy old cooks, who are the best in the world, and not to forget that in thy ambulatory seraglio there are three dozen pretty faces, which Bababalouk hath not yet unveiled. I myself have a great desire to watch over thy conduct, and visit the subterranean palace, which no doubt contains whatever can interest persons like us; there is nothing so pleasing as retiring to caverns; my taste for dead bodies and everything mummy-like is decided; and I am confident thou wilt see the most exquisite of their kind. Forget me not, then, but the moment thou art in possession of the talismans which are to open to thee the mineral kingdoms and the centre of the earth itself, fail not to despatch some trusty genius to take me and my cabinet, for the oil of the serpents I have pinched to death will be a pretty present to the Giaour, who cannot but be charmed with such dainties.'

Scarcely had Carathis ended this edifying discourse when the sun, setting behind the Mountain of the Four Fountains, gave place to the rising moon; this planet, being that evening at full, appeared of unusual beauty and magnitude in the eyes of the women, the eunuchs, and the pages, who were all impatient to set forward. The city re-echoed with shouts of joy and flourishing of trumpets; nothing was visible but plumes nodding on pavilions, and aigrets shining in the mild lustre of the moon; the spacious square resembled an immense parterre, variegated with the most stately tulips of the East.

Arrayed in the robes which were only worn at the most distinguished ceremonials, and supported by his vizir and Bababalouk, the Caliph descended the grand staircase of the tower in the sight of all his people; he could not forbear pausing at intervals to admire the superb appearance which everywhere courted his view, whilst the whole multitude, even to the camels with their sumptuous burdens, knelt down before him. For some time a general stillness prevailed, which nothing happened to disturb but the shrill screams of some eunuchs in the rear; these vigilant guards, having remarked certain cages of the ladies swagging somewhat awry, and discovered that a few adventurous gallants had contrived to get in, soon dislodged the enraptured culprits, and consigned them, with good commendations, to the surgeons of the serail. The majesty of so magnificent a spectacle was not, however, violated by incidents like these. Vathek meanwhile saluted the moon with an idolatrous air, that neither pleased Moraka-nabad nor the Doctors of the Law, any more than the vizirs and the grandees of his court, who were all assembled to enjoy the last view of their sovereign.

At length the clarions and trumpets from the top of the tower announced the prelude of departure; though the instruments were in unison with each other, yet a singular dissonance was blended with their sounds; this proceeded from Carathis, who was singing her direful orisons to the Giaour, whilst the negresses and mutes supplied thorough-base without articulating a word. The good Mussulmans fancied that they heard the sullen hum of those nocturnal insects which presage evil, and importuned Vathek to beware how he vent-ured his sacred person.

On a given signal the great standard of the Califat was displayed; twenty thousand lances shone around it, and the Caliph, treading loyally on the cloth of gold which had been spread for his feet, ascended his litter amidst the general acclamations of his subjects.

The expedition commenced with the utmost order, and so entire a silence, that even the locusts were heard from the thickets on the plain of Catoul. Gaiety and good-humour prevailing, they made six good leagues before dawn; and the morning star was still glittering in the firmament when the whole of this numerous train had halted on the banks of the Tigris, where they encamped to repose for the rest of the day.

The three days that followed were spent in the same manner; but on the fourth the heavens looked angry, lightnings broke forth in frequent flashes, re-echoing peals of thunder succeeded, and the trembling Circassians clung with all their might to their ugly guard-ians. The Caliph himself was greatly inclined to take shelter in the large town of Gulchissar, the governor of which came forth to meet him, and tendered every kind of refreshment the place could supply; but, having examined his tablets, he suffered the rain to soak him almost to the bone, notwithstanding the importunity of his first favourites. Though he began to regret the palace of the senses, yet he lost not sight of his enterprise, and his sanguine expectations confirmed his resolution; his geographers were ordered to attend him, but the weather proved so terrible that these poor people exhibited a lamentable appearance; and their maps of the different countries, spoiled by the rain, were in a still worse plight than themselves. As no long journeys had been undertaken since the time of Haroun al Raschid, everyone was ignorant which way to turn; for Vathek, though well versed in the course of the heavens, no longer knew his situation on earth; he thundered even louder than the elements, and muttered forth certain hints of the bow-string, which were not very soothing to literary ears. Disgusted at the toilsome weariness of the way, he determined to cross over the craggy heights and follow the guidance of a peasant, who undertook to bring him in four days to Rocnabad. Remonstrances were all to no purpose; his resolution was fixed.

The females and eunuchs uttered shrill wailings at the sight of the precipices below them, and the dreary prospects that opened in the vast gorges of the mountains. Before they could reach the ascent of the steepest rock, night overtook them, and a boisterous tempest arose, which, having rent the awnings of the palanquins and cages, exposed to the raw gusts the poor ladies within, who had never before felt so piercing a cold. The dark clouds that overcast the face of the sky deepened the horrors of this disastrous night, insomuch that nothing could be heard distinctly but the mewling of pages and lamentations of sultanas.

To increase the general misfortune, the frightful uproar of wild beasts resounded at a distance, and there were soon perceived, in the forest they were skirting, the glaring of eyes which could belong only to devils or tigers. The pioneers, who, as well as they could, had marked out a track, and a part of the advanced guard, were devoured before they had been in the least apprised of their danger. The confusion that prevailed was extreme: wolves, tigers, and other carnivorous animals, invited by the howling of their companions, flocked together from every quarter; the crashing of bones was heard on all sides, and a fearful rush of wings overhead, for now vultures also began to be of the party.

The terror at length reached the main body of the troops which surrounded the monarch and his harem, at the distance of two leagues from the scene. Vathek (voluptuously reposed in his capacious litter upon cushions of silk, with two little pages beside him of complexions more fair than the enamel of Franguestan, who were occupied in keeping off flies) was soundly asleep, and contemplating in his dreams the treasures of Soliman. The shrieks, however, of his wives awoke him with a start, and, instead of the Giaour with his key of gold, he beheld Bababalouk full of consternation.

'Sire,' exclaimed this good servant of the most potent of monarchs, 'misfortune is arrived at its height; wild beasts, who entertain no more reverence for your sacred person than for that of a dead ass, have beset your camels and their drivers; thirty of the richest laden are already become their prey, as well as your confectioners, your cooks, and purveyors; and, unless our holy Prophet should protect us, we shall have all eaten our last meal.'

At the mention of eating the Caliph lost all patience; he began to bellow, and even beat himself (for there was no seeing in the dark). The rumour every instant increased, and Bababalouk, finding no good could be done with his master, stopped both his ears against the hurly-burly of the harem, and called out aloud: 'Come, ladies and brothers! All hands to work! Strike light in a moment! Never shall it be said that the Commander of the Faithful served to regale these infidel brutes.'

Though there wanted not in this bevy of beauties a sufficient number of capricious and wayward, yet on the present occasion they were all compliance; fires were visible in a twinkling in all their cages; ten thousand torches were lighted at once; the Caliph himself seized a large one of wax; every person followed his example, and, by kindling ropes' ends dipped in oil and fastened on poles, an amazing blaze was spread. The rocks were covered with the splendour of sunshine; the trails of sparks wafted by the wind communicated to the dry fern, of which there was plenty. Serpents were observed to crawl forth from their retreats with amazement and hissings, whilst the horses snorted, stamped the ground, tossed their noses in the air, and plunged about without mercy.

One of the forests of cedar that bordered their way took fire, and the branches that overhung the path, extending their flames to the muslins and chintzes which covered the cages of the ladies, obliged them to jump out, at the peril of their necks. Vathek, who vented on the occasion a thousand blasphemies, was himself compelled to touch with his sacred feet the naked earth.

Never had such an incident happened before. Full of mortification, shame, and despondence, and not knowing how to walk, the ladies fell into the dirt. 'Must I go on foot?' said one. 'Must I wet my feet?' cried another. 'Must I soil my dress?' asked a third. 'Execrable Bababalouk!' exclaimed all. 'Outcast of hell! what hadst thou to do with torches? Better were it to be eaten by tigers than to fall into our present condition! We are for ever undone! Not a porter is there in the army, nor a currier of camels, but hath seen some part of our bodies, and, what is worse, our very faces!' On saying this the most bashful amongst them hid their foreheads on the ground, whilst such as had more boldness flew at Bababalouk; but he, well apprised of their humour, and not wanting in shrewdness, betook himself to his heels along with his comrades, all dropping their torches and striking their tymbals.

It was not less light than in the brightest of the dog-days, and the weather was hot in proportion; but how degrading was the spectacle, to behold the Caliph bespattered like an ordinary mortal! As the exercise of his faculties seemed to be suspended, one of his Ethiopian wives (for he delighted in variety) clasped him in her arms, threw him upon her shoulder like a sack of dates, and finding that the fire was hemming them in, set off with no small expedition, considering the weight of her burden. The other ladies, who had just learnt the use of their feet, followed her, their guards galloped after, and the camel-drivers brought up the rear as fast as their charge would permit.

They soon reached the spot where the wild beasts had commenced the carnage, and which they had too much spirit to leave, notwithstanding the approaching tumult and the luxurious supper they had made; Bababalouk nevertheless seized on a few of the plumpest, which were unable to budge from the place, and began to flay them with admirable adroitness. The cavalcade being got so far from the conflagration as that the heat felt rather grateful than violent, it was immediately resolved on to halt. The tattered chintzes were picked up, the scraps left by the wolves and tigers interred, and vengeance was taken on some dozens of vultures that were too much glutted to rise on the wing. The camels, which had been left unmolested to make sal ammoniac, being numbered, and the ladies once more enclosed in their cages, the imperial tent was pitched on the levellest ground they could find.

Vathek, reposing upon a mattress of down, and tolerably recovered from the jolting of the Ethiopian, who to his feelings seemed the roughest trotting jade he had hitherto mounted, called out for something to eat. But, alas! those delicate cakes which had been baked in silver ovens for his royal mouth, those rich manchets, amber comfits, flagons of Schiraz wine, porcelain vases of snow, and grapes from the banks of the Tigris, were all irremediably lost! And nothing had Bababalouk to present in their stead but a roasted wolf, vultures *à la daube*, aromatic herbs of the most acrid poignancy, rotten truffles, boiled thistles, and such other wild plants as must ulcerate the throat and parch up the tongue. Nor was he better provided in the article of drink, for he could procure nothing to accompany these irritating viands but a few vials of abominable brandy, which had been secreted by the scullions in their slippers. Vathek made wry faces at so savage a repast, and Bababalouk answered them with shrugs and contortions; the Caliph, however, ate with tolerable appetite, and fell into a nap that lasted six hours.

The splendour of the sun, reflected from the white cliffs of the mountains, in spite of the curtains that enclosed him, at length disturbed his repose; he awoke terrified, and stung to the quick by those wormwood-coloured flies, which emit from their wings a suffocating stench. The miserable monarch was perplexed how to act, though his wits were not idle in seeking expedients, whilst Bababalouk lay snoring amidst a swarm of those insects, that busily thronged to pay court to his nose. The little pages, famished with hunger, had dropped their fans on the ground, and exerted their dying voices in bitter reproaches on the Caliph, who now for the first time heard the language of truth.

Thus stimulated, he renewed his imprecations against the Giaour, and bestowed upon Mahomet some soothing expressions. 'Where am I?' cried he. 'What are these dreadful rocks? these valleys of darkness? Are we arrived at the horrible Kaf? Is the Simurgh coming to pluck out my eyes, as a punishment for undertaking this impious enterprise!' Having said this, he bellowed like a calf and turned himself towards an outlet in the side of his pavilion; but, alas! what objects occurred to his view! On one side a plain of black sand that appeared to be unbounded, and on the other perpendicular crags, bristled over with those abominable thistles which had so severely lacerated his tongue. He fancied, however, that he perceived, amongst the brambles and briers, some gigantic flowers, but was mistaken; for these were only the dangling palampores and variegated tatters of his gay retinue. As there were several clefts in the rock from whence water seemed to have flowed, Vathek applied his ear, with the hope of catching the sound of some latent runnel, but could only distinguish the low murmurs of his people, who were repining at their journey, and complaining for the want of water.

'To what purpose,' asked they, 'have we been brought hither? Hath our Caliph another tower to build? Or have the relentless afrits, whom Carathis so much loves, fixed in this place their abode?'

At the name of Carathis Vathek recollected the tablets he had received from his mother, who assured him they were fraught with preternatural qualities, and advised him to consult them as emergencies might require. Whilst he was engaged in turning them over he

heard a shout of joy and a loud clapping of hands; the curtains of his
pavilion were soon drawn back, and he beheld Bababalouk, followed
by a troop of his favourites, conducting two dwarfs, each a cubit
high, who brought between them a large basket of melons, oranges,
and pomegranates. They were singing in the sweetest tones the
words that follow.

'We dwell on the top of these rocks in a cabin of rushes and canes;
the eagles envy us our nest; a small spring supplies us with water for
the Abdest, and we daily repeat prayers which the Prophet approves.
We love you, O Commander of the Faithful! Our master, the good
Emir Fakreddin, loves you also; he reveres in your person the vicegerent of Mahomet. Little as we are, in us he confides; he knows our
hearts to be good as our bodies are contemptible, and hath placed us
here to aid those who are bewildered on these dreary mountains.
Last night, whilst we were occupied within our cell in reading the
holy Koran, a sudden hurricane blew out our lights and rocked our
habitation; for two whole hours a palpable darkness prevailed, but we
heard sounds at a distance which we conjectured to proceed from the
bells of a Cafila passing over the rocks; our ears were soon filled with
deplorable shrieks, frightful roarings, and the sound of tymbals.
Chilled with terror, we concluded that the Deggial, with his extermin-
inating angels, had sent forth his plagues on the earth. In the midst
of these melancholy reflections we perceived flames of the deepest
red glow in the horizon, and found ourselves in a few moments
covered with flakes of fire; amazed at so strange an appearance, we
took up the volume dictated by the blessed Intelligence, and kneeling, by the light of the fire that surrounded us, we recited the verse
which says: "Put no trust in anything but the mercy of Heaven; there
is no help save in the holy Prophet; the mountain of Kaf itself may
tremble, it is the power of Allah only that cannot be moved." After
having pronounced these words we felt consolation, and our minds
were hushed into a sacred repose; silence ensued, and our ears clearly
distinguished a voice in the air, saying: "Servants of my faithful
servant! Go down to the happy valley of Fakreddin; tell him that
an illustrious opportunity now offers to satiate the thirst of his
hospitable heart. The Commander of true believers is this day
bewildered amongst these mountains, and stands in need of thy
aid." We obeyed with joy the angelic mission, and our master, filled
with pious zeal, hath culled with his own hands these melons,
oranges, and pomegranates; he is following us with a hundred dromedaries laden with the purest waters of his fountains, and is coming

to kiss the fringe of your consecrated robe, and implore you to enter his humble habitation, which, placed amidst these barren wilds, resembles an emerald set in lead.' The dwarfs, having ended their address, remained still standing, and, with hands crossed upon their bosoms, preserved a respectful silence.

Vathek, in the midst of this curious harangue, seized the basket, and long before it was finished the fruits had dissolved in his mouth; as he continued to eat his piety increased, and in the same breath which recited his prayers he called for the Koran and sugar.

Such was the state of his mind when the tablets, which were thrown by at the approach of the dwarfs, again attracted his eye; he took them up, but was ready to drop on the ground when he beheld, in large red characters, these words inscribed by Carathis, which were indeed enough to make him tremble.

'Beware of thy old doctors, and their puny messengers of but one cubit high; distrust their pious frauds, and, instead of eating their melons, impale on a spit the bearers of them. Shouldst thou be such a fool as to visit them, the portal of the subterranean palace will be shut in thy face, and with such force as shall shake thee asunder; thy body shall be spit upon, and bats will engender in thy belly.'

'To what tends this ominous rhapsody?' cried the Caliph. 'And must I then perish in these deserts with thirst, whilst I may refresh myself in the valley of melons and cucumbers! Accursed be the Giaour, with his portal of ebony! He hath made me dance attendance too long already. Besides, who shall prescribe laws to me? I forsooth must not enter anyone's habitation! Be it so; but what one can I enter that is not my own?'

Bababalouk, who lost not a syllable of this soliloquy, applauded it with all his heart, and the ladies for the first time agreed with him in opinion.

The dwarfs were entertained, caressed, and seated with great ceremony on little cushions of satin. The symmetry of their persons was the subject of criticism; not an inch of them was suffered to pass unexamined; knick-knacks and dainties were offered in profusion, but all were declined with respectful gravity. They clambered up the sides of the Caliph's seat, and, placing themselves each on one of his shoulders, began to whisper prayers in his ears; their tongues quivered like the leaves of a poplar, and the patience of Vathek was almost exhausted, when the acclamations of the troops announced the approach of Fakreddin, who was come with a hundred old grey-beards and as many Korans and dromedaries; they instantly set about their ablutions, and began to repeat the Bismillah; Vathek, to get rid of these officious monitors, followed their example, for his hands were burning.

The good Emir, who was punctiliously religious, and likewise a great dealer in compliments, made an harangue five times more prolix and insipid than his harbingers had already delivered. The Caliph, unable any longer to refrain, exclaimed – 'For the love of Mahomet, my dear Fakreddin, have done! Let us proceed to your valley, and enjoy the fruits that Heaven hath vouchsafed you.'

The hint of proceeding put all into motion; the venerable attendants of the Emir set forward somewhat slowly, but Vathek, having ordered his little pages in private to goad on the dromedaries, loud fits of laughter broke forth from the cages, for the unwieldy curveting of these poor beasts, and the ridiculous distress of their superannuated riders, afforded the ladies no small entertainment.

They descended, however, unhurt into the valley, by the large steps which the Emir had cut in the rock; and already the murmuring of streams and the rustling of leaves began to catch their attention. The cavalcade soon entered a path which was skirted by flowering shrubs, and extended to a vast wood of palm-trees, whose branches overspread a building of hewn stone. This edifice was crowned with nine domes, and adorned with as many portals of bronze, on which was engraven the following inscription: 'This is the asylum of pilgrims, the refuge of travellers, and the depository of secrets from all parts of the world.'

Nine pages, beautiful as the day, and clothed in robes of Egyptian linen, very long and very modest, were standing at each door. They received the whole retinue with an easy and inviting air. Four of the most amiable placed the Caliph on a magnificent taktrevan, four others, somewhat less graceful, took charge of Bababalouk, who capered for joy at the snug little cabin that fell to his share; the pages that remained waited on the rest of the train.

Every man being gone out of sight, the gate of a large enclosure on the right turned on its harmonious hinges and a young female of a slender form came forth; her light brown hair floated in the hazy breeze of the twilight; a troop of young maidens, like the Pleiades, attended her on tiptoe. They hastened to the pavilions that contained the sultanas, and the young lady, gracefully bending, said to them: 'Charming princesses, everything is ready; we have prepared beds for your repose, and strewed your apartments with jasmine; no insects will keep off slumber from visiting your eyelids,

we will dispel them with a thousand plumes; come then, amiable
ladies! refresh your delicate feet and your ivory limbs in baths of rose
water; and by the light of perfumed lamps, your servants will amuse
you with tales.'

The sultanas accepted with pleasure these obliging offers, and
followed the young lady to the Emir's harem, where we must for a
moment leave them, and return to the Caliph.

Vathek found himself beneath a vast dome, illuminated by a thousand lamps of rock crystal; as many vases of the same material, filled
with excellent sherbet, sparkled on a large table, where a profusion of
viands were spread; amongst others were sweetbreads stewed in milk
of almonds, saffron soups, and lamb *à la crème*, of all which the
Caliph was amazingly fond. He took of each as much as he was able,
testified his sense of the Emir's friendship by the gaiety of his heart,
and made the dwarfs dance against their will, for these little devotees
durst not refuse the Commander of the Faithful; at last he spread
himself on the sofa, and slept sounder than he had ever before.

Beneath this dome a general silence prevailed, for there was nothing
to disturb it but the jaws of Bababalouk, who had untrussed himself
to eat with greater advantage, being anxious to make amends for his
fast in the mountains. As his spirits were too high to admit of his
sleeping, and not loving to be idle, he proposed with himself to visit
the harem, and repair to his charge of the ladies, to examine if they
had been properly lubricated with the balm of Mecca, if their eye-
brows and tresses were in order, and, in a word, to perform all the
little offices they might need. He sought for a long time together,
but without being able to find out the door; he durst not speak aloud,
for fear of disturbing the Caliph, and not a soul was stirring in the
precincts of the palace; he almost despaired of effecting his purpose,
when a low whispering just reached his ear; it came from the dwarfs
who were returned to their old occupation, and for the nine hundred
and ninety-ninth time in their lives, were reading over the Koran.
They very politely invited Bababalouk to be of their party, but his
head was full of other concerns. The dwarfs, though scandalised at
his dissolute morals, directed him to the apartments he wanted to
find; his way thither lay through a hundred dark corridors, along
which he groped as he went, and at last began to catch from the
extremity of a passage the charming gossiping of the women, which
not a little delighted his heart. 'Ah, ha! what, not yet asleep!' cried he;
and, taking long strides as he spoke. 'Did you not suspect me of
abjuring my charge? I stayed but to finish what my master had left.'

Two of the black eunuchs, on hearing a voice so loud, detached a party in haste, sabre in hand, to discover the cause; but presently was repeated on all sides: ''Tis only Bababalouk! No one but Bababalouk!' This circumspect guardian, having gone up to a thin veil of carnation-coloured silk that hung before the doorway, distinguished, by means of the softened splendour that shone through it, an oval bath of dark porphyry, surrounded by curtains festooned in large folds; through the apertures between them, as they were not drawn close, groups of young slaves were visible, amongst whom Bababalouk perceived his pupils, indulgingly expanding their arms, as if to embrace the perfumed water and refresh themselves after their fatigues. The looks of tender languor, their confidential whispers, and the enchanting smiles with which they were imparted, the exquisite fragrance of the roses, all combined to inspire a voluptuousness, which even Bababalouk himself was scarce able to withstand.

He summoned up, however, his usual solemnity, and, in the peremptory tone of authority, commanded the ladies instantly to leave the bath. Whilst he was issuing these mandates the young Nouronihar, daughter of the Emir, who was sprightly as an antelope, and full of wanton gaiety, beckoned one of her slaves to let down the great swing, which was suspended to the ceiling by cords of silk, and whilst this was doing, winked to her companions in the bath, who, chagrined to be forced from so soothing a state of indolence, began to twist and entangle their hair to plague and detain Bababalouk, and teased him, besides, with a thousand vagaries.

Nouronihar, perceiving that he was nearly out of patience, accosted him, with an arch air of respectful concern, and said: 'My lord, it is not by any means decent that the chief eunuch of the Caliph, our Sovereign, should thus continue standing; deign but to recline your graceful person upon this sofa, which will burst with vexation if it have not the honour to receive you.'

Caught by these flattering accents, Bababalouk gallantly replied: 'Delight of the apple of my eye! I accept the invitation of thy honeyed lips; and, to say truth, my senses are dazzled with the radiance that beams from thy charms.'

'Repose, then, at your ease,' replied the beauty, and placed him on the pretended sofa, which, quicker than lightning, gave way all at once. The rest of the women, having aptly conceived her design, sprang naked from the bath, and plied the swing with such unmerciful jerks, that it swept through the whole compass of a very lofty dome, and took from the poor victim all power of respiration;

sometimes his feet rased the surface of the water, and at others the skylight almost flattened his nose; in vain did he pierce the air with the cries of a voice that resembled the ringing of a cracked basin, for their peals of laughter were still more predominant.

Nouronihar, in the inebriety of youthful spirits, being used only to eunuchs of ordinary harems, and having never seen anything so royal and disgusting, was far more diverted than all of the rest; she began to parody some Persian verses, and sang with an accent most demurely piquant:

> O gentle white dove, as thou soar'st through the air,
> Vouchsafe one kind glance on the mate of thy love;
> Melodious Philomel, I am thy rose;
> Warble some couplet to ravish my heart!

The sultanas and their slaves, stimulated by these pleasantries, persevered at the swing with such unremitted assiduity, that at length the cord which had secured it snapped suddenly asunder, and Baba-balouk fell floundering like a turtle to the bottom of the bath. This accident occasioned a universal shout; twelve little doors, till now unobserved, flew open at once, and the ladies in an instant made their escape, after throwing all the towels on his head, and putting out the lights that remained.

The deplorable animal, in water to the chin, overwhelmed with darkness, and unable to extricate himself from the wrap that em-barrassed him, was still doomed to hear for his further consolation the fresh bursts of merriment his disaster occasioned. He bustled, but in vain, to get from the bath, for the margin was become so slippery with the oil spilt in breaking the lamps, that at every effort he slid back with a plunge, which resounded aloud through the hollow of the dome. These cursed peals of laughter at every relapse were redoubled; and he, who thought the place infested rather by devils than women, resolved to cease groping, and abide in the bath, where he amused himself with soliloquies, interspersed with imprecations, of which his malicious neighbours reclining on down suffered not an accent to escape. In this delectable plight the morn-ing surprised him. The Caliph, wondering at his absence, had caused him to be everywhere sought for. At last he was drawn forth, almost smothered from the wisp of linen, and wet even to the marrow. Limping and chattering his teeth, he appeared before his master, who inquired what was the matter, and how he came soused in so strange a pickle.

'And why did you enter this cursed lodge?' answered Bababalouk, gruffly. 'Ought a monarch like you to visit with his harem the abode of a grey-bearded Emir, who knows nothing of life? And with what gracious damsels doth the place, too, abound! Fancy to yourself how they have soaked me like a burnt crust, and made me dance like a jack-pudding the livelong night through, on their damnable swing! What an excellent lesson for your sultanas to follow, into whom I have instilled such reserve and decorum!'

Vathek, comprehending not a syllable of all this invective, obliged him to relate minutely the transaction; but instead of sympathising with the miserable sufferer, he laughed immoderately at the device of the swing, and the figure of Bababalouk mounting upon it. The stung eunuch could scarcely preserve the semblance of respect. 'Ay, laugh, my lord! laugh,' said he. 'But I wish this Nouronihar would play some trick on you; she is too wicked to spare even majesty itself.' Those words made for the present but a slight impression on the Caliph; but they not long after recurred to his mind.

This conversation was cut short by Fakreddin, who came to request that Vathek would join in the prayers and ablutions to be solemnised on a spacious meadow, watered by innumerable streams. The Caliph found the waters refreshing, but the prayers abominably irksome; he diverted himself, however, with the multitude of calenders, santons, and dervishes, who were continually coming and going, but especially with the brahmins, fakirs, and other enthusiasts, who had travelled from the heart of India, and halted on their way with the Emir. These latter had, each of them, some mummery peculiar to himself. One dragged a huge chain wherever he went, another an orangoutang, whilst a third was furnished with scourges, and all performed to a charm; some clambered up trees, holding one foot in the air; others poised themselves over a fire, and without mercy filliped their noses. There were some amongst them that cherished vermin, which were not ungrateful in requiting their caresses. These rambling fanatics revolted the hearts of the dervishes, the calenders, and santons; however, the vehemence of their aversion soon subsided, under the hope that the presence of the Caliph would cure their folly, and convert them to the Mussulman faith; but, alas! how great was their disappointment! For Vathek, instead of preaching to them, treated them as buffoons, bade them present his compliments to Visnow and Ixhora, and discovered a predilection for a squat old man from the isle of Serendib, who was more ridiculous than any of the rest.

'Come!' said he, 'for the love of your gods bestow a few slaps on your chops to amuse me.'

The old fellow, offended at such an address, began loudly to weep; but, as he betrayed a villainous drivelling in his tears, the Caliph turned his back and listened to Bababalouk, who whispered, whilst he held the umbrella over him: 'Your Majesty should be cautious of this odd assembly which hath been collected I know not for what. Is it necessary to exhibit such spectacles to a mighty potentate, with interludes of talapoins more mangy than dogs? Were I you, I would command a fire to be kindled, and at once purge the earth of the Emir, his harem, and all his menagerie.'

'Tush, dolt!' answered Vathek. 'And know that all this infinitely charms me; nor shall I leave the meadow till I have visited every hive of these pious mendicants.'

Wherever the Caliph directed his course, objects of pity were sure to swarm round him: the blind, the purblind, smarts without noses, damsels without ears, each to extol the munificence of Fakreddin, who, as well as his attendant greybeards, dealt about, gratis, plasters and cataplasms to all that applied. At noon a superb corps of cripples made its appearance, and soon after advanced by platoons on the plain, the completest association of invalids that had ever been embodied till then. The blind went groping with the blind, the lame limped on together, and the maimed made gestures to each other with the only arm that remained; the sides of a considerable waterfall were crowded by the deaf, amongst whom were some from Pegu with ears uncommonly handsome and large, but still less able to hear than the rest; nor were there wanting others in abundance with hump-backs, wenny necks, and even horns of an exquisite polish.

The Emir, to aggrandise the solemnity of the festival in honour of his illustrious visitant, ordered the turf to be spread on all sides with skins and table-cloths, upon which were served up for the good Mussulmans pilaus of every hue, with other orthodox dishes; and, by the express order of Vathek, who was shamefully tolerant, small plates of abominations were prepared, to the great scandal of the faithful. The holy assembly began to fall to. The Caliph, in spite of every remonstrance from the chief of his eunuchs, resolved to have a dinner dressed on the spot. The complaisant Emir immediately gave orders for a table to be placed in the shade of the willows. The first service consisted of fish, which they drew from a river flowing over sands of gold at the foot of a lofty hill; these were broiled as fast as taken, and served up with a sauce of vinegar, and small herbs that grow on Mount Sinai; for everything with the Emir was excellent and pious.

The dessert was not quite set on when the sound of lutes from the hill was repeated by the echoes of the neighbouring mountains. The Caliph, with an emotion of pleasure and surprise, had no sooner raised up his head than a handful of jasmine dropped on his face; an abundance of tittering succeeded the frolic, and instantly appeared through the bushes the elegant forms of several young females, skipping and bounding like roes. The fragrance diffused from their hair struck the sense of Vathek, who, in an ecstasy, suspending his repast, said to Bababalouk: 'Are the Peris come down from their spheres? Note her in particular whose form is so perfect, venturously running on the brink of the precipice, and turning back her head, as regardless of nothing but the graceful flow of her robe; with what captivating impatience doth she contend with the bushes for her veil! Could it be she who threw the jasmine at me?'

'Ay! she it was; and you too would she throw from the top of the rock,' answered Bababalouk. 'For that is my good friend Nouronihar, who so kindly lent me her swing; my dear lord and master,' added he, twisting a twig that hung by the rind from a willow, 'let me correct her for want of respect; the Emir will have no reason to complain, since (bating what I owe to his piety) he is much to be censured for keeping a troop of girls on the mountains, where the sharpness of the air gives their blood too brisk a circulation.'

'Peace, blasphemer!' said the Caliph. 'Speak not thus of her who over her mountains leads my heart a willing captive; contrive rather that my eyes may be fixed upon hers, that I may respire her sweet breath, as she bounds panting along these delightful wilds!' On saying these words, Vathek extended his arms towards the hill, and directing his eyes with an anxiety unknown to him before, endeavoured to keep within view the object that enthralled his soul; but her course was as difficult to follow as the flight of one of those beautiful blue butterflies of Cashmere, which are at once so volatile and rare.

The Caliph, not satisfied with seeing, wished also to hear Nouronihar, and eagerly turned to catch the sound of her voice; at last he distinguished her whispering to one of her companions behind the thicket from whence she had thrown the jasmine: 'A Caliph, it must be owned, is a fine thing to see, but my little Gulchenrouz is much more amiable; one lock of his hair is of more value to me than the richest embroidery of the Indies; I had rather that his teeth should mischievously press my finger than the richest ring of the imperial treasure. Where have you left him, Sutlememe? And why is he now not here?'

The agitated Caliph still wished to hear more, but she immediately retired, with all her attendants; the fond monarch pursued her with his eyes till she was gone out of sight, and then continued like a bewildered and benighted traveller, from whom the clouds had obscured the constellation that guided his way; the curtain of night seemed dropped before him; everything appeared discoloured; the falling waters filled his soul with dejection, and his tears trickled down the jasmines he had caught from Nouronihar, and placed in his inflamed bosom; he snatched up a shining pebble, to remind him of the scene where he felt the first tumults of love. Two hours were elapsed, and evening drew on before he could resolve to depart from the place; he often, but in vain, attempted to go; a soft languor enervated the powers of his mind; extending himself on the brink of the stream, he turned his eyes towards the blue summits of the mountain, and exclaimed: 'What concealest thou behind thee? What is passing in thy solitudes? Whither is she gone? O Heaven! perhaps she is now wandering in thy grottos, with her happy Gulchenrouz!'

In the meantime the damps began to descend, and the Emir, solicitous for the health of the Caliph, ordered the imperial litter to be brought. Vathek, absorbed in his reveries, was imperceptibly removed, and conveyed back to the saloon that received him the evening before. But let us leave the Caliph, immersed in his new passion, and attend Nouronihar beyond the rocks, where she had again joined her beloved Gulchenrouz.

This Gulchenrouz was the son of Ali Hassan, brother to the Emir, and the most delicate and lovely creature in the world. Ali Hassan, who had been absent ten years on a voyage to the unknown seas, committed at his departure this child, the only survivor of many, to the care and protection of his brother. Gulchenrouz could write in various characters with precision, and paint upon vellum the most elegant arabesques that fancy could devise; his sweet voice accompanied the lute in the most enchanting manner, and when he sang the loves of Megnoun and Leileh, or some unfortunate lovers of ancient days, tears insensibly overflowed the cheeks of his auditors; the verses he composed (for, like Megnoun, he too was a poet) inspired that unresisting languor so frequently fatal to the female heart; the women all doted upon him; for though he had passed his thirteenth year, they still detained him in the harem; his dancing was light as the gossamer waved by the zephyrs of spring, but his arms, which twined so gracefully with those of the young girls in the dance, could neither dart the lance in the chase, nor curb the steeds that pastured his uncle's domains. The bow, however, he drew with a certain aim, and would have excelled his competitors in the race, could he have broken the ties that bound him to Nouronihar.

The two brothers had mutually engaged their children to each other, and Nouronihar loved her cousin more than her eyes; both had the same tastes and amusements, the same long, languishing looks, the same tresses, the same fair complexions, and when Gulchenrouz appeared in the dress of his cousin he seemed to be more feminine than even herself. If at any time he left the harem to visit Fakreddin, it was with all the bashfulness of a fawn, that consciously ventures from the lair of its dam; he was however, wanton enough to mock the solemn old greybeards to whom he was subject, though sure to be rated without mercy in return; whenever this happened he would plunge into the recesses of the harem, and sobbing, take refuge in the arms of Nouronihar, who loved even his faults beyond the virtues of others.

It fell out this evening that, after leaving the Caliph in the meadow, she ran with Gulchenrouz over the green sward of the mountain that sheltered the vale where Fakreddin had chosen to reside. The sun was dilated on the edge of the horizon; and the young people, whose fancies were lively and inventive, imagined they beheld in the gorgeous clouds of the west the domes of Shadukiam and Amberabad, where the Peris have fixed their abode. Nouronihar, sitting on the slope of the hill, supported on her knees the perfumed head of Gulchenrouz; the air was calm, and no sound stirred but the voices of other young girls, who were drawing cool water from the streams below. The unexpected arrival of the Caliph, and the splendour that marked his appearance, had already filled with emotion the ardent soul of Nouronihar; her vanity irresistibly prompted her to pique the prince's attention, and this she before took good care to effect whilst he picked up the jasmine she had thrown upon him. But when Gulchenrouz asked after the flowers he had culled for her bosom, Nouronihar was all in confusion; she hastily kissed his forehead, arose in a flutter, and walked with unequal steps on the border of the precipice. Night advanced, and the pure gold of the setting sun had yielded to a sanguine red, the glow of which, like the reflection of a burning furnace, flushed Nouronihar's animated countenance. Gulchenrouz, alarmed at the agitation of his cousin, said to her with a supplicating accent: 'Let us be gone; the sky looks portentous, the tamarisks tremble more than common, and the raw wind chills my very heart; come! let us be gone; 'tis a melancholy night!' Then, taking hold of her hand, he drew it towards the path he besought her to go. Nouronihar unconsciously followed the attraction, for a thousand strange imaginations occupied her spirit; she passed the large round of honeysuckles, her favourite resort, without ever vouchsafing it a glance, yet Gulchenrouz could not help snatching off a few shoots in his way, though he ran as if a wild beast were behind.

The young females, seeing him approach in such haste, and according to custom expecting a dance, instantly assembled in a circle, and took each other by the hand; but Gulchenrouz, coming up out of breath, fell down at once on the grass. This accident struck with consternation the whole of this frolicsome party; whilst Nouronihar, half distracted, and overcome both by the violence of her exercise and the tumult of her thoughts, sunk feebly down at his side, cherished his cold hands in her bosom, and chafed his temples with a fragrant unguent. At length he came to himself and, wrapping up his head in the robe of his cousin, entreated that she would not return to the harem; he was afraid of being snapped at by Shaban, his tutor, a wrinkled old eunuch of a surly disposition; for having interrupted the stated walk of Nouronihar, he dreaded lest the churl should take it amiss. The whole of this sprightly group, sitting round upon a mossy knoll, began to entertain themselves with various pastimes, whilst their superintendents the eunuchs were gravely conversing at a distance. The nurse of the Emir's daughter, observing her pupil sit ruminating with her eyes on the ground, endeavoured to amuse her with diverting tales, to which Gulchenrouz, who had already forgotten his inquietudes, listened with a breathless attention; he laughed, he clapped his hands, and passed a hundred little tricks on the whole of the company, without omitting the eunuchs, whom he provoked to run after him, in spite of their age and decrepitude.

During these occurrences the moon arose, the wind subsided, and the evening became so serene and inviting, that a resolution was taken to sup on the spot. Sutlememe, who excelled in dressing a salad, having filled large bowls of porcelain with eggs of small birds, curds turned with citron juice, slices of cucumber, and the inmost leaves of delicate herbs, handed it round from one to another, and gave each their shares in a large spoon of cocknos. Gulchenrouz, nestling as usual in the bosom of Nouronihar, pouted out his vermilion little lips against the offer of Sutlememe, and would take it only from the hand of his cousin, on whose mouth he hung like a bee inebriated with the quintessence of flowers.

In the midst of this festive scene there appeared a light on the top of the highest mountain, which attracted the notice of every eye; this light was not less bright than the moon when at full, and might have been taken for her, had it not been that the moon was already risen. The phenomenon occasioned a general surprise, and no one could conjecture the cause; it could not be a fire, for the light was clear and bluish, nor had meteors ever been seen of that magnitude or splendour. This strange light faded for a moment, and immediately renewed its brightness; it first appeared motionless at the foot of the rock, whence it darted in an instant to sparkle in a thicket of palm-trees; from thence it glided along the torrent, and at last fixed in a glen that was narrow and dark. The moment it had taken its direction, Gulchenrouz, whose heart always trembled at anything sudden or rare, drew Nouronihar by the robe, and anxiously requested her to return to the harem; the women were importunate in seconding the entreaty, but the curiosity of the Emir's daughter prevailed; she not only refused to go back, but resolved at all hazards to pursue the appearance.

Whilst they were debating what was best to be done, the light shot forth so dazzling a blaze, that they all fled away shrieking; Nouronihar followed them a few steps, but, coming to the turn of a little by-path, stopped, and went back alone; as she ran with an alertness peculiar to herself, it was not long before she came to the place where they had just been supping. The globe of fire now appeared stationary in the glen, and burned in majestic stillness. Nouronihar, compressing her hands upon her bosom, hesitated for some moments to advance; the solitude of her situation was new, the silence of the night awful, and every object inspired sensations which till then she never had felt: the affright of Gulchenrouz recurred to her mind, and she a thousand times turned to go back, but this luminous appearance was always before her; urged on by an irresistible impulse, she continued to approach it, in defiance of every obstacle that opposed her progress.

At length she arrived at the opening of the glen; but, instead of coming up to the light, she found herself surrounded by darkness, excepting that at a considerable distance a faint spark glimmered by fits. She stopped a second time; the sound of waterfalls mingling their murmurs, the hollow rustlings amongst the palm-branches, and the funereal screams of the birds from their rifted trunks, all conspired to fill her with terror; she imagined every moment that she trod on some venomous reptile; all the stories of malignant dives and dismal ghouls thronged into her memory; but her curiosity was, notwithstanding, more predominant than her fears; she therefore firmly entered a winding track that led towards the spark, but, being a stranger to the path, she had not gone far till she began to repent of her rashness.

'Alas!' said she, 'that I were but in those secure and illuminated apartments where my evenings glided on with Gulchenrouz! Dear child! how would thy heart flutter with terror wert thou wandering in these wild solitudes like me!' At the close of this apostrophe she regained her road, and, coming to steps hewn out in the rock, ascended them undismayed; the light, which was now gradually enlarging, appeared above her on the summit of the mountain; at length she distinguished a plaintive and melodious union of voices, proceeding from a sort of cavern, that resembled the dirges which are sung over tombs; a sound, likewise, like that which arises from the filling of baths, at the same time struck her ear; she continued ascending, and discovered large wax torches in full blaze planted here and there in the fissures of the rock; this preparation filled her with fear, whilst the subtle and potent odour which the torches exhaled caused her to sink, almost lifeless, at the entrance of the grot.

Casting her eyes within in this kind of trance, she beheld a large cistern of gold filled with a water, whose vapour distilled on her face a dew of the essence of roses; a soft symphony resounded through the grot; on the sides of the cistern she noticed appendages of royalty, diadems, and feathers of the heron, all sparkling with carbuncles; whilst her attention was fixed on this display of magnificence, the music ceased, and a voice instantly demanded: 'For what monarch were these torches kindled, this bath prepared, and these habiliments, which belong, not only to the sovereigns of the earth, but even to the talismanic powers?'

To which a second voice answered: 'They are for the charming daughter of the Emir Fakreddin.'

'What,' replied the first, 'for that trifler, who consumes her time with a giddy child, immersed in softness, and who at best can make but a pitiful husband?'

'And can she,' rejoined the other voice, 'be amused with such empty toys, whilst the Caliph, the sovereign of the world, he who is destined to enjoy the treasures of the pre-Adamite sultans, a prince six feet high, and whose eyes pervade the inmost soul of a female, is inflamed with the love of her. No! she will be wise enough to answer that passion alone that can aggrandise her glory; no doubt she will, and despise the puppet of her fancy. Then all the riches this place contains, as well as the carbuncle of Giamschid, shall be hers.'

'You judge right,' returned the first voice, 'and I haste to Istakar to prepare the palace of subterranean fire for the reception of the bridal pair.'

The voices ceased, the torches were extinguished, the most entire darkness succeeded, and Nouronihar, recovering with a start, found herself reclined on a sofa in the harem of her father. She clapped her hands, and immediately came together Gulchenrouz and her women, who, in despair at having lost her, had despatched eunuchs to seek her in every direction; Shaban appeared with the rest, and began to reprimand her with an air of consequence: 'Little impertinent,' said he, 'whence got you false keys? Or are you beloved of some Genius that hath given you a pick-lock? I will try the extent of your power; come, to your chamber! Through the two skylights; and expect not the company of Gulchenrouz; be expeditious! I will shut you up, and turn the key twice upon you!'

At these menaces Nouronihar indignantly raised her head, opened on Shaban her black eyes, which, since the important dialogue of the enchanted grot, were considerably enlarged, and said: 'Go, speak thus to slaves, but learn to reverence her who is born to give laws, and subject all to her power.'

Proceeding in the same style, she was interrupted by a sudden exclamation of 'The Caliph! The Caliph!' The curtains at once were thrown open, and the slaves prostrate in double rows, whilst poor little Gulchenrouz hid himself beneath the elevation of a sofa. At first appeared a file of black eunuchs, trailing after them long trains of muslin embroidered with gold, and holding in their hands censers, which dispensed as they passed the grateful perfume of the wood of aloes; next marched Bababalouk with a solemn strut, and tossing his head as not over-pleased at the visit; Vathek came close after, superbly robed; his gait was unembarrassed and noble, and his presence would have engaged admiration, though he had not been the sovereign of the world; he approached Nouronihar with a throbbing heart, and seemed enraptured at the full effulgence of her radiant eyes, of which he had before caught but a few glimpses; but she instantly depressed them, and her confusion augmented her beauty.

Bababalouk, who was a thorough adept in coincidences of this nature, and knew that the worst game should be played with the

best face, immediately made a signal for all to retire; and no sooner
did he perceive beneath the sofa the little one's feet, than he
drew him forth without ceremony, set him upon his shoulders,
and lavished on him as he went off a thousand odious caresses;
Gulchenrouz cried out, and resisted till his cheeks became the
colour of the blossom of the pomegranate, and the tears that started
into his eyes shot forth a gleam of indignation; he cast a significant
glance at Nouronihar, which the Caliph noticing, asked: 'Is that
then your Gulchenrouz?'

'Sovereign of the world,' answered she, 'spare my cousin, whose
innocence and gentleness deserve not your anger.'

'Take comfort,' said Vathek, with a smile. 'He is in good hands.
Bababalouk is fond of children, and never goes without sweetmeats
and comfits.'

The daughter of Fakreddin was abashed, and suffered Gulchenrouz to be borne away without adding a word. The tumult of her
bosom betrayed her confusion; and Vathek, becoming still more
impassioned, gave a loose to his frenzy, which had only not subdued
the last faint strugglings of reluctance, when the Emir, suddenly
bursting in, threw his face upon the ground at the feet of the Caliph,
and said: 'Commander of the Faithful! abase not yourself to the
meanness of your slave.'

'No, Emir,' replied Vathek. 'I raise her to an equality with myself;
I declare her my wife, and the glory of your race shall extend from
one generation to another.'

'Alas! my lord,' said Fakreddin, as he plucked off a few grey hairs of
his beard, 'cut short the days of your faithful servant, rather than
force him to depart from his word. Nouronihar, as her hands evince,
is solemnly promised to Gulchenrouz, the son of my brother Ali
Hassan; they are united also in heart, their faith is mutually plighted,
and affiances so sacred cannot be broken.'

'What then!' replied the Caliph, bluntly, 'would you surrender this
divine beauty to a husband more womanish than herself? And can
you imagine that I will suffer her charms to decay in hands so
inefficient and nerveless? No! she is destined to live out her life
within my embraces: such is my will; retire, and disturb not the time
I devote to the homage of her charms.'

The irritated Emir drew forth his sabre, presented it to Vathek,
and stretching out his neck, said in a firm tone of voice: 'Strike your
unhappy host, my lord! He has lived long enough, since he hath seen
the Prophet's vicegerent violate the rites of hospitality.'

At his uttering these words Nouronihar, unable to support any longer the conflict of her passions, sank down in a swoon. Vathek, both terrified for her life and furious at an opposition to his will, bade Fakreddin assist his daughter, and withdrew, darting his terrible look at the unfortunate Emir, who suddenly fell backward, bathed in a sweat cold as the damp of death.

Gulchenrouz, who had escaped from the hands of Bababalouk, and was that instant returned, called out for help as loudly as he could, not having strength to afford it himself. Pale and panting, the poor child attempted to revive Nouronihar by caresses; and it happened that the thrilling warmth of his lips restored her to life.

Fakreddin, beginning also to recover from the look of the Caliph, with difficulty tottered to a seat, and after warily casting round his eye to see if this dangerous prince was gone, sent for Shaban and Sutlememe, and said to them apart: 'My friends! violent evils require as violent remedies; the Caliph has brought desolation and horror into my family, and how shall we resist his power? Another of his looks will send me to my grave. Fetch then that narcotic powder which the dervish brought me from Aracan; a dose of it, the effect of which will continue three days, must be administered to each of these children; the Caliph will believe them to be dead, for they will have all the appearance of death; we shall go as if to inter them in the cave of Meimouné, at the entrance of the great desert of sand, and near the cabin of my dwarfs. When all the spectators shall be withdrawn, you, Shaban, and four select eunuchs, shall convey them to the lake, where provisions shall be ready to support them a month; for one day allotted to the surprise this event will occasion, five to the tears, a fortnight to reflection, and the rest to prepare for renewing his progress, will, according to my calcul- ation, fill up the whole time that Vathek will tarry, and I shall then be freed from his intrusion.'

'Your plan,' said Sutlememe, 'is a good one, if it can but be effected. I have remarked that Nouronihar is well able to support the glances of the Caliph, and that he is far from being sparing of them to her; be assured, therefore, notwithstanding her fondness for Gulchenrouz, she will never remain quiet while she knows him to be here, unless we can persuade her that both herself and Gulchenrouz are really dead, and that they were conveyed to those rocks for a limited season to expiate the little faults of which their love was the cause; we will add that we killed ourselves in despair, and that your dwarfs, whom they never yet saw, will preach to them

delectable sermons. I will engage that everything shall succeed to
the bent of your wishes.'

'Be it so!' said Fakreddin. 'I approve your proposal; let us lose not a
moment to give it effect.'

They hastened to seek for the powder, which, being mixed in a
sherbet, was immediately drunk by Gulchenrouz and Nouronihar.
Within the space of an hour both were seized with violent palpit-
ations, and a general numbness gradually ensued; they arose from
the floor, where they had remained ever since the Caliph's departure,
and, ascending to the sofa, reclined themselves at full length upon it,
clasped in each other's embraces.

'Cherish me, my dear Nouronihar!' said Gulchenrouz. 'Put thy
hand upon my heart, for it feels as if it were frozen. Alas! thou
art as cold as myself! Hath the Caliph murdered us both with his
terrible look?'

'I am dying!' cried she in a faltering voice. 'Press me closer; I am
ready to expire!'

'Let us die then together,' answered the little Gulchenrouz, whilst
his breast laboured with a convulsive sigh. 'Let me at least breathe
forth my soul on thy lips!' They spoke no more, and became as dead.

Immediately the most piercing cries were heard through the harem,
whilst Shaban and Sutlememe personated with great adroitness the
parts of persons in despair. The Emir, who was sufficiently mortified
to be forced into such untoward expedients, and had now for the first
time made a trial of his powder, was under no necessity of counter-
feiting grief. The slaves, who had flocked together from all quarters,
stood motionless at the spectacle before them; all lights were extinguished save two lamps, which shed a wan glimmering over the faces
of these lovely flowers, that seemed to be faded in the springtime of
life; funeral vestments were prepared, their bodies were washed with
rose-water, their beautiful tresses were braided and incensed, and
they were wrapped in simars whiter than alabaster.

At the moment that their attendants were placing two wreaths of
their favourite jasmines on their brows, the Caliph, who had just
heard of the tragical catastrophe, arrived; he looked not less pale
and haggard than the ghouls, that wander at night among graves;
forgetful of himself and everyone else, he broke through the midst of
the slaves, fell prostrate at the foot of the sofa, beat his bosom, called
himself 'atrocious murderer!' and invoked upon his head a thousand
imprecations; with a trembling hand he raised the veil that covered
the countenance of Nouronihar, and, uttering a loud shriek, fell

lifeless on the floor. The chief of the eunuchs dragged him off with horrible grimaces, and repeated as he went: 'Ay, I foresaw she would play you some ungracious turn!'

No sooner was the Caliph gone than the Emir commanded biers to be brought, and forbad that anyone should enter the harem. Every window was fastened, all instruments of music were broken, and the imams began to recite their prayers; towards the close of this melancholy day Vathek sobbed in silence, for they had been forced to compose with anodynes his convulsions of rage and desperation.

At the dawn of the succeeding morning the wide folding doors of the palace were set open, and the funeral procession moved forward for the mountain. The wailful cries of 'La Ilah illa Allah!' reached to the Caliph, who was eager to cicatrise himself and attend the ceremonial; nor could he have been dissuaded, had not his excessive weakness disabled him from walking; at the few first steps he fell on the ground, and his people were obliged to lay him on a bed, where he remained many days in such a state of insensibility as excited compassion in the Emir himself.

When the procession was arrived at the grot of Meimouné, Shaban and Sutlememe dismissed the whole of the train, excepting the four confidential eunuchs who were appointed to remain. After resting some moments near the biers, which had been left in the open air, they caused them to be carried to the brink of a small lake, whose banks were overgrown with a hoary moss; this was the great resort of herons and storks, which preyed continually on little blue fishes. The dwarfs, instructed by the Emir, soon repaired thither, and, with the help of the eunuchs, began to construct cabins of rushes and reeds, a work in which they had admirable skill; a magazine also was contrived for provisions, with a small oratory for themselves, and a pyramid of wood neatly piled, to furnish the necessary fuel, for the air was bleak in the hollows of the mountains.

At evening two fires were kindled on the brink of the lake, and the two lovely bodies, taken from their biers, were carefully deposited upon a bed of dried leaves within the same cabin. The dwarfs began to recite the Koran with their clear shrill voices, and Shaban and Sutlememe stood at some distance, anxiously waiting the effects of the powder. At length Nouronihar and Gulchenrouz faintly stretched out their arms, and gradually opening their eyes, began to survey with looks of increasing amazement every object around them; they even attempted to rise, but for want of strength fell back again; Sutlememe on this administered a cordial, which the Emir had taken care to provide.

Gulchenrouz, thoroughly aroused, sneezed out aloud, and raising himself with an effort that expressed his surprise, left the cabin, and inhaled the fresh air with the greatest avidity. 'Yes,' said he, 'I breathe again! Again do I exist! I hear sounds! I behold a firmament spangled over with stars!'

Nouronihar, catching these beloved accents, extricated herself from the leaves, and ran to clasp Gulchenrouz to her bosom. The first objects she remarked were their long simars, their garlands of flowers, and their naked feet; she hid her face in her hands to reflect; the vision of the enchanted bath, the despair of her father, and, more vividly than both, the majestic figure of Vathek recurred to her memory; she recollected also that herself and Gulchenrouz had been sick and dying; but all these images bewildered her mind. Not knowing where she was, she turned her eyes on all sides, as if to recognise the surrounding scene; this singular lake, those flames reflected from its glassy surface, the pale hues of its banks, the romantic cabins, the bulrushes that sadly waved their drooping heads, the storks whose melancholy cries blended with the shrill voices of the dwarfs, everything conspired to persuade them that the Angel of Death had opened the portal of some other world.

Gulchenrouz on his part, lost in wonder, clung to the neck of his cousin: he believed himself in the region of phantoms, and was terrified at the silence she preserved; at length addressing her: 'Speak,' said he, 'where are we? Do you not see those spectres that are stirring the burning coals? Are they Monker and Nakir, come to throw us into them? Does the fatal bridge cross this lake, whose solemn stillness perhaps conceals from us an abyss, in which for whole ages we shall be doomed incessantly to sink?'

'No, my children!' said Sutlememe, going towards them, 'take comfort! The exterminating angel, who conducted our souls hither after yours, hath assured us that the chastisement of your indolent and voluptuous life shall be restricted to a certain series of years, which you must pass in this dreary abode, where the sun is scarcely visible, and where the soil yields neither fruits nor flowers. These,' continued she, pointing to the dwarfs, 'will provide for our wants, for souls so mundane as ours retain too strong a tincture of their earthly extraction; instead of meats your food will be nothing but rice, and your bread shall be moistened in the fogs that brood over the surface of the lake.'

At this desolating prospect the poor children burst into tears, and prostrated themselves before the dwarfs, who perfectly supported their characters, and delivered an excellent discourse of a customary length upon the sacred camel, which after a thousand years was to convey them to the paradise of the faithful.

The sermon being ended, and ablutions performed, they praised Allah and the Prophet, supped very indifferently, and retired to their withered leaves. Nouronihar and her little cousin consoled themselves on finding that, though dead, they yet lay in one cabin. Having slept well before, the remainder of the night was spent in conversation on what had befallen them, and both, from a dread of apparitions, betook themselves for protection to one another's arms.

In the morning, which was lowering and rainy, the dwarfs mounted high poles like minarets, and called them to prayers; the whole congregation, which consisted of Sutlememe, Shaban, the four eunuchs, and some storks, were already assembled. The two children came forth from their cabin with a slow and dejected pace; as their minds were in a tender and melancholy mood, their devotions were performed with fervour. No sooner were they finished, than Gulchenrouz demanded of Sutlememe and the rest, 'how they happened to die so opportunely for his cousin and himself.'

'We killed ourselves,' returned Sutlememe, 'in despair at your death.'

On this, Nouronihar, who, notwithstanding what was past, had not yet forgotten her vision, said: 'And the Caliph! Is he also dead of his grief? And will he likewise come hither?'

The dwarfs, who were prepared with an answer, most demurely replied: 'Vathek is damned beyond all redemption!'

'I readily believe so,' said Gulchenrouz, 'and I am glad from my heart to hear it; for I am convinced it was his horrible look that sent us hither to listen to sermons and mess upon rice.'

One week passed away on the side of the lake unmarked by any variety; Nouronihar ruminating on the grandeur of which death had deprived her, and Gulchenrouz applying to prayers and to panniers, along with the dwarfs, who infinitely pleased him.

Whilst this scene of innocence was exhibiting in the mountains, the Caliph presented himself to the Emir in a new light; the instant he recovered the use of his senses, with a voice that made Bababalouk quake, he thundered out: 'Perfidious Giaour! I renounce thee for ever! It is thou who hast slain my beloved Nouronihar! and I supplicate the pardon of Mahomet, who would have preserved her to me had I been more wise; let water be brought to perform my ablutions, and let the pious Fakreddin be called to offer up his prayers with mine, and reconcile me to him; afterwards we will go together and visit the sepulchre of the unfortunate Nouronihar; I am resolved to become a hermit, and consume the residue of my days on this mountain, in hope of expiating my crimes.'

'And what do you intend to live upon there?' enquired Bababalouk.

'I hardly know,' replied Vathek, 'but I will tell you when I feel hungry – which, I believe, will not soon be the case.'

The arrival of Fakreddin put a stop to this conversation. As soon as Vathek saw him, he threw his arms around his neck, bedewed his face with a torrent of tears, and uttered things so affecting, so pious, that the Emir, crying for joy, congratulated himself in his heart for having performed so admirable and unexpected a conversion. As for the pilgrimage to the mountain, Fakreddin had his own reasons not to oppose it; therefore, each ascending his own litter, they started.

Notwithstanding the vigilance with which his attendants watched the Caliph, they could not prevent his harrowing his cheeks with a few scratches, when on the place where he was told Nouronihar had been buried; they were even obliged to drag him away, by force of hands, from the melancholy spot. However he swore, with a solemn oath, that he would return thither every day. This resolution did not exactly please the Emir – yet he flattered himself that the Caliph might not proceed farther, and would merely perfom his devotions in the cavern of Meimouné. Besides, the lake was so completely concealed within the solitary bosom of those tremendous rocks, that he thought it utterly impossible anyone could ever find it. This security of Fakreddin was also considerably strengthened by the conduct of Vathek, who performed his vow most scrupulously, and returned daily from the hill so devout and so contrite, that all the greybeards were in a state of ecstasy on account of it.

Nouronihar was not altogether so content, for though she felt a fondness for Gulchenrouz, who, to augment the attachment, had been left at full liberty with her, yet she still regarded him as but a bauble, that bore no competition with the carbuncle of Giamschid. At times she indulged doubts on the mode of her being, and scarcely could believe that the dead had all the wants and the whims of the living. To gain satisfaction, however, on so perplexing a topic, she arose one morning whilst all were asleep, with a breathless caution,

from the side of Gulchenrouz, and, after having given him a soft
kiss, began to follow the windings of the lake till it terminated with a
rock, whose top was accessible, though lofty; this she clambered up
with considerable toil, and having reached the summit, set forward
in a run, like a doe that unwittingly follows her hunter; though
she skipped along with the alertness of an antelope, yet at intervals
she was forced to desist, and rest beneath the tamarisks to recover
her breath. Whilst she, thus reclined, was occupied with her little
reflections on the apprehension that she had some knowledge of the
place, Vathek, who, finding himself that morning but ill at ease, had
gone forth before the dawn, presented himself on a sudden to her
view; motionless with surprise, he durst not approach the figure
before him, which lay shrouded up in a simar, extended on the
ground, trembling and pale, but yet lovely to behold. At length
Nouronihar, with a mixture of pleasure and affliction, raising her
fine eyes to him, said: 'My lord, are you come hither to eat rice and
hear sermons with me?'

'Beloved phantom!' cried Vathek. 'Dost thou speak? Hast thou
the same graceful form? The same radiant features? Art thou palpable likewise?' And, eagerly embracing her, added: 'here are limbs
and a bosom animated with a gentle warmth! What can such a
prodigy mean?'

Nouronihar with diffidence answered: 'You know, my lord, that I
died on the night you honoured me with your visit; my cousin
maintains it was from one of your glances, but I cannot believe him;
for to me they seem not so dreadful. Gulchenrouz died with me,
and we were both brought into a region of desolation, where we are
fed with a wretched diet. If you be dead also, and are come hither
to join us, I pity your lot; for you will be stunned with the noise of
the dwarfs and the storks; besides, it is mortifying in the extreme
that you, as well as myself, should have lost the treasures of the
subterranean palace.'

At the mention of the subterranean palace the Caliph suspended
his caresses, to seek from Nouronihar an explanation of her meaning. She then recapitulated her vision, what immediately followed,
and the history of her pretended death, adding also a description
of the place of expiation from whence she had fled, and all in a
manner that would have extorted his laughter, had not the thoughts
of Vathek been too deeply engaged. No sooner, however, had she
ended, than he again clasped her to his bosom, and said: 'Light of my
eyes! the mystery is unravelled. We both are alive! Your father is a

cheat, who, for the sake of dividing, hath deluded us both; and the Giaour, whose design, as far as I can discover, is that we shall proceed together, seems scarce a whit better; it shall be some time at least before he find us in his palace of fire. Your lovely little person in my estimation is far more precious than all the treasures of the pre-Adamite sultans, and I wish to possess it at pleasure, and in open day, for many a moon, before I go to burrow underground like a mole. Forget this little trifler, Gulchenrouz, and – '

'Ah! my lord!' interposed Nouronihar, 'let me entreat that you do him no evil.'

'No, no!' replied Vathek, 'I have already bid you forbear to alarm yourself for him; he has been brought up too much on milk and sugar to stimulate my jealousy; we will leave him with the dwarfs, who, by the bye, are my old acquaintances; their company will suit him far better than yours. As to other matters, I will return no more to your father's. I want not to have my ears dinned by him and his dotards with the violation of the rites of hospitality; as if it were less an honour for you to espouse the sovereign of the world than a girl dressed up like a boy!'

Nouronihar could find nothing to oppose in a discourse so eloquent; she only wished the amorous monarch had discovered more ardour for the carbuncle of Giamschid; but flattered herself it would gradually increase, and therefore yielded to his will with the most bewitching submission.

When the Caliph judged it proper, he called for Bababalouk, who was asleep in the cave of Meimouné, and dreaming that the phantom of Nouronihar, having mounted him once more on her swing, had just given him such a jerk that he one moment soared above the mountains, and the next sunk into the abyss; starting from his sleep at the voice of his master, he ran gasping for breath, and had nearly fallen backward at the sight, as he believed, of the spectre by whom he had so lately been haunted in his dream.

'Ah, my lord!' cried he, recoiling ten steps, and covering his eyes with both hands: 'do you then perform the office of a ghoul? 'Tis true you have dug up the dead, yet hope not to make her your prey; for after all she hath caused me to suffer, she is even wicked enough to prey upon you.'

'Cease thy folly,' said Vathek, 'and thou shalt soon be convinced that it is Nouronihar herself, alive and well, whom I clasp to my breast; go only and pitch my tents in the neighbouring valley; there will I fix my abode with this beautiful tulip, whose colours I soon shall restore; there exert thy best endeavours to procure whatever can augment the enjoyments of life, till I shall disclose to thee more of my will.'

The news of so unlucky an event soon reached the ears of the Emir, who abandoned himself to grief and despair, and began, as did all his old greybeards, to begrime his visage with ashes. A total supineness ensued, travellers were no longer entertained, no more plaisters were spread, and, instead of the charitable activity that had distinguished this asylum, the whole of its inhabitants exhibited only faces of a half cubit long, and uttered groans that accorded with their forlorn situation.

Though Fakreddin bewailed his daughter as lost to him for ever, yet Gulchenrouz was not forgotten. He despatched immediate instruction to Sutlememe, Shaban, and the dwarfs, enjoining them not to undeceive the child in respect to his state, but, under some pretence, to convey him far from the lofty rock at the extremity of the lake, to a place which he should appoint, as safer from danger; for he suspected that Vathek intended him evil.

Gulchenrouz in the meanwhile was filled with amazement at not finding his cousin; nor were the dwarfs at all less surprised; but Sutlememe, who had more penetration, immediately guessed what had happened. Gulchenrouz was amused with the delusive hope of once more embracing Nouronihar in the interior recesses of the mountains, where the ground, strewed over with orange blossoms and jasmines, offered beds much more inviting than the withered leaves in their cabin, where they might accompany with their voices the sounds of their lutes, and chase butterflies in concert. Sutlememe was far gone in this sort of description, when one of the four eunuchs beckoned her aside to apprise her of the arrival of a messenger from their fraternity, who had explained the secret of the flight of Nouronihar, and brought the commands of the Emir. A council with Shaban and the dwarfs was immediately held; their baggage being stowed in consequence of it, they embarked in a shallop, and quietly sailed with the little one, who acquiesced in all their proposals; their voyage proceeded in the same manner till they came to the place where the lake sinks beneath the hollow of the rock; but as soon as the bark had entered it, and Gulchenrouz found himself surrounded with darkness, he was seized with a dreadful consternation, and incessantly uttered the most piercing outcries; for he now was persuaded he should actually be damned for having taken too many little freedoms in his lifetime with his cousin.

But let us return to the Caliph and her who ruled over his heart. Bababalouk had pitched the tents, and closed up the extremities of the valley with magnificent screens of India cloth, which were guarded by Ethiopian slaves with their drawn sabres; to preserve the verdure of this beautiful enclosure in its natural freshness, the white eunuchs went continually round it with their red water-vessels. The waving of fans was heard near the imperial pavilion, where, by the voluptuous light that glowed through the muslins, the Caliph enjoyed at full view all the attractions of Nouron-ihar. Inebriated with delight, he was all ear to her charming voice, which accompanied the lute; while she was not less captivated with his descriptions of Samarah and the tower full of wonders, but especially with his relation of the adventure of the ball, and the chasm of the Giaour, with its ebony portal.

In this manner they conversed for a day and a night; they bathed together in a basin of black marble, which admirably relieved the fairness of Nouronihar. Bababalouk, whose good graces this beauty had regained, spared no attention that their repasts might be served up with the minutest exactness; some exquisite rarity was ever placed before them; and he sent even to Schiraz for that fragrant and delicious wine which had been hoarded up in bottles prior to the birth of Mahomet; he had excavated little ovens in the rock to bake the nice manchets which were prepared by the hands of Nouronihar, from whence they had derived a flavour so grateful to Vathek, that he regarded the ragouts of his other wives as entirely mawkish; whilst they would have died at the Emir's of chagrin at finding themselves so neglected, if Fakreddin, notwithstanding his resentment, had not taken pity upon them.

The Sultana Dilara, who till then had been the favourite, took this dereliction of the Caliph to heart with a vehemence natural to her character, for during her continuance in favour she had imbibed from Vathek many of his extravagant fancies, and was fired with impatience to behold the superb tombs of Istakar, and the palace of forty columns; besides, having been brought up amongst the Magi, she had fondly cherished the idea of the Caliph's devoting himself to the worship of fire; thus his voluptuous and desultory life with her rival was to her a double source of affliction. The transient piety of Vathek had occasioned her some serious alarms, but the present was an evil of far greater magnitude; she resolved, therefore, without hesitation, to write to Carathis, and acquaint her that all things went ill; that they had eaten, slept, and revelled at an old emir's,

whose sanctity was very formidable, and that after all, the prospect
of possessing the treasures of the pre-Adamite sultans was no less
remote than before. This letter was entrusted to the care of two
woodmen, who were at work on one of the great forests of the
mountains, and, being acquainted with the shortest cuts, arrived in
ten days at Samarah.

The Princess Carathis was engaged at chess with Morakanabad,
when the arrival of these wood-fellers was announced. She, after
some weeks of Vathek's absence, had forsaken the upper regions of
her tower, because everything appeared in confusion among the
stars, whom she consulted relative to the fate of her son. In vain did
she renew her fumigations, and extend herself on the roof to obtain
mystic visions; nothing more could she see in her dreams than pieces
of brocade, nosegays of flowers, and other unmeaning gewgaws.
These disappointments had thrown her into a state of dejection,
which no drug in her power was sufficient to remove; her only
resource was in Morakanabad, who was a good man, and endowed
with a decent share of confidence, yet whilst in her company he
never thought himself on roses.

No person knew aught of Vathek, and a thousand ridiculous stories
were propagated at his expense. The eagerness of Carathis may be
easily guessed at receiving the letter, as well as her rage at reading
the dissolute conduct of her son. 'Is it so?' said she. 'Either I will
perish, or Vathek shall enter the palace of fire. Let me expire in
flames, provided he may reign on the throne of Soliman!' Having
said this, and whirled herself round in a magical manner, which
struck Morakanabad with such terror as caused him to recoil, she
ordered her great camel Alboufaki to be brought, and the hideous
Nerkes with the unrelenting Cafour to attend. 'I require no other
retinue,' said she to Morakanabad. 'I am going on affairs of emerg-
ency; a truce therefore to parade! Take you care of the people; fleece
them well in my absence; for we shall expend large sums, and one
knows not what may betide.'

The night was uncommonly dark, and a pestilential blast ravaged
the plain of Catoul that would have deterred any other traveller,
however urgent the call; but Carathis enjoyed most whatever filled
others with dread. Nerkes concurred in opinion with her, and Cafour
had a particular predilection for a pestilence. In the morning this
accomplished caravan, with the wood-fellers who directed their route,
halted on the edge of an extensive marsh, from whence so noxious a
vapour arose as would have destroyed any animal but Alboufaki, who

naturally inhaled these malignant fogs. The peasants entreated their
convoy not to sleep in this place.

'To sleep,' cried Carathis. 'What an excellent thought! I never
sleep but for visions; and, as to my attendants, their occupations are
too many to close the only eye they each have.'

The poor peasants, who were not over-pleased with their party,
remained open-mouthed with surprise.

Carathis alighted, as well as her negresses, and severally stripping
off their outer garments, they all ran in their drawers, to cull from
those spots where the sun shone fiercest the venomous plants that
grew on the marsh; this provision was made for the family of the
Emir, and whoever might retard the expedition to Istakar. The
woodmen were overcome with fear when they beheld these three
horrible phantoms run, and, not much relishing the company of
Alboufaki, stood aghast at the command of Carathis to set forward,
notwithstanding it was noon, and the heat fierce enough to calcine
even rocks. In spite, however, of every remonstrance, they were
forced implicitly to submit.

Alboufaki, who delighted in solitude, constantly snorted whenever
he perceived himself near a habitation; and Carathis, who was apt to
spoil him with indulgence, as constantly turned him aside, so that the
peasants were precluded from procuring subsistence; for the milch
goats and ewes, which Providence had sent towards the district they
traversed, to refresh travellers with their milk, all fled at the sight of
the hideous animal and his strange riders. As to Carathis, she needed
no common aliment, for her invention had previously furnished her
with an opiate to stay her stomach, some of which she imparted to
her mutes.

At dusk Alboufaki, making a sudden stop, stamped with his foot,
which to Carathis, who understood his paces, was a certain indication
that she was near the confines of some cemetery. The moon shed a
bright light on the spot, which served to discover a long wall, with a
large door in it standing ajar, and so high that Alboufaki might easily
enter. The miserable guides, who perceived their end approaching,
humbly implored Carathis, as she had now so good an opportunity, to
inter them, and immediately gave up the ghost. Nerkes and Cafour,
whose wit was of a style peculiar to themselves, were by no means
parsimonious of it on the folly of these poor people, nor could anything have been found more suited to their tastes than the site of the
burying-ground, and the sepulchres which its precincts contained;
there were at least two thousand of them on the declivity of a hill:

some in the form of pyramids, others like columns, and, in short, the variety of their shapes was endless. Carathis was too much immersed in her sublime contemplations to stop at the view, charming as it appeared in her eyes; pondering the advantages that might accrue from her present situation, she said to herself: 'So beautiful a cemetery must be haunted by ghouls! And they want not for intelligence; having heedlessly suffered my guides to expire, I will apply for directions to them, and as an inducement will invite them to regale on these fresh corpses.' After this wise soliloquy she beckoned to Nerkes and Cafour, and made signs with her fingers, as much as to say, 'Go, knock against the sides of the tombs, and strike up your delightful warblings.'

The negresses, full of joy at the behests of their mistress, and promising themselves much pleasure from the society of the ghouls, went with an air of conquest, and began their knockings at the tombs; as their strokes were repeated a hollow noise was heard in the earth, the surface hove up into heaps, and the ghouls on all sides protruded their noses, to inhale the effluvia which the carcases of the woodmen began to emit.

They assembled before a sarcophagus of white marble, where Carathis was seated between the bodies of her miserable guides; the princess received her visitants with distinguished politeness, and, when supper was ended, proceeded with them to business. Having soon learnt from them everything she wished to discover, it was her intention to set forward forthwith on her journey, but her negresses, who were forming tender connections with the ghouls, importuned her with all their fingers to wait at least till the dawn. Carathis, however, being chastity in the abstract, and an implacable enemy to love and repose, at once rejected their prayer, mounted Alboufaki, and commanded them to take their seats in a moment; four days and four nights she continued her route, without turning to the right hand or left; on the fifth she traversed the mountains and half-burnt forests, and arrived on the sixth before the beautiful screens which concealed from all eyes the voluptuous wanderings of her son.

It was daybreak, and the guards were snoring on their posts in careless security, when the rough trot of Alboufaki awoke them in consternation. Imagining that a group of spectres ascended from the abyss was approaching, they all without ceremony took to their heels. Vathek was at that instant with Nouronihar in the bath, hearing tales, and laughing at Bababalouk, who related them; but no sooner did the outcry of his guards reach him, than he flounced from the water like a carp, and as soon threw himself back at the sight of Carathis, who, advancing with her negresses upon Albou-faki, broke through the muslin awnings and veils of the pavilion; at this sudden apparition Nouronihar (for she was not at all times free from remorse) fancied that the moment of celestial vengeance was come, and clung about the Caliph in amorous despondence.

Carathis, still seated on her camel, foamed with indignation at the spectacle which obtruded itself on her chaste view; she thundered forth without check or mercy: 'Thou double-headed and four-legged monster! What means all this winding and writhing? Art thou not ashamed to be seen grasping this limber sapling, in preference to the sceptre of the pre-Adamite sultans? Is it then for this paltry doxy that thou hast violated the conditions in the parchment of our Giaour? Is it on her thou hast lavished thy precious moments? Is this the fruit of the knowledge I have taught thee? Is this the end of thy journey? Tear thyself from the arms of this little simpleton, drown her in the water before me, and instantly follow my guidance.'

In the first ebullition of his fury Vathek resolved to rip open the body of Alboufaki, and to stuff it with those of the negresses and Carathis herself; but the remembrance of the Giaour, the palace of Istakar, the sabres and the talismans, flashing before his imagination with the simultaneousness of lightning, he became more moderate, and said to his mother, in a civil but decisive tone: 'Dread lady! you shall be obeyed, but I will not drown Nouronihar; she is sweeter to me than a Myrabolan comfit, and is enamoured of carbuncles, especially that of Giamschid, which hath also been promised to be conferred upon her; she therefore shall go along with us, for I intend to repose with her beneath the canopies of Soliman; I can sleep no more without her.'

'Be it so!' replied Carathis, alighting, and at the same time committing Alboufaki to the charge of her women.

Nouronihar, who had not yet quitted her hold, began to take courage, and said, with an accent of fondness to the Caliph: 'Dear Sovereign of my soul! I will follow thee, if it be thy will, beyond the Kaf in the land of the afrits; I will not hesitate to climb for thee the nest of the Simurgh, who, this lady excepted, is the most awful of created beings.'

'We have here then,' subjoined Carathis, 'a girl both of courage and science!'

Nouronihar had certainly both; but, notwithstanding all her firmness, she could not help casting back a look of regret upon the graces

of her little Gulchenrouz, and the days of tenderness she had participated with him; she even dropped a few tears (which Carathis
observed), and inadvertently breathed out with a sigh: 'Alas! my
gentle cousin! What will become of thee?'

Vathek at this apostrophe knitted up his brows, and Carathis enquired what it could mean.

'She is preposterously sighing after a stripling with languishing
eyes and soft hair, who loves her,' said the Caliph.

'Where is he?' asked Carathis. 'I must be acquainted with this pretty
child; for,' added she, lowering her voice, 'I design before I depart to
regain the favour of the Giaour; there is nothing so delicious in his
estimation as the heart of a delicate boy, palpitating with the first
tumults of love.'

Vathek, as he came from the bath, commanded Bababalouk to
collect the women and other movables of his harem, embody his
troops, and hold himself in readiness to march in three days; whilst
Carathis retired alone to a tent, where the Giaour solaced her with
encouraging visions; but at length waking, she found at her feet
Nerkes and Cafour, who informed her by their signs that, having led
Alboufaki to the borders of a lake, to browse on some moss that
looked tolerably venomous, they had discovered certain blue fishes
of the same kind with those in the reservoir on the top of the tower.

'Ah! ha!' said she, 'I will go thither to them; these fish are past
doubt of a species that, by a small operation, I can render oracular;
they may tell me where this little Gulchenrouz is, whom I am bent
upon sacrificing.' Having thus spoken, she immediately set out with
her swarthy retinue.

It being but seldom that time is lost in the accomplishment of
a wicked enterprise, Carathis and her negresses soon arrived at the
lake, where, after burning the magical drugs with which they were
always provided, they stripped themselves naked, and waded to their
chins, Nerkes and Cafour waving torches around them, and Carathis
pronouncing her barbarous incantations. The fishes with one accord
thrust forth their heads from the water, which was violently rippled by
the flutter of their fins, and, at length finding themselves constrained
by the potency of the charm, they opened their piteous mouths, and
said: 'From gills to tail we are yours; what seek ye to know?'

'Fishes,' answered she, 'I conjure you, by your glittering scales, tell
me where now is Gulchenrouz?'

'Beyond the rock,' replied the shoal in full chorus. 'Will this content you? For we do not delight in expanding our mouths.'

'It will,' returned the princess. 'I am not to learn that you like not long conversations; I will leave you therefore to repose, though I had other questions to propound.'

The instant she had spoken the water became smooth, and the fishes at once disappeared.

Carathis, inflated with the venom of her projects, strode hastily over the rock, and found the amiable Gulchenrouz asleep in an arbour, whilst the two dwarfs were watching at his side, and ruminating their accustomed prayers. These diminutive personages possessed the gift of divining whenever an enemy to good Mussulmans approached; thus they anticipated the arrival of Carathis, who, stopping short, said to herself: 'How placidly doth he recline his lovely little head! how pale and languishing are his looks! It is just the very child of my wishes!'

The dwarfs interrupted this delectable soliloquy by leaping instantly upon her, and scratching her face with their utmost zeal. But Nerkes and Cafour, betaking themselves to the succour of their mistress, pinched the dwarfs so severely in return, that they both gave up the ghost, imploring Mahomet to inflict his sorest vengeance upon this wicked woman and all her household.

At the noise which this strange conflict occasioned in the valley, Gulchenrouz awoke, and, bewildered with terror, sprung impetuously upon an old fig tree that rose against the acclivity of the rocks; from thence gained their summits, and ran for two hours without once looking back. At last, exhausted with fatigue, he fell as if dead into the arms of a good old Genius, whose fondness for the company of children had made it his sole occupation to protect them, and who, whilst performing his wonted rounds through the air, happening on the cruel Giaour at the instant of his growling in the horrible chasm, rescued the fifty little victims which the impiety of Vathek had devoted to his maw; these the Genius brought up in nests still higher than the clouds, and himself fixed his abode in a nest more capacious than the rest, from which he had expelled the rocs that had built it.

These inviolable asylums were defended against the dives and the afrits by waving streamers, on which were inscribed, in characters of gold that flashed like lightning, the names of Allah and the Prophet. It was there that Gulchenrouz, who as yet remained undeceived with respect to his pretended death, thought himself in the mansions of eternal peace; he admitted without fear the congratulations of his little friends, who were all assembled in the nest of the venerable Genius, and vied with each other in kissing his serene forehead and beautiful eyelids. This he found to be the state congenial to his soul; remote from the inquietudes of earth, the impertinence of harems, the brutality of eunuchs, and the lubricity of women: in this peaceable society, his days, months, and years glided on; nor was he less happy than the rest of his companions; for the Genius, instead of burthening his pupils with perishable riches and the vain sciences of the world, conferred upon them the boon of perpetual childhood.

Carathis, unaccustomed to the loss of her prey, vented a thousand execrations on her negresses for not seizing the child, instead of amusing themselves with pinching to death the dwarfs, from which they could gain no advantage. She returned into the valley murmuring, and finding that her son was not risen from the arms of Nouronihar, discharged her ill-humour upon both. The idea, however, of departing next day for Istakar, and cultivating, through the good offices of the Giaour, an intimacy with Eblis himself, at length consoled her chagrin. But Fate had ordained it otherwise.

In the evening, as Carathis was conversing with Dilara, who, through her contrivance, had become of the party, and whose taste resembled her own, Bababalouk came to acquaint her 'that the sky towards Samarah looked of a fiery red, and seemed to portend some alarming disaster.' Immediately recurring to her astrolabes and instruments of magic, she took the altitude of the planets, and discovered by her calculations, to her great mortification, that a formidable revolt had taken place at Samarah; that Motavakel, availing himself of the disgust which was inveterate against his brother, had incited commotions amongst the populace, made himself master of the palace, and actually invested the great tower, to which Morakanabad had retired, with a handful of the few that still remained faithful to Vathek.

'What!' exclaimed she. 'Must I lose then my tower! my mutes! my negresses! my mummies! and, worse than all, the laboratory in which I have spent so many a night, without knowing at least if my hairbrained son will complete his adventure? No! I will not be the dupe! Immediately will I speed to support Morakanabad; by my formidable art the clouds shall sleet hailstones in the faces of the assailants, and shafts of red-hot iron on their heads; I will spring mines of serpents and torpedos from beneath them, and we shall soon see the stand they will make against such an explosion!'

Having thus spoken, Carathis hastened to her son, who was tranquilly banqueting with Nouronihar in his superb carnation-coloured tent. 'Glutton that thou art!' cried she. 'Were it not for me, thou

wouldst soon find thyself the commander only of pies. Thy faithful
subjects have abjured the faith they swore to thee; Motavakel, thy
brother, now reigns on the Hill of Pied Horses, and had I not some
slight resources in the tower, would not be easily persuaded to ab-
dicate; but, that time may not be lost, I shall only add a few words:
Strike tent tonight, set forward, and beware how thou loiterest again
by the way; though thou hast forfeited the conditions of the parchment, I am not yet without hope; for it cannot be denied that thou
hast violated, to admiration, the laws of hospitality, by seducing the
daughter of the Emir, after having partaken of his bread and his salt.
Such a conduct cannot but be delightful to the Giaour; and if on thy
march thou canst signalise thyself by an additional crime, all will still
go well, and thou shalt enter the palace of Soliman in triumph.
Adieu! Alboufaki and my negresses are waiting at the door.'

The Caliph had nothing to offer in reply; he wished his mother a
prosperous journey, and ate on till he had finished his supper. At
midnight the camp broke up, amidst the flourishing of trumpets and
other martial instruments; but loud indeed must have been the sound
of the tymbals to overpower the blubbering of the Emir and his long-
beards, who, by an excessive profusion of tears, had so far exhausted
the radical moisture, that their eyes shrivelled up in their sockets, and
their hairs dropped off by the roots. Nouronihar, to whom such a
symphony was painful, did not grieve to get out of hearing; she
accompanied the Caliph in the imperial litter, where they amused
themselves with imagining the splendour which was soon to surround
them. The other women, overcome with dejection, were dolefully
rocked in their cages, whilst Dilara consoled herself with anticipating
the joy of celebrating the rites of fire on the stately terraces of Istakar.

In four days they reached the spacious valley of Rocnabad. The
season of spring was in all its vigour, and the grotesque branches of
the almond trees in full blossom fantastically chequered the clear
blue sky; the earth, variegated with hyacinths and jonquils, breathed
forth a fragrance which diffused through the soul a divine repose;
myriads of bees, and scarce fewer of santons, had there taken up
their abode; on the banks of the stream hives and oratories were
alternately ranged, and their neatness and whiteness were set off by
the deep green of the cypresses that spired up amongst them. These
pious personages amused themselves with cultivating little gardens
that abounded with flowers and fruits, especially musk-melons of the
best flavour that Persia could boast; sometimes, dispersed over the
meadow, they entertained themselves with feeding peacocks whiter

than snow, and turtles more blue than the sapphire; in this manner were they occupied when the harbingers of the imperial procession began to proclaim: 'Inhabitants of Rocnabad! prostrate yourselves on the brink of your pure waters, and tender your thanksgivings to Heaven, that vouchsafeth to show you a ray of its glory; for lo! the Commander of the Faithful draws near.'

The poor santons, filled with holy energy, having bustled to light up wax torches in their oratories and expand the Koran on their ebony desks, went forth to meet the Caliph with baskets of honey-comb, dates, and melons. But, whilst they were advancing in solemn procession and with measured steps, the horses, camels, and guards wantoned over their tulips and other flowers, and made a terrible havoc amongst them. The santons could not help casting from one eye a look of pity on the ravages committing around them, whilst the other was fixed upon the Caliph and heaven. Nouronihar, enraptured with the scenery of a place which brought back to her remembrance the pleasing solitudes where her infancy had passed, entreated Vathek to stop; but he, suspecting that each oratory might be deemed by the Giaour a distinct habitation, commanded his pioneers to level them all; the santons stood motionless with horror at the barbarous man-date, and at last broke out into lamentations; but these were uttered with so ill a grace, that Vathek bade his eunuchs to kick them from his presence. He then descended from the litter with Nouronihar; they sauntered together in the meadow, and amused themselves with culling flowers, and passing a thousand pleasantries on each other. But the bees, who were staunch Mussulmans, thinking it their duty to revenge the insult on their dear masters the santons, assembled so zealously to do it with effect, that the Caliph and Nouronihar were glad to find their tents prepared to receive them.

Bababalouk, who in capacity of purveyor had acquitted himself with applause as to peacocks and turtles, lost no time in consigning some dozens to the spit, and as many more to be fricasseed. Whilst they were feasting, laughing, carousing, and blaspheming at pleasure on the banquet so liberally furnished, the mullahs, the sheiks, the cadis and imams of Schiraz (who seemed not to have met the santons) arrived, leading by bridles of riband inscribed from the Koran, a train of asses, which were loaded with the choicest fruits the country could boast; having presented their offerings to the Caliph, they petitioned him to honour their city and mosques with his presence.

'Fancy not,' said Vathek, 'that you can detain me; your presents I condescend to accept, but beg you will let me be quiet, for I am not

over-fond of resisting temptation; retire, then; yet, as it is not decent
for personages so reverend to return on foot, and as you have not the
appearance of expert riders, my eunuchs shall tie you on your asses,
with the precaution that your backs be not turned towards me, for
they understand etiquette.'

In this deputation were some high-stomached sheiks, who, taking
Vathek for a fool, scrupled not to speak their opinion. These Bababalouk girded with double cords, and, having well disciplined their
asses with nettles behind, they all started with a preternatural alertness, plunging, kicking, and running foul of each other in the most
ludicrous manner imaginable.

Nouronihar and the Caliph mutually contended who should most
enjoy so degrading a sight; they burst out in volleys of laughter to see
the old men and their asses fall into the stream; the leg of one was
fractured, the shoulder of another dislocated, the teeth of a third
dashed out, and the rest suffered still worse.

Two days more, undisturbed by fresh embassies, having been
devoted to the pleasures of Rocnabad, the expedition proceeded,
leaving Shiraz on the right, and verging towards a large plain, from
whence were discernible on the edge of the horizon the dark summits of the mountains of Istakar.

At this prospect the Caliph and Nouronihar were unable to repress
their transports; they bounded from their litter to the ground, and
broke forth into such wild exclamations, as amazed all within hearing.
Interrogating each other, they shouted, 'Are we not approaching the
radiant palace of light? Or gardens more delightful than those of
Sheddad?' Infatuated mortals! They thus indulged delusive conjecture,
unable to fathom the decrees of the Most High!

The good Genii, who had not totally relinquished the superin-
tendence of Vathek, repairing to Mahomet in the seventh heaven,
said: 'Merciful Prophet! stretch forth thy propitious arms towards
thy vicegerent, who is ready to fall irretrievably into the snare
which his enemies, the dives, have prepared to destroy him; the
Giaour is awaiting his arrival in the abominable palace of fire,
where, if he once set his foot, his perdition will be inevitable.'

Mahomet answered with an air of indignation: 'He hath too well
deserved to be resigned to himself, but I permit you to try if one
effort more will be effectual to divert him from pursuing his ruin.'

One of these beneficent Genii, assuming without delay the exterior
of a shepherd, more renowned for his piety than all the dervishes and
santons of the region, took his station near a flock of white sheep on

the slope of a hill, and began to pour forth from his flute such airs of pathetic melody as subdued the very soul, and, awakening remorse, drove far from it every frivolous fancy. At these energetic sounds the sun hid himself beneath a gloomy cloud, and the waters of two little lakes, that were naturally clearer than crystal, became of a colour like blood. The whole of this superb assembly was involuntarily drawn towards the declivity of the hill; with downcast eyes they all stood abashed, each upbraiding himself with the evil he had done; the heart of Dilara palpitated, and the chief of the eunuchs with a sigh of contrition implored pardon of the women, whom for his own satisfaction he had so often tormented.

Vathek and Nouronihar turned pale in their litter, and, regarding each other with haggard looks, reproached themselves – the one with a thousand of the blackest crimes, a thousand projects of impious ambition – the other with the desolation of her family, and the perdition of the amiable Gulchenrouz. Nouronihar persuaded herself that she heard in the fatal music the groans of her dying father, and Vathek the sobs of the fifty children he had sacrificed to the Giaour. Amidst these complicated pangs of anguish they perceived themselves impelled towards the shepherd, whose countenance was so commanding, that Vathek for the first time felt overawed, whilst Nouronihar concealed her face with her hands.

The music paused, and the Genius, addressing the Caliph, said: 'Deluded prince! to whom Providence hath confided the care of innumerable subjects, is it thus that thou fulfillest thy mission? Thy crimes are already completed, and art thou now hastening towards thy punishment? Thou knowest that beyond these mountains Eblis and his accursed dives hold their infernal empire; and, seduced by a malignant phantom, thou art proceeding to surrender thyself to them! This moment is the last of grace allowed thee; abandon thy atrocious purpose; return; give back Nouronihar to her father, who still retains a few sparks of life; destroy thy tower with all its abominations; drive Carathis from thy councils; be just to thy subjects; respect the ministers of the Prophet; compensate for thy impieties by an exemplary life; and, instead of squandering thy days in voluptuous indulgence, lament thy crimes on the sepulchres of thy ancestors. Thou beholdest the clouds that obscure the sun; at the instant he recovers his splendour, if thy heart be not changed, the time of mercy assigned thee will be passed for ever.'

Vathek, depressed with fear, was on the point of prostrating himself at the feet of the shepherd, whom he perceived to be of a nature

superior to man; but, his pride prevailing, he audaciously lifted his
head, and, glancing at him one of his terrible looks, said: 'Whoever
thou art, withhold thy useless admonitions; thou wouldst either
delude me, or art thyself deceived. If what I have done be so criminal
as thou pretendest, there remains not for me a moment of grace; I
have traversed a sea of blood to acquire a power which will make
thy equals tremble; deem not that I shall retire when in view of the
port, or that I will relinquish her who is dearer to me than either my
life or thy mercy. Let the sun appear! Let him illumine my career!
It matters not where it may end.' On uttering these words, which
made even the Genius shudder, Vathek threw himself into the arms
of Nouronihar, and commanded that his horse should be forced
back to the road.

There was no difficulty in obeying these orders, for the attraction
had ceased; the sun shone forth in all his glory, and the shepherd
vanished with a lamentable scream.

The fatal impression of the music of the Genius remained, notwithstanding, in the heart of Vathek's attendants; they viewed each
other with looks of consternation; at the approach of night almost
all of them escaped, and of this numerous assemblage there only
remained the chief of the eunuchs, some idolatrous slaves, Dilara and
a few other women, who, like herself, were votaries of the religion
of the Magi.

The Caliph, fired with the ambition of prescribing laws to the
Intelligences of Darkness, was but little embarrassed at this dereliction; the impetuosity of his blood prevented him from sleeping,
nor did he encamp any more as before. Nouronihar, whose impatience, if possible, exceeded his own, importuned him to hasten
his march, and lavished on him a thousand caresses to beguile all
reflection; she fancied herself already more potent than Balkis,
and pictured to her imagination the Genii falling prostrate at the
foot of her throne. In this manner they advanced by moonlight, till
they came within view of the two towering rocks that form a kind
of portal to the valley, at whose extremity rose the vast ruins of
Istakar. Aloft on the mountain glimmered the fronts of various
royal mausoleums, the horror of which was deepened by the shadows of night. They passed through two villages almost deserted, the
only inhabitants remaining being a few feeble old men, who, at the
sight of horses and litters, fell upon their knees and cried out: 'O
Heaven! is it then by these phantoms that we have been for six
months tormented? Alas! it was from the terror of these spectres

and the noise beneath the mountains, that our people have fled, and left us at the mercy of maleficent spirits!'

The Caliph, to whom these complaints were but unpromising auguries, drove over the bodies of these wretched old men, and at length arrived at the foot of the terrace of black marble; there he descended from his litter, handing down Nouronihar; both with beating hearts stared wildly around them, and expected with an apprehensive shudder the approach of the Giaour; but nothing as yet announced his appearance.

A death-like stillness reigned over the mountain and through the air; the moon dilated on a vast platform the shades of the lofty columns, which reached from the terrace almost to the clouds; the gloomy watch-towers, whose numbers could not be counted, were veiled by no roof, and their capitals, of an architecture unknown in the records of the earth, served as an asylum for the birds of darkness, which, alarmed at the approach of such visitants, fled away croaking.

The chief of the eunuchs, trembling with fear, besought Vathek that a fire might be kindled.

'No!' replied he, 'there is no time left to think of such trifles; abide where thou art, and expect my commands.'

Having thus spoken, he presented his hand to Nouronihar, and, ascending the steps of a vast staircase, reached the terrace, which was flagged with squares of marble, and resembled a smooth expanse of water, upon whose surface not a leaf ever dared to vegetate; on the right rose the watch-towers, ranged before the ruins of an immense palace, whose walls were embossed with various figures; in front stood forth the colossal forms of four creatures, composed of the leopard and the griffin; and, though but of stone, inspired emotions of terror; near these were distinguished by the splendour of the moon, which streamed full on the place, characters like those on the sabres of the Giaour, that possessed the same virtue of changing every moment; these, after vacillating for some time, at last fixed in Arabic letters, and prescribed to the Caliph the following words.

'Vathek! thou hast violated the conditions of my parchment, and deservest to be sent back; but, in favour to thy companion, and as the meed for what thou hast done to obtain it, Eblis permitteth that the portal of his palace shall be opened, and the subterranean fire will receive thee into the number of its adorers.'

He scarcely had read these words before the mountain against which the terrace was reared trembled, and the watch-towers were ready to topple headlong upon them; the rock yawned, and disclosed

within it a staircase of polished marble that seemed to approach
the abyss; upon each stair were planted two large torches, like
those Nouronihar had seen in her vision, the camphorated vapour
ascending from which gathered into a cloud under the hollow of
the vault.

This appearance, instead of terrifying, gave new courage to the
daughter of Fakreddin. Scarcely deigning to bid adieu to the moon
and the firmament, she abandoned without hesitation the pure
atmosphere to plunge into these infernal exhalations. The gait of
those impious personages was haughty and determined; as they
descended by the effulgence of the torches they gazed on each
other with mutual admiration, and both appeared so resplendent,
that they already esteemed themselves spiritual Intelligences; the
only circumstance that perplexed them was their not arriving at the
bottom of the stairs; on hastening their descent with an ardent
impetuosity, they felt their steps accelerated to such a degree, that
they seemed not walking, but falling from a precipice. Their progress, however, was at length impeded by a vast portal of ebony,
which the Caliph without difficulty recognised; here the Giaour
awaited them with the key in his hand.

'Ye are welcome,' said he to them, with a ghastly smile, 'in spite
of Mahomet and all his dependants. I will now admit you into that
palace where you have so highly merited a place.' Whilst he was
uttering these words he touched the enamelled lock with his key,
and the doors at once expanded, with a noise still louder than the
thunder of mountains, and as suddenly recoiled the moment they
had entered.

The Caliph and Nouronihar beheld each other with amazement,
at finding themselves in a place which, though roofed with a vaulted
ceiling, was so spacious and lofty that at first they took it for an
immeasurable plain. But their eyes at length growing familiar to the
grandeur of the objects at hand, they extended their view to those
at a distance, and discovered rows of columns and arcades, which
gradually diminished till they terminated in a point, radiant as the
sun when he darts his last beams athwart the ocean; the pavement,
strewed over with gold dust and saffron, exhaled so subtle an odour
as almost overpowered them; they, however, went on, and observed
an infinity of censers, in which ambergris and the wood of aloes
were continually burning; between the several columns were placed
tables, each spread with a profusion of viands, and wines of every
species sparkling in vases of crystal. A throng of Genii and other

fantastic spirits of each sex danced lasciviously at the sound of music which issued from beneath.

In the midst of this immense hall a vast multitude was incessantly passing, who severally kept their right hands on their hearts, without once regarding anything around them; they had all the livid paleness of death; their eyes, deep sunk in their sockets, resembled those phosphoric meteors that glimmer by night in places of interment. Some stalked slowly on, absorbed in profound reverie; some, shrieking with agony, ran furiously about, like tigers wounded with poisoned arrows; whilst others, grinding their teeth in rage, foamed along, more frantic than the wildest maniac. They all avoided each other, and, though surrounded by a multitude that no one could number, each wandered at random, unheedful of the rest, as if alone on a desert which no foot had trodden.

Vathek and Nouronihar, frozen with terror at a sight so baleful, demanded of the Giaour what these appearances might mean, and why these ambulating spectres never withdrew their hands from their hearts.

'Perplex not yourselves,' replied he bluntly, 'with so much at once. You will soon be acquainted with all; let us haste and present you to Eblis.'

They continued their way through the multitude but, notwithstanding their confidence at first, they were not sufficiently composed to examine with attention the various perspectives of halls and of galleries that opened on the right hand and left, which were all illuminated by torches and braziers, whose flames rose in pyramids to the centre of the vault. At length they came to a place where long curtains, brocaded with crimson and gold, fell from all parts in striking confusion; here the choirs and dances were heard no longer; the light which glimmered came from afar.

After some time Vathek and Nouronihar perceived a gleam brightening through the drapery, and entered a vast tabernacle carpeted with the skins of leopards; an infinity of elders with streaming beards, and afrits in complete armour, had prostrated themselves before the ascent of a lofty eminence, on the top of which, upon a globe of fire, sat the formidable Eblis. His person was that of a young man, whose noble and regular features seemed to have been tarnished by malignant vapours; in his large eyes appeared both pride and despair; his flowing hair retained some resemblance to that of an angel of light; in his hand, which thunder had blasted, he swayed the iron sceptre that causes the monster Ouranabad, the afrits, and all the powers of the abyss to tremble; at his presence the heart of the Caliph sank within him, and for the first time he fell prostrate on his face.

Nouronihar, however, though greatly dismayed, could not help admiring the person of Eblis; for she expected to have seen some stupendous giant. Eblis, with a voice more mild than might be imagined, but such as transfused through the soul the deepest melancholy, said: 'Creatures of clay, I receive you into mine empire; ye are numbered amongst my adorers; enjoy whatever this palace affords; the treasures of the pre-Adamite sultans, their bickering sabres, and those talismans that compel the dives to open the subterranean expanses of the mountain of Kaf, which communicate with these; there, insatiable as your curiosity may be, shall you find sufficient to gratify it; you shall possess the exclusive privilege of entering the fortress of Aherman, and the halls of Argenk, where are portrayed all creatures endowed with intelligence, and the various animals that inhabited the earth prior to the creation of that contemptible being whom ye denominate the Father of Mankind.'

Vathek and Nouronihar, feeling themselves revived and encouraged by this harangue, eagerly said to the Giaour: 'Bring us instantly to the place which contains these precious talismans.'

'Come!' answered this wicked dive, with his malignant grin. 'Come! and possess all that my sovereign hath promised, and more.'

He then conducted them into a long aisle adjoining the tabernacle, preceding them with hasty steps, and followed by his disciples with the utmost alacrity. They reached, at length, a hall of great extent, and covered with a lofty dome, around which appeared fifty portals of bronze, secured with as many fastenings of iron; a funereal gloom prevailed over the whole scene; here, upon two beds of incorruptible cedar, lay recumbent the fleshless forms of the pre-Adamite kings, who had been monarchs of the whole earth; they still possessed enough of life to be conscious of their deplorable condition; their eyes retained a melancholy motion; they regarded each other with looks of the deepest dejection, each holding his right hand motionless on his heart; at their feet were inscribed the events of their several reigns, their power, their pride, and their crimes: Soliman Raad, Soliman Daki, and Soliman Di Gian Ben Gian, who, after having chained up the dives in the dark caverns of Kaf, became so presumptuous as to doubt of the Supreme Power; all these maintained great state, though not to be compared with the eminence of Soliman Ben Daoud.

This king, so renowned for his wisdom, was on the loftiest elevation, and placed immediately under the dome; he appeared to
possess more animation than the rest; though from time to time he
laboured with profound sighs, and, like his companions, kept his
right hand on his heart; yet his countenance was more composed,
and he seemed to be listening to the sullen roar of a vast cataract,
visible in part through the grated portals: this was the only sound
that intruded on the silence of these doleful mansions. A range of
broken cases surrounded the elevation.

'Remove the covers from these cabalistic depositories,' said the
Giaour to Vathek, 'and avail thyself of the talismans, which will
break asunder all these gates of bronze; and not only render thee
master of the treasures contained within them, but also of the spirits
by which they are guarded.'

The Caliph, whom this ominous preliminary had entirely discon-
certed, approached the vases with faltering footsteps, and was ready
to sink with terror when he heard the groans of Soliman. As he
proceeded a voice from the livid lips of the Prophet articulated
these words: 'In my lifetime I filled a magnificent throne, having on
my right hand twelve thousand seats of gold, where the patriarchs
and the prophets heard my doctrines; on my left the sages and
doctors, upon as many thrones of silver, were present at all my
decisions. Whilst I thus administered justice to innumerable multi-
tudes, the birds of the air hovering over me served as a canopy from
the rays of the sun; my people flourished, and my palace rose to the
clouds; I erected a temple to the Most High, which was the wonder
of the universe; but I basely suffered myself to be seduced by the
love of women, and a curiosity that could not be restrained by
sublunary things; I listened to the counsels of Aherman and the
daughter of Pharaoh, and adored fire and the hosts of heaven;
I forsook the holy city, and commanded the Genii to rear the
stupendous palace of Istakar, and the terrace of the watch-towers,
each of which was consecrated to a star; there for a while I enjoyed
myself in the zenith of glory and pleasure; not only men, but supernatural existences were subject also to my will. I began to think,
as these unhappy monarchs around had already thought, that the
vengeance of Heaven was asleep, when at once the thunder burst
my structures asunder and precipitated me hither; where, however,
I do not remain, like the other inhabitants, totally destitute of hope,
for an angel of light hath revealed that, in consideration of the piety
of my early youth, my woes shall come to an end when this cataract

shall for ever cease to flow; till then I am in torments, ineffable torments! An unrelenting fire preys on my heart.'

Having uttered this exclamation, Soliman raised his hands towards heaven, in token of supplication, and the Caliph discerned through his bosom, which was transparent as crystal, his heart enveloped in flames. At a sight so full of horror Nouronihar fell back, like one petrified, into the arms of Vathek, who cried out with a convulsive sob: 'O Giaour! whither hast thou brought us? Allow us to depart, and I will relinquish all thou hast promised. O Mahomet! remains there no more mercy?'

'None! none!' replied the malicious dive. 'Know, miserable prince! thou art now in the abode of vengeance and despair; thy heart also will be kindled, like those of the other votaries of Eblis. A few days are allotted thee previous to this fatal period; employ them as thou wilt; recline on these heaps of gold; command the infernal potentates; range at thy pleasure through these immense subterr- anean domains; no barrier shall be shut against thee; as for me, I have fulfilled my mission; I now leave thee to thyself.' At these words he vanished.

The Caliph and Nouronihar remained in the most abject affliction; their tears unable to flow, scarcely could they support themselves. At length, taking each other despondingly by the hand, they went faltering from this fatal hall, indifferent which way they turned their steps; every portal opened at their approach; the dives fell prostrate before them; every reservoir of riches was disclosed to their view; but they no longer felt the incentives of curiosity, pride, or avarice. With like apathy they heard the chorus of Genii, and saw the stately banquets prepared to regale them; they went wandering on from chamber to chamber, hall to hall, and gallery to gallery, all without bounds or limit, all distinguishable by the same lowering gloom, all adorned with the same awful grandeur, all traversed by persons in search of repose and consolation, but who sought them in vain; for everyone carried within him a heart tormented in flames: shunned by these various sufferers, who seemed by their looks to be upbraiding the partners of their guilt, they withdrew from them to wait in direful suspense the moment which should render them to each other the like objects of terror.

'What!' exclaimed Nouronihar, 'will the time come when I shall snatch my hand from thine!'

'Ah!' said Vathek, 'and shall my eyes ever cease to drink from thine long draughts of enjoyment! Shall the moments of our reciprocal ecstasies be reflected on with horror? It was not thou that broughtest me hither; the principles by which Carathis perverted my youth have been the sole cause of my perdition!' Having given vent to these painful expressions, he called to an afrit, who was stirring up one of the braziers, and bade him fetch the Princess Carathis from the palace of Samarah.

After issuing these orders, the Caliph and Nouronihar continued walking amidst the silent crowd, till they heard voices at the end of the gallery; presuming them to proceed from some unhappy beings, who, like themselves, were awaiting their final doom, they followed the sound, and found it to come from a small square chamber, where they discovered sitting on sofas four young men of goodly figure, and a lovely female, who were all holding a melancholy conversation by the glimmering of a lonely lamp; each had a gloomy and forlorn air, and two of them were embracing each other with great tenderness.

On seeing the Caliph and the daughter of Fakreddin enter, they arose, saluted, and gave them place; then he who appeared the most considerable of the group addressed himself thus to Vathek: 'Strangers! who doubtless are in the same state of suspense with ourselves, as you do not yet bear your hands on your hearts, if you are come hither to pass the interval allotted previous to the infliction of our common punishment, condescend to relate the adventures that have brought you to this fatal place, and we in return will acquaint you with ours, which deserve but too well to be heard; we will trace back our crimes to their source, though we are not permitted to repent; this is the only employment suited to wretches like us!'

The Caliph and Nouronihar assented to the proposal, and Vathek began, not without tears and lamentations, a sincere recital of every circumstance that had passed. When the afflicting narrative was closed, the young man entered on his own. Each person proceeded in order, and when the fourth prince had reached the midst of his adventures, a sudden noise interrupted him, which caused the vault to tremble and to open.

Immediately a cloud descended, which gradually dissipating, discovered Carathis on the back of an afrit, who grievously complained of his burden. She, instantly springing to the ground, advanced towards her son, and said: 'What dost thou here in this little square chamber? As the dives are become subject to thy beck, I expected to have found thee on the throne of the pre-Adamite kings.'

'Execrable woman!' answered the Caliph. 'Cursed be the day thou gavest me birth! Go, follow this afrit; let him conduct thee to the hall of the Prophet Soliman; there thou wilt learn to what these palaces are destined, and how much I ought to abhor the impious knowledge thou hast taught me.'

'The height of power to which thou art arrived has certainly turned thy brain,' answered Carathis. 'But I ask no more than permission to show my respect for Soliman the Prophet. It is, however, proper thou shouldest know, that (as the afrit has informed me neither of us shall return to Samarah) I requested his permission to arrange my affairs, and he politely consented; availing myself, therefore, of the few moments allowed me, I set fire to the tower, and consumed in it the mutes, negresses, and serpents which have rendered me so much good service; nor should I have been less kind to Morakanabad, had he not prevented me by deserting at last to thy brother. As for Bababalouk, who had the folly to return to Samarah, to provide husbands for thy wives, I undoubtedly would have put him to the torture, could I but have allowed the time; being, however, in a hurry, I only hung him after having caught him in a snare with thy wives, whilst them I buried alive by the help of my negresses, who thus spent their last moments greatly to their satisfaction. With respect to Dilara, who ever stood high in my favour, she hath evinced the greatness of her mind by fixing herself near in the service of one of the Magi, and I think will soon be one of our society.'

Vathek, too much cast down to express the indignation excited by such a discourse, ordered the afrit to remove Carathis from his presence, and continued immersed in thought, which his companions durst not disturb.

Carathis, however, eagerly entered the dome of Soliman, and, without regarding in the least the groans of the Prophet, undauntedly removed the covers of the vases, and violently seized on the talismans; then, with a voice more loud than had hitherto been heard within these mansions, she compelled the dives to disclose to her the most secret treasures, the most profound stores, which the afrit himself had not seen; she passed by rapid descents, known only to Eblis and his most favoured potentates, and thus penetrated the very entrails of the earth, where breathes the Sansar, or icy wind of death; nothing appalled her dauntless soul; she perceived, however, in all the inmates who bore their hands on their hearts, a little singularity not much to her taste.

As she was emerging from one of the abysses, Eblis stood forth to her view; but, notwithstanding he displayed the full effulgence of his infernal majesty, she preserved her countenance unaltered, and even paid her compliments with considerable firmness.

This superb monarch thus answered: 'Princess, whose knowledge and whose crimes have merited a conspicuous rank in my empire, thou dost well to employ the leisure that remains; for the flames and torments, which are ready to seize on thy heart, will not fail to provide thee with full employment.' He said this, and was lost in the curtains of his tabernacle.

Carathis paused for a moment with surprise; but, resolved to follow the advice of Eblis, she assembled all the choirs of Genii, and all the dives, to pay her homage; thus marched she in triumph through a vapour of perfumes, amidst the acclamations of all the malignant spirits, with most of whom she had formed a previous acquaintance; she even attempted to dethrone one of the Solimans for the purpose of usurping his place, when a voice, proceeding from the abyss of Death, proclaimed, 'All is accomplished!' Instantaneously the haughty forehead of the intrepid princess was corrugated with agony; she uttered a tremendous yell, and fixed, no more to be withdrawn, her right hand upon her heart, which was become a receptacle of eternal fire.

In this delirium, forgetting all ambitious projects and her thirst for that knowledge which should ever be hidden from mortals, she overturned the offerings of the Genii, and, having execrated the hour she was begotten and the womb that had borne her, glanced off in a whirl that rendered her invisible, and continued to revolve without intermission.

At almost the same instant the same voice announced to the Caliph, Nouronihar, the four princes, and the princess, the awful and irrevocable decree. Their hearts immediately took fire, and they at once lost the most precious of the gifts of Heaven – hope. These unhappy beings recoiled with looks of the most furious distraction; Vathek beheld in the eyes of Nouronihar nothing but rage and vengeance, nor could she discern aught in his but aversion and despair. The two princes who were friends, and till that moment had preserved their attachment, shrank back, gnashing their teeth with mutual and unchangeable hatred. Kalilah and his sister made reciprocal gestures of imprecation, whilst the two other princes testified their horror for each other by the most ghastly convulsions, and screams that could not be smothered. All severally plunged themselves into the accursed multitude, there to wander in an eternity of unabating anguish.

Such was, and such should be, the punishment of unrestrained passions and atrocious actions! Such is, and such should be, the chastisement of blind ambition, that would transgress those bounds which the Creator hath prescribed to human knowledge; and, by aiming at discoveries reserved for beings of a supernatural order, acquire that infatuated pride which perceives not that the condition appointed to man is to be – humble and ignorant.

Thus the Caliph Vathek, who, for the sake of empty pomp and forbidden power, had sullied himself with a thousand crimes, became a prey to grief without end, and remorse without mitigation; whilst the humble and despised Gulchenrouz passed whole ages in undisturbed tranquillity, and the pure happiness of childhood.

NIGHTMARE ABBEY

There's a dark lantern of the spirit,
Which none see by but those who bear it,
That makes them in the dark see visions
And hag themselves with apparitions,
Find racks for their own minds, and vaunt
Of their own misery and want.

BUTLER

MATTHEW. Oh! it's your only fine humour, sir. Your true melancholy breeds your perfect fine wit, sir. I am melancholy myself, divers times, sir; and then do I no more but take pen and paper presently, and overflow you half a score or a dozen of sonnets at a sitting.

STEPHEN. Truly, sir, and I love such things out of measure.

MATTHEW. Why, I pray you, sir, make use of my study: it's at your service.

STEPHEN. I thank you, sir, I shall be bold, I warrant you. Have you a stool there, to be melancholy upon?

BEN JONSON, *Every Man in his Humour*, Act 3, Scene 1

Ay esleu gazouiller et siffler oye, comme dit le commun proverbe, entre les cygnes, plutoust que d'estre entre tant de gentils poëtes et faconds orateurs mut du tout estimé.

RABELAIS, *Prol. L.* 5

Chapter One

Nightmare Abbey, a venerable family-mansion, in a highly pictur-esque state of semi-dilapidation, pleasantly situated on a strip of dry land between the sea and the fens, at the verge of the county of Lincoln, had the honour to be the seat of Christopher Glowry, Esquire. This gentleman was naturally of an atrabilarious temperament, and much troubled with those phantoms of indigestion which are commonly called *blue devils*. He had been deceived in an early friendship: he had been crossed in love; and had offered his hand, from pique, to a lady, who accepted it from interest, and who, in so doing, violently tore asunder the bonds of a tried and youthful attachment. Her vanity was gratified by being the mistress of a very extensive, if not very lively, establishment; but all the springs of her sympathies were frozen. Riches she possessed, but that which enriches them, the participation of affection, was wanting. All that they could purchase for her became indifferent to her, because that which they could not purchase, and which was more valuable than themselves, she had, for their sake, thrown away. She discovered, when it was too late, that she had mistaken the means for the end – that riches, rightly used, are instruments of happiness, but are not in themselves happiness. In this wilful blight of her affections, she found them valueless as means: they had been the end to which she had immolated all her affections, and were now the only end that remained to her. She did not confess this to herself as a principle of action, but it operated through the medium of unconscious self-deception, and terminated in inveterate avarice. She laid on external things the blame of her mind's internal disorder, and thus became by degrees an accomplished scold. She often went her daily rounds through a series of deserted apartments, every creature in the house vanishing at the creak of her shoe, much more at the sound of her voice, to which the nature of things affords no simile; for, as far as the voice of woman, when attuned by gentleness and love, transcends all other sounds in harmony, so far does it surpass all others in discord, when stretched into unnatural shrillness by anger and impatience.

Mr Glowry used to say that his house was no better than a spacious kennel, for everyone in it led the life of a dog. Disappointed both in love and in friendship, and looking upon human learning as vanity, he had come to a conclusion that there was but one good thing in the world, *videlicet*, a good dinner; and this his parsimonious lady seldom suffered him to enjoy: but, one morning, like Sir Leoline in *Christabel*, 'he woke and found his lady dead', and remained a very consolate widower, with one small child.

This only son and heir Mr Glowry had christened Scythrop, from the name of a maternal ancestor, who had hanged himself one rainy day in a fit of *taedium vitae*, and had been eulogised by a coroner's jury in the comprehensive phrase of *felo de se*; on which account, Mr Glowry held his memory in high honour, and made a punchbowl of his skull.

When Scythrop grew up, he was sent, as usual, to a public school, where a little learning was painfully beaten into him, and from thence to the university, where it was carefully taken out of him; and he was sent home like a well-threshed ear of corn, with nothing in his head: having finished his education to the high satisfaction of the master and fellows of his college, who had, in testimony of their approbation, presented him with a silver fish-slice, on which his name figured at the head of a laudatory inscription in some semi-barbarous dialect of Anglo-Saxonised Latin.

His fellow-students, however, who drove tandem and random in great perfection, and were connoisseurs in good inns, had taught him to drink deep ere he departed. He had passed much of his time with these choice spirits, and had seen the rays of the midnight lamp tremble on many a lengthening file of empty bottles. He passed his vacations sometimes at Nightmare Abbey, sometimes in London, at the house of his uncle, Mr Hilary, a very cheerful and elastic gentleman, who had married the sister of the melancholy Mr Glowry. The company that frequented his house was the gayest of the gay. Scythrop danced with the ladies and drank with the gentlemen, and was pronounced by both a very accomplished charming fellow, and an honour to the university.

At the house of Mr Hilary, Scythrop first saw the beautiful Miss Emily Girouette. He fell in love; which is nothing new. He was favourably received; which is nothing strange. Mr Glowry and Mr Girouette had a meeting on the occasion, and quarrelled about the terms of the bargain; which is neither new nor strange. The lovers were torn asunder, weeping and vowing everlasting constancy; and, in three weeks after this tragical event, the lady was led a smiling bride to the altar, by the Honourable Mr Lackwit; which is neither strange nor new.

Scythrop received this intelligence at Nightmare Abbey, and was half distracted on the occasion. It was his first disappointment, and preyed deeply on his sensitive spirit. His father, to comfort him, read him a *Commentary on Ecclesiastes*, which he had himself composed, and which demonstrated incontrovertibly that all is vanity. He insisted particularly on the text, 'One man among a thousand have I found, but a woman amongst all those have I not found.'

'How could he expect it,' said Scythrop, 'when the whole thousand were locked up in his seraglio? His experience is no precedent for a free state of society like that in which we live.'

'Locked up or at large,' said Mr Glowry, 'the result is the same: their minds are always locked up, and vanity and interest keep the key. I speak feelingly, Scythrop.'

'I am sorry for it, sir,' said Scythrop. 'But how is it that their minds are locked up? The fault is in their artificial education, which studiously models them into mere musical dolls, to be set out for sale in the great toy-shop of society.'

'To be sure,' said Mr Glowry, 'their education is not so well finished as yours has been; and your idea of a musical doll is good. I bought one myself, but it was confoundedly out of tune; but, whatever be the cause, Scythrop, the effect is certainly this, that one is pretty nearly as good as another, as far as any judgment can be formed of them before marriage. It is only after marriage that they show their true qualities, as I know by bitter experience. Marriage is, therefore, a lottery, and the less choice and selection a man bestows on his ticket the better; for, if he has incurred considerable pains and expense to obtain a lucky number, and his lucky number proves a blank, he experiences not a simple, but a complicated disappointment; the loss of labour and money being superadded to the disappointment of drawing a blank, which, constituting simply and entirely the grievance of him who has chosen his ticket at random, is, from its simplicity, the more endurable.' This very excellent reasoning was thrown away upon Scythrop, who retired to his tower as dismal and disconsolate as before.

The tower which Scythrop inhabited stood at the south-eastern angle of the Abbey; and, on the southern side, the foot of the tower opened on a terrace, which was called the garden, though nothing grew on it but ivy, and a few amphibious weeds. The south-western tower, which was ruinous and full of owls, might, with equal propriety, have been called the aviary. This terrace or garden, or terrace-garden, or garden-terrace (the reader may name it *ad libitum*), took in an oblique view of the open sea, and fronted a long tract of level sea-coast, and a fine monotony of fens and windmills.

The reader will judge, from what we have said, that this building was a sort of castellated abbey; and it will, probably, occur to him to inquire if it had been one of the strongholds of the ancient church militant. Whether this was the case, or how far it had been indebted to the taste of Mr Glowry's ancestors for any transmutations from its original state, are, unfortunately, circumstances not within the pale of our knowledge.

The north-western tower contained the apartments of Mr Glowry. The moat at its base, and the fens beyond, comprised the whole of his prospect. This moat surrounded the Abbey, and was in immediate contact with the walls on every side but the south.

The north-eastern tower was appropriated to the domestics, whom Mr Glowry always chose by one of two criterions – a long face, or a dismal name. His butler was Raven; his steward was Crow; his valet was Skellet. Mr Glowry maintained that the valet was of French extraction, and that his name was Squelette. His grooms were Mattocks and Graves. On one occasion, being in want of a footman, he received a letter from a person signing himself Diggory Deathshead, and lost no time in securing this acquisition; but on Diggory's arrival, Mr Glowry was horror-struck by the sight of a round ruddy face, and a pair of laughing eyes. Deathshead was always grinning – not a ghastly smile, but the grin of a comic mask; and disturbed the echoes of the hall with so much unhallowed laughter, that Mr Glowry gave him his discharge. Diggory, however, had stayed long enough to make conquests of all the old gentleman's maids, and left him a flourishing colony of young Deathsheads to join chorus with the owls, that had before been the exclusive choristers of Nightmare Abbey.

The main body of the building was divided into rooms of state, spacious apartments for feasting, and numerous bedrooms for visitors, who, however, were few and far between.

Family interests compelled Mr Glowry to receive occasional visits from Mr and Mrs Hilary, who paid them from the same motive; and, as the lively gentleman on these occasions found few conductors for his exuberant gaiety, he became like a double-charged electric jar, which often exploded in some burst of outrageous merriment, to the signal discomposure of Mr Glowry's nerves.

Another occasional visitor, much more to Mr Glowry's taste, was Mr Flosky,* a very lachrymose and morbid gentleman, of some note in the literary world, but in his own estimation of much more merit than name. The part of his character which recommended him to Mr Glowry, was his very fine sense of the grim and the tearful. No one could relate a dismal story with so many minutiae of supererogatory wretchedness. No one could call up a *raw-head and bloody-bones* with so many adjuncts and circumstances of ghastliness. Mystery was his mental element. He lived in the midst of that visionary world in which nothing is but what is not. He dreamed with his eyes open, and saw ghosts dancing round him at noontide. He had been in his youth an enthusiast for liberty, and had hailed the dawn of the French Revolution as the promise of a day that was to banish war and slavery, and every form of vice and misery, from the face of the earth. Because all this was not done, he deduced that nothing was done; and from this deduction, according to his system of logic, he drew a conclusion that worse than nothing was done; that the overthrow of the feudal fortresses of tyranny and superstition was the greatest calamity that had ever befallen mankind; and that their only hope now was to rake the rubbish together, and rebuild it without any of those loopholes by which the light had originally crept in. To qualify himself for a coadjutor in this laudable task, he plunged into the central opacity of Kantian metaphysics, and lay *perdu* several years in transcendental darkness, till the common daylight of common sense became intolerable to his eyes. He called the sun an *ignis fatuus*; and exhorted all who would listen to his friendly voice, which were about as many as called 'God save King Richard', to shelter themselves from its delusive radiance in the obscure haunt of Old Philosophy. This word Old had great charms for him. The good old times were always on his lips; meaning the days when polemic theology was in its prime, and rival prelates beat the drum ecclesiastic with Herculean vigour, till the one wound up his series of syllogisms with the very orthodox conclusion of roasting the other.

* *Mr Flosky*: A corruption of Filosky, quasi Φιλόσκιος, a lover, or sector, of shadows.

But the dearest friend of Mr Glowry, and his most welcome guest, was Mr Toobad, the Manichaean Millennarian. The twelfth verse of the twelfth chapter of *Revelations* was always in his mouth: 'Woe to the inhabiters of the earth and of the sea! for the devil is come among you, having great wrath, because he knoweth that he hath but a short time.' He maintained that the supreme dominion of the world was, for wise purposes, given over for a while to the Evil Principle; and that this precise period of time, commonly called the enlightened age, was the point of his plenitude of power. He used to add that by and by he would be cast down, and a high and happy order of things succeed; but he never omitted the saving clause, 'Not in our time'; which last words were always echoed in doleful response by the sympathetic Mr Glowry.

Another and very frequent visitor, was the Reverend Mr Larynx, the vicar of Claydyke, a village about ten miles distant – a good-natured accommodating divine, who was always most obligingly ready to take a dinner and a bed at the house of any country gentle-man in distress for a companion. Nothing came amiss to him – a game at billiards, at chess, at draughts, at backgammon, at piquet, or at all-fours in a *tête-à-tête* – or any game on the cards, round, square, or triangular, in a party of any number exceeding two. He would even dance among friends, rather than that a lady, even if she were on the wrong side of thirty, should sit still for want of a partner. For a ride, a walk, or a sail, in the morning – a song after dinner, a ghost story after supper – a bottle of port with the squire, or a cup of green tea with his lady – for all or any of these, or for anything else that was agreeable to anyone else, consistently with the dye of his coat, the Reverend Mr Larynx was at all times equally ready. When at Night-mare Abbey, he would condole with Mr Glowry – drink madeira with Scythrop – crack jokes with Mr Hilary – hand Mrs Hilary to the piano, take charge of her fan and gloves, and turn over her music with surprising dexterity – quote *Revelations* with Mr Toobad – and lament the good old times of feudal darkness with the transcendental Mr Flosky.

Chapter Two

Shortly after the disastrous termination of Scythrop's passion for Miss Emily Girouette, Mr Glowry found himself, much against his will, involved in a lawsuit, which compelled him to dance attendance on the High Court of Chancery. Scythrop was left alone at Nightmare Abbey. He was a burnt child, and dreaded the fire of female eyes. He wandered about the ample pile, or along the garden-terrace, with 'his cogitative faculties immersed in cogibundity of cogitation'. The terrace terminated at the south-western tower, which, as we have said, was ruinous and full of owls. Here would Scythrop take his evening seat, on a fallen fragment of mossy stone, with his back resting against the ruined wall – a thick canopy of ivy, with an owl in it, over his head – and the *Sorrows of Werter* in his hand. He had some taste for romance reading before he went to the university, where, we must confess in justice to his college, he was cured of the love of reading in all its shapes; and the cure would have been radical, if disappointment in love, and total solitude, had not conspired to bring on a relapse. He began to devour romances and German tragedies, and, by the recommendation of Mr Flosky, to pore over ponderous tomes of transcendental philosophy, which reconciled him to the labour of studying them by their mystical jargon and necromantic imagery. In the congenial solitude of Nightmare Abbey, the distempered ideas of metaphysical romance and romantic metaphysics had ample time and space to germinate into a fertile crop of chimeras, which rapidly shot up into vigorous and abundant vegetation.

He now became troubled with the *passion for reforming the world.** He built many castles in the air, and peopled them with secret tribunals, and bands of illuminati, who were always the imaginary instruments of his projected regeneration of the human species. As he intended to institute a perfect republic, he invested himself with absolute sovereignty over these mystical dispensers of liberty. He slept with *Horrid Mysteries* under his pillow, and dreamed of venerable

---

* *passion for reforming the world*: See Forsyth's *Principles of Moral Science*.

eleutherarchs and ghastly confederates holding midnight conventions in subterranean caves. He passed whole mornings in his study, immersed in gloomy reverie, stalking about the room in his nightcap, which he pulled over his eyes like a cowl, and folding his striped calico dressing-gown about him like the mantle of a conspirator.

'Action,' thus he soliloquised, 'is the result of opinion, and to new-model opinion would be to new-model society. Knowledge is power; it is in the hands of a few, who employ it to mislead the many, for their own selfish purposes of aggrandisement and appropriation. What if it were in the hands of a few who should employ it to lead the many? What if it were universal, and the multitude were enlightened? No. The many must be always in leading-strings; but let them have wise and honest conductors. A few to think, and many to act; that is the only basis of perfect society. So thought the ancient philosophers: they had their esoterical and exoterical doctrines. So thinks the sublime Kant, who delivers his oracles in language which none but the initiated can comprehend. Such were the views of those secret associations of illuminati, which were the terror of superstition and tyranny, and which, carefully selecting wisdom and genius from the great wilderness of society, as the bee selects honey from the flowers of the thorn and the nettle, bound all human excellence in a chain, which, if it had not been prematurely broken, would have commanded opinion, and regenerated the world.'

Scythrop proceeded to meditate on the practicability of reviving a confederation of regenerators. To get a clear view of his own ideas, and to feel the pulse of the wisdom and genius of the age, he wrote and published a treatise, in which his meanings were carefully wrapped up in the monk's hood of transcendental technology, but filled with hints of matter deep and dangerous, which he thought would set the whole nation in a ferment; and he awaited the result in awful expectation, as a miner who has fired a train awaits the explosion of a rock. However, he listened and heard nothing; for the explosion, if any ensued, was not sufficiently loud to shake a single leaf of the ivy on the towers of Nightmare Abbey; and some months afterwards he received a letter from his bookseller, informing him that only seven copies had been sold, and concluding with a polite request for the balance.

Scythrop did not despair. 'Seven copies,' he thought, 'have been sold. Seven is a mystical number, and the omen is good. Let me find the seven purchasers of my seven copies, and they shall be the seven golden candlesticks with which I will illuminate the world.'

Scythrop had a certain portion of mechanical genius, which his romantic projects tended to develop. He constructed models of cells and recesses, sliding panels and secret passages, that would have baffled the skill of the Parisian police. He took the opportunity of his father's absence to smuggle a dumb carpenter into the Abbey, and between them they gave reality to one of these models in Scythrop's tower. Scythrop foresaw that a great leader of human regeneration would be involved in fearful dilemmas, and determined, for the benefit of mankind in general, to adopt all possible precautions for the preservation of himself.

The servants, even the women, had been tutored into silence. Profound stillness reigned throughout and around the Abbey, except when the occasional shutting of a door would peal in long reverberations through the galleries, or the heavy tread of the pensive butler would wake the hollow echoes of the hall. Scythrop stalked about like the Grand Inquisitor, and the servants flitted past him like familiars. In his evening meditations on the terrace, under the ivy of the ruined tower, the only sounds that came to his ear were the rustling of the wind in the ivy, the plaintive voices of the feathered choristers, the owls, the occasional striking of the Abbey clock, and the monotonous dash of the sea on its low and level shore. In the mean time, he drank madeira, and laid deep schemes for a thorough repair of the crazy fabric of human nature.

Chapter Three

Mr Glowry returned from London with the loss of his lawsuit. Justice was with him, but the law was against him. He found Scythrop in a mood most sympathetically tragic; and they vied with each other in enlivening their cups by lamenting the depravity of this degenerate age, and occasionally interspersing divers grim jokes about graves, worms, and epitaphs. Mr Glowry's friends, whom we have mentioned in the first chapter, availed themselves of his return to pay him a simultaneous visit. At the same time arrived Scythrop's friend and fellow-collegian, the Honourable Mr Listless. Mr Glowry had discovered this fashionable young gentleman in London, 'stretched on the rack of a too easy chair', and devoured with a gloomy and misanthropical *nil curo*, and had pressed him so earnestly to take the benefit of the pure country air at Nightmare Abbey, that Mr Listless, finding it would give him more trouble to refuse than to comply, summoned his French valet, Fatout, and told him he was going to Lincolnshire. On this simple hint, Fatout went to work, and the imperials were packed, and the post-chariot was at the door, without the Honourable Mr Listless having said or thought another syllable on the subject.

Mr and Mrs Hilary brought with them an orphan niece, a daughter of Mr Glowry's youngest sister, who had made a runaway love-match with an Irish officer. The lady's fortune disappeared in the first year: love, by a natural consequence, disappeared in the second: the Irishman himself, by a still more natural consequence, disappeared in the third. Mr Glowry had allowed his sister an annuity, and she had lived in retirement with her only daughter, whom, at her death, which had recently happened, she commended to the care of Mrs Hilary.

Miss Marionetta Celestina O'Carroll was a very blooming and accomplished young lady. Being a compound of the *Allegro Vivace* of the O'Carrolls, and of the *Andante Doloroso* of the Glowries, she exhibited in her own character all the diversities of an April sky. Her hair was light-brown; her eyes hazel, and sparkling with a mild but fluctuating light; her features regular; her lips full, and of equal size; and her person surpassingly graceful. She was a proficient in music. Her conversation was sprightly, but always on subjects light in their nature and limited in their interest: for moral sympathies, in any general sense, had no place in her mind. She had some coquetry, and more caprice, liking and disliking almost in the same moment; pursuing an object with earnestness while it seemed unattainable, and rejecting it when in her power as not worth the trouble of possession.

Whether she was touched with a *penchant* for her cousin Scythrop, or was merely curious to see what effect the tender passion would have on so *outré* a person, she had not been three days in the Abbey before she threw out all the lures of her beauty and accomplishments to make a prize of his heart. Scythrop proved an easy conquest. The image of Miss Emily Girouette was already sufficiently dimmed by the power of philosophy and the exercise of reason: for to these influences, or to any influence but the true one, are usually ascribed the mental cures performed by the great physician Time. Scythrop's romantic dreams had indeed given him many pure *anticipated cognitions* of combinations of beauty and intelligence, which, he had some misgivings, were not exactly realised in his cousin Marionetta; but, in spite of these misgivings, he soon became distractedly in love; which, when the young lady clearly perceived, she altered her tactics, and assumed as much coldness and reserve as she had before shown ardent and ingenuous attachment. Scythrop was confounded at the sudden change; but, instead of falling at her feet and requesting an explanation, he retreated to his tower, muffled himself in his nightcap, seated himself in the president's chair of his imaginary secret tribunal, summoned Marionetta with all terrible formalities, frightened her out of her wits, disclosed himself, and clasped the beautiful penitent to his bosom.

While he was acting this reverie – in the moment in which the awful president of the secret tribunal was throwing back his cowl and his mantle, and discovering himself to the lovely culprit as her adoring and magnanimous lover, the door of the study opened, and the real Marionetta appeared.

The motives which had led her to the tower were a little penitence, a little concern, a little affection, and a little fear as to what the sudden secession of Scythrop, occasioned by her sudden change of manner, might portend. She had tapped several times unheard, and of course unanswered; and at length, timidly and cautiously opening the door, she discovered him standing up before a black velvet chair, which was mounted on an old oak table, in the act of throwing open his striped calico dressing-gown, and flinging away his nightcap – which is what the French call an imposing attitude.

Each stood a few moments fixed in their respective places – the lady in astonishment, and the gentleman in confusion. Marionetta was the first to break silence. 'For heaven's sake,' said she, 'my dear Scythrop, what is the matter?'

'For heaven's sake, indeed!' said Scythrop, springing from the table; 'for your sake, Marionetta, and you are my heaven – distraction is the matter. I adore you, Marionetta, and your cruelty drives me mad.' He threw himself at her knees, devoured her hand with kisses, and breathed a thousand vows in the most passionate language of romance.

Marionetta listened a long time in silence, till her lover had exhausted his eloquence and paused for a reply. She then said, with a very arch look, 'I prithee deliver thyself like a man of this world.' The levity of this quotation, and of the manner in which it was delivered, jarred so discordantly on the high-wrought enthusiasm of the romantic inamorato, that he sprang upon his feet, and beat his forehead with his clenched fist. The young lady was terrified; and, deeming it expedient to soothe him, took one of his hands in hers, placed the other hand on his shoulder, looked up in his face with a winning seriousness, and said, in the tenderest possible tone, 'What would you have, Scythrop?'

Scythrop was in heaven again. 'What would I have? What but you, Marionetta? You, for the companion of my studies, the partner of my thoughts, the auxiliary of my great designs for the emancipation of mankind.'

'I am afraid I should be but a poor auxiliary, Scythrop. What would you have me do?'

'Do as Rosalia does with Carlos, divine Marionetta. Let us each open a vein in the other's arm, mix our blood in a bowl, and drink it as a sacrament of love. Then we shall see visions of transcendental illumination, and soar on the wings of ideas into the space of pure intelligence.'

Marionetta could not reply; she had not so strong a stomach as Rosalia, and turned sick at the proposition. She disengaged herself suddenly from Scythrop, sprang through the door of the tower, and fled with precipitation along the corridors. Scythrop pursued her, crying, 'Stop, stop, Marionetta – my life, my love!' and was gaining rapidly on her flight, when, at an ill-omened corner, where two corridors ended in an angle, at the head of a staircase, he came into sudden and violent contact with Mr Toobad, and they both plunged together to the foot of the stairs, like two billiard-balls into one pocket. This gave the young lady time to escape, and enclose herself in her chamber; while Mr Toobad, rising slowly, and rubbing his knees and shoulders, said, 'You see, my dear Scythrop, in this little incident, one of the innumerable proofs of the temporary supremacy of the devil; for what but a systematic design and concurrent contrivance of evil could have made the angles of time and place coincide in our unfortunate persons at the head of this accursed staircase?'

'Nothing else, certainly,' said Scythrop: 'you are perfectly in the right, Mr Toobad. Evil, and mischief, and misery, and confusion, and vanity, and vexation of spirit, and death, and disease, and assassination, and war, and poverty, and pestilence, and famine, and avarice, and selfishness, and rancour, and jealousy, and spleen, and malevolence, and the disappointments of philanthropy, and the faithlessness of friendship, and the crosses of love – all prove the accuracy of your views, and the truth of your system; and it is not impossible that the infernal interruption of this fall downstairs may throw a colour of evil on the whole of my future existence.'

'My dear boy,' said Mr Toobad, 'you have a fine eye for consequences.'

So saying, he embraced Scythrop, who retired, with a disconsolate step, to dress for dinner; while Mr Toobad stalked across the hall, repeating, 'Woe to the inhabiters of the earth, and of the sea, for the devil is come among you, having great wrath.'

Chapter Four

The flight of Marionetta, and the pursuit of Scythrop, had been witnessed by Mr Glowry, who, in consequence, narrowly observed his son and his niece in the evening; and, concluding from their manner, that there was a better understanding between them than he wished to see, he determined on obtaining the next morning from Scythrop a full and satisfactory explanation. He, therefore, shortly after breakfast, entered Scythrop's tower, with a very grave face, and said, without ceremony or preface, 'So, sir, you are in love with your cousin.'

Scythrop, with as little hesitation, answered, 'Yes, sir.'

'That is candid, at least; and she is in love with you.'

'I wish she were, sir.'

'You know she is, sir.'

'Indeed, sir, I do not.'

'But you hope she is.'

'I do, from my soul.'

'Now that is very provoking, Scythrop, and very disappointing: I could not have supposed that you, Scythrop Glowry, of Nightmare Abbey, would have been infatuated with such a dancing, laughing, singing, thoughtless, careless, merry-hearted thing, as Marionetta – in all respects the reverse of you and me. It is very disappointing, Scythrop. And do you know, sir, that Marionetta has no fortune?'

'It is the more reason, sir, that her husband should have one.'

'The more reason for her; but not for you. My wife had no fortune, and I had no consolation in my calamity. And do you reflect, sir, what an enormous slice this lawsuit has cut out of our family estate? We who used to be the greatest landed proprietors in Lincolnshire.'

'To be sure, sir, we had more acres of fen than any man on this coast: but what are fens to love? What are dykes and windmills to Marionetta?'

'And what, sir, is love to a windmill? Not grist, I am certain: besides, sir, I have made a choice for you. I have made a choice for you, Scythrop. Beauty, genius, accomplishments, and a great fortune

into the bargain. Such a lovely, serious creature, in a fine state of
high dissatisfaction with the world, and everything in it. Such a
delightful surprise I had prepared for you. Sir, I have pledged my
honour to the contract – the honour of the Glowries of Nightmare
Abbey: and now, sir, what is to be done?'

'Indeed, sir, I cannot say. I claim, on this occasion, that liberty of
action which is the co-natal prerogative of every rational being.'

'Liberty of action, sir? There is no such thing as liberty of action.
We are all slaves and puppets of a blind and unpathetic necessity.'

'Very true, sir; but liberty of action, between individuals, consists
in their being differently influenced, or modified, by the same universal necessity; so that the results are unconsentaneous, and their
respective necessitated volitions clash and fly off in a tangent.'

'Your logic is good, sir: but you are aware, too, that one individual
may be a medium of adhibiting to another a mode or form of necessity, which may have more or less influence in the production of
consentaneity; and, therefore, sir, if you do not comply with my
wishes in this instance (you have had your own way in everything
else), I shall be under the necessity of disinheriting you, though I
shall do it with tears in my eyes.' Having said these words, he
vanished suddenly, in the dread of Scythrop's logic.

Mr Glowry immediately sought Mrs Hilary, and communicated to
her his views of the case in point. Mrs Hilary, as the phrase is, was as
fond of Marionetta as if she had been her own child: but – there is
always a *but* on these occasions – she could do nothing for her in the
way of fortune, as she had two hopeful sons, who were finishing their
education at Brazen-nose, and who would not like to encounter any
diminution of their prospects, when they should be brought out
of the house of mental bondage – i.e. the university – to the land
flowing with milk and honey – i.e. the west end of London.

Mrs Hilary hinted to Marionetta, that propriety, and delicacy, and
decorum, and dignity, &c. &c. &c.,* would require them to leave
the Abbey immediately. Marionetta listened in silent submission,
for she knew that her inheritance was passive obedience; but, when
Scythrop, who had watched the opportunity of Mrs Hilary's departure, entered, and, without speaking a word, threw himself at her
feet in a paroxysm of grief, the young lady, in equal silence and
sorrow, threw her arms round his neck and burst into tears. A very
tender scene ensued, which the sympathetic susceptibilities of the

---

* *decorum, and dignity, &c. &c. &c.*: We are not masters of the whole vocabulary.
See any novel by any literary lady.

soft-hearted reader can more accurately imagine than we can delin-
eate. But when Marionetta hinted that she was to leave the Abbey
immediately, Scythrop snatched from its repository his ancestor's
skull, filled it with madeira, and presenting himself before Mr
Glowry, threatened to drink off the contents if Mr Glowry did not
immediately promise that Marionetta should not be taken from the
Abbey without her own consent. Mr Glowry, who took the madeira
to be some deadly brewage, gave the required promise in dismal
panic. Scythrop returned to Marionetta with a joyful heart, and
drank the madeira by the way.

Mr Glowry, during his residence in London, had come to an agree-
ment with his friend Mr Toobad, that a match between Scythrop and
Mr Toobad's daughter would be a very desirable occurrence. She
was finishing her education in a German convent, but Mr Toobad
described her as being fully impressed with the truth of his Ahrimanic philosophy,* and being altogether as gloomy and antithalian
a young lady as Mr Glowry himself could desire for the future
mistress of Nightmare Abbey. She had a great fortune in her own
right, which was not, as we have seen, without its weight in inducing
Mr Glowry to set his heart upon her as his daughter-in-law that was
to be; he was therefore very much disturbed by Scythrop's untoward
attachment to Marionetta. He condoled on the occasion with Mr
Toobad; who said, that he had been too long accustomed to the
intermeddling of the devil in all his affairs, to be astonished at this
new trace of his cloven claw; but that he hoped to outwit him yet, for
he was sure there could be no comparison between his daughter and
Marionetta in the mind of anyone who had a proper perception of
the fact that, the world being a great theatre of evil, seriousness and
solemnity are the characteristics of wisdom, and laughter and merriment make a human being no better than a baboon. Mr Glowry

---

* *his Ahrimanic philosophy*: Ahrimanes, in the Persian mythology, is the evil power,
the prince of the kingdom of darkness. He is the rival of Oromazes, the prince
of the kingdom of light. These two powers have divided and equal dominion.
Sometimes one of the two has a temporary supremacy. – According to Mr Toobad, the present period would be the reign of Ahrimanes. Lord Byron seems to
be of the same opinion, by the use he has made of Ahrimanes in *Manfred*; where
the great Alastor, or κακὸς δαίμων, of Persia, is hailed king of the world by the
Nemesis of Greece, in concert with three of the Scandinavian Valkyrae, under
the name of the Destinies; the astrological spirits of the alchemists of the middle
ages; an elemental witch, transplanted from Denmark to the Alps; and a chorus
of Dr Faustus's devils, who come in the last act for a soul. It is difficult to
conceive where this heterogeneous mythological company could have originally
met, except at a *table d'hôte*, like the six kings in *Candide*.

comforted himself with this view of the subject, and urged Mr Toobad to expedite his daughter's return from Germany. Mr Toobad said he was in daily expectation of her arrival in London, and would set off immediately to meet her, that he might lose no time in bringing her to Nightmare Abbey. 'Then,' he added, 'we shall see whether Thalia or Melpomene – whether the Allegra or the Penserosa – will carry off the symbol of victory.' – 'There can be no doubt,' said Mr Glowry, 'which way the scale will incline, or Scythrop is no true scion of the venerable stem of the Glowries.'

Chapter Five

Marionetta felt secure of Scythrop's heart; and notwithstanding the difficulties that surrounded her, she could not debar herself from the pleasure of tormenting her lover, whom she kept in a perpetual fever. Sometimes she would meet him with the most unqualified affection; sometimes with the most chilling indifference; rousing him to anger by artificial coldness – softening him to love by eloquent tenderness – or inflaming him to jealousy by coquetting with the Honourable Mr Listless, who seemed, under her magical influence, to burst into sudden life, like the bud of the evening primrose. Sometimes she would sit by the piano, and listen with becoming attention to Scythrop's pathetic remonstrances; but, in the most impassioned part of his oratory, she would convert all his ideas into a chaos, by striking up some *Rondo Allegro*, and saying, 'Is it not pretty?' Scythrop would begin to storm; and she would answer him with,

Zitti, zitti, piano, piano,
Non facciamo confusione,

or some similar *facezia*, till he would start away from her, and enclose himself in his tower, in an agony of agitation, vowing to renounce her, and her whole sex, for ever; and returning to her presence at the summons of the billet, which she never failed to send with many expressions of penitence and promises of amendment. Scythrop's schemes for regenerating the world, and detecting his seven golden candlesticks, went on very slowly in this fever of his spirit.

Things proceeded in this train for several days, and Mr Glowry began to be uneasy at receiving no intelligence from Mr Toobad; when one evening the latter rushed into the library, where the family and the visitors were assembled, vociferating, 'The devil is come among you, having great wrath!' He then drew Mr Glowry aside into another apartment, and after remaining some time together, they re-entered the library with faces of great dismay, but did not condescend to explain to anyone the cause of their discomfiture.

The next morning, early, Mr Toobad departed. Mr Glowry sighed and groaned all day, and said not a word to anyone. Scythrop had quarrelled, as usual, with Marionetta, and was enclosed in his tower, in a fit of morbid sensibility. Marionetta was comforting herself at the piano, with singing the airs of *Nina pazza per amore*; and the Honourable Mr Listless was listening to the harmony, as he lay supine on the sofa, with a book in his hand, into which he peeped at intervals. The Reverend Mr Larynx approached the sofa, and proposed a game at billiards.

THE HONOURABLE MR LISTLESS

Billiards! Really I should be very happy; but, in my present exhausted state, the exertion is too much for me. I do not know when I have been equal to such an effort. [*he rang the bell for his valet. Fatout entered*] Fatout! when did I play at billiards last?

FATOUT

De fourteen December de last year, Monsieur. [*Fatout bowed and retired*]

THE HONOURABLE MR LISTLESS

So it was. Seven months ago. You see, Mr Larynx; you see, sir. My nerves, Miss O'Carroll, my nerves are shattered. I have been advised to try Bath. Some of the faculty recommend Cheltenham. I think of trying both, as the seasons don't clash. The season, you know, Mr Larynx – the season, Miss O'Carroll – the season is everything.

MARIONETTA

And health is something. *N'est-ce pas*, Mr Larynx?

THE REVEREND MR LARYNX

Most assuredly, Miss O'Carroll. For, however reasoners may dispute about the *summum bonum*, none of them will deny that a very good dinner is a very good thing: and what is a good dinner without a good appetite? and whence is a good appetite but from good health? Now, Cheltenham, Mr Listless, is famous for good appetites.

THE HONOURABLE MR LISTLESS

The best piece of logic I ever heard, Mr Larynx; the very best, I assure you. I have thought very seriously of Cheltenham: very seriously and profoundly. I thought of it – let me see – when did I think of it? [*he rang again, and Fatout reappeared*] Fatout! when did I think of going to Cheltenham, and did not go?

FATOUT

De Juillet twenty-von, de last summer, Monsieur. [*Fatout retired*]

THE HONOURABLE MR LISTLESS

So it was. An invaluable fellow that, Mr Larynx – invaluable, Miss O'Carroll.

MARIONETTA

So I should judge, indeed. He seems to serve you as a walking memory, and to be a living chronicle, not of your actions only, but of your thoughts.

THE HONOURABLE MR LISTLESS

An excellent definition of the fellow, Miss O'Carroll – excellent, upon my honour. Ha! ha! he! Heigho! Laughter is pleasant, but the exertion is too much for me.

A parcel was brought in for Mr Listless; it had been sent express. Fatout was summoned to unpack it; and it proved to contain a new novel, and a new poem, both of which had long been anxiously expected by the whole host of fashionable readers; and the last number of a popular Review, of which the editor and his coadjutors were in high favour at court, and enjoyed ample pensions* for their services to church and state. As Fatout left the room, Mr Flosky entered, and curiously inspected the literary arrivals.

MR FLOSKY

[*turning over the leaves*] *Devilman, a novel*. Hm. Hatred – revenge – misanthropy – and quotations from the Bible. Hm. This is the morbid anatomy of black bile. – *Paul Jones, a poem*. Hm. I see how it is. Paul Jones, an amiable enthusiast – disappointed in his affections – turns pirate from ennui and magnanimity – cuts various masculine throats, wins various feminine hearts – is hanged at the yard-arm! The catastrophe is very awkward, and very unpoetical. – *The Downing Street Review*. Hm. First article – An Ode to the Red Book, by Roderick Sackbut, Esquire. Hm. His own poem reviewed by himself. Hm – m – m.

[*Mr Flosky proceeded in silence to look over the other articles of the review; Marionetta inspected the novel, and Mr Listless the poem*]

---

* *pensions*: 'Pension. Pay given to a slave of state for treason to his country.' – Johnson's *Dictionary*.

THE REVEREND MR LARYNX

For a young man of fashion and family, Mr Listless, you seem to be of a very studious turn.

THE HONOURABLE MR LISTLESS

Studious! You are pleased to be facetious, Mr Larynx. I hope you do not suspect me of being studious. I have finished my education. But there are some fashionable books that one must read, because they are ingredients of the talk of the day; otherwise, I am no fonder of books than I dare say you yourself are, Mr Larynx.

THE REVEREND MR LARYNX

Why, sir, I cannot say that I am indeed particularly fond of books; yet neither can I say that I never do read. A tale or a poem, now and then, to a circle of ladies over their work, is no very heterodox employment of the vocal energy. And I must say, for myself, that few men have a more Job-like endurance of the eternally recurring questions and answers that interweave themselves, on these occasions, with the crisis of an adventure, and heighten the distress of a tragedy.

THE HONOURABLE MR LISTLESS

And very often make the distress when the author has omitted it.

MARIONETTA

I shall try your patience some rainy morning, Mr Larynx; and Mr Listless shall recommend us the very newest new book, that everybody reads.

THE HONOURABLE MR LISTLESS

You shall receive it, Miss O'Carroll, with all the gloss of novelty; fresh as a ripe greengage in all the downiness of its bloom. A mail-coach copy from Edinburgh, forwarded express from London.

MR FLOSKY

This rage for novelty is the bane of literature. Except my works and those of my particular friends, nothing is good that is not as old as Jeremy Taylor: and, *entre nous*, the best parts of my friends' books were either written or suggested by myself.

THE HONOURABLE MR LISTLESS

Sir, I reverence you. But I must say, modern books are very consolatory and congenial to my feelings. There is, as it were, a delightful north-east wind, an intellectual blight breathing through them; a

delicious misanthropy and discontent, that demonstrates the null-
ity of virtue and energy, and puts me in good humour with myself
and my sofa.

MR FLOSKY

Very true, sir. Modern literature is a north-east wind – a blight of
the human soul. I take credit to myself for having helped to make it
so. The way to produce fine fruit is to blight the flower. You call
this a paradox. Marry, so be it. Ponder thereon.

The conversation was interrupted by the reappearance of Mr
Toobad, covered with mud. He just showed himself at the door,
muttered 'The devil is come among you!' and vanished. The road
which connected Nightmare Abbey with the civilised world, was
artificially raised above the level of the fens, and ran through them in
a straight line as far as the eye could reach, with a ditch on each side,
of which the water was rendered invisible by the aquatic vegetation
that covered the surface. Into one of these ditches the sudden action
of a shy horse, which took fright at a windmill, had precipitated the
travelling chariot of Mr Toobad, who had been reduced to the
necessity of scrambling in dismal plight through the window. One of
the wheels was found to be broken; and Mr Toobad, leaving the
postilion to get the chariot as well as he could to Claydyke for the
purpose of cleaning and repairing, had walked back to Nightmare
Abbey, followed by his servant with the imperial, and repeating all
the way his favourite quotation from the *Revelations*.

Chapter Six

Mr Toobad had found his daughter Celinda in London, and after the first joy of meeting was over, told her he had a husband ready for her. The young lady replied, very gravely, that she should take the liberty to choose for herself. Mr Toobad said he saw the devil was determined to interfere with all his projects, but he was resolved on his own part, not to have on his conscience the crime of passive obedience and non-resistance to Lucifer, and therefore she should marry the person he had chosen for her. Miss Toobad replied, *très posément*, she assuredly would not. 'Celinda, Celinda,' said Mr Toobad, 'you most assuredly shall.' – 'Have I not a fortune in my own right, sir?' said Celinda. 'The more is the pity,' said Mr Toobad: 'but I can find means, miss; I can find means. There are more ways than one of breaking in obstinate girls.' They parted for the night with the expression of opposite resolutions, and in the morning the young lady's chamber was found empty, and what was become of her Mr Toobad had no clue to conjecture. He continued to investigate town and country in search of her, visiting and revisiting Nightmare Abbey at intervals, to consult with his friend, Mr Glowry. Mr Glowry agreed with Mr Toobad that this was a very flagrant instance of filial disobedience and rebellion; and Mr Toobad declared, that when he discovered the fugitive, she should find that 'the devil was come unto her, having great wrath.'

In the evening, the whole party met, as usual, in the library. Marionetta sat at the harp; the Honourable Mr Listless sat by her and turned over her music, though the exertion was almost too much for him. The Reverend Mr Larynx relieved him occasionally in this delightful labour. Scythrop, tormented by the demon Jealousy, sat in the corner biting his lips and fingers. Marionetta looked at him every now and then with a smile of most provoking good humour, which he pretended not to see, and which only the more exasperated his troubled spirit. He took down a volume of Dante, and pretended to be deeply interested in the *Purgatorio*, though he knew not a word he was reading, as Marionetta was well aware; who, tripping across the room, peeped into his book, and said to him, 'I see you are in the middle of *Purgatory*.' – 'I am in the middle of hell,' said Scythrop furiously. 'Are you?' said she; 'then come across the room, and I will sing you the finale of *Don Giovanni*.'

'Let me alone,' said Scythrop. Marionetta looked at him with a deprecating smile, and said, 'You unjust, cross creature, you.' – 'Let me alone,' said Scythrop, but much less emphatically than at first, and by no means wishing to be taken at his word. Marionetta left him immediately, and returning to the harp, said, just loud enough for Scythrop to hear – 'Did you ever read Dante, Mr Listless? Scythrop is reading Dante, and is just now in *Purgatory*.' – 'And I,' said the Honourable Mr Listless, 'am not reading Dante, and am just now in Paradise,' bowing to Marionetta.

MARIONETTA

You are very gallant, Mr Listless; and I dare say you are very fond of reading Dante.

THE HONOURABLE MR LISTLESS

I don't know how it is, but Dante never came in my way till lately. I never had him in my collection, and if I had had him I should not have read him. But I find he is growing fashionable, and I am afraid I must read him some wet morning.

MARIONETTA

No, read him some evening, by all means. Were you ever in love, Mr Listless?

THE HONOURABLE MR LISTLESS

I assure you, Miss O'Carroll, never – till I came to Nightmare Abbey. I dare say it is very pleasant; but it seems to give so much trouble that I fear the exertion would be too much for me.

MARIONETTA

Shall I teach you a compendious method of courtship, that will give you no trouble whatever?

THE HONOURABLE MR LISTLESS

You will confer on me an inexpressible obligation. I am all impatience to learn it.

MARIONETTA

Sit with your back to the lady and read Dante; only be sure to begin in the middle, and turn over three or four pages at once –

backwards as well as forwards, and she will immediately perceive that you are desperately in love with her – desperately.

[the Honourable Mr Listless, sitting between Scythrop and Marionetta, and fixing all his attention on the beautiful speaker, did not observe Scythrop, who was doing as she described]

THE HONOURABLE MR LISTLESS
You are pleased to be facetious, Miss O'Carroll. The lady would infallibly conclude that I was the greatest brute in town.

MARIONETTA
Far from it. She would say, perhaps, some people have odd methods of showing their affection.

THE HONOURABLE MR LISTLESS
But I should think, with submission –

MR FLOSKY *[joining them from another part of the room]*
Did I not hear Mr Listless observe that Dante is becoming fashionable?

THE HONOURABLE MR LISTLESS
I did hazard a remark to that effect, Mr Flosky, though I speak on such subjects with a consciousness of my own nothingness, in the presence of so great a man as Mr Flosky. I know not what is the colour of Dante's devils, but as he is certainly becoming fashionable I conclude they are blue; for the blue devils, as it seems to me, Mr Flosky, constitute the fundamental feature of fashionable literature.

MR FLOSKY
The blue are, indeed, the staple commodity; but as they will not always be commanded, the black, red, and grey may be admitted as substitutes. Tea, late dinners, and the French Revolution, have played the devil, Mr Listless, and brought the devil into play.

MR TOOBAD *[starting up]*
Having great wrath.

MR FLOSKY
This is no play upon words, but the sober sadness of veritable fact.

THE HONOURABLE MR LISTLESS
Tea, late dinners, and the French Revolution. I cannot exactly see the connection of ideas.

MR FLOSKY

I should be sorry if you could; I pity the man who can see the connection of his own ideas. Still more do I pity him, the connection of whose ideas any other person can see. Sir, the great evil is, that there is too much commonplace light in our moral and political literature; and light is a great enemy to mystery, and mystery is a great friend to enthusiasm. Now the enthusiasm for abstract truth is an exceedingly fine thing, as long as the truth which is the object of the enthusiasm, is so completely abstract as to be altogether out of the reach of the human faculties; and, in that sense, I have myself an enthusiasm for truth, but in no other, for the pleasure of metaphysical investigation lies in the means, not in the end; and if the end could be found, the pleasure of the means would cease. The mind, to be kept in health, must be kept in exercise. The proper exercise of the mind is elaborate reasoning. Analytical reasoning is a base and mechanical process, which takes to pieces and examines, bit by bit, the rude material of knowledge, and extracts therefrom a few hard and obstinate things called facts, everything in the shape of which I cordially hate. But synthetical reasoning, setting up as its goal some unattainable abstraction, like an imaginary quantity in algebra, and commencing its course with taking for granted some two assertions which cannot be proved, from the union of these two assumed truths produces a third assumption, and so on in infinite series, to the unspeakable benefit of the human intellect. The beauty of this process is, that at every step it strikes out into two branches, in a compound ratio of ramification; so that you are perfectly sure of losing your way, and keeping your mind in perfect health, by the perpetual exercise of an interminable quest; and for these reasons I have christened my eldest son Emanuel Kant Flosky.

THE REVEREND MR LARYNX

Nothing can be more luminous.

THE HONOURABLE MR LISTLESS

And what has all that to do with Dante, and the blue devils?

MR HILARY

Not much, I should think, with Dante, but a great deal with the blue devils.

MR FLOSKY

It is very certain, and much to be rejoiced at, that our literature is hag-ridden. Tea has shattered our nerves; late dinners make us slaves of indigestion; the French Revolution has made us shrink from the name of philosophy, and has destroyed, in the more refined part of the community (of which number I am one), all enthusiasm for political liberty. That part of the *reading public* which shuns the solid food of reason for the light diet of fiction, requires a perpetual adhibition of *sauce piquante* to the palate of its depraved imagination. It lived upon ghosts, goblins, and skeletons (I and my friend Mr Sackbut served up a few of the best), till even the devil himself, though magnified to the size of Mount Athos, became too base, common, and popular, for its surfeited appetite. The ghosts have therefore been laid, and the devil has been cast into outer darkness, and now the delight of our spirits is to dwell on all the vices and blackest passions of our nature, tricked out in a masquerade dress of heroism and disappointed benevolence; the whole secret of which lies in forming combinations that contradict all our experience, and affixing the purple shred of some particular virtue to that precise character, in which we should be most certain not to find it in the living world; and making this single virtue not only redeem all the real and manifest vices of the character, but make them actually pass for necessary adjuncts, and indispensable accompaniments and characteristics of the said virtue.

MR TOOBAD

That is, because the devil is come among us, and finds it for his interest to destroy all our perceptions of the distinctions of right and wrong.

MARIONETTA

I do not precisely enter into your meaning, Mr Flosky, and should be glad if you would make it a little more plain to me.

MR FLOSKY

One or two examples will do it, Miss O'Carroll. If I were to take all the mean and sordid qualities of a money-dealing Jew, and tack on to them, as with a nail, the quality of extreme benevolence, I should have a very decent hero for a modern novel; and should contribute my quota to the fashionable method of administering a mass of vice, under a thin and unnatural covering of virtue, like a spider wrapt in a bit of gold leaf, and administered as a wholesome pill. On the same principle, if a man knocks me down, and takes my purse and watch by main force, I turn him to account, and set him forth in a tragedy as a dashing young fellow, disinherited for his romantic generosity, and full of a most amiable hatred of the world in general, and his own country in particular, and of a most enlightened and chivalrous affection for himself: then, with the addition of a wild girl to fall in love with him, and a series of adventures in which they break all the Ten Commandments in succession (always, you will observe, for some sublime motive, which must be carefully analysed in its progress), I have as amiable a pair of tragic characters as ever issued from that new region of the *belles lettres*, which I have called the Morbid Anatomy of Black Bile, and which is greatly to be admired and rejoiced at, as affording a fine scope for the exhibition of mental power.

MR HILARY

Which is about as well employed as the power of a hothouse would be in forcing up a nettle to the size of an elm. If we go on in this way, we shall have a new art of poetry, of which one of the first rules will be: To remember to forget that there are any such things as sunshine and music in the world.

THE HONOURABLE MR LISTLESS

It seems to be the case with us at present, or we should not have interrupted Miss O'Carroll's music with this exceedingly dry conversation.

MR FLOSKY

I should be most happy if Miss O'Carroll would remind us that there are yet both music and sunshine –

THE HONOURABLE MR LISTLESS

In the voice and the smile of beauty. May I entreat the favour of – [*turning over the pages of music*]

All were silent, and Marionetta sung:

> Why are thy looks so blank, grey friar?
>   Why are thy looks so blue?
> Thou seem'st more pale and lank, grey friar,
>   Than thou wast used to do –
>   Say, what has made thee rue?
>
> Thy form was plump, and a light did shine
>   In thy round and ruby face,
> Which showed an outward visible sign
>   Of an inward spiritual grace –
>   Say, what has changed thy case?

Yet will I tell thee true, grey friar,
  I very well can see,
That, if thy looks are blue, grey friar,
  'Tis all for love of me –
  'Tis all for love of me.

But breathe not thy vows to me, grey friar,
  Oh, breathe them not, I pray;
For ill beseems in a reverend friar,
  The love of a mortal may;
  And I needs must say thee nay.

But, could'st thou think my heart to move
  With that pale and silent scowl,
Know, he who would win a maiden's love,
  Whether clad in cap or cowl,
  Must be more of a lark than an owl.

Scythrop immediately replaced Dante on the shelf, and joined the circle round the beautiful singer. Marionetta gave him a smile of approbation that fully restored his complacency, and they continued on the best possible terms during the remainder of the evening. The Honourable Mr Listless turned over the leaves with double alacrity, saying, 'You are severe upon invalids, Miss O'Carroll: to escape your satire, I must try to be sprightly, though the exertion is too much for me.'

Chapter Seven

A new visitor arrived at the Abbey, in the person of Mr Asterias, the ichthyologist. This gentleman had passed his life in seeking the living wonders of the deep through the four quarters of the world; he had a cabinet of stuffed and dried fishes, of shells, sea-weeds, corals, and madrepores, that was the admiration and envy of the Royal Society. He had penetrated into the watery den of the Sepia Octopus, disturbed the conjugal happiness of that turtle-dove of the ocean, and come off victorious in a sanguinary conflict. He had been becalmed in the tropical seas, and had watched, in eager expectation, though unhappily always in vain, to see the colossal polypus rise from the water, and entwine its enormous arms round the masts and the rigging. He maintained the origin of all things from water, and insisted that the polypodes were the first of animated things, and that, from their round bodies and many-shooting arms, the Hindoos had taken their gods, the most ancient of deities. But the chief object of his ambition, the end and aim of his researches, was to discover a triton and a mermaid, the existence of which he most potently and implicitly believed, and was prepared to demonstrate, *a priori, a posteriori, a fortiori*, synthetically and analytically, syllogistically and inductively, by arguments deduced both from acknowledged facts and plausible hypotheses. A report that a mermaid had been seen 'sleeking her soft alluring locks' on the sea-coast of Lincolnshire, had brought him in great haste from London, to pay a long-promised and often-postponed visit to his old acquaintance, Mr Glowry.

Mr Asterias was accompanied by his son, to whom he had given the name of Aquarius – flattering himself that he would, in the process of time, become a constellation among the stars of ichthyological science. What charitable female had lent him the mould in which this son was cast, no one pretended to know; and, as he never dropped the most distant allusion to Aquarius' mother, some of the wags of London maintained that he had received the favours of a mermaid, and that the scientific perquisitions which kept him always prowling about the sea-shore, were directed by the less philosophical motive of regaining his lost love.

Mr Asterias perlustrated the sea-coast for several days, and reaped disappointment, but not despair. One night, shortly after his arrival, he was sitting in one of the windows of the library, looking towards the sea, when his attention was attracted by a figure which was moving near the edge of the surf, and which was dimly visible through the moonless summer night. Its motions were irregular, like those of a person in a state of indecision. It had extremely long hair, which floated in the wind. Whatever else it might be, it certainly was not a fisherman. It might be a lady; but it was neither Mrs Hilary nor Miss O'Carroll, for they were both in the library. It might be one of the female servants; but it had too much grace, and too striking an air of habitual liberty, to render it probable. Besides, what should one of the female servants be doing there at this hour, moving to and fro, as it seemed, without any visible purpose? It could scarcely be a stranger; for Claydyke, the nearest village, was ten miles distant; and what female would come ten miles across the fens, for no purpose but to hover over the surf under the walls of Nightmare Abbey? Might it not be a mermaid? It was possibly a mermaid. It was probably a mermaid. It was very probably a mermaid. Nay, what else could it be but a mermaid? It certainly was a mermaid. Mr Asterias stole out of the library on tiptoe, with his finger on his lips, having beckoned Aquarius to follow him.

The rest of the party was in great surprise at Mr Asterias' movement, and some of them approached the window to see if the locality would tend to elucidate the mystery. Presently they saw him and Aquarius cautiously stealing along on the other side of the moat, but they saw nothing more; and Mr Asterias returning, told them, with accents of great disappointment, that he had had a glimpse of a mermaid, but she had eluded him in the darkness, and was gone, he presumed, to sup with some enamoured triton, in a submarine grotto.

'But, seriously, Mr Asterias,' said the Honourable Mr Listless, 'do you positively believe there are such things as mermaids?'

MR ASTERIAS
Most assuredly; and tritons too.

THE HONOURABLE MR LISTLESS
What! things that are half human and half fish?

MR ASTERIAS

Precisely. They are the oran-outangs of the sea. But I am persuaded that there are also complete sea men, differing in no respect from us, but that they are stupid, and covered with scales; for, though our organisation seems to exclude us essentially from the class of amphibious animals, yet anatomists well know that the *foramen ovale* may remain open in an adult, and that respiration is, in that case, not necessary to life: and how can it be otherwise explained that the Indian divers, employed in the pearl fishery, pass whole hours under the water; and that the famous Swedish gardener of Troningholm lived a day and a half under the ice without being drowned? A nereid, or mermaid, was taken in the year 1403 in a Dutch lake, and was in every respect like a French woman, except that she did not speak. Towards the end of the seventeenth century, an English ship, a hundred and fifty leagues from land, in the Greenland seas, discovered a flotilla of sixty or seventy little skiffs, in each of which was a triton, or sea man: at the approach of the English vessel the whole of them, seized with simultaneous fear, disappeared, skiffs and all, under the water, as if they had been a human variety of the nautilus. The illustrious Don Feijoo has preserved an authentic and well-attested story of a young Spaniard, named Francis de la Vega, who, bathing with some of his friends in June, 1674, suddenly dived under the sea and rose no more. His friends thought him drowned; they were plebeians and pious Catholics, but a philosopher might very legitimately have drawn the same conclusion.

THE REVEREND MR LARYNX

Nothing could be more logical.

MR ASTERIAS

Five years afterwards, some fishermen near Cadiz found in their nets a triton, or sea man; they spoke to him in several languages –

THE REVEREND MR LARYNX

They were very learned fishermen.

MR HILARY

They had the gift of tongues by especial favour of their brother fisherman, Saint Peter.

THE HONOURABLE MR LISTLESS

Is Saint Peter the tutelar saint of Cadiz?

[*none of the company could answer this question, and Mr Asterias proceeded*]

MR ASTERIAS

They spoke to him in several languages, but he was as mute as a fish. They handed him over to some holy friars, who exorcised him; but the devil was mute too. After some days he pronounced the name Lierganes. A monk took him to that village. His mother and brothers recognised and embraced him; but he was as insensible to their caresses as any other fish would have been. He had some scales on his body, which dropped off by degrees; but his skin was as hard and rough as shagreen. He stayed at home nine years, without recovering his speech or his reason: he then disappeared again; and one of his old acquaintance, some years after, saw him pop his head out of the water near the coast of the Asturias. These facts were certified by his brothers, and by Don Gaspardo de la Riba Aguero, Knight of Saint James, who lived near Lierganes, and often had the pleasure of our triton's company to dinner. – Pliny mentions an embassy of the Olyssiponians to Tiberius, to give him intelligence of a triton which had been heard playing on its shell in a certain cave; with several other authenticated facts on the subject of tritons and nereids.

THE HONOURABLE MR LISTLESS

You astonish me. I have been much on the sea-shore, in the season, but I do not think I ever saw a mermaid. [*he rang, and summoned Fatout, who made his appearance half-seas-over*] Fatout! did I ever see a mermaid?

FATOUT

Mermaid! mer-r-m-m-aid! Ah! merry maid! *Oui, monsieur*! Yes, sir, very many. I vish dere vas von or two here in de kitchen – *ma foi*! Dey be all as melancholic as so many tombstone.

THE HONOURABLE MR LISTLESS

I mean, Fatout, an odd kind of human fish.

FATOUT

De odd fish! Ah, oui! I understand de phrase: ve have seen nothing else since ve left town – *ma foi*!

THE HONOURABLE MR LISTLESS

You seem to have a cup too much, sir.

FATOUT

Non, monsieur: de cup too little. De fen be very unwholesome, and I drink-a-de ponch vid Raven de butler, to keep out de bad air.

THE HONOURABLE MR LISTLESS

Fatout! I insist on your being sober.

FATOUT

Oui, monsieur; I vil be as sober as de reverendissime *père* Jean. I should be ver glad of de merry maid; but de butler be de odd fish, and he swim in de bowl de ponch. Ah! ah! I do recollect de leetle-a song – 'About fair maids, and about fair maids, and about my merry maids all.' [*Fatout reeled out, singing*]

THE HONOURABLE MR LISTLESS

I am overwhelmed: I never saw the rascal in such a condition before. But will you allow me, Mr Asterias, to inquire into the *cui bono* of all the pains and expense you have incurred to discover a mermaid? The *cui bono*, sir, is the question I always take the liberty to ask when I see anyone taking much trouble for any object. I am myself a sort of Signor Pococurante, and should like to know if there be anything better or pleasanter, than the state of existing and doing nothing?

MR ASTERIAS

I have made many voyages, Mr Listless, to remote and barren shores: I have travelled over desert and inhospitable lands: I have defied danger – I have endured fatigue – I have submitted to privation. In the midst of these I have experienced pleasures which I would not at any time have exchanged for that of existing and doing nothing. I have known many evils, but I have never known the worst of all, which, as it seems to me, are those which are comprehended in the inexhaustible varieties of *ennui*: spleen, chagrin, vapours, blue devils, time-killing, discontent, misanthropy, and all their interminable train of fretfulness, querulousness, suspicions, jealousies, and fears, which have alike infected society, and the literature of society; and which would make an arctic ocean of the human mind, if the more humane pursuits of philosophy and science did not keep alive the better feelings and more valuable energies of our nature.

THE HONOURABLE MR LISTLESS

You are pleased to be severe upon our fashionable *belles lettres*.

MR ASTERIAS

Surely not without reason, when pirates, highwaymen, and other varieties of the extensive genus Marauder, are the only *beau idéal* of the active, as splenetic and railing misanthropy is of the speculative energy. A gloomy brow and a tragical voice seem to have been of late the characteristics of fashionable manners: and a morbid, withering, deadly, antisocial sirocco, loaded with moral and political despair, breathes through all the groves and valleys of the modern Parnassus; while science moves on in the calm dignity of its course, affording to youth delights equally pure and vivid – to maturity, calm and grateful occupation – to old age, the most pleasing recollections and inexhaustible materials of agreeable and salutary reflection; and, while its votary enjoys the disinterested pleasure of enlarging the intellect and increasing the comforts of society, he is himself independent of the caprices of human intercourse and the accidents of human fortune. Nature is his great and inexhaustible treasure. His days are always too short for his enjoyment: *ennui*, is a stranger to his door. At peace with the world and with his own mind, he suffices to himself, makes all around him happy, and the close of his pleasing and beneficial existence is the evening of a beautiful day.*

THE HONOURABLE MR LISTLESS

Really I should like very well to lead such a life myself, but the exertion would be too much for me. Besides, I have been at college. I contrive to get through my day by sinking the morning in bed, and killing the evening in company; dressing and dining in the intermediate space, and stopping the chinks and crevices of the few vacant moments that remain with a little easy reading. And that amiable discontent and antisociality which you reprobate in our present drawing-room-table literature, I find, I do assure you, a very fine mental tonic, which reconciles me to my favourite pursuit of doing nothing, by showing me that nobody is worth doing anything for.

MARIONETTA

But is there not in such compositions a kind of unconscious self-detection, which seems to carry their own antidote with them? For surely no one who cordially and truly either hates or despises the world will publish a volume every three months to say so.

* *of a beautiful day*: see Denys Montfort, *Histoire Naturelle des Mollusques; Vues Generales*, pp.37,38.

MR FLOSKY

There is a secret in all this, which I will elucidate with a dusky remark. According to Berkeley, the *esse* of things is *percipi*. They exist as they are perceived. But, leaving for the present, as far as relates to the material world, the materialists, hyloists and anti-hyloists, to settle this point among them, which is indeed

> A subtle question, raised among
> Those out o' their wits, and those i' the wrong:

for only we transcendentalists are in the right: we may very safely assert that the *esse* of happiness is *percipi*. It exists as it is perceived. 'It is the mind that maketh well or ill.' The elements of pleasure and pain are everywhere. The degree of happiness that any circum- stances or objects can confer on us depends on the mental dispos- ition with which we approach them. If you consider what is meant by the common phrases, a happy disposition and a discontented temper, you will perceive that the truth for which I am contending is universally admitted.

[*Mr Flosky suddenly stopped: he found himself unintentionally trespassing within the limits of common sense*]

MR HILARY

It is very true; a happy disposition finds materials of enjoyment everywhere. In the city, or the country – in society, or in solitude – in the theatre, or the forest – in the hum of the multitude, or in the silence of the mountains, are alike materials of reflection and elements of pleasure. It is one mode of pleasure to listen to the music of *Don Giovanni*, in a theatre glittering with light and crowded with elegance and beauty: it is another to glide at sunset over the bosom of a lonely lake, where no sound disturbs the silence but the motion of the boat through the waters. A happy disposition derives pleasure from both, a discontented temper from neither, but is always busy in detecting deficiencies, and feeding dissatisfaction with comparisons. The one gathers all the flowers, the other all the nettles, in its path. The one has the faculty of en- joying everything, the other of enjoying nothing. The one realises all the pleasure of the present good; the other converts it into pain, by pining after something better, which is only better because it is not present, and which, if it were present, would not be enjoyed. These morbid spirits are in life what professed critics are in liter- ature; they see nothing but faults, because they are predetermined to shut their eyes to beauties. The critic does his utmost to blight genius in its infancy; that which rises in spite of him he will not see; and then he complains of the decline of literature. In like manner, these cankers of society complain of human nature and society, when they have wilfully debarred themselves from all the good they contain, and done their utmost to blight their own happiness and that of all around them. Misanthropy is sometimes the product of disappointed benevolence; but it is more frequently the offspring of overweening and mortified vanity, quarrelling with the world for not being better treated than it deserves.

SCYTHROP [*to Marionetta*]
These remarks are rather uncharitable. There is great good in human nature, but it is at present ill-conditioned. Ardent spirits cannot but be dissatisfied with things as they are; and according to their views of the probabilities of amelioration, they will rush into the extremes of either hope or despair – of which the first is enthusiasm, and the second misanthropy; but their sources in this case are the same, as the Severn and the Wye run in different directions, and both rise in Plinlimmon.

MARIONETTA
'And there is salmon in both;' for the resemblance is about as close as that between Macedon and Monmouth.

Chapter Eight

Marionetta observed the next day a remarkable perturbation in Scythrop, for which she could not imagine any probable cause. She was willing to believe at first that it had some transient and trifling source, and would pass off in a day or two; but, contrary to this expectation, it daily increased. She was well aware that Scythrop had a strong tendency to the love of mystery, for its own sake; that is to say, he would employ mystery to serve a purpose, but would first choose his purpose by its capability of mystery. He seemed now to have more mystery on his hands than the laws of the system allowed, and to wear his coat of darkness with an air of great discomfort. All her little playful arts lost by degrees much of their power either to irritate or to soothe; and the first perception of her diminished influence produced in her an immediate depression of spirits, and a consequent sadness of demeanour, that rendered her very interesting to Mr Glowry; who, duly considering the improbability of accomplishing his wishes with respect to Miss Toobad (which improbability naturally increased in the diurnal ratio of that young lady's absence), began to reconcile himself by degrees to the idea of Marionetta being his daughter.

Marionetta made many ineffectual attempts to extract from Scythrop the secret of his mystery; and, in despair of drawing it from himself, began to form hopes that she might find a clue to it from Mr Flosky, who was Scythrop's dearest friend, and was more frequently than any other person admitted to his solitary tower. Mr Flosky, however, had ceased to be visible in a morning. He was engaged in the composition of a dismal ballad; and, Marionetta's uneasiness overcoming her scruples of decorum, she determined to seek him in the apartment which he had chosen for his study. She tapped at the door, and at the sound 'Come in', entered the apartment. It was noon, and the sun was shining in full splendour, much to the annoyance of Mr Flosky, who had obviated the inconvenience by closing the shutters, and drawing the window-curtains. He was sitting at his table by the light of a solitary candle, with a pen in one hand, and a muffineer in the other, with which he occasionally sprinkled salt on the wick, to make it burn blue. He sate with 'his eye in a fine frenzy rolling', and turned his inspired gaze on Marionetta as if she had been the ghastly ladie of a magical vision; then placed his hand before his eyes, with an appearance of manifest pain – shook his head – withdrew his hand – rubbed his eyes, like a waking man – and said, in a tone of ruefulness most jeremitaylorically pathetic, 'To what am I to attribute this very unexpected pleasure, my dear Miss O'Carroll?'

MARIONETTA

I must apologise for intruding on you, Mr Flosky; but the interest which I – you – take in my cousin Scythrop –

MR FLOSKY

Pardon me, Miss O'Carroll; I do not take any interest in any person or thing on the face of the earth; which sentiment, if you analyse it, you will find to be the quintessence of the most refined philanthropy.

MARIONETTA

I will take it for granted that it is so, Mr Flosky; I am not conversant with metaphysical subtleties, but –

MR FLOSKY

Subtleties! my dear Miss O'Carroll. I am sorry to find you participating in the vulgar error of the *reading public*, to whom an unusual collocation of words, involving a juxtaposition of antiperistatical ideas, immediately suggests the notion of hyperoxysophistical paradoxology.

MARIONETTA

Indeed, Mr Flosky, it suggests no such notion to me. I have sought you for the purpose of obtaining information.

MR FLOSKY [*shaking his head*]

No one ever sought me for such a purpose before.

MARIONETTA

I think, Mr Flosky – that is, I believe – that is, I fancy – that is, I imagine –

MR FLOSKY

The τουτέστι, the *id est*, the *cioè*, the *c'est à dire*, the *that is*, my dear Miss O'Carroll, is not applicable in this case – if you will permit me to take the liberty of saying so. Think is not synonymous with believe – for belief, in many most important particulars, results from the total absence, the absolute negation of thought, and is thereby the sane and orthodox condition of mind; and thought and belief are both essentially different from fancy, and fancy, again, is distinct from imagination. This distinction between fancy and imagination is one of the most abstruse and important points of metaphysics. I have written seven hundred pages of promise to elucidate it, which promise I shall keep as faithfully as the bank will its promise to pay.

MARIONETTA

I assure you, Mr Flosky, I care no more about metaphysics than I do about the bank; and, if you will condescend to talk to a simple girl in intelligible terms –

MR FLOSKY

Say not condescend! Know you not that you talk to the most humble of men, to one who has buckled on the armour of sanctity, and clothed himself with humility as with a garment?

MARIONETTA

My cousin Scythrop has of late had an air of mystery about him, which gives me great uneasiness.

MR FLOSKY

That is strange: nothing is so becoming to a man as an air of mystery. Mystery is the very keystone of all that is beautiful in poetry, all that is sacred in faith, and all that is recondite in transcendental psychology. I am writing a ballad which is all mystery; it is 'such stuff as dreams are made of', and is, indeed, stuff made of a dream; for, last night, I fell asleep as usual over my book, and had a vision of pure reason. I composed five hundred lines in my sleep; so that, having had a dream of a ballad, I am now officiating as my own Peter Quince, and making a ballad of my dream, and it shall be called 'Bottom's Dream', because it has no bottom.

MARIONETTA

I see, Mr Flosky, you think my intrusion unseasonable, and are inclined to punish it, by talking nonsense to me. [*Mr Flosky gave a start at the word nonsense, which almost overturned the table*] I assure you, I would not have intruded if I had not been very much interested in the question I wish to ask you. – [*Mr Flosky listened in sullen dignity*] – My cousin Scythrop seems to have some secret preying on his mind. – [*Mr Flosky was silent*] – He seems very unhappy – Mr Flosky. – Perhaps you are acquainted with the cause. – [*Mr Flosky was still silent*] – I only wish to know – Mr Flosky – if it is anything – that could be remedied by anything – that anyone – of whom I know anything – could do.

MR FLOSKY [*after a pause*]

There are various ways of getting at secrets. The most approved methods, as recommended both theoretically and practically in philosophical novels, are eavesdropping at keyholes, picking the locks of chests and desks, peeping into letters, steaming wafers, and insinuating hot wire under sealing wax; none of which methods I hold it lawful to practise.

MARIONETTA

Surely, Mr Flosky, you cannot suspect me of wishing to adopt or encourage such base and contemptible arts.

MR FLOSKY

Yet are they recommended, and with well-strung reasons, by writers of gravity and note, as simple and easy methods of studying character, and gratifying that laudable curiosity which aims at the knowledge of man.

MARIONETTA

I am as ignorant of this morality which you do not approve, as of the metaphysics which you do: I should be glad to know by your means, what is the matter with my cousin; I do not like to see him unhappy, and I suppose there is some reason for it.

MR FLOSKY

Now I should rather suppose there is no reason for it: it is the fashion to be unhappy. To have a reason for being so would be exceedingly commonplace: to be so without any is the province of genius: the art of being miserable for misery's sake, has been brought to great perfection in our days; and the ancient *Odyssey*, which held forth a shining example of the endurance of real misfortune, will give place to a modern one, setting out a more instructive picture of querulous impatience under imaginary evils.

MARIONETTA

Will you oblige me, Mr Flosky, by giving me a plain answer to a plain question?

MR FLOSKY

It is impossible, my dear Miss O'Carroll. I never gave a plain answer to a question in my life.

MARIONETTA

Do you, or do you not, know what is the matter with my cousin?

MR FLOSKY

To say that I do not know, would be to say that I am ignorant of something; and God forbid, that a transcendental metaphysician, who has pure anticipated cognitions of everything, and carries the whole science of geometry in his head without ever having looked into Euclid, should fall into so empirical an error as to declare himself ignorant of anything: to say that I do know, would be to pretend to positive and circumstantial knowledge touching present matter of fact, which, when you consider the nature of evidence, and the various lights in which the same thing may be seen –

MARIONETTA

I see, Mr Flosky, that either you have no information, or are determined not to impart it; and I beg your pardon for having given you this unnecessary trouble.

MR FLOSKY

My dear Miss O'Carroll, it would have given me great pleasure to have said anything that would have given you pleasure; but if any person living could make report of having obtained any information on any subject from Ferdinando Flosky, my transcendental reputation would be ruined for ever.

Chapter Nine

Scythrop grew every day more reserved, mysterious, and distrait; and gradually lengthened the duration of his diurnal seclusions in his tower. Marionetta thought she perceived in all this very manifest symptoms of a warm love cooling.

It was seldom that she found herself alone with him in the morning, and, on these occasions, if she was silent in the hope of his speaking first, not a syllable would he utter; if she spoke to him indirectly, he assented monosyllabically; if she questioned him, his answers were brief, constrained, and evasive. Still, though her spirits were depressed, her playfulness had not so totally forsaken her, but that it illuminated at intervals the gloom of Nightmare Abbey; and if, on any occasion, she observed in Scythrop tokens of unextinguished or returning passion, her love of tormenting her lover immediately got the better both of her grief and her sympathy, though not of her curiosity, which Scythrop seemed determined not to satisfy. This playfulness, however, was in a great measure artificial, and usually vanished with the irritable Strephon, to whose annoyance it had been exerted. The Genius Loci, the *tutela* of Nightmare Abbey, the spirit of black melancholy, began to set his seal on her pallescent countenance. Scythrop perceived the change, found his tender sympathies awakened, and did his utmost to comfort the afflicted damsel, assuring her that his seeming inattention had only proceeded from his being involved in a profound meditation on a very hopeful scheme for the regeneration of human society. Marionetta called him ungrateful, cruel, cold-hearted, and accompanied her reproaches with many sobs and tears; poor Scythrop growing every moment more soft and submissive – till, at length, he threw himself at her feet, and declared that no competition of beauty, however dazzling, genius, however transcendent, talents, however cultivated, or philosophy, however enlightened, should ever make him renounce his divine Marionetta.

'Competition!' thought Marionetta, and suddenly, with an air of the most freezing indifference, she said, 'You are perfectly at liberty, sir, to do as you please; I beg you will follow your own plans, without any reference to me.'

Scythrop was confounded. What was become of all her passion and her tears? Still kneeling, he kissed her hand with rueful timidity, and said, in most pathetic accents, 'Do you not love me, Marionetta?'

'No,' said Marionetta, with a look of cold composure: 'No.' Scythrop still looked up incredulously. 'No, I tell you.'

'Oh! very well, madam,' said Scythrop, rising, 'if that is the case, there are those in the world – '

'To be sure there are, sir – and do you suppose I do not see through your designs, you ungenerous monster?'

'My designs? Marionetta!'

'Yes, your designs, Scythrop. You have come here to cast me off, and artfully contrive that it should appear to be my doing, and not yours, thinking to quiet your tender conscience with this pitiful stratagem. But do not suppose that you are of so much consequence to me: do not suppose it: you are of no consequence to me at all – none at all: therefore, leave me: I renounce you: leave me; why do you not leave me?'

Scythrop endeavoured to remonstrate, but without success. She reiterated her injunctions to him to leave her, till, in the simplicity of his spirit, he was preparing to comply. When he had nearly reached the door, Marionetta said, 'Farewell.' Scythrop looked back. 'Farewell, Scythrop,' she repeated, 'you will never see me again.'

'Never see you again, Marionetta?'

'I shall go from hence tomorrow, perhaps today; and before we meet again, one of us will be married, and we might as well be dead, you know, Scythrop.'

The sudden change of her voice in the last few words, and the burst of tears that accompanied them, acted like electricity on the tender-hearted youth; and, in another instant, a complete reconciliation was accomplished without the intervention of words.

There are, indeed, some learned casuists, who maintain that love has no language, and that all the misunderstandings and dissensions of lovers arise from the fatal habit of employing words on a subject to which words are inapplicable; that love, beginning with looks, that is to say, with the physiognomical expression of congenial mental dispositions, tends through a regular gradation of signs and symbols of affection, to that consummation which is most devoutly to be wished; and that it neither is necessary that there should be, nor probable that there would be, a single word spoken from first to last between two sympathetic spirits, were it not that the arbitrary institutions of society have raised, at every step of this very simple process, so many complicated impediments and barriers in the shape of settlements and ceremonies, parents and guardians, lawyers, Jew-brokers, and parsons, that many an adventurous knight (who, in order to obtain the conquest of the Hesperian fruit, is obliged to fight his way through all these monsters), is either repulsed at the onset, or vanquished before the achievement of his enterprise: and such a quantity of unnatural talking is rendered inevitably necessary through all the stages of the progression, that the tender and volatile spirit of love often takes flight on the pinions of some of the ἔπεα πτερόεντα, or *winged words*, which are pressed into his service in despite of himself.

At this conjuncture, Mr Glowry entered, and sitting down near them, said, 'I see how it is; and, as we are all sure to be miserable do what we may, there is no need of taking pains to make one another more so; therefore, with God's blessing and mine, there' – joining their hands as he spoke.

Scythrop was not exactly prepared for this decisive step; but he could only stammer out, 'Really, sir, you are too good;' and Mr Glowry departed to bring Mr Hilary to ratify the act.

Now, whatever truth there may be in the theory of love and language, of which we have so recently spoken, certain it is, that during Mr Glowry's absence, which lasted half an hour, not a single word was said by either Scythrop or Marionetta.

Mr Glowry returned with Mr Hilary, who was delighted at the prospect of so advantageous an establishment for his orphan niece, of whom he considered himself in some manner the guardian, and nothing remained, as Mr Glowry observed, but to fix the day.

Marionetta blushed, and was silent. Scythrop was also silent for a time, and at length hesitatingly said, 'My dear sir, your goodness overpowers me; but really you are so precipitate.'

Now, this remark, if the young lady had made it, would, whether she thought it or not – for sincerity is a thing of no account on these occasions, nor indeed on any other, according to Mr Flosky – this remark, if the young lady had made it, would have been perfectly *comme il faut*; but, being made by the young gentleman, it was *toute autre chose*, and was, indeed, in the eyes of his mistress, a most heinous and irremissible offence. Marionetta was angry, very angry, but she concealed her anger, and said, calmly and coldly, 'Certainly, you are much too precipitate, Mr Glowry. I assure you, sir, I have by no means made up my mind; and, indeed, as far as I know it, it inclines the other way; but it will be quite time enough to think of these matters seven years hence. Before surprise permitted reply, the young lady had locked herself up in her own apartment.

'Why, Scythrop,' said Mr Glowry, elongating his face exceedingly, 'the devil is come among us sure enough, as Mr Toobad observes: I thought you and Marionetta were both of a mind.'

'So we are, I believe, sir,' said Scythrop, gloomily, and stalked away to his tower.

'Mr Glowry,' said Mr Hilary, 'I do not very well understand all this.'

'Whims, brother Hilary,' said Mr Glowry; 'some little foolish love quarrel, nothing more. Whims, freaks, April showers. They will be blown over by tomorrow.'

'If not,' said Mr Hilary, 'these April showers have made us April fools.'

'Ah!' said Mr Glowry, 'you are a happy man, and in all your afflictions you can console yourself with a joke, let it be ever so bad, provided you crack it yourself. I should be very happy to laugh with you, if it would give you any satisfaction; but, really, at present, my heart is so sad, that I find it impossible to levy a contribution on my muscles.'

Chapter Ten

On the evening on which Mr Asterias had caught a glimpse of a female figure on the sea-shore, which he had translated into the visual sign of his interior cognition of a mermaid, Scythrop, retiring to his tower, found his study preoccupied. A stranger, muffled in a cloak, was sitting at his table. Scythrop paused in surprise. The stranger rose at his entrance, and looked at him intently a few minutes, in silence. The eyes of the stranger alone were visible. All the rest of the figure was muffled and mantled in the folds of a black cloak, which was raised, by the right hand, to the level of the eyes. This scrutiny being completed, the stranger, dropping the cloak, said, 'I see, by your physiognomy, that you may be trusted;' and revealed to the astonished Scythrop a female form and countenance of dazzling grace and beauty, with long flowing hair of raven blackness, and large black eyes of almost oppressive brilliancy, which strikingly contrasted with a complexion of snowy whiteness. Her dress was extremely elegant, but had an appearance of foreign fashion, as if both the lady and her mantua-maker were of 'a far countree'.

> I guess 'twas frightful there to see
> A lady so richly clad as she,
> Beautiful exceedingly.'

For, if it be terrible to one young lady to find another under a tree at midnight, it must, *a fortiori*, be much more terrible to a young gentleman to find a young lady in his study at that hour. If the logical consecutiveness of this conclusion be not manifest to my readers, I am sorry for their dulness, and must refer them, for more ample elucidation, to a treatise which Mr Flosky intends to write, on the Categories of Relation, which comprehend Substance and Accident, Cause and Effect, Action and Re-action.

Scythrop, therefore, either was or ought to have been frightened; at all events, he was astonished; and astonishment, though not in itself fear, is nevertheless a good stage towards it, and is, indeed, as it were, the half-way house between respect and terror, according to Mr Burke's graduated scale of the sublime.*

'You are surprised,' said the lady; 'yet why should you be surprised? If you had met me in a drawing-room, and I had been introduced to you by an old woman, it would have been a matter of course: can the division of two or three walls, and the absence of an unimportant personage, make the same object essentially different in the perception of a philosopher?'

'Certainly not,' said Scythrop; 'but when any class of objects has habitually presented itself to our perceptions in invariable conjunction with particular relations, then, on the sudden appearance of one object of the class divested of those accompaniments, the essential difference of the relation is, by an involuntary process, transferred to the object itself, which thus offers itself to our perceptions with all the strangeness of novelty.'

'You are a philosopher,' said the lady, 'and a lover of liberty. You are the author of a treatise, called "Philosophical Gas; or, a Project for a General Illumination of the Human Mind." '

'I am,' said Scythrop, delighted at this first blossom of his renown.

'I am a stranger in this country,' said the lady; 'I have been but a few days in it, yet I find myself immediately under the necessity of seeking refuge from an atrocious persecution. I had no friend to whom I could apply; and, in the midst of my difficulties, accident threw your pamphlet in my way. I saw that I had, at least, one kindred mind in this nation, and determined to apply to you.'

'And what would you have me do?' said Scythrop, more and more amazed, and not a little perplexed.

---

* *Mr Burke's graduated scale of the sublime*: There must be some mistake in this, for the whole honourable band of gentlemen-pensioners has resolved unanimously, that Mr Burke was a very sublime person, particularly after he had prostituted his own soul, and betrayed his country and mankind, for 1200*l.* a year: yet he does not appear to have been a very terrible personage, and certainly went off with a very small portion of human respect, though he contrived to excite, in a great degree, the astonishment of all honest men. Our immaculate laureate (who gives us to understand that, if he had not been purified by holy matrimony into a mystical type, he would have died a virgin,) is another sublime gentleman of the same genus: he very much astonished some persons when he sold his birthright for a pot of sack; but not even his *Sosia* has a grain of respect for him, though, doubtless, he thinks his name very terrible to the enemy, when he flourishes his criticopoeticopolitical tomahawk, and sets up his Indian yell for the blood of his old friends: but, at best, he is a mere political scarecrow, a man of straw, ridiculous to all who know of what materials he is made; and to none more so, than to those who have stuffed him, and set him up, as the Priapus of the garden of the golden apples of corruption.

'I would have you,' said the young lady, 'assist me in finding some place of retreat, where I can remain concealed from the indefatigable search that is being made for me. I have been so nearly caught once or twice already, that I cannot confide any longer in my own ingenuity.'

Doubtless, thought Scythrop, this is one of my golden candle-sticks. 'I have constructed,' said he, 'in this tower, an entrance to a small suite of unknown apartments in the main building, which I defy any creature living to detect. If you would like to remain there a day or two, till I can find you a more suitable concealment, you may rely on the honour of a transcendental eleutherarch.'

'I rely on myself,' said the lady. 'I act as I please, go where I please, and let the world say what it will. I am rich enough to set it at defiance. It is the tyrant of the poor and the feeble, but the slave of those who are above the reach of its injury.'

Scythrop ventured to inquire the name of his fair *protegée*. 'What is a name?' said the lady: 'any name will serve the purpose of distinction. Call me Stella. I see by your looks,' she added, 'that you think all this very strange. When you know me better, your surprise will cease. I submit not to be an accomplice in my sex's slavery. I am, like yourself, a lover of freedom, and I carry my theory into practice. *They alone are subject to blind authority who have no reliance on their own strength.*'

Stella took possession of the recondite apartments. Scythrop intended to find her another asylum; but from day to day he postponed his intention, and by degrees forgot it. The young lady reminded him of it from day to day, till she also forgot it. Scythrop was anxious to learn her history; but she would add nothing to what she had already communicated, that she was shunning an atrocious persecution. Scythrop thought of Lord C. and the Alien Act, and said, 'As you will not tell your name, I suppose it is in the green bag.' Stella, not understanding what he meant, was silent; and Scythrop, translating silence into acquiescence, concluded that he was sheltering an *illuminée* whom Lord S. suspected of an intention to take the Tower, and set fire to the Bank: exploits at least as likely to be accomplished by the hands and eyes of a young beauty, as by a drunken cobbler and doctor, armed with a pamphlet and an old stocking.

Stella, in her conversations with Scythrop, displayed a highly cultiv-ated and energetic mind, full of impassioned schemes of liberty, and impatience of masculine usurpation. She had a lively sense of all the oppressions that are done under the sun; and the vivid pictures which her imagination presented to her of the numberless scenes of injustice and misery which are being acted at every moment in every part of the inhabited world, gave an habitual seriousness to her physiognomy, that made it seem as if a smile had never once hovered on her lips. She was intimately conversant with the German language and literature; and Scythrop listened with delight to her repetitions of her favourite passages from Schiller and Goethe, and to her encomiums on the sublime Spartacus Weishaupt, the immortal founder of the sect of the Illuminati. Scythrop found that his soul had a greater capacity of love than the image of Marionetta had filled. The form of Stella took possession of every vacant corner of the cavity, and by degrees displaced that of Marionetta from many of the outworks of the citadel; though the latter still held possession of the *keep*. He judged, from his new friend calling herself Stella, that, if it were not her real name, she was an admirer of the principles of the German play from which she had taken it, and took an opportunity of leading the conversation to that subject; but to his great surprise, the lady spoke very ardently of the singleness and exclusiveness of love, and declared that the reign of affection was one and indivisible; that it might be transferred, but could not be participated. 'If I ever love,' said she, 'I shall do so without limit or restriction. I shall hold all difficulties light, all sacrifices cheap, all obstacles gossamer. But for love so total, I shall claim a return as absolute. I will have no rival: whether more or less favoured will be of little moment. I will be neither first nor second – I will be alone. The heart which I shall possess I will possess entirely, or entirely renounce.'

Scythrop did not dare to mention the name of Marionetta; he trembled lest some unlucky accident should reveal it to Stella, though he scarcely knew what result to wish or anticipate, and lived in the double fever of a perpetual dilemma. He could not dissemble to himself that he was in love, at the same time, with two damsels of minds and habits as remote as the antipodes. The scale of predilection always inclined to the fair one who happened to be present; but the absent was never effectually outweighed, though the degrees of exaltation and depression varied according to accidental variations in the outward and visible signs of the inward and spiritual graces of his respective charmers. Passing and repassing several times a day from the company of the one to that of the other, he was like a shuttlecock between two battledores, changing its direction as rapidly as the oscillations of a pendulum, receiving many a hard knock on the cork of a sensitive heart, and flying from point to point on the feathers of a super-sublimated head. This was an awful state of things. He had now

as much mystery about him as any romantic transcendentalist or
transcendental romancer could desire. He had his esoterical and his
exoterical love. He could not endure the thought of losing either of
them, but he trembled when he imagined the possibility that some
fatal discovery might deprive him of both. The old proverb concerning two strings to a bow gave him some gleams of comfort; but that
concerning two stools occurred to him more frequently, and covered
his forehead with a cold perspiration. With Stella, he could indulge
freely in all his romantic and philosophical visions. He could build
castles in the air, and she would pile towers and turrets on the imaginary edifices. With Marionetta it was otherwise: she knew nothing of
the world and society beyond the sphere of her own experience. Her
life was all music and sunshine, and she wondered what anyone could
see to complain of in such a pleasant state of things. She loved Scythrop, she hardly knew why; indeed she was not always sure that she
loved him at all: she felt her fondness increase or diminish in an
inverse ratio to his. When she had manoeuvred him into a fever of
passionate love, she often felt and always assumed indifference: if she
found that her coldness was contagious, and that Scythrop either was,
or pretended to be, as indifferent as herself, she would become doubly
kind, and raise him again to that elevation from which she had previously thrown him down. Thus, when his love was flowing, hers was
ebbing: when his was ebbing, hers was flowing. Now and then there
were moments of level tide, when reciprocal affection seemed to
promise imperturbable harmony; but Scythrop could scarcely resign
his spirit to the pleasing illusion, before the pinnace of the lover's
affections was caught in some eddy of the lady's caprice, and he was
whirled away from the shore of his hopes, without rudder or compass,
into an ocean of mists and storms. It resulted, from this system of
conduct, that all that passed between Scythrop and Marionetta, consisted in making and unmaking love. He had no opportunity to take
measure of her understanding by conversations on general subjects,
and on his favourite designs; and, being left in this respect to the
exercise of indefinite conjecture, he took it for granted, as most lovers
would do in similar circumstances, that she had great natural talents,
which she wasted at present on trifles: but coquetry would end with
marriage, and leave room for philosophy to exert its influence on her
mind. Stella had no coquetry, no disguise: she was an enthusiast in
subjects of general interest; and her conduct to Scythrop was always
uniform, or rather showed a regular progression of partiality which
seemed fast ripening into love.

Chapter Eleven

Scythrop, attending one day the summons to dinner, found in the drawing-room his friend Mr Cypress the poet, whom he had known at college, and who was a great favourite of Mr Glowry. Mr Cypress said, he was on the point of leaving England, but could not think of doing so without a farewell look at Nightmare Abbey and his respected friends, the moody Mr Glowry and the mysterious Mr Scythrop, the sublime Mr Flosky and the pathetic Mr Listless; to all of whom, and the morbid hospitality of the melancholy dwelling in which they were then assembled, he assured them he should always look back with as much affection as his lacerated spirit could feel for anything. The sympathetic condolence of their respective replies was cut short by Raven's announcement of 'dinner on table'.

The conversation that took place when the wine was in circulation, and the ladies were withdrawn, we shall report with our usual scrupulous fidelity.

MR GLOWRY

You are leaving England, Mr Cypress. There is a delightful melancholy in saying farewell to an old acquaintance, when the chances are twenty to one against ever meeting again. A smiling bumper to a sad parting, and let us all be unhappy together.

MR CYPRESS [*filling a bumper*]

This is the only social habit that the disappointed spirit never unlearns.

THE REVEREND MR LARYNX [*filling*]

It is the only piece of academical learning that the finished educatee retains.

MR FLOSKY [*filling*]

It is the only objective fact which the sceptic can realise.

SCYTHROP [*filling*]

It is the only styptic for a bleeding heart.

THE HONOURABLE MR LISTLESS [*filling*]

It is the only trouble that is very well worth taking.

MR ASTERIAS [*filling*]

It is the only key of conversational truth.

MR TOOBAD [*filling*]

It is the only antidote to the great wrath of the devil.

MR HILARY [*filling*]

It is the only symbol of perfect life. The inscription 'HIC NON BIBITUR' will suit nothing but a tombstone.

MR GLOWRY

You will see many fine old ruins, Mr Cypress; crumbling pillars, and mossy walls – many a one-legged Venus and headless Minerva – many a Neptune buried in sand – many a Jupiter turned topsy-turvy – many a perforated Bacchus doing duty as a waterpipe – many reminiscences of the ancient world, which I hope was better worth living in than the modern; though, for myself, I care not a straw more for one than the other, and would not go twenty miles to see anything that either could show.

MR CYPRESS

It is something to seek, Mr Glowry. The mind is restless, and must persist in seeking, though to find is to be disappointed. Do you feel no aspirations towards the countries of Socrates and Cicero? No wish to wander among the venerable remains of the greatness that has passed for ever?

MR GLOWRY

Not a grain.

SCYTHROP

It is, indeed, much the same as if a lover should dig up the buried form of his mistress, and gaze upon relics which are anything but herself, to wander among a few mouldy ruins, that are only imperfect indexes to lost volumes of glory, and meet at every step the more melancholy ruins of human nature – a degenerate race of stupid and shrivelled slaves, grovelling in the lowest depths of servility and superstition.

THE HONOURABLE MR LISTLESS

It is the fashion to go abroad. I have thought of it myself, but am hardly equal to the exertion. To be sure, a little eccentricity and originality are allowable in some cases; and the most eccentric and original of all characters is an Englishman who stays at home.

SCYTHROP

I should have no pleasure in visiting countries that are past all hope of regeneration. There is great hope of our own; and it seems to me that an Englishman who, either by his station in society, or by his genius, or (as in your instance, Mr Cypress) by both, has the power of essentially serving his country in its arduous struggle with its domestic enemies, yet forsakes his country, which is still so rich in hope, to dwell in others which are only fertile in the ruins of memory, does what none of those ancients, whose fragmentary memorials you venerate, would have done in similar circumstances.

MR CYPRESS

Sir, I have quarrelled with my wife; and a man who has quarrelled with his wife is absolved from all duty to his country. I have written an ode to tell the people as much, and they may take it as they list.

SCYTHROP

Do you suppose, if Brutus had quarrelled with his wife, he would have given it as a reason to Cassius for having nothing to do with his enterprise? Or would Cassius have been satisfied with such an excuse?

MR FLOSKY

Brutus was a senator; so is our dear friend: but the cases are different. Brutus had some hope of political good: Mr Cypress has none. How should he, after what we have seen in France?

SCYTHROP

A Frenchman is born in harness, ready saddled, bitted, and bridled, for any tyrant to ride. He will fawn under his rider one moment, and throw him and kick him to death the next; but another adventurer springs on his back, and by dint of whip and spur on he goes as before. We may, without much vanity, hope better of ourselves.

MR CYPRESS

I have no hope for myself or for others. Our life is a false nature; it is not in the harmony of things; it is an all-blasting upas, whose root is earth, and whose leaves are the skies which rain their poison-dews upon mankind. We wither from our youth; we gasp with unslaked thirst for unattainable good; lured from the first to the last by phantoms – love, fame, ambition, avarice – all idle, and all ill – one meteor of many names, that vanishes in the smoke of death.*

MR FLOSKY

A most delightful speech, Mr Cypress. A most amiable and instructive philosophy. You have only to impress its truth on the minds of all living men, and life will then, indeed, be the desert and the solitude; and I must do you, myself, and our mutual friends, the justice to observe, that let society only give fair play at one and the same time, as I flatter myself it is inclined to do, to your system of morals, and my system of metaphysics, and Scythrop's system of politics, and Mr Listless's system of manners, and Mr Toobad's system of religion, and the result will be as fine a mental chaos as even the immortal Kant himself could ever have hoped to see; in the prospect of which I rejoice.

MR HILARY

'Certainly, ancient, it is not a thing to rejoice at:' I am one of those who cannot see the good that is to result from all this mystifying and blue-devilling of society. The contrast it presents to the cheerful and solid wisdom of antiquity is too forcible not to strike anyone who has the least knowledge of classical literature. To represent vice and misery as the necessary accompaniments of genius, is as mischievous as it is false, and the feeling is as unclassical as the language in which it is usually expressed.

MR TOOBAD

It is our calamity. The devil has come among us, and has begun by taking possession of all the cleverest fellows. Yet, forsooth, this is the enlightened age. Marry, how? Did our ancestors go peeping about with dark lanterns, and do we walk at our ease in broad sunshine? Where is the manifestation of our light? By what symptoms do you recognise it? What are its signs, its tokens, its symptoms, its symbols, its categories, its conditions? What is it, and why? How, where, when is it to be seen, felt, and understood? What do we see by it which our ancestors saw not, and which at the same time is worth seeing? We see a hundred men hanged, where they saw one. We see five hundred transported, where they saw one. We see five thousand in the workhouse, where they saw one. We see scores of Bible Societies, where they saw none. We see

* *vanishes in the smoke of death*: Childe Harold, canto 4:124,126

paper, where they saw gold. We see men in stays, where they saw men in armour. We see painted faces, where they saw healthy ones. We see children perishing in manufactories, where they saw them flourishing in the fields. We see prisons, where they saw castles. We see masters, where they saw representatives. In short, they saw true men, where we see false knaves. They saw Milton, and we see Mr Sackbut.

MR FLOSKY

The false knave, sir, is my honest friend; therefore, I beseech you, let him be countenanced. God forbid but a knave should have some countenance at his friend's request.

MR TOOBAD

'Good men and true' was their common term, like the καλὸς κἀγαθὸς of the Athenians. It is so long since men have been either good or true, that it is to be questioned which is most obsolete, the fact or the phraseology.

MR CYPRESS

There is no worth nor beauty but in the mind's idea. Love sows the wind and reaps the whirlwind.* Confusion, thrice confounded, is the portion of him who rests even for an instant on that most brittle of reeds – the affection of a human being. The sum of our social destiny is to inflict or to endure.†

MR HILARY

Rather to bear and forbear, Mr Cypress – a maxim which you perhaps despise. Ideal beauty is not the mind's creation: it is real beauty, refined and purified in the mind's alembic, from the alloy which always more or less accompanies it in our mixed and imperfect nature. But still the gold exists in a very ample degree. To expect too much is a disease in the expectant, for which human nature is not responsible; and, in the common name of humanity, I protest against these false and mischievous ravings. To rail against humanity for not being abstract perfection, and against human love for not realising all the splendid visions of the poets of chivalry, is to rail at the summer for not being all sunshine, and at the rose for not being always in bloom.

* *and reaps the whirlwind*: *Childe Harold*, canto 4:123.
† *or to endure*: *Ibid.* canto 3:71.

MR CYPRESS

Human love! Love is not an inhabitant of the earth. We worship him as the Athenians did their unknown god: but broken hearts are the martyrs of his faith, and the eye shall never see the form which phantasy paints, and which passion pursues through paths of delusive beauty, among flowers whose odours are agonies, and trees whose gums are poison.*

MR HILARY

You talk like a Rosicrucian, who will love nothing but a sylph, who does not believe in the existence of a sylph, and who yet quarrels with the whole universe for not containing a sylph.

MR CYPRESS

The mind is diseased of its own beauty, and fevers into false creation. The forms which the sculptor's soul has seized exist only in himself.†

MR FLOSKY

Permit me to discept. They are the mediums of common forms combined and arranged into a common standard. The ideal beauty of the Helen of Zeuxis was the combined medium of the real beauty of the virgins of Crotona.

MR HILARY

But to make ideal beauty the shadow in the water, and, like the dog in the fable, to throw away the substance in catching at the shadow, is scarcely the characteristic of wisdom, whatever it may be of genius. To reconcile man as he is to the world as it is, to preserve and improve all that is good, and destroy or alleviate all that is evil, in physical and moral nature – have been the hope and aim of the greatest teachers and ornaments of our species. I will say, too, that the highest wisdom and the highest genius have been invariably accompanied with cheerfulness. We have sufficient proofs on record that Shakspeare and Socrates were the most festive of companions. But now the little wisdom and genius we have seem to be entering into a conspiracy against cheerfulness.

MR TOOBAD

How can we be cheerful with the devil among us?

---

* *whose gums are poison*: *Childe Harold*, canto 4:121,136.
† *exist only in himself*: *Ibid.*, canto 4:122.

THE HONOURABLE MR LISTLESS

How can we be cheerful when our nerves are shattered?

MR FLOSKY

How can we be cheerful when we are surrounded by a *reading public* that is growing too wise for its betters?

SCYTHROP

How can we be cheerful when our great general designs are crossed every moment by our little particular passions?

MR CYPRESS

How can we be cheerful in the midst of disappointment and despair?

MR GLOWRY

Let us all be unhappy together.

MR HILARY

Let us sing a catch.

MR GLOWRY

No: a nice tragical ballad. The Norfolk Tragedy to the tune of the Hundredth Psalm.

MR HILARY

I say a catch.

MR GLOWRY

I say no. A song from Mr Cypress.

ALL

A song from Mr Cypress.

MR CYPRESS [*sung*] –

> There is a fever of the spirit,
>   The brand of Cain's unresting doom,
> Which in the lone dark souls that bear it
>   Glows like the lamp in Tullia's tomb:
> Unlike that lamp, its subtle fire
>   Burns, blasts, consumes its cell, the heart,
> Till, one by one, hope, joy, desire,
>   Like dreams of shadowy smoke depart.
>
> When hope, love, life itself, are only
>   Dust – spectral memories – dead and cold –
> The unfed fire burns bright and lonely,
>   Like that undying lamp of old:

>And by that drear illumination,
> Till time its clay-built home has rent,
>Thought broods on feeling's desolation –
> The soul is its own monument.

MR GLOWRY

Admirable. Let us all be unhappy together.

MR HILARY

Now, I say again, a catch.

THE REVEREND MR LARYNX

I am for you.

MR HILARY

'Seamen three'.

THE REVEREND MR LARYNX

Agreed. I'll be Harry Gill, with the voice of three. Begin.

MR HILARY AND THE REVEREND MR LARYNX

>Seamen three! I What men be ye?
>Gotham's three wise men we be.
>Whither in your bowl so free?
>To rake the moon from out the sea.
>The bowl goes trim. The moon doth shine.
>And our ballast is old wine;
> And your ballast is old wine.

>Who art thou, so fast adrift?
>I am he they call Old Care.
>Here on board we will thee lift.
>No: I may not enter there.
>Wherefore so? 'Tis Jove's decree,
>In a bowl Care may not be;
> In a bowl Care may not be.

>Fear ye not the waves that roll?
>No: in charmèd bowl we swim.
>What the charm that floats the bowl?
>Water may not pass the brim.
>The bowl goes trim. The moon doth shine.
>And our ballast is old wine;
> And your ballast is old wine.

This catch was so well executed by the spirit and science of Mr Hilary, and the deep tri-une voice of the reverend gentleman, that the whole party, in spite of themselves, caught the contagion, and joined in chorus at the conclusion, each raising a bumper to his lips:

> The bowl goes trim. The moon doth shine.
> And our ballast is old wine;

Mr Cypress, having his ballast on board, stepped, the same evening, into his bowl, or travelling chariot, and departed to rake seas and rivers, lakes and canals, for the moon of ideal beauty.

Chapter Twelve

It was the custom of the Honourable Mr Listless, on adjourning from the bottle to the ladies, to retire for a few moments to make a second toilette, that he might present himself in becoming taste. Fatout, attending as usual, appeared with a countenance of great dismay, and informed his master that he had just ascertained that the abbey was haunted. Mrs Hilary's *gentlewoman*, for whom Fatout had lately conceived a *tendresse*, had been, as she expressed it, 'fritted out of her seventeen senses' the preceding night, as she was retiring to her bedchamber, by a ghastly figure which she had met stalking along one of the galleries, wrapped in a white shroud, with a bloody turban on its head. She had fainted away with fear; and, when she recovered, she found herself in the dark, and the figure was gone. '*Sacré – cochon – bleu!*' exclaimed Fatout, giving very deliberate emphasis to every portion of his terrible oath – 'I vould not meet de *revenant*, de ghost – *non* – not for all de *bowl-de-ponch* in de vorld.'

'Fatout,' said the Honourable Mr Listless, 'did I ever see a ghost?'

'*Jamais, monsieur*, never.'

'Then I hope I never shall, for, in the present shattered state of my nerves, I am afraid it would be too much for me. There – loosen the lace of my stays a little, for really this plebeian practice of eating – not too loose – consider my shape. That will do. And I desire that you bring me no more stories of ghosts; for, though I do not believe in such things, yet, when one is awake in the night, one is apt, if one thinks of them, to have fancies that give one a kind of a chill, particularly if one opens one's eyes suddenly on one's dressing gown, hanging in the moonlight, between the bed and the window.'

The Honourable Mr Listless, though he had prohibited Fatout from bringing him any more stories of ghosts, could not help thinking of that which Fatout had already brought; and, as it was uppermost in his mind, when he descended to the tea and coffee cups, and the rest of the company in the library, he almost involuntarily asked Mr Flosky, whom he looked up to as a most oraculous personage, whether any story of any ghost that had ever appeared to anyone, was entitled to any degree of belief?

MR FLOSKY

By far the greater number, to a very great degree.

THE HONOURABLE MR LISTLESS

Really, that is very alarming!

MR FLOSKY

Sunt geminae somni portae. There are two gates through which ghosts find their way to the upper air: fraud and self-delusion. In the latter case, a ghost is a *deceptio visus*, an ocular spectrum, an idea with the force of a sensation. I have seen many ghosts myself. I dare say there are few in this company who have not seen a ghost.

THE HONOURABLE MR LISTLESS

I am happy to say, I never have, for one.

THE REVEREND MR LARYNX

We have such high authority for ghosts, that it is rank scepticism to disbelieve them. Job saw a ghost, which came for the express purpose of asking a question, and did not wait for an answer.

THE HONOURABLE MR LISTLESS

Because Job was too frightened to give one.

THE REVEREND MR LARYNX

Spectres appeared to the Egyptians during the darkness with which Moses covered Egypt. The witch of Endor raised the ghost of Samuel. Moses and Elias appeared on Mount Tabor. An evil spirit was sent into the army of Sennacherib, and exterminated it in a single night.

MR TOOBAD

Saying, The devil is come among you, having great wrath.

MR FLOSKY

Saint Macarius interrogated a skull, which was found in the desert, and made it relate, in presence of several witnesses, what was going forward in hell. Saint Martin of Tours, being jealous of a pretended martyr, who was the rival saint of his neighbourhood, called up his ghost, and made him confess that he was damned. Saint Germain, being on his travels, turned out of an inn a large party of ghosts, who had every night taken possession of the *table d'hôte*, and consumed a copious supper.

MR HILARY

Jolly ghosts, and no doubt all friars. A similar party took possession of the cellar of M. Swebach, the painter, in Paris, drank his wine, and threw the empty bottles at his head.

THE REVEREND MR LARYNX

An atrocious act.

MR FLOSKY

Pausanias relates, that the neighing of horses and the tumult of combatants were heard every night on the field of Marathon: that those who went purposely to hear these sounds suffered severely for their curiosity; but those who heard them by accident passed with impunity.

THE REVEREND MR LARYNX

I once saw a ghost myself, in my study, which is the last place where anyone but a ghost would look for me. I had not been into it for three months, and was going to consult Tillotson, when, on opening the door, I saw a venerable figure in a flannel dressing gown, sitting in my armchair, and reading my Jeremy Taylor. It vanished in a moment, and so did I; and what it was or what it wanted I have never been able to ascertain.

MR FLOSKY

It was an idea with the force of a sensation. It is seldom that ghosts appeal to two senses at once; but, when I was in Devonshire, the following story was well attested to me. A young woman, whose lover was at sea, returning one evening over some solitary fields, saw her lover sitting on a stile over which she was to pass. Her first emotions were surprise and joy, but there was a paleness and seriousness in his face that made them give place to alarm. She advanced towards him, and he said to her, in a solemn voice, 'The eye that hath seen me shall see me no more. Thine eye is upon me, but I am not.' And with these words he vanished; and on that very day and hour, as it afterwards appeared, he had perished by shipwreck.

The whole party now drew round in a circle, and each related some ghostly anecdote, heedless of the flight of time, till, in a pause of the conversation, they heard the hollow tongue of midnight sounding twelve.

MR HILARY

All these anecdotes admit of solution on psychological principles. It is more easy for a soldier, a philosopher, or even a saint, to be frightened at his own shadow, than for a dead man to come out of his grave. Medical writers cite a thousand singular examples of the force of imagination. Persons of feeble, nervous, melancholy temperament, exhausted by fever, by labour, or by spare diet, will readily conjure up, in the magic ring of their own phantasy, spectres, gorgons, chimeras, and all the objects of their hatred and their love. We are most of us like Don Quixote, to whom a windmill was a giant, and Dulcinea a magnificent princess: all more or less the dupes of our own imagination, though we do not all go so far as to see ghosts, or to fancy ourselves pipkins and teapots.

MR FLOSKY

I can safely say I have seen too many ghosts myself to believe in their external existence. I have seen all kinds of ghosts: black spirits and white, red spirits and grey. Some in the shapes of venerable old men, who have met me in my rambles at noon; some of beautiful young women, who have peeped through my curtains at midnight.

THE HONOURABLE MR LISTLESS

And have proved, I doubt not, 'palpable to feeling as to sight'.

MR FLOSKY

By no means, sir. You reflect upon my purity. Myself and my friends, particularly my friend Mr Sackbut, are famous for our purity. No, sir, genuine untangible ghosts. I live in a world of ghosts. I see a ghost at this moment.

Mr Flosky fixed his eyes on a door at the farther end of the library. The company looked in the same direction. The door silently opened, and a ghastly figure, shrouded in white drapery, with the semblance of a bloody turban on its head, entered and stalked slowly up the apartment. Mr Flosky, familiar as he was with ghosts, was not prepared for this apparition, and made the best of his way out at the opposite door. Mrs Hilary and Marionetta followed, screaming. The Honourable Mr Listless, by two turns of his body, rolled first off the sofa and then under it. The Reverend Mr Larynx leaped up and fled with so much precipitation, that he overturned the table on the foot of Mr Glowry. Mr Glowry roared with pain in the ear of Mr Toobad. Mr Toobad's alarm so bewildered his senses, that, missing the door, he threw up one of the windows, jumped out in his panic, and plunged over head and ears in the moat. Mr Asterias and his son, who were on the watch for their mermaid, were attracted by the splashing, threw a net over him, and dragged him to land.

Scythrop and Mr Hilary meanwhile had hastened to his assistance, and, on arriving at the edge of the moat, followed by several servants with ropes and torches, found Mr Asterias and Aquarius busy in endeavouring to extricate Mr Toobad from the net, who was entangled in the meshes, and floundering with rage. Scythrop was lost in amazement; but Mr Hilary saw, at one view, all the circumstances of the adventure, and burst into an immoderate fit of laughter; on recovering from which, he said to Mr Asterias, 'You have caught an odd fish, indeed.' Mr Toobad was highly exasperated at this unseasonable pleasantry; but Mr Hilary softened his anger, by producing a knife, and cutting the Gordian knot of his reticular envelopment. 'You see,' said Mr Toobad, 'you see, gentlemen, in my unfortunate person proof upon proof of the present dominion of the devil in the affairs of this world; and I have no doubt but that the apparition of this night was Apollyon himself in disguise, sent for the express purpose of terrifying me into this complication of misadventures. The devil is come among you, having great wrath, because he knoweth that he hath but a short time.'

Chapter Thirteen

Mr Glowry was much surprised, on occasionally visiting Scythrop's tower, to find the door always locked, and to be kept sometimes waiting many minutes for admission: during which he invariably heard a heavy rolling sound like that of a ponderous mangle, or of a waggon on a weighing-bridge, or of theatrical thunder.

He took little notice of this for some time; at length his curiosity was excited, and, one day, instead of knocking at the door, as usual, the instant he reached it, he applied his ear to the key-hole, and like Bottom, in the *Midsummer Night's Dream*, 'spied a voice', which he guessed to be of the feminine gender, and knew to be not Scythrop's, whose deeper tones he distinguished at intervals. Having attempted in vain to catch a syllable of the discourse, he knocked violently at the door, and roared for immediate admission. The voices ceased, the accustomed rolling sound was heard, the door opened, and Scythrop was discovered alone. Mr Glowry looked round to every corner of the apartment, and then said, 'Where is the lady?'

'The lady, sir?' said Scythrop.

'Yes, sir, the lady.'

'Sir, I do not understand you.'

'You don't, sir?'

'No, indeed, sir. There is no lady here.'

'But, sir, this is not the only apartment in the tower, and I make no doubt there is a lady upstairs.'

'You are welcome to search, sir.'

'Yes, and while I am searching, she will slip out from some lurking place, and make her escape.'

'You may lock this door, sir, and take the key with you.'

'But there is the terrace door: she has escaped by the terrace.'

'The terrace, sir, has no other outlet, and the walls are too high for a lady to jump down.'

'Well, sir, give me the key.'

Mr Glowry took the key, searched every nook of the tower, and returned.

'You are a fox, Scythrop; you are an exceedingly cunning fox, with that demure visage of yours. What was that lumbering sound I heard before you opened the door?'

'Sound, sir?'

'Yes, sir, sound.'

'My dear sir, I am not aware of any sound, except my great table, which I moved on rising to let you in.'

'The table! – let me see that. No, sir; not a tenth part heavy enough, not a tenth part.'

'But, sir, you do not consider the laws of acoustics: a whisper becomes a peal of thunder in the focus of reverberation. Allow me to explain this: sounds striking on concave surfaces are reflected from them, and, after reflection, converge to points which are the foci of these surfaces. It follows, therefore, that the ear may be so placed in one, as that it shall hear a sound better than when situated nearer to the point of the first impulse: again, in the case of two concave surfaces placed opposite to each other – '

'Nonsense, sir. Don't tell me of foci. Pray, sir, will concave surfaces produce two voices when nobody speaks? I heard two voices, and one was feminine; feminine, sir: what say you to that?'

'Oh, sir, I perceive your mistake: I am writing a tragedy, and was acting over a scene to myself. To convince you, I will give you a specimen; but you must first understand the plot. It is a tragedy on the German model. The Great Mogul is in exile, and has taken lodgings at Kensington, with his only daughter, the Princess Rantro-rina, who takes in needlework, and keeps a day school. *The princess is discovered hemming a set of shirts for the parson of the parish: they are to be marked with a large R. Enter to her the Great Mogul. A pause, during which they look at each other expressively. The princess changes colour several times. The Mogul takes snuff in great agitation. Several grains are heard to fall on the stage. His heart is seen to beat through his upper benjamin.* – THE MOGUL [*with a mournful look at his left shoe*]. 'My shoe-string is broken.' – THE PRINCESS [*after an interval of melancholy reflection*]. 'I know it.' THE MOGUL. 'My second shoe-string! The first broke when I lost my empire: the second has broken today. When will my poor heart break?' – THE PRINCESS. 'Shoe-strings, hearts, and empires! Mysterious sympathy!'

'Nonsense, sir,' interrupted Mr Glowry. 'That is not at all like the voice I heard.'

'But, sir,' said Scythrop, 'a keyhole may be so constructed as to act like an acoustic tube, and an acoustic tube, sir, will modify sound in a very remarkable manner. Consider the construction of the ear, and the nature and causes of sound. The external part of the ear is a cartilaginous funnel.'

'It won't do, Scythrop. There is a girl concealed in this tower, and find her I will. There are such things as sliding panels and secret closets.' – He sounded round the room with his cane, but detected no hollowness. – 'I have heard, sir,' he continued, 'that during my absence, two years ago, you had a dumb carpenter closeted with you day after day. I did not dream that you were laying contrivances for carrying on secret intrigues. Young men will have their way: I had my way when I was a young man: but, sir, when your cousin Marionetta – '

Scythrop now saw that the affair was growing serious. To have clapped his hand upon his father's mouth, to have entreated him to be silent, would, in the first place, not have made him so; and, in the second, would have shown a dread of being overheard by somebody. His only resource, therefore, was to try to drown Mr Glowry's voice; and, having no other subject, he continued his description of the ear, raising his voice continually as Mr Glowry raised his.

'When your cousin Marionetta,' said Mr Glowry, 'whom you profess to love – whom you profess to love, sir – '

'The internal canal of the ear,' said Scythrop, 'is partly bony and partly cartilaginous. This internal canal is – '

'Is actually in the house, sir; and, when you are so shortly to be – as I expect – '

'Closed at the further end by the *membrana tympani* – '

'Joined together in holy matrimony – '

'Under which is carried a branch of the fifth pair of nerves – '

'I say, sir, when you are so shortly to be married to your cousin Marionetta – '

'The *cavitas tympani* – '

A loud noise was heard behind the book-case, which, to the astonishment of Mr Glowry, opened in the middle, and the massy compartments, with all their weight of books, receding from each other in the manner of a theatrical scene, with a heavy rolling sound (which Mr Glowry immediately recognised to be the same which had excited his curiosity), disclosed an interior apartment, in the entrance of which stood the beautiful Stella, who, stepping forward, exclaimed, 'Married! Is he going to be married? The profligate!'

'Really, madam,' said Mr Glowry, 'I do not know what he is going to do, or what I am going to do, or what anyone is going to do; for all this is incomprehensible.'

'I can explain it all,' said Scythrop, 'in a most satisfactory manner, if you will but have the goodness to leave us alone.'

'Pray, sir, to which act of the tragedy of the Great Mogul does this incident belong?'

'I entreat you, my dear sir, leave us alone.'

Stella threw herself into a chair, and burst into a tempest of tears. Scythrop sat down by her, and took her hand. She snatched her hand away, and turned her back upon him. He rose, sat down on the other side, and took her other hand. She snatched it away, and turned from him again. Scythrop continued entreating Mr Glowry to leave them alone; but the old gentleman was obstinate, and would not go.

'I suppose, after all,' said Mr Glowry maliciously, 'it is only a phenomenon in acoustics, and this young lady is a reflection of sound from concave surfaces.'

Someone tapped at the door: Mr Glowry opened it, and Mr Hilary entered. He had been seeking Mr Glowry, and had traced him to Scythrop's tower. He stood a few moments in silent surprise, and then addressed himself to Mr Glowry for an explanation.

'The explanation,' said Mr Glowry, 'is very satisfactory. The Great Mogul has taken lodgings at Kensington, and the external part of the ear is a cartilaginous funnel.'

'Mr Glowry, that is no explanation.'

'Mr Hilary, it is all I know about the matter.'

'Sir, this pleasantry is very unseasonable. I perceive that my niece is sported with in a most unjustifiable manner, and I shall see if she will be more successful in obtaining an intelligible answer.' And he departed in search of Marionetta.

Scythrop was now in a hopeless predicament. Mr Hilary made a hue and cry in the abbey, and summoned his wife and Marionetta to Scythrop's apartment. The ladies, not knowing what was the matter, hastened in great consternation. Mr Toobad saw them sweeping along the corridor, and judging from their manner that the devil had manifested his wrath in some new shape, followed from pure curiosity.

Scythrop meanwhile vainly endeavoured to get rid of Mr Glowry and to pacify Stella. The latter attempted to escape from the tower, declaring she would leave the abbey immediately, and he should never see her or hear of her more. Scythrop held her hand and detained her by force, till Mr Hilary reappeared with Mrs Hilary and Marionetta. Marionetta, seeing Scythrop grasping the hand of a strange beauty, fainted away in the arms of her aunt. Scythrop flew to her assistance; and Stella with redoubled anger sprang towards the door, but was intercepted in her intended flight by being caught in the arms of Mr Toobad, who exclaimed – 'Celinda!'

'Papa!' said the young lady disconsolately.

'The devil is come among you,' said Mr Toobad. 'How came my daughter here?'

'Your daughter!' exclaimed Mr Glowry.

'Your daughter!' exclaimed Scythrop, and Mr and Mrs Hilary.

'Yes,' said Mr Toobad, 'my daughter Celinda.'

Marionetta opened her eyes and fixed them on Celinda; Celinda in return fixed hers on Marionetta. They were at remote points of the apartment. Scythrop was equidistant from both of them, central and motionless, like Mahomet's coffin.

'Mr Glowry,' said Mr Toobad, 'can you tell by what means my daughter came here?'

'I know no more,' said Mr Glowry, 'than the Great Mogul.'

'Mr Scythrop,' said Mr Toobad, 'how came my daughter here?'

'I did not know, sir, that the lady was your daughter.'

'But how came she here?'

'By spontaneous locomotion,' said Scythrop, sullenly.

'Celinda,' said Mr Toobad, 'what does all this mean?'

'I really do not know, sir.'

'This is most unaccountable. When I told you in London that I had chosen a husband for you, you thought proper to run away from him; and now, to all appearance, you have run away to him.'

'How, sir! was that your choice?'

'Precisely; and if he is yours too we shall be both of a mind, for the first time in our lives.'

'He is not my choice, sir. This lady has a prior claim: I renounce him.'

'And I renounce him,' said Marionetta.

Scythrop knew not what to do. He could not attempt to conciliate the one without irreparably offending the other; and he was so fond of both, that the idea of depriving himself for ever of the society of either was intolerable to him: he therefore retreated into his stronghold, mystery; maintained an impenetrable silence; and contented himself with stealing occasionally a deprecating glance at each of the objects of his idolatry. Mr Toobad and Mr Hilary, in the meantime, were each insisting on an explanation from Mr Glowry, who they thought had been playing a double game on this occasion. Mr Glowry was vainly endeavouring to persuade them of his innocence in the whole transaction. Mrs Hilary was endeavouring to mediate between her husband and brother. The Honourable Mr Listless, the Reverend Mr Larynx, Mr Flosky, Mr Asterias, and Aquarius, were attracted by the tumult to the scene of action, and were appealed to severally and conjointly by the respective disputants. Multitudinous questions, and answers *en masse*, composed a *charivari*, to which the genius of Rossini alone could have given a suitable accompaniment, and which was only terminated by Mrs Hilary and Mr Toobad retreating with the captive damsels. The whole party followed, with the exception of Scythrop, who threw himself into his armchair, crossed his left foot over his right knee, placed the hollow of his left hand on the interior ankle of his left leg, rested his right elbow on the elbow of the chair, placed the ball of his right thumb against his right temple, curved the forefinger along the upper part of his forehead, rested the point of the middle finger on the bridge of his nose, and the points of the two others on the lower part of the palm, fixed his eyes intently on the veins in the back of his left hand, and sat in this position like the immovable Theseus, who, as is well known to many who have not been at college, and to some few who have, *sedet, aeternumque sedebit.** We hope the admirers of the *minutiae* in poetry and romance will appreciate this accurate description of a pensive attitude.

---

* *sedet, aeternumque sedebit*: sits, and will sit for ever.

Chapter Fourteen

Scythrop was still in this position when Raven entered to announce that dinner was on table.

'I cannot come,' said Scythrop.

Raven sighed. 'Something is the matter,' said Raven: 'but man is born to trouble.'

'Leave me,' said Scythrop: 'go, and croak elsewhere.'

'Thus it is,' said Raven. 'Five-and-twenty years have I lived in Nightmare Abbey, and now all the reward of my affection is – Go, and croak elsewhere. I have danced you on my knee, and fed you with marrow.'

'Good Raven,' said Scythrop, 'I entreat you to leave me.'

'Shall I bring your dinner here?' said Raven. 'A boiled fowl and a glass of madeira are prescribed by the faculty in cases of low spirits. But you had better join the party: it is very much reduced already.'

'Reduced! How?'

'The Honourable Mr Listless is gone. He declared that, what with family quarrels in the morning, and ghosts at night, he could get neither sleep nor peace; and that the agitation was too much for his nerves: though Mr Glowry assured him that the ghost was only poor Crow walking in his sleep, and that the shroud and bloody turban were a sheet and a red nightcap.'

'Well, sir?'

'The Reverend Mr Larynx has been called off on duty, to marry or bury (I don't know which) some unfortunate person or persons, at Claydyke: but man is born to trouble!'

'Is that all?'

'No. Mr Toobad is gone too, and a strange lady with him.'

'Gone!'

'Gone. And Mr and Mrs Hilary, and Miss O'Carroll: they are all gone. There is nobody left but Mr Asterias and his son, and they are going tonight.'

'Then I have lost them both.'

'Won't you come to dinner?'

'No.'

'Shall I bring your dinner here?'

'Yes.'

'What will you have?'

'A pint of port and a pistol.'*

'A pistol!'

'And a pint of port. I will make my exit like Werter. Go. Stay. Did Miss O'Carroll say anything?'

'No.'

'Did Miss Toobad say anything?'

'The strange lady? No.'

'Did either of them cry?'

'No.'

'What did they do?'

'Nothing.'

'What did Mr Toobad say?'

'He said, fifty times over, the devil was come among us.'

'And they are gone?'

'Yes; and the dinner is getting cold. There is a time for everything under the sun. You may as well dine first, and be miserable afterwards.'

'True, Raven. There is something in that. I will take your advice: therefore, bring me – '

'The port and the pistol?'

'No; the boiled fowl and madeira.'

Scythrop had dined, and was sipping his madeira alone, immersed in melancholy musing, when Mr Glowry entered, followed by Raven, who, having placed an additional glass and set a chair for Mr Glowry, withdrew. Mr Glowry sat down opposite Scythrop. After a pause, during which each filled and drank in silence, Mr Glowry said, 'So, sir, you have played your cards well. I proposed Miss Toobad to you: you refused her. Mr Toobad proposed you to her: she refused you. You fell in love with Marionetta, and were going to poison yourself, because, from pure fatherly regard to your temporal interests, I withheld my consent. When, at length, I offered you my consent, you told me I was too precipitate. And, after all, I find you and Miss Toobad living together in the same tower, and behaving in every respect like two plighted lovers. Now, sir, if there be any rational solution of all this absurdity, I shall be very much obliged to you for a small glimmering of information.'

* *a pint of port and a pistol*: see *The Sorrows of Werter*, Letter 93.

'The solution, sir, is of little moment; but I will leave it in writing for your satisfaction. The crisis of my fate is come: the world is a stage, and my direction is *exit*.'

'Do not talk so, sir – do not talk so, Scythrop. What would you have?'

'I would have my love.'

'And pray, sir, who is your love?'

'Celinda – Marionetta – either – both.'

'Both! That may do very well in a German tragedy; and the Great Mogul might have found it very feasible in his lodgings at Kensington; but it will not do in Lincolnshire. Will you have Miss Toobad?'

'Yes.'

'And renounce Marionetta?'

'No.'

'But you must renounce one.'

'I cannot.'

'And you cannot have both. What is to be done?'

'I must shoot myself.'

'Don't talk so, Scythrop. Be rational, my dear Scythrop. Consider, and make a cool, calm choice, and I will exert myself in your behalf.'

'Why should I choose, sir? Both have renounced *me*: I have no hope of either.'

'Tell me which you will have, and I will plead your cause irresistibly.'

'Well, sir – I will have – no, sir, I cannot renounce either. I cannot choose either. I am doomed to be the victim of eternal disappointments; and I have no resource but a pistol.'

'Scythrop – Scythrop – if one of them should come to you – what then?'

'That, sir, might alter the case: but that cannot be.'

'It can be, Scythrop; it will be: I promise you it will be. Have but a little patience – but a week's patience; and it shall be.'

'A week, sir, is an age: but, to oblige you, as a last act of filial duty, I will live another week. It is now Thursday evening, twenty-five minutes past seven. At this hour and minute, on Thursday next, love and fate shall smile on me, or I will drink my last pint of port in this world.'

Mr Glowry ordered his travelling chariot, and departed from the abbey.

Chapter Fifteen

The day after Mr Glowry's departure was one of incessant rain, and Scythrop repented of the promise he had given. The next day was one of bright sunshine: he sat on the terrace, read a tragedy of Sophocles, and was not sorry, when Raven announced dinner, to find himself alive. On the third evening, the wind blew, and the rain beat, and the owl flapped against his windows; and he put a new flint in his pistol. On the fourth day, the sun shone again; and he locked the pistol up in a drawer, where he left it undisturbed, till the morning of the eventful Thursday, when he ascended the turret with a telescope, and spied anxiously along the road that crossed the fens from Claydyke: but nothing appeared on it. He watched in this manner from ten a.m. till Raven summoned him to dinner at five, when he stationed Crow at the telescope, and descended to his own funeral-feast. He left open the communications between the tower and turret, and called aloud at intervals to Crow – 'Crow, Crow, is anything coming?' Crow answered, 'The wind blows, and the windmills turn, but I see nothing coming;' and, at every answer, Scythrop found the necessity of raising his spirits with a bumper. After dinner, he gave Raven his watch to set by the abbey clock. Raven brought it, Scythrop placed it on the table, and Raven departed. Scythrop called again to Crow; and Crow, who had fallen asleep, answered mechanically, 'I see nothing coming.' Scythrop laid his pistol between his watch and his bottle. The hour-hand passed the vii – the minute-hand moved on – it was within three minutes of the appointed time. Scythrop called again to Crow: Crow answered as before. Scythrop rang the bell: Raven appeared.

'Raven,' said Scythrop, 'the clock is too fast.'

'No, indeed,' said Raven, who knew nothing of Scythrop's intentions; 'if anything, it is too slow.'

'Villain!' said Scythrop, pointing the pistol at him; 'it is too fast.'

'Yes – yes – too fast, I meant,' said Raven, in manifest fear.

'How much too fast?' said Scythrop.

'As much as you please,' said Raven.

'How much, I say?' said Scythrop, pointing the pistol again.

'An hour, a full hour, sir,' said the terrified butler.

'Put back my watch,' said Scythrop.

Raven, with trembling hand, was putting back the watch, when the rattle of wheels was heard in the court; and Scythrop, springing down the stairs by three steps together, was at the door in sufficient time to have handed either of the young ladies from the carriage, if she had happened to be in it; but Mr Glowry was alone.

'I rejoice to see you,' said Mr Glowry; 'I was fearful of being too late, for I waited till the last moment in the hope of accomplishing my promise; but all my endeavours have been vain, as these letters will show.'

Scythrop impatiently broke the seals. The contents were these:

Almost a stranger in England, I fled from parental tyranny, and the dread of an arbitrary marriage, to the protection of a stranger and a philosopher, whom I expected to find something better than, or at least something different from, the rest of his worthless species. Could I, after what has occurred, have expected nothing more from you than the commonplace impertinence of sending your father to treat with me, and with mine, for me? I should be a little moved in your favour, if I could believe you capable of carrying into effect the resolutions which your father says you have taken, in the event of my proving inflexible; though I doubt not you will execute them, as far as relates to the pint of wine, twice over, at least. I wish you much happiness with Miss O'Carroll. I shall always cherish a grateful recollection of Nightmare Abbey, for having been the means of introducing me to a true transcendentalist; and, though he is a little older than myself, which is all one in Germany, I shall very soon have the pleasure of subscribing myself

CELINDA FLOSKY

I hope, my dear cousin, that you will not be angry with me, but that you will always think of me as a sincere friend, who will always feel interested in your welfare; I am sure you love Miss Toobad much better than me, and I wish you much happiness with her. Mr Listless assures me that people do not kill themselves for love nowadays, though it is still the fashion to talk about it. I shall, in a very short time, change my name and